THE ART of Falling

DANI COJO

THE ART of Falling

DANI COJO

For Kaylen and Tryst
Our daydreams are finally a reality.

PART *One*

CHAPTER *One*

*T*HE SMALL OF Madeline's back was pushed back against the island in her kitchen, her blouse hitching up slightly so her skin touched the cold marble countertop. She nearly dropped the chef knife she was holding as her boyfriend kissed her deeply.

Instead, she set it down carefully and brought her hands up to tangle in his salt-and-pepper hair. She loved the way he wore it slightly too long, so it hung into his face and tickled her cheeks when they kissed; almost as much as she loved him smelling of rosemary and basil after volunteering at *Restos du Coeur,* or how his eyes seemed to turn different shades of gray in the light.

Madeline adored everything about Jacque, which is why she allowed herself to be a little reckless whenever they were alone.

His hand grazed along her waist, resting on her hip but going no lower. She was adamant about not going against her beliefs for one night of bliss. The moral ramifications were far too high. As a true gentleman, he always respected her boundaries and never once pushed her to go farther than she wanted.

However, there was no denying that in their four months of dating, their connection had transformed from roses into fireworks. She knew they were soulmates from the day they first met in the Parc de Belleville. He was an artist who dreamed of one day having a family of his own, while she was studying to teach French to children in other parts of the world. She played violin, and he was an excellent chef. They were a perfect match, both spiritually and physically.

She felt him press against her thigh, and she shivered.

Madeline never thought that she might throw away her Catholic upbringing and give herself up to a man before marriage.

9

But tonight she just might.

The pot of pasta water boiled over, splashing onto the electric stove and sizzling. They both jumped back, startled. Jacque hurried over to stir the contents and clean up the mess, while Madeline shifted her shirt back into place and took a deep, slow breath.

No, she couldn't let herself get too careless.

"Are you okay?" Jacque asked as he walked back over to her, leaning onto the counter. "I didn't go too far, did I?"

"No, you were fine," she assured him. She picked the knife back up to continue chopping vegetables, ignoring the way her hands trembled as adrenaline coursed through her veins. "But I think we should focus on cooking dinner."

Jacque chuckled. "Of course, beautiful." He reached out and brushed a strand of hair away from her cheek before turning his attention back to the alfredo sauce bubbling on the stove. They worked in silence, the sexual tension between them crackling in the air like static.

She knew that Jacque was dangerous. Not because he would ever hurt her, but because she could easily lose control around him.

Madeline carried the tossed salad out to the terrace. After smoothing out the wrinkles in the tablecloth and lighting the tea lights, Jacque came out behind her and set down the bowl of fettucine and pulled out the chair for her to sit.

They held hands as she prayed over their meal, and the two ate quietly as they enjoyed the spring evening. Everything about the dinner was perfect, from the setting, to the food, to the man sitting beside her.

Then, she began to feel like something wasn't right.

At first she tried to ignore it. She didn't want to cut their date short due to her head feeling dizzy. As they finished, she noticed that she was starting to feel flushed and her stomach was queasy. She excused herself to the bathroom, but stumbled as the world spun under her feet.

"Madeline, what's wrong?" Jacque asked as he hurried up to steady her.

"I'm not sure," she said shakily. "I just don't feel well all of a sudden."

"Was it the food?"

She smiled and shook her head. "No, of course not. It was delicious. I might just be coming down with something."

"Why don't you go lie down for a while, see if that helps."

"But what about the movie?"

Jacque guided her toward the bedroom. "Don't worry about that. We can watch it another time. You just rest, and I'll clean up everything."

Madeline leaned into him and kissed his shoulder. "You're too good to me."

"You deserve all of the luxury and romance a man like myself can offer."

He helped lay Madeline into bed and tucked her in, fetching a glass of water to set on her nightstand and drawing the curtains closed so the light streaming in wouldn't bother her.

"Is that better?"

She nodded a bit, her eyes feeling heavy. "Yeah. I didn't realize how tired I was..."

"Well, you have been studying for exams like crazy, and you've been volunteering more time at the church. Maybe you've just pushed yourself too hard."

"It never used to bother me before..." She thought that she heard her words slurring together, but couldn't tell if it was just in her head.

Jacque held her hand and squeezed. "I'm going to clean up the kitchen. If you need anything, just call."

The Art of Falling

Madeline closed her eyes and quickly slipped into unconsciousness before she realized what was happening. Jacque could feel her slow and steady pulse through her wrist.

He smiled.

His plan had gone without a hitch. It had taken quite a few weeks to get Madeline to warm up to him, to fall so head over heels for the vision of a man she so desperately wanted. That was the one benefit to the religious types: their sexual repression often reared its ugly head when they think they've found an angel on earth.

Humans were so easy to trick.

Regal hated the identity he had to take on to please her. He knew nothing of art, except what his stepmother had taught him, and he nearly gagged every time she would say a prayer. He made sure to repeat the words, only murmuring and nodding his head. Even that was almost too much to bear. But it was the fantasy that Madeline had clung to, so Jacque was born.

Honestly, he hadn't expected to act on his plans that evening. He had planned to fake a marriage proposal after five months of "dating" to get her to finally give in to him; but when she became so flustered and distracted by their impromptu makeout session in the kitchen, he didn't miss the opportunity to grab some medications from the cabinet above the stove and mix them into the pasta sauce. It wasn't nearly enough to make someone like him succumb, but more than enough to knock her out for hours.

Regal pulled out his silver pocket watch and looked at the time. Normally it took someone an hour and a half until they were deep in REM sleep, but he expected this timeframe to be sped up from the drugs. As he waited patiently, he cleaned up the kitchen and made sure that it looked like he had never been there. It wouldn't matter in the morning. Even if her parents suspected her new boyfriend to be the culprit, he would already have vanished into thin air.

When he thought Madeline was finally ready, he entered the bedroom once more and locked the door behind him. He approached and watched as her eyelids fluttered from her dreams. *Excellent.*

Regal crawled over her body slowly, deliberately shifting his weight so he didn't rock the bed. After nearly a century of practice, he was a pro. He slithered forward and loomed over her without the slightest disturbance.

Dreamwalking was a skill that he, and all other incubi, were born with; but it was more than a skill. It was an art that required delicate and slow maneuvers through each stage of sleep: beta, alpha, theta, and delta—in that order. It needed to be performed with the perfect balance of ambition and patience.

Those who didn't train as much as him would try to jump in the moment the victim fell asleep, but there were risks for being too eager. They might wake up too soon, and if the dreams weren't fully formed, the invader could become trapped inside. It was far too easy to make a mistake on the outer layers of the subconscious, and his father has made sure that lesson was drilled into his head long before he allowed him to hunt.

Father will be pleased that I've coveted another religious soul for his kingdom, he thought proudly as he held his hands over Madeline's head.

A blinding light flooded the bedroom. The incubus fell back with an agonized cry. Black wings unfurled from his shoulder blades, phasing through his dress shirt without tearing the fabric. They curled around him, trying to block out the burning glow.

Who the hell...?

Regal peered through his feathers to try and see who had interrupted him. He growled as the angel materialized in the room, hovering over Madeline. She didn't even flinch.

13

"Don't touch her," the ethereal being commanded, his voice tense. He was young. A new angel in Gloria's army.

Regal chuckled lowly. "I don't listen to those who are beneath me."

"My name is Keir, Angel of Kindness under the guidance of Michaelangelo and Gloria, and you are—"

"Regal. Son of Jackal, heir to the throne of Hell." He stood up and stretched his wings threateningly, his once-gentle gray eyes turning to a cold, black hue. "By rank alone, you are outmatched. I suggest you run back to Heaven so I can finish my job."

The angel flinched, but he didn't flee back through the portal from whence he'd come. "By Her command you will leave this place this instant!"

"Or else what? You're going to stop me?"

"I have my orders," Keir stated with wavering authority.

Regal shrugged. "Then why not settle this outside, hmm?"

He launched himself forward, baring his fangs as clawed hands reached out for the angel. Keir gasped in surprise, his fists clenching as the demon lunged at him. The angel swiftly dodged the attack, twisting his body to avoid getting scratched as he moved away from Madeline. Regal hovered over her body like an animal guarding a fresh kill. He was surprised at the angel's speed, even more so at the angel's strength. He shot forward, but Keir firmly grabbed his shoulders and jammed his knee up into the demon's stomach.

Choking from the pain, Regal staggered back and leaned against the far wall. He stared wide-eyed at Keir standing tall before him. Was he really being outdone by an angel? Even worse, an angel *in training*? His face grew red from mortification for a moment as Keir straightened his stance. There was no way this angel was smarter or stronger than him.

His angered expression melted away and turned into one of fear and surrender as a tricky idea formed in his head.

"All right, you've got me." He raised one hand as a sign of mercy. As he did so, his other hand slipped into his pocket to grab his watch. It lay heavy in his hand, the chain coiled around his fingers.

"Wise choice." As Keir took a step toward Regal to make sure he left the premises, the incubus swung his arm around sharply. The pocket watch flung forward, wrapping around the angel's ankle. The metal chain, coated in demonic silver, embedded itself into Keir's skin, scorching it. Keir cried out in pain as Regal pulled the chain taut and yanked Keir's foot forward, causing him to fall onto his back.

Regal violently tugged his watch from around Keir's ankle and swung it in large circles by his side. As it spun, it grew in size until it resembled a razor-edged disc and chain more than a timepiece. With a grunt, Regal leapt forward to try and land a finishing blow at Keir's head.

Keir, somewhat stunned and off-guard, saw the heavy object coming toward his head in a large arc. His hand reached up to his throat, his fingertips touching the cross necklace hanging loosely around his neck. It glowed for a moment, the light blinding Regal as the pendant expanded into a large golden shield with intricate carvings around the border. An image of the earth, Gloria's symbol, was in the center.

Regal's weapon bounced off the shield with a loud *clang* and ricocheted into the air. He pulled it back with a jerk of his wrist and spun it by his side, preparing to attack again.

However, Keir was ready. When Regal moved to strike again, Keir tossed his shield to the side and rolled up onto his back. He curled his legs up and kicked at Regal, his foot connecting with the demon's stomach and forcing him up and into the air, over Keir. The thin, gold halo wrapped around Keir's ankle and skimmed past Regal's body. The demon hissed in agony as the holy instrument singed his flesh.

Regal tumbled to the floor, slamming into the wall. He staggered to his feet, his vision blurry as he tried to catch his breath. Before he could regain his composure, Keir had firmly grabbed his shield once more and swung it up to smash into Regal's chest. The force shoved him right through the window.

The glass shattered, spraying everywhere as Regal hurtled toward the ground. The demon tumbled head over heels, his heavy ball and chain dragging him through the air. Dazed, he turned his weapon back into a simple pocket watch and gripped it tightly in his fist. In an instant, Regal's wings stretched out and caught the air, catching him roughly from falling.

He hovered for a moment, his shoulders aching from the sudden stop. Grunting in pain, Regal looked down at the small red mark where the halo had brushed against his skin. He then saw the glass littering the sidewalk below, and turned himself invisible before any humans saw him.

A rustle of feathers caught his attention. He looked up to see Keir jumping through the window, his body shooting down at Regal like a holy missile. Regal burst back into action, pumping his wings to guide him down to the empty back roads of the city as the angel chased after him.

The demon wasn't one to flee from a fight, but he knew that if he were to keep fighting, he would grow weaker and be unable to finish his job. He needed to focus on his assignment, not on some annoying angel. Once he was done, he could get his revenge on the angel later for disrupting his plans.

Keir tracked Regal as they wove their way between buildings. The incubus pulled himself up, spiraling upward into the sky. He gained speed, pushing himself to the limit as he struggled to lose track of Keir.

He couldn't help but wonder who this angel was anyways, and why he had to interrupt at such a perfect moment. If his father caught wind of this, he would surely clip his wings and send him back to caring for the infant demons.

Regal twisted and turned, diving down close to the streets. With a desperate attempt to confuse the angel, he landed on the ground and slid to a stop among a crowd of unsuspecting humans. He spun around to face his assailant, who dove at him, but slowed his speed to avoid accidentally harming an innocent bystander. Regal took this moment to twist the dial on his pocket watch, opening a secret compartment that released a dense plume of black and violet smoke.

The smog was heavy and clung to Regal as he backed away into the crowd of people, who were confused by the sudden fog. He watched as Keir clumsily flew into the cloud, coughing heavily as he tried to blow the smoke away with his wings. Regal held back his laughter as he darted away. Once he shook off the lingering fog from his wings, he took flight and doubled back to return to Madeline's apartment. If she was still unconscious, he could force his way into her mind and quickly finish his job.

Landing back in her room, Regal saw that luck was still on his side. She remained sedated, despite the battle raging around her. He slunk over to her, his eyes grazing over her limp body. He hovered over her form in silence, savoring her soul's lively energy, before forcing himself into her mind. It was easy, with her numb and unable to push him back. He could manipulate her cloudy dreams to make her submit completely to his influence. Within moments her soul was taken; delicately ripped from her body, never to return.

Grinning with success, he pulled himself away from her. He could see the vapor-like essence floating outside of her body, searching for a new host. All living creatures had an aura connected to their souls, each one its own unique blend of colors and emotion. They were the most valuable form of currency in Hell, and Madeline's obnoxious yellow hue would be fought over by the highest bidder.

He took out his pocket watch and opened it up, exposing the face of the clock to the dissociated aura. It acted as a container that her soul was sucked into. Now that it was collected, his job was complete, and he could return home.

The incubus took one last look at his victim. From the outside, she looked like she was merely sleeping, no damage to her body. On the inside she was empty, a husk of what she used to be. Smiling, he took the blankets and covered her, in his own way mocking her for trying to remain celibate and faithful to God.

The room felt empty without the life force of Madeline resonating off the walls with each heartbeat. All that was left was the soothing warmth of an angel's divine determination trying to melt away the icy chill of a demon's work.

"You took her soul..."

Regal turned, seeing the winded angel floating in front of the window with a look of despair and horror plastered on his face. A wicked grin tugged at the demon's lips.

"You monster," Keir said lowly, his eyes blazing brightly.

Regal burst into laughter. "You're as much as a monster as I am, if not worse for being so pure," he sneered.

Keir launched himself forward, filled with anger fueled by holy justice. Regal had been expecting the angel to get angry, but was not prepared for him to brazenly instigate an attack. Regal swiftly moved to the side, Keir's shield knocking into his arm and leaving a gash in his bicep. Black ichor began to well at the edges, pooling for a moment before dripping down his arm.

The demon, just as trained and skilled as the angel before him, allowed his pocket watch to expand again to become a deadly long-range weapon once more. To hell with being careful; he was going to teach this angel a lesson.

Crying out in rage, Regal leapt forward and whipped his chain toward Keir. The watch bounced off of Keir's shield as he held it up to protect him, leaving a large gash into the hardened metal. Regal pulled his weapon back toward him, swinging it around his body before lashing back at Keir. The angel leapt over Madeline's soulless body, dodging Regal's attack. The demon's watch was buried into the plaster wall, refusing to be yanked out easily. Regal discarded his pocket watch and grabbed the stool in front of the vanity just as Keir swung his shield down onto his back.

Keir's weapon collided with the chair as Regal used it as protection. The wooden legs splintered off as Regal pushed back at Keir's advances. He flapped his wings to help give him an extra boost of power. Keir pressed forward with equal strength, and the two found themselves in a stalemate.

Growing more infuriated, Regal let go of the remains of the stool, causing Keir to stumble forward in surprise. He swung his leg under Keir's feet to trip him. The angel's shield clattered to the ground as they both went tumbling down.

Each weaponless and desperate to overpower the other, they continued to fight with their bare hands. They clawed and scratched like wild animals, ripping out feathers and leaving red welts and scratches on their once-flawless skin. They tumbled and rolled across the floor, knocking into furniture and breaking property. Finally, Regal managed to gain the upper hand and pinned Keir to the floor, his fingers clasped around the angel's neck.

"Huh... you know, angel, you're not too bad of a fighter," Regal grunted, panting as he caught his breath. "Michaelangelo must have taught you well."

"Trying to use your abilities to seduce me, demon?" he gagged as he tried to pry away the fingers around his throat. "It won't work!"

Regal cocked a brow. That was definitely an amusing idea. He chuckled. "You think? I'm sure I can prove you wrong and make you fall."

He yanked Keir's face forward, kissing him forcefully. The taste of an angel's lips was sweeter than any other human's. They were constantly warm and tingled with pure energy. It burned Regal's mouth to have something so innocent and pure so close to him, but the pain was worth it. To feel the angel squirm under his touch, fighting back the urge to give into his power until he couldn't any longer was satisfying. As Regal continued to force his darkness onto the angel, Keir's white aura grew weaker until he had no chance of breaking free. Keir fell limp with a soft whimper of defeat.

The incubus chuckled lowly. This was almost too easy. Regal let go of his grip, standing up to tower over the angel's crumpled form. Spitting out the aftertaste, he stepped over Keir to pluck out a single feather from his wing. It burned to the touch, but it no longer held the same glow that once blinded him.

"A souvenir, for the day I influenced an angel."

He walked over to the wall where his pocket watch was still embedded, and pulled it free. He slipped the feather into an empty slot normally meant for souls and snapped it shut. He put the watch back in his pocket and looked around the room. What a mess. This would definitely look like a homicide with how disastrous the room was. Yet another problem the angel had caused him that night.

Regal fled from the scene, knowing that the angel would eventually pull himself out from his numb state. He wished he could have finished off Keir in that instant, but the laws of Heaven and Hell state that a demon cannot kill an angel, and an angel cannot kill a demon. Doing so without proof of corruption would start a war between the afterlives, and all balance in the world would be lost. Although discord seemed like a fantastic idea, that was under the control of the sole enemy to both Heaven and Hell: Chaos.

But Regal could dream as he flew away, leaving the consequences of his infernal deeds behind him.

CHAPTER *Two*

REGAL DIDN'T WASTE his time hunting in rural areas. There wasn't enough prey to kill without someone noticing a pattern. He preferred working in built-up urban cities like San Diego, where one missing person or two wouldn't create much of a stir. Yet, in the small town of Woodburn, Iowa, everybody knew everybody. The risk of being caught was too high, even though he was sure that would never happen.

The one good thing about rural communities is that they were the perfect place to relax after a long weekend of work. That is, if you could find a place to settle.

He had managed to find a new diner toward the middle of town called The Goldfinch. It was a small establishment, resembling a wooden cabin to give it the homey feel that made it the most successful diner in the area. During the day it was filled with customers, mainly elderly couples in the afternoon, and families in the evening. However, as the sun set and night approached, the diner became empty.

This is when The Goldfinch became a haven for people with big dreams. It was home for teenagers and young adults who were looking to become something greater than what the town had to offer. They gathered at dusk to eat and drink while their friends stood in front of the diner to recite poems and play instruments. Next to woodworking and welding, being a musician or slam poet was considered the next best job opportunity.

By day, they dressed like well-to-do gentlemen and proper ladies, but at night they became wild. They wore racy clothes, listened to secular music, and cheered on their fellow poets and musicians with snaps and whistles. They would mutter amongst themselves, discussing the deeper meaning and the flow of poetry and literature.

Regal thought it was all a load of nonsense.

Sitting in the darkest corner of the room, he leaned back in his seat and watched the newest performer walk onto the stage. In his limp grip was a lukewarm cup of black coffee, which he swirled with lackluster. His gray eyes glazed over with boredom as yet another annoying and monotone voice rang in his ears.

I should kill him, he thought tiredly as he closed his eyes. *I'm sure he won't be missed.* Regal probably would have done so, too, if he weren't too tired to bother.

Regal took a sip of his coffee. He wrinkled his nose as the bitter liquid touched his tongue. He couldn't stand coffee. Yet the dark and quiet ambiance of the diner after dark was soothing. So, he continued to drink it, blending in as best as he could.

Whether he liked it or not, this was his crowd. They drove him insane, but they didn't question his presence. To them, he was "cool," and he didn't judge them for wanting more out of life than being a lumberjack.

He couldn't wait to get out of there and head back to New York City. That's where all of the interesting souls lived.

Regal preferred hunting the Mythos over humans. The fabled creatures were more of a challenge; some of the put up a fight, and others sensed the danger that came off of him before he could get close. The resistance made it more fun.

Many of the people in Woodburn were normal humans— boring and stupid. However, there was a surprising amount of Mythos visiting The Goldfinch that night, which is why Regal hadn't decided to leave earlier.

He continued to lazily watch the crowd, taking note of the Mythos: a male pixie worked behind the counter serving shitty lattes, and the small pack of she-wolves gossiped amongst themselves at one of the tables. Even the young man playing guitar on stage resembled one of the mer-folk despite his human scent. Yet none of them fully roused his appetite.

Out of the corner of his eye, he caught sight of a young woman in her late 20s searching for a place to sit. As she came closer, Regal examined her: wavy brown hair, dark chocolate eyes, and an average face; he had seen much better. She wore a tight blue and black sweater, cute stilettos, and chunky bracelets.

He watched her with dark eyes, scanning her body up and down. From what he could tell, she was a normal human with no signs of any mythological bloodlines. He could do better, and he wasn't in the mood to try and seduce her; he was still exhausted from his last catch in Des Moines.

Fate seemed to be on his side that night, as her gaze connected with his own. Regal perked up as she walked over to him, her hips swaying in time with the clicking of her heels on the wooden floor. She didn't seem to be the shy type, which was a welcome change of pace for Regal. For once, he wouldn't be the one chasing after the women—not that it was ever much of a chase anyways. He caught the smell of her perfume as she came closer. It was sweet, just like the smile on her face as her dark red lips curled up to show perfect white teeth.

"Hey there," she said. "Mind if I have a seat?"

"The pleasure is all mine, beautiful," Regal replied smoothly.

The woman chuckled at his response and sat down beside him. She crossed her legs, subtly flashing him some skin. Regal smirked as she leaned closer until their shoulders were brushing.

"My name is Jen."

Regal smiled despite his urge to roll his eyes. Hell, even her *name* was boring. "Eric."

"You're not from around here, are you?" Jen asked with a seductive grin. She twirled a piece of her hair around her finger. Regal had learned to pick up on these classic cliché signs of flirting after years of experience.

He acted surprised by her statement. "How'd you know?"

"I think I would remember someone like you."

Regal's smirk grew, eyes narrowing just enough to let her notice. Ah, so she was playing *that* game. Too bad he wasn't in the mood for compliments or flirting. He wanted something much more... instinctual.

"Just passing through, actually," he stated, leaning back into his chair as he sipped his coffee again. It had already grown cold, but he wouldn't show it. It wasn't "sexy" to gag on your stale drink.

Jen frowned, her lower lip pouting. "That's too bad. I'd love to show you around the town."

There isn't much of a town to show, he thought cynically. "I'd like that too," he lied with a coy grin he had mastered with practice. It was the subtle reactions that always did the best job at making women swoon. His playful smile and subtle hint of interest did the job, causing her cheeks to flush a bit and her pupils to dilate with desire.

"You don't seem like you're enjoying this place very much," she cooed, glancing around the café.

Regal shrugged in response. "It's alright."

Focusing back on him, she scooted closer in her seat, brushing her leg against his. "We can always ditch this place and have fun elsewhere."

Now *that* was what he wanted to hear.

"Sounds good to me," he purred as he ran a hand against her thigh. She shivered under the gentle touch. Regal loved it when they reacted the way they were supposed to. It was even better when they willingly came to him. He didn't have to work hard to flatter and seduce them. "Where would you like to go?"

"I know a club in the next town over. They have a fantastic DJ and the best drinks," Jen said eagerly, biting her lip to try and not seem too fervent. Her excitement was a turn on for Regal. Like a predator, her high levels of adrenaline and arousal spiked his desire to hunt. He decided that his exhaustion could be ignored if it would land him another woman to win over.

"I'll take your word for it." Regal smiled as he stood up, lending his hand out for her.

"Oh," she said suddenly. Regal could feel waves of anxiety rolling off of her. "You are twenty-one, right? I don't want to rob the cradle or drag a kid out to a club when they shouldn't be there..."

I wonder why that is? Regal thought. *Worried that past mistakes of fooling around with minors will come back to haunt you?* He chuckled, pretending that he found her question funny. "I get that a lot. I may look young, but I am over the age of twenty-one," he assured her. *Much older, actually.*

"Great," she sighed with relief. She took his hand and got to her feet, masterfully balancing on her six-inch heels.

Discarding his drink in the nearest trash bin, Regal slipped his hand around her waist and pulled her close. "Just lead the way, beautiful."

Jen giggled again, her eyes dancing in the dim lighting. She was clearly flattered by the pet-name Regal gave her, and he could feel the energy sparking between them, building up rapidly. As she led him toward the front door, he began to plan his final night in Woodburn with this vixen.

A warm sensation washed over him. It was an unnatural feeling and it made his stomach churn. He paused and stared out the front window in surprise. Watching hard for a moment, he waited for the warmth that surrounded his body to fade. Instead, it came back even stronger as he caught sight of a thin man walking toward the diner. His face was hidden underneath his mop of blond hair that glistened under the "OPEN" sign in the window. Fixating his gaze on the stranger, Regal caught sight of glowing blue eyes.

Dammit, he's here?

Regal turned around, holding tightly onto the woman in his arms for balance. He hissed under his breath with annoyance. Who would have thought *he* would think of searching for him in a place like this?

"Are you okay, Eric?" Jen asked with concern, her voice slightly higher from being spun around. She noticed that Regal was considerably paler in complexion and seemed nervous.

"Yes, fine," he said quickly, his mind reeling as he tried to think. He was so close to claiming another victim, but he couldn't stay here. It was too dangerous now. With a soft sigh, he pulled his arm from the woman's waist. "I'm sorry, beautiful, but I have to go. An emergency turned up." He turned, cupping her face in his hand before placing a soft kiss on her cheek. "Perhaps next time."

As soon as the last syllable fell from his mouth, he left her side and headed for the back exit, pushing people out of his way as he fled. The bell on the front door jingled as it opened and another strong wave of warmth crashed into him. He wove around tables and chairs until he reached the back exit. He shoved the door open and hurried out, not bothering to make sure that it was closed as he fled from the diner.

Guided by the barely-present crescent moon, Regal sprinted down the back alley toward the edge of town. The darkness of the night charged him, making him feel stronger, but it did nothing to protect him from the light that was close behind.

He could sense Keir on his tail. Regal glanced behind him, catching sight of the ethereal glow reflecting on the brick walls. He kept running and examined his surroundings. The alley was too tight; he would never be able to escape upward. His only choice was to run straight.

Clearing the end of the alley, he headed for the woods across the dirt road. Like the flick of a switch, Regal activated the innate celestial charm of invisibility that hid him from the sight of humans and mythos alike. However, those like him could still see him. His only chance at escaping was to get lost in the cover of the trees and put plenty of distance between them.

He sprinted for another several feet, his shoes crushing the grass and weeds of the unkempt meadow. As soon as his foot hit the edge of the forest, he let out a deep breath and leapt into the air. His wings shot out from his back, the tips brushing the ground as he attempted to become airborne. His feathers caught in the tree branches. The forest was denser than he expected. Cursing, he grabbed a thick branch and curled his wings in. He'd have to climb to the top before he could fly freely.

He only made it halfway up the tree before he felt a hand grip his ankle. Hissing, Regal kicked back at his assailant. His eyes turned black with rage as he swiped at his attacker with a clawed hand.

"Regal, stop!"

Regal ignored his pleas and continued to climb. He yanked on a tree branch and let it whip back. It smacked Keir in the chest. A mixture of green, red, and yellow leaves fluttered to the ground as Regal pushed his way to the top of the canopy. However, Keir was persistent and climbed up after him with little hesitation. Although he was not as nimble, he managed to catch up to Regal.

Unfurling his dark wings once more, Regal leaped off the top of the tree. Black feathers dropped behind him as he pumped his wings, desperately trying to climb higher into the air.

"Please, wait!" Keir called out as he chased after him.

Regal grunted with annoyance, forcing himself to fly faster and higher. Yet no matter the power he put into each stroke, his stalker could match it.

If I can't outpace him, I'll have to outsmart him.

He suddenly changed direction, dive-bombing toward the ground. He tucked his wings in, gaining speed as he headed for the forest. The rush of wind in his face, tugging at his feathers and pricking his skin, was exhilarating.

Regal glanced behind him and smirked when he saw no sight of Keir. Before he hit the ground, he extended his wings again, catching the air to slow him down. He angled his feet for the floor, landing smoothly as his heels dug into the soft dirt. He began to sprint once he was on steady ground again. Tucking in his wings, he ran under the cover of the canopy of trees.

He panted, walking toward a natural cave near the edge of the forest. Welcoming the darkness, Regal sighed and sat down against the wall and closed his eyes, basking in the cool dampness of the cave. Soft squeaks of bats greeted him, and he couldn't help but smile.

This was his domain, his home. Any dark cavern or shadowed room was his safe haven. He felt protected here.

He wasn't expecting the warm—almost affectionate—sensation to hit him so hard again and ruin his moment of peace. Before he could even pull himself to his feet and flee, his stalker was blocking the exit.

"Didn't think you'd lose me again with that trick, did you?" Keir said smugly, proud of cornering the demon.

Regal hissed, flaring his wings in an attempt to prevent the man from trapping him. However, all it did was cause the other man do the same, his wings casting a bright light into the cave. Regal winced and hid behind his wings to block out the holy aura with darkness.

"Please don't run anymore. I need to talk to you."

The demon peeked through his feathers, groaning as the glow shone through. With the walls of the cave reflecting the light and trapping the heavenly essence inside, it was like flying too close to the sun. "Put those damned things away and *maybe* I'll listen."

Keir did as he was told. Regal sighed, his body aching from the concentrated exposure to the warm aura. He stood up straighter, in an effort to look strong and unaffected by the other's holy essence. Keir smiled warmly, causing Regal to sneer.

"Thank you—"

"Tell me what you want."

Keir stepped back a bit, his expression growing nervous. Regal watched as he toyed with his hands, as if uncertain of what to say.

"Spit it out!" he barked impatiently.

"I can't just spit it out," Keir replied, his voice wavering with apprehension. "I have to word it carefully."

Regal sighed heavily, moving from his place in the shadows to walk closer to Keir. "You have been chasing me down for over a year. I suggest you say what you want before I rip your wings from your sockets," he growled. The guttural sound ripped from his chest as his fangs flashed again in warning.

Keir's eyes widened in fear. He knew Regal could easily dislodge his wings if he wanted. "I... I want you..." he squeaked quickly, his face flushing.

Regal laughed, his voice echoing in the cave and making him sound louder. "I knew I was good, but not *that* good."

Keir's flustered expression hardened at Regal's reaction. He looked Regal straight in the eye and continued, "I mean... I... I love you."

Regal's stroked ego deflated as he stared at Keir, his lips curled in a repulsed snarl. "No, you don't."

"Yes, I do."

The demon reached out to grab the collar of Keir's shirt in his hand, dragging him closer until they were face to face. "Then you're delusional."

The angel yelped, his hands flying up to claw at Regal's grip. "I'm not delusional! Ever since I met you, I've loved you," he all but screamed in panic.

"That's not how I remember it."

"Who cares how it happened?"

"Angels don't fall in love with demons. It's wrong. Even for a demon, it's *wrong*."

"But isn't that your specialty?" Keir shot back, growing a bit braver as they argued.

Regal scoffed. "I'm an incubus. I don't play with your concept of love."

"Haven't you already proven how talented you are? Because here I am, and I will not leave so easily."

They stood in the mouth of the cave, their eyes glowing dangerously in the dark as they stared each other down. Around them, the wildlife grew silent. Crickets stopped chirping, deer huddled in high grass, and families of rabbits shook with fear. They could sense the struggle that was mounting between two beings much more powerful than anything in their world.

A demon from the deepest pits of Hell and an angel from the gates of Heaven were never meant to interact except in battle. They were never meant to be friendly toward one another.

They certainly were never meant to fall in love.

CHAPTER *Three*

DO YOU EVEN realize how ridiculous you sound?" Regal asked, laughing at the absurdity of the whole ordeal. "What were you expecting, some sort of heartwarming confession? Demons can't love. We are nothing but rage, and lust, and every horrible nightmare you pure little *things* are not."

"I know you can't love me back!" Keir barked with frustration. Regal watched him sternly as the angel fell silent. Keir remained quiet for a minute before hanging his head. "I know what you are, and I know what you do."

"So why did you hunt me down if you knew it was for nothing?" Regal asked impatiently, confused at the angel's bewildering actions. "Have you forgotten that getting into a relationship with a demon is forbidden? You can be exiled from Heaven."

Now, *that* was an interesting idea.

"I know, but... ever since that day, I've been smitten for you and I can't fight it," Keir explained. "It was driving me insane! I had to find you and tell you despite the risks."

"Well, it was a waste of your time." He still couldn't comprehend Keir's reasoning. It was foolish and pathetic.

"It's never a waste of time to go after something you love."

"I can't decide if I should kill you now, or let you suffer with your unrequited feelings of *love*," Regal grumbled under his breath. He was growing more irritated by Keir's statements. Deciding it was best to let it go, he released his grip on Keir's shirt and pushed past him to leave.

"There is one more reason why I came here. One I think you'll like better," Keir said desperately, turning to face Regal's back. The incubus stopped for a moment, staring at the mouth

32

of the cave. He could sense Keir's strength and power coming off him in waves, slamming into Regal's own dark aura. It made him nauseated, and immensely curious.

"You have ten seconds to explain."

With a shuddered breath, Keir whispered, "I also came to... serve you..."

"Serve me?" Regal asked with surprise, looking back at the irrational angel. "Like a slave? You've got to be—"

"I can't face Gloria anymore," Keir blurted, cutting Regal off. "Now that I've fallen in love with a demon..."

"How do I know that this isn't a trick? Your Mother is just as crafty as my father. This could easily be a ploy to capture me."

"Angels don't lie."

"Everyone lies," Regal scoffed. He hated how angels thought of themselves as superior. They were just as flawed as demons; which was why he was skeptical of Keir's request. Warning signals were going off in his head, yelling at him to turn away. He knew it was dangerous to affiliate himself with angels, and he'd be better off rejecting the angel's advances. However, Regal was certain that an angel had never asked to be a demon's servant in the history of the universe. If Keir were telling the truth... Regal could go down in history as the first demon to *own* an angel.

The temptation was too great to overcome.

"Alright."

Keir blinked with surprise. "Really?"

Regal nodded. "I'll let you tag along with me, and I'll keep quiet about it to your Mother."

"Thank you, Regal!" Keir cried out happily, rushing forward to hug him tightly. Regal stiffened, expecting pain to seize him; but the angel's embrace caused him no harm, only discomfort.

He fought back the urge to flee and growled, shoving Keir back enough to force him onto the ground. "Not so fast, angel.

It's not that easy. I'll give you the opportunity to stay by my side... if you agree to do your part as well. What are you willing to give to be with a *lowly* demon like myself?"

This was the ultimatum. If Keir backed away, Regal would be free. However, if Keir accepted Regal's demands, he would have an angelic servant. It was a win-win situation. Everything was up to fate now.

After a moment, Keir finally spoke up. "I... give you my body to... use as you please..." he uttered, shuddering. Regal began to laugh again. Annoyed by his response, Keir regained his composure. "That is what you want, isn't it, incubus?"

The incubus grinned viciously. "Fair enough." He closed the distance between them, a glint in his eye. "Of course, I will do what every demon does: mark his territory."

Keir's bravado flickered away, and the flash of fear in his eyes made Regal swell with pride. Fear was going to be his biggest ally in claiming this holy being.

"Mark your territory?" Keir asked nervously.

Regal smiled. "Are you frightened to give up your flawless hide for a demon who will put a permanent scar on your body?"

Keir shuddered at the thought. It was the last thing he wanted, but it was necessary in the process of bonding ethereal beings. Angels left white tattoos as a way to mate for life, and Keir assumed demons had their own version of it. If Keir wanted the bond between them to be legitimate, he had to allow Regal to brand him.

He gulped and closed his eyes. His wings collapsed out of him, unable to hold them inside any longer. They draped weakly on the ground behind him like a battered swan's.

Regal cringed and glanced away from him. "Those have to be gone."

Keir looked at his wings solemnly for a moment and stroked

them. He pulled them back slowly, reluctant to let Regal hurt them in any way.

"They are gone..."

"Trust me, I can tell," Regal sighed as he flared out his wings to block out all the light. The darkness enveloped them as he leaned closer to the angel.

The desire to overpower Keir was immense. The predator within Regal was dying to come out. He wanted to pin the angel down, terrify him, destroy him, tear him to pieces and savor every inch of his tanned skin. He wanted him to suffer, but something inside of him fought against it: mercy, kindness, sympathy? All traits of angels. It disgusted him to know that such emotions clawed at his conscience.

Regal sighed, trying to sort out the conflicting thoughts in his head. He stared at Keir, his eyes soaking in every feature of the angel's disgustingly perfect face.

Damn it all.

"Say the vow," Regal commanded.

"I can't remember it all by heart..." Keir said with embarrassment, his face flushing.

Regal sighed with annoyance and shook his head. "Repeat after me: I, Keir, vow in the name of Gloria..."

Keir smiled warmly. "If it's easier, don't worry trying to edit it for me. I'll tweak it as needed."

Regal grimaced at Keir's dumb, love-struck face, and rambled off the vow quickly out of spite, hoping Keir would have a hard time catching it all: "I, Regal, in the name of Jackal, and by the life that courses within my blood, take you, Keir, under my wing and into my spirit as my life-bound partner. I shall forever be your ruler, and you shall forever be my servant. I vow to protect you and follow you to the end of days."

Keir repeated the vow, switching out Regal's and Jackal's

names for his own and Gloria's. When he stumbled, forgetting the words, Regal would remind him impatiently, until Keir had said everything correctly.

As soon as Keir finished, they could sense their auras stretching to link together, with Regal's taking the dominant role of master. Now it was time to physically mark his property.

The demon grasped the angel's chin roughly and tilted his head up to stare directly at him. Regal's eyes turned black, the whites of his eyes fading into nothing, and his claws scraping at the soft skin on his cheeks. Despite his rough actions, he did not harm the flesh.

Keir didn't seem deterred by Regal's unhinged power. Regal wondered for a moment if he should be concerned that Keir seemed too calm all of a sudden, but pushed aside his worries.

He closed the gap, pressing his mouth against the angel's just as he did the night they first met, causing Keir to gasp lightly. Regal tilted his head slightly, making sure no part of Keir's lips was untouched. He allowed his dark energy to flow through him into the angel; he could sense the corruption destroying Keir from within. The light that radiated from inside faded away until it was almost unnoticeable.

Keir's courage vanished. His eyes were wide as he felt the darkness creeping into his soul. It burned as it trickled down his throat, into his stomach, and outward through his veins to reach every part of his body. He felt like he was being torn apart from inside. His eyes shut tight as he gave into Regal, knowing there was no turning back now.

Then, a terrifying question appeared in Keir's mind: was this Regal's version of affection? If so, was this the best Keir had to look forward to? Would he be able to withstand it without feeling such pain?

I must, Keir thought diligently. *I'll teach him how to love.*

The angel focused on the light shining behind his eyelids as Regal's wings lowered to allow the dim moonlight to shine over them. He clung to that image, willing the strength to move forward with his plan. Placing his hands on Regal's cheek, he pulled him closer and kissed back. Regal seemed to pay no mind to the angel's actions, and in fact mirrored him by moving his hands up to cup Keir's cheeks. He was solely focused on draining the holy energy from Keir's soul and replacing it with his darkness, riding along the high that came with such a potent ritual.

It was in this moment, when Regal was engrossed in claiming Keir as his own, that the angel acted on his true intentions. Although noticeably fainter, the heavenly light within the angel returned. Slowly, it entered Regal's body. It was warm, not at all painful, and it coursed through the demon's veins like new blood. It lapped at the darkness of his soul like waves on a beach. Regal hardly noticed it and continued to complete his own task.

Keir allowed his wings out, their shine now gone due to Regal's ritual. They were pale and white, although the darkness easily broke through its translucent gaps.

Regal pulled away, looking at his handiwork. The brands on Keir were subtle, but obvious to those who knew what they were. Keir's lips were tinged darker, and his cheeks were stained with Regal's fingerprints. They looked like symmetrical wing-shaped birthmarks. The angel's wings were translucent as well, yet another sign of their pledge. He grinned, pleased with his achievement, and stood up.

"Come now. We have business to do."

Keir nodded and stood shakily. He wrapped his wings around himself, holding them close as though he was cold. He couldn't believe that they were no longer the bright, pure white that they once were.

"Where are we going?" he asked meekly.

Regal smiled. "To see my Father. He would like to see my latest catch."

"What? You said that you would keep quiet!" Keir squeaked, stepping back. This caused the demon to laugh.

"To *your* creator. I never said anything about keeping secrets from mine." Regal spread out his wings widely, the force of their opening causing feathers to fall around his feet. To Keir, he looked like a fallen angel.

Just then, Regal caught the glimpse of a feather as it landed by the angel's feet. He noticed how the normally pitch-black feather was now a thin gray. It was translucent. Tainted.

Regal's eyes widened, turning black immediately in rage. "What did you do?"

Keir grit his teeth, taking another step back. "I had to make sure that you wouldn't mark me and then run off," he retorted. He furrowed his brow at the demon. "I wasn't going to botch a year of chasing after you without a plan in mind. I may not be as calculating or as cunning as you, but I *do* think ahead."

"You *marked* me!" Regal roared, his wings fluttering around him angrily as his fingernails turned into sharp claws. "I should exterminate you for this."

"It's your own fault you were marked," Keir growled, his eyes flashing with the intensity his wings had once held. "You didn't think of the possibility of me retaliating. You made the mistake in trusting me to be a blind, lovesick fool, and you were arrogant enough to rush through the vow without thinking of the consequences."

They both knew that Keir was right. The angel had not said anything about not marking Regal back, and Regal had underestimated the validity of his oath. Regal hissed, cursing himself silently for allowing the angel to trick him. He suppressed his anger and clenched his fist, drawing blood. The black liquid dripped down his hand, spilling onto the ground.

"You're lucky we're bound. If I were to kill you now, I would die, too." He turned swiftly and let his once-dark wings spread out. "We're leaving."

Regal leapt into the air, his wings beating down hard. The tips of his feathers brushed the cave floor for a moment before he was airborne and soaring away without looking back.

Keir sighed and followed the demon, his wings flapping effortlessly after him. He wrapped his arms around himself as he flew after Regal, who continued to soar higher until he was far past the clouds.

He let his wings beat slowly, keeping him suspended in the air. As Keir flew up beside him, shivering from the cool breeze, he pulled out his pocket watch and checked the time briefly before turning the dial on the side three times.

One of many small secret compartments slid out from the bottom. Inside was a small, black crystal that resembled a chunk of obsidian. It glistened with purple highlights that bounced off the crystal's cleavage and onto the inside of the slot. Keir recognized it as a demonic nomad stone. It was similar to the gems that archangels used to travel from Heaven to Earth. The only difference was that an angelic nomad stone was pure quartz white.

Keir watched as Regal took out the stone and took a deep breath. The demon closed his eyes and clasped his hands together, holding the crystal within his palms, and bringing them to his chest. He could almost see the light flickering from between his fingers.

Regal squeezed tightly, increasing the heat and pressure on the gem. A bright light flashed, and Regal reopened his palm. The black crystal had melted to form a malleable gel. The liquid mass hovered over his hands, shimmering with a dark and powerful light.

He murmured his desired destination: the outskirts. He then spread out his wings swiftly to create a large gust of wind. The breeze caused the gel to quickly expand into a large portal, the center swirling with dark energy.

Keir glided near Regal, staring at the portal. The aura radiating from the gateway made his stomach churn with anxiety. Keir was used to traveling through the portals, thanks to his mentor's constant training, but he had never encountered one with such a foreboding presence.

"I can't go in there."

"Yes, you can. Now get in the portal."

"You know what the rules are. Angels aren't allowed in—"

"Get your ass in the portal right now!" Regal commanded.

The two glared at each other, each too stubborn to give in to the other's demands. Their wills clashed like bulls locking horns, refusing to give ground. Eventually, the combination of the portal's negative energy and the force of Regal's resolve caused Keir to waver.

He broke eye contact, looking toward the ground. Regal smirked, feeling triumphant. The angel glanced over toward the portal and sighed, his shoulders sagging with defeat.

"After you," Regal gloated.

Keir looked between Regal and the dark portal. He shuddered heavily, and took a steadying breath. He closed his eyes and shot through the portal in one wing beat. Regal followed after, the seams of the portal stitching shut behind him. He saw Keir hovering above the ground, looking around wildly at his new surroundings.

Regal smiled as he took in a deep breath. He enjoyed the slightly stale and damp breeze that pulled at his feathers. The sickly-sweet smell of rotten souls being swept away in the River Styx comforted him.

He was back in Hell.

He was home.

CHAPTER *Four*

*T*HIS WAS THE realm of the dead and the damned. This was the home of all demons, and the most feared place of mortals and pure beings. It was a dark and desolate abode, crawling with demons and lesser beings who were deemed unworthy to go to Heaven.

Gray dust kicked up around them as they landed on the dried and cracked ground. With the swirling vortex now closed, the two were now stranded on the outskirts of Hell. Only the weakest demons who strayed far from the rivers leading toward the city resided here. Although it was nothing like the comfortable royal life Regal was used to, simply being within this ethereal plane was comforting.

Keir, however, felt queasy and lightheaded. His heart pounded as he felt a wave of unease crash into him. This place was forbidden, toxic, and dangerous for an angel. He stepped closer to Regal, seeking comfort. The incubus sneered in disgust as their shoulders brushed. Keir coughed slightly and waved his hand to disperse the dense fog that surrounded him.

"Don't bother. Until we get closer to the main city, the fog won't get any thinner. Keep walking with me, and don't bother trying to fly, either. You'll be as blind as a bat with only Purgatory to light your way," Regal directed harshly as he began his trek back home.

Keir looked up at the heavy clouds above them and could see the faint glow of many moons hanging between the realms of Heaven and Hell. These were the homes to the mysterious lesser gods that ranked under Gloria. Keir had never met any of them, but he knew of their power. Three of the moons were completely

42

dark, left abandoned by their gods. However, the brightest of the moons was Purgatory, home of the dragon god Malektil. Souls of the deceased were judged there to determine whether they would spend their afterlife in Heaven, Hell, or in Chaos' Realm.

"How long of a walk will it be?" he asked with a shiver, jogging to keep up with Regal's quick pace.

"About twenty minutes." Regal's voice was still bitter.

Keir gulped silently, his mouth dry from fear. However, he didn't stray from Regal's side. The demon was the only person who could protect him in this realm.

As they walked, Keir kept an eye out for danger. Contrary to popular belief, the realm was not a pit of fire and brimstone. Rather, it was a desert wasteland. Above them was a dense blanket of smog that would make it impossible for anyone to see the ground from above. The earth was dull gray with flecks of black ash and cracks along the surface. It was dry and flaked as they walked across it. In the distance, he could see dark murky rivers lapping against the desolate shore. Keir immediately recognized it as one of the five rivers that used to carry unfortunate souls toward the city. The most famous of the five was the River Styx. This was where the ferryman Charon swept freshly damned souls into the center of Hell on his rickety gondola.

Regal took Keir near one of the rivers. The angel recoiled from the water's edge. Keir could see the faint forms of souls being pulled along by icy currents, desperate hands reaching out to try and pull Keir and Regal in. The waves of the river mixed with their cries for help, and Keir felt his stomach flip in agony at the sight of their mouth hanging open. The incubus got a sadistic kick out of seeing Keir squirm.

"Sad, isn't it? So many souls deemed unworthy of going to Heaven," Regal mused as he kept their greedy hands away from

Keir. "Looks like Heaven has strict rules for admission."

"Malektil judged them accordingly," Keir replied with a huff.

The fog began to thin as they made their way through the outskirts and closer to the Kingdom. They could both see the outline of the massive castle in the center of a giant industrialized city. It stood out amongst the metal and glass of the surrounding buildings. The castle was built out of black and red stone and silver: the colors of Hell. Tall towers jutted up toward the sky, their roofs sharpening into arrows that pointed toward Heaven. A large gate made of black iron surrounded the castle's property, to keep out unwanted guests. The only visible door was made of silver and sat underneath a giant arch.

Keir knew that the moment they stepped through the front gates, he would be making history. It was rare that angels ever stepped foot in Hell, let alone inside of the castle. The last one who did had fallen from grace and had wreaked havoc among both kingdoms.

Everyone in Heaven and Hell knew the story. It was a legend that haunted all souls, young or old. The elder angels were always wary, afraid that the events may happen again. Keir was certain the demons were just as anxious.

Originally, Hell was known as Hades, named after the original ruler of the Underworld. Hades ruled his domain with a kind heart. He was humble and treated his people less like slaves and more like independent demons. His time as ruler was prosperous, and many were happy with his childish, yet modest ways of judgment.

However, the only remaining evidence of his reign was now in ruins. His kingdom was destroyed during the civil war that ended with his death. Keir could see them in the distance, looming over the barren ground like a dead carcass. His blue eyes were locked on the rubble. He could only imagine the horrors that took place at those ruins so long ago, the terror and confusion that was caused by the treachery of Satan, the most famous fallen angel in history.

Satan was corrupted by Chaos, the enemy of both Gloria and Hades. After he and his best friend, Lucifer, fell from Heaven and took residence in the Underworld, Satan's greed developed into a desire to claim his new home as his own domain. To accomplish this goal, he lulled Hades into trusting him until he was named the Prince of Wrath.

Once his title was secured, he began to establish a legion of demons who wanted to take control of the kingdom. He was able to successfully find allies in three of the other six princes to join him. On the night of the battle, while his allies started a civil war against the other three princes who denied Satan's offer, he focused on assassinating Hades. Satan managed to separate the god from his loyal guard, a demon named Ephysto, and brutally attacked him. He then murdered Hades in cold blood, blasting a hole through his chest before Erebos—Hades' best friend, partner, and protector—could stop him.

Erebos and Satan battled for ages, fighting for revenge and power. Their unholy fight finally ended when Ephysto collected the last remaining ounces of energy within him and released them in an unhallowed burst. However, his aim was off, and the spell meant to destroy Satan hit Erebos as well. As a result, the two souls combined to create a new being. Too weak to correct the spell, Ephysto died soon after and Jackal was born.

At that moment, he became the new ruler of Hades. Jackal appointed new princes to replace the ones who had lost their lives during the war. He then renamed the realm *Hell*, as a symbol of rebirth and renewal, but kept the remains of Hades as a reminder of their past. He never wanted the inhabitants of Hell to forget the battle that took place and the great loss they had experienced.

This decision appeased the elder demons, who believed that Jackal shouldn't have been given the throne so easily.

A shiver ran down Keir's spine at the thought of it all, causing Regal to laugh lowly. "It's amusing how mere ruins can make you so uncomfortable."

"It's horrific what happened there," Keir stated, his voice wavering slightly. He cleared his throat a bit before he continued, "For both Kingdoms. We lost a powerful angel and you lost a powerful ruler."

Regal shrugged. "I wasn't alive to witness it, so I don't hold any opinions on it."

"None?" Keir asked in surprise. "I find that hard to believe. I mean, if Gloria had been lost, I'm sure all of the angels would have felt despair for many centuries."

"That's because you're all *Her* children," Regal snapped, glaring at the angel beside him. His fists clenched with annoyance. "Hades is not my father. Jackal is. I follow his commands, not those of a deceased king."

Regal was silent for the rest of the journey, except to scold Keir for using his wings for balance as they walked along the worn bridge that crossed over the deep chasm separating the outskirts from the city. Keir didn't bother arguing with him, knowing that it was dangerous to reveal that he was an angel in a place full of demons.

Soon after entering the slums, which consisted mainly of run-down shacks and apartments with crumbling walls and broken windows, they could both feel the ground quaking beneath their feet. Keir instantly flapped his wings to bring himself off the ground. Regal reached up to grab Keir's wrist to pull him back down.

"How many times do I have to tell you to keep those in?" he hissed.

"What was that?" Keir asked nervously.

"Tartarus, The Glutton, whatever else you wish to call it," Regal explained tersely. "It's the beast that Hell is built upon."

Keir gasped in shock. "Tartarus? As in the Titan, the son of Chaos?"

Regal shot an annoyed look at Keir. "Yes. Don't they teach you anything in Heaven?"

Tartarus resembled a large inky mass more than an actual creature. Its skin was burnt and peeling, black ooze dripping from its torn open wounds. It reeked of ash and brimstone, black plumes rising up and creating the dense smog that covered the outskirts. As its name suggested, it was a gluttonous creature that was never satisfied. It swallowed anything that fell off the edge of the floating island.

"I knew of Tartarus, I just didn't know that Hell was built on his back," the angel murmured. Heaven rested upon dense clouds that could support the weight of the kingdom.

"Where else did you expect Hell to stand?" Regal scoffed. "Beneath Tartarus is the Sea of Discord—you *do* know what that is, don't you?"

Keir flushed, refusing to come across as uneducated again. "It's where Chaos lives, and where souls too damned for Hell go as well."

Regal nodded. "If we didn't have The Glutton, we would have nothing to support us or protect us from being dragged under into the slick. We are lucky that it decided to side with Hades and not with its father."

"That makes sense. I guess I just assumed Hell would float like Heaven does."

"That's not how it works in the Underworld. Gravity is more of a bitch." Regal glanced around at the lesser demons who were passing by, begging for food and staring at them as they passed. Even with his wings tucked in, they could sense something was off about the newcomer. Regal glared at them as they crossed into the middle-class portion of the kingdom.

It looked like New York City: large skyscrapers and buildings scattered about within the large walls. These buildings held many lower-class demons who, instead of paying rent, went out in search of souls to feed Tartarus. Regal's job was similar, but the souls he collected were more prized, and were used for labor instead of nourishment. With how much Tartarus moved around, some buildings needed severe renovation.

Here, more demons seemed to pay attention to them, peering through windows of their homes and shops to see who Regal had brought home. It wasn't strange to see an incubus with a new mate, but they too could sense that something was different about Keir. The angel kept close to Regal, who wrapped his arm around Keir's shoulder to establish dominance. This convinced most of the onlookers to mind their own business.

As they approached the main gates that separated Jackal's castle from the rest of the city, Regal stopped Keir. "Turn invisible and keep quiet."

"You're going to try and sneak me in?" Keir asked with a small laugh. "You know that won't work!"

"You're going to have to trust me."

"Trust you?"

Regal continued toward the gates, leaving Keir behind. The angel hurried forward, turning himself invisible as Regal had asked, and kept close to his side.

Standing in front of the doorway was a silent guard, covered in full red and silver armor. He held a long spear in one hand and stood still like a statue. All that could be seen were his red eyes that fixated on Regal for a moment, as if trying to identify him. His grip on the spear tightened.

"I sense an outsider," the guard said. His voice echoed underneath his helmet.

Keir glanced at Regal with surprise. The guard couldn't see him? That meant he wasn't from the ethereal planes...

Regal feigned a sense of being hurt. "Ouch, and I thought you were fond of me."

"Not you. Someone else."

"I'm the only one here, as you can see. Now let me in."

The guard stayed still. "I cannot open the gates if I sense a threat."

"I get that security has been high ever since Hades died, but this *is* my home."

"I apologize, but I cannot—"

"Do you know who I am?" Regal snapped, his voice rising to a yell, causing bystanders to turn and look at the scene. "I can have you stripped of your title, cast off to the outskirts in exile, or thrown to the Glutton. I command that you let me enter before I bring my father into this."

Growling lowly, the guard reluctantly opened the gates to allow the son of Jackal inside.

"Wise decision," Regal spat as he walked forward.

Keir stood close beside him, holding his breath as he tried to be as quiet as he could. He didn't want the guard to change his mind. "He didn't see me," he whispered once they were out of earshot, leaning close to Regal.

"I told you to trust me."

"He wasn't a demon, was he?"

"He was a mythos who was damned to guard Jackal's kingdom until the end of time. I don't remember what he did during his life that left him destined to serve the devil himself..."

"Why didn't you just say so in the first place?" Keir asked with exasperation.

Regal grinned. "You're young for an angel, aren't you?"

Keir glared back at Regal. "What makes you say that?"

"First of all, you have a baby face."

"So do cherubs, but they're some of the oldest angels in Heaven."

"You're also pretty naïve."

Keir crossed his arms over his chest defiantly. "If you were forced to visit Heaven without any explanation of how things worked, I think you would be pretty clueless as well!"

Regal snickered, taking pleasure in getting on Keir's nerves. He turned around to salute the guard who watched him warily. The gates closed behind them with a loud squeal, sealing them inside of the courtyard to await their visit with the Lord of Hell.

CHAPTER *Five*

REGAL TOOK A deep breath and sighed. This was his true home. No smog from Tartarus or the Sea of Discord. No unfortunate souls trying to grab at him whenever he walked past. No lesser demons trying to gain his affection. There was only safety and comfort within the walls of his father's castle.

It was built up in the center of the city, and was by far the most elaborate and well-kept building here. This was where Jackal lived, along with his most favored demons and servants. Regal was one of them.

"Every inch of this kingdom will be mine someday," Regal said as he stopped in the center of the plaza. Running along the ground were small demons known as furies, who scavenged and roamed in search of a meal. One slipped through the fence and ran close by Regal and Keir, causing the angel to gasp in surprise. His hand flew up to his pendant, prepared to release the shield that could protect him from an attack. However, the fury did not dare come closer to them. Regal gave off a presence of importance and reeked of high status. He chuckled at their reaction and turned toward Keir.

"So, you're actually Jackal's son?"

"Unlike you angels, who call Gloria your Mother regardless of whom you're born to, I'm actually related to Jackal. You should feel proud that you're bonded with royalty," Regal bragged, grinning from ear to ear.

"I suppose. I don't care much about status. Hierarchies don't matter in our kingdoms," Keir mused, gaining a small ounce of enjoyment out of Regal's annoyance. Even though Regal was an incubus, he still had a lot of pride within him, and teasing him by pretending not to care made Keir feel better. Two could play the mind games. "How long until we meet your father?"

"It may be a while, so sit and enjoy the view," Regal said as he walked up to the edge of the fountain in the center of the plaza and sat on the edge.

Keir sighed and sat beside Regal. Although he honestly did love the incubus, he was finding staying with him more difficult than he had imagined. He looked around curiously, his eyes wide and bright as he took everything in. He ran his hands along the cool stonework of the fountain and soon recognized the structure. There was a fountain similar to this one in Heaven, except the one back home was gold and white in color instead of black and silver.

They were called the Fountains of Fate. Despite looking similar, each fountain told a different story. The one Keir and Regal sat on described the nine levels of Hell where damned souls resided. The water feature made of dark marble and steel no longer ran. It was a tiered structure, composed of three large basins supported by thick pillars.

The bottom of the fountain—now dried up and covered in dust—was shaped like a pentagon and once held clear, shimmering water. Five pillars, one at each point, jutted out and supported the second basin. This basin looked like a large bowl with holes cut out in the bottom to let the water flow down like rain. Three more pillars extended from this basin to hold up the final cup. A single pillar rose up from the center with a statue of Hades balancing on the top. The basins were carved with incantations and ancient runes that told the story of Hades' downfall, as well as the birth of Jackal. The nine pillars were decorated with detailed sculptures representing the different levels of Hell: Limbo, Lust, Gluttony, Greed, Anger, Heresy, Violence, Fraud, and Treachery. These factions were hidden within the body of Tartarus, and sinners were sent to live the rest of their afterlife in the group that suited them best.

The fountain represented everything Hell had to offer to those who sinned, including disobedient demons.

"Is this the center of Hell?" Keir asked as he stared straight up into the sky. The incubus glanced over at him, sighing.

"Yes. Why do you ask?" he questioned, hoping that the angel wouldn't actually give him an answer.

Keir felt a strange sense of peace, knowing that he was still connected to Heaven even while being in Hell. "Heaven is directly above us, then." Keir's comforted smile made Regal gag. However, Regal did not have to suffer in Keir's company for long. Soon after, Persephone, the Queen of Hell, came walking down one of the corridors toward them.

Persephone wore a red gown and silver jewelry that accentuated her short, curvy figure. Her brown eyes looked dull and lacking in enjoyment. It was no secret that she despised having to live in Hell during the fall and winter seasons, especially now that Hades was dead and she was Jackal's inherited wife. Her hair was currently a deep brown that was tipped with red, orange, and yellow. Her curly locks fell to her shoulders and framed her round face. Her appearance indicated that she had recently arrived back in Hell after spending the summer on Earth. As the fall turned to winter, her body would become thin and sharp, and her hair would turn white.

"Welcome home, Regal," she said sweetly. Her voice was warm and loving, still full with the joys of summer.

"Thank you, Persephone." Regal stood up from his seat and bowed. "Would you be able to inform my father of my return?"

"Of course." Persephone turned to head back to the castle, but paused briefly to look at Regal. She raised her eyebrows in slight surprise and smiled before continuing on her way.

"She can see me?"

"Well, she is a goddess. Invisibility charms don't exactly work on them."

"Why is she still here?" Keir thought absentmindedly. "I thought she was only bound to the Underworld as long as she was married to Hades."

"Her contract with this realm didn't end with Hades death," Regal explained. "Unlike your customs, it is not 'until death do us part.' Once damned to Hell, that's where you stay. Persephone will never be able to leave except for during the spring and summer, and she will be courtesan to every ruler of Hell until her death."

"So she'll be your wife one day."

Regal nodded, standing when he saw his father walking out from the shadows of the corridors leading to the castle.

Jackal was tall, towering over both Regal and Keir. He looked like a giant compared to other demons. He had bronze-colored skin and pointed ears, with earrings made of silver and gold dangling from the lobes. His long hair was a fiery orange and it fell down past his shoulders. On his chin, he had a goatee that matched the color of his locks, and golden eyes that seemed to glow menacingly in the dark. Jutting from his head were two large horns that curled to resemble a ram. He wore an ornate overcoat that was decorated with silver runes and symbols. Beneath, he wore a simple black tunic, black dress pants, and dress shoes.

Keir, although trying to act brave, cowered at the sight of the god. The power that radiated off of him was more than any power the angel had ever experienced before. This was Gloria's complement, Her perfect match in power after Hades' death. For the first time since meeting Regal, Keir became afraid of death.

The ruler of Hell smiled as he came closer, his fangs gleaming in the dim light of the realm. He drew an apple from thin air, a symbol commonly associated with him. It made Keir shiver again, causing Jackal to laugh as he took a large bite of its juicy flesh.

"Regal... and company..." he mused after he finished chewing. He held the apple in the air and let his hand fall away. The fruit stayed suspended in midair as he made a simple gesture with his hand. All of the Furies and lesser demons saw the wave of the hand and understood that they needed to leave. In a few moments, the plaza was empty except for Regal, Keir, and Jackal.

Regal smiled and bowed slightly. "Father." He stood up proudly and grinned. "I've marked a great catch."

"So it seems," Jackal mused. Keir swallowed the lump in his throat, anxiously watching as Jackal moved closer to him. "Well done," the god purred, brushing Regal's head affectionately with a hand. "Now, drop your charm, angel. I wish to see you without a slight glamour over you."

Keir hesitated, frightened to become fully visible before the god. Regal growled lowly and the angel obeyed his order. The veil of security peeled away to leave Keir vulnerable and exposed.

"He's one of Gloria's favorites... seems they're *all* Her favorite, hmm?" Jackal said as he grabbed Keir's face in his hand and pulled it close for inspection. Keir squeaked in fear at the touch. "I can still feel your mark lingering; very powerful." He grinned, forcing the poor angel to look him in the eyes. "Good. The stronger the mark, the weaker the angel."

Regal beamed, feeling proud and respected. "I kept that in mind. I placed a powerful sin on him. His wings are barely noticeable." He still felt Jackal's palm lingering on his head. The simple gesture made him feel like he was one of the chosen demons; one of the ones that Jackal favored most. As if confirming him, Jackal smiled and shifted his gaze to Regal.

"You become stronger every time, too. Can you feel the power growing? Let it breed inside of you. Let the energy thrive," he instructed, releasing Keir.

Keir collapsed on the floor, absolutely terrified. Jackal laid a hand against Regal's cheek and opened his mouth to praise him some more before he blinked and frowned.

"What is it, Father?" Regal asked.

"Hmm. The angel was able to mark you as well, though... such a pity..." He let out a soft tsk of disappointment. He closed his eyes and shook his head. In an instant, his calm expression burst into anger. He whipped his hand around and smacked Regal across his cheek.

Regal stumbled back from the force, gasping as the breath was knocked out of him. Stars twinkled in his vision as his head swam.

Keir also cried out and doubled over, clutching his face as if he had been the one to be smacked. The pain Regal felt resonated through the bond between them.

"You imbecile," Jackal barked, his eyes burning black.

Regal cringed, the sudden ferocity in Jackal's voice sending a shiver down his spine. "I... I didn't know he would dare try to mark me." He refused to move from his spot, but his skin was crawling and his legs were itching to take a few steps back. However, he knew the consequences of running; it would only make his punishment worse.

"It's an angel. They're made to leave delicious gooey lovey-dovey mush all over you. Do not assume the next time that they will not mark you back," Jackal hissed.

"Yes, Father," Regal murmured with a nod. He could feel Jackal's eyes boring into his soul. He started shaking and clenched his fist angrily. His claws pierced his skin, the pricks beading with ichor. The pain was welcoming, and much more pleasing that his father's glare.

Jackal sighed, suddenly seeming tired as he ran his hand through his hair. "But it couldn't have been helped. The poor whelp was just trying to please you..." he mumbled to himself, shaking his head. Jackal placed his hand on Regal's shoulder, glancing back over at Keir. "If you excuse me, my son and I need to have a private chat."

Keir's eyes widened with dread. He didn't want to leave Regal's side, especially not in a place like this. But what could he do? He didn't dare speak out against the Lord of the Underworld. Instead, he bit his lip and put on a brave face, determined to not show Jackal or Regal his intimidation or fear. He was an angel of Gloria's, and he would not be looked down upon! He merely blinked and took one brave step back, showing that he would be fine being alone for a moment— even if he was scared out of his mind.

Jackal pulled Regal aside and walked with him toward the castle entrance. Once they were out of Keir's earshot, he leaned close and murmured in Regal's ear. "You really put yourself into a unique situation this time... a demon in possession of an angel in possession of a demon... who would have thought."

Regal was too nervous to speak up. Normally, he wasn't afraid to talk to his father, but now he felt utterly defeated. All the time and care he took into placing Sins on others and all his hard work for killing his prey. It all went to waste after this extreme mistake.

"I understand if you wish to exile me," he said finally, shame overwhelming him.

"I would never exile you," Jackal assured him, squeezing Regal's shoulder firmly. There was warmth in Jackal's eyes that was rarely seen. "You're my son, and I will always be on your side. All I ever ask is that you return to me whenever you are in need."

"Yes, Father."

"Now, how are we going to fix this... minor inconvenience?"

"Would you be able to reverse it? After all, you are a god. Don't you have the power to make it like it never happened?"

Jackal shook his head. "Only Gloria or Chaos have the power to sever a bond like this without deadly consequences." He paused, and then grinned deviously. "However, I do think that you may have figured out a way to bend the rules in your favor." He wrapped his arm around his son's shoulder and pulled him close. "You need to make the angel fall from grace."

"How will that help me?" Regal asked, confused and uncertain about how making Keir fall would solve their problem. They were still bonded, regardless of their alignment with Heaven or Hell, weren't they?

"When an angel falls, they must go to Purgatory to receive proper judgment. When they are there, all of their sins and virtues are wiped clean." Jackal started, smiling when he saw the realization growing in Regal's eyes.

"You think it will strip away the vow as well?"

"I believe that is the only option you have."

Regal nodded with a sly smirk. By making an angel fall from grace, he was converting them into a new breed of demon: a fallen angel. Not only was this the only way to fix his problem, but it would also win Jackal another soul. However, it was dangerous. Making Keir fall would be a long, time-consuming process, and there was a danger of the angel trying to cause the demon to ascend into Heaven; not to mention that there was the threat of having their bond sever and kill them both. Even if Regal succeeded, he might have to face Gloria's wrath.

Jackal could see the hesitant determination in Regal's eyes. "Are you up to it, or shall I have a more experienced prince take care of it? Kasdeya, perhaps?" he asked.

Kasdeya was the demon who had replaced Satan as the Prince of Wrath. He followed Jackal's orders with reverence and conviction, and he was willing to do anything to please the satanic side of him. Jackal often used Kasdeya to finish tasks he was too lazy to do himself or to clean up messes like the one Regal made.

Regal pulled away, scowling. "I can make him fall myself. He may own my soul, but I owned him first."

"Are you certain about that?" Jackal questioned. "Angels are crafty."

"I have him wrapped around my finger. I have dirt on him that he doesn't hold above me. He won't betray my commands," Regal said boldly.

"Excellent! Good to know you aren't out of commission yet. I trust you to keep a firm leash on that one," he said as he gave Regal a pat on the head.

"I will," Regal promised, turning to head back to Keir.

"Oh, before you go, there is one catch."

"Catch?"

Jackal smirked deviously. "Yes. I don't want this issue to end up lasting a lifetime. So there is a time limit."

Regal's eyes flashed darkly as he snarled. "You're giving me a time limit? I'm not a child."

"When you're as old as I am..."

"Don't you trust me to redeem myself?"

"I trust you, my son. However, I do not trust *him*," Jackal grumbled as he glanced back at Keir. "I do not believe he will make it easy for him to fall. He will fight back and try to cause you to ascend. I am not willing to let that happen."

Regal frowned, crossing his arms with a sigh. "Then how long do I have before you decide to interfere?"

"One month. I feel that is plenty of time for an experienced incubus such as yourself, but is still a short enough time to make sure you don't slack off."

Regal growled, annoyed that he was given such a short amount of time. He wondered whether or not Jackal was trying to help him.

His father smiled sweetly, as if nothing wrong had happened. "Now go and make me proud. And remember, one month. Watch the moon to keep track. One day later and I'll step in."

Regal narrowed his eyes and bowed his head curtly. "Of course, Father. I won't let you down." He walked quickly to Keir, and reopened a portal with his nomad stone. He nodded his head toward it, gesturing for the angel to pass through. Keir flew through the gateway, relieved to get away as quickly as possible.

"Oh, and Regal," Jackal said before Regal stepped through. "Don't forget your other duties as well."

Regal frowned and nodded, flying through the portal.

Jackal watched quietly as the portal closed, amused at Regal's predicament. Who would have thought that an incubus like Regal, one who was so careful and precise with his actions, would mess up so badly?

CHAPTER *Six*

KEIR AND REGAL walked out of the portal and began to free fall. Regal easily caught the air with his wings, flying down through the clouds below them. He shot past Keir, who had been caught off-guard and was tumbling through the air as he tried to catch the wind. Regal laughed as he dive-bombed through the blanket of clouds.

Regal sighed with a relaxed smile. He opened his wings again and let the draft pull him up so he glided gently. He turned and looked up toward the crescent moon that was beginning to set. The lunar cycle was beginning, and Regal was at his strongest. He knew he would have to act fast and plan on placing his sins on Keir before the full moon. Then he would be weaker, possibly too weak to do any lasting damage to Keir.

The angel caught up to Regal, following him silently. Keir also cherished the wind, but the darkness made him uncomfortable. He wished the sun was shining. "Where are we going?" he asked when he was next to Regal.

"Your new home." Regal soared over the buildings, angling his wings as he lowered himself carefully on the roof of an apartment complex. He tucked his wings back, fixing his sweater. Keir landed softly next to him, ruffling his feathers and pulling them close.

"You live in New York City?" Keir asked as he recognized the dim silhouette of the Statue of Liberty on the horizon.

"When I'm not in Hell, this is where I prefer to stay. Plus my next assignment happens to be here," Regal explained as he walked to the rooftop door, brushing his fingertips against the lock. He let his energy flow through, twisting the gears inside. Heat radiated off the metal door handle for a moment before it clicked. Regal easily opened the now-unlocked door and headed down the dark stairwell.

He welcomed the darkness, enjoying the shadows that rejuvenated him. He easily moved down the stairwell, his footsteps barely making a sound.

Keir was hesitant to follow, and took a tentative step onto the stairs. He could barely see, and his balance was off. His hand shot out to grab the railing, gripping it tightly until his knuckles turned white.

The angel felt drained after a long day of hunting Regal down. Being in the dark for so long weakened an angel. Now that he was marked, he felt even more tired than usual.

"I... I can't see..." he whispered, reaching out with his other hand for Regal blindly. He heard the demon sigh with exasperation and grasp his wrist, yanking him down the next few steps onto the top floor's platform.

"Keep up."

"S-sorry..." Keir gasped, stumbling after Regal as best as he could. They continued down the spiraling stairwell. Keir tried to keep up with Regal's pace, but just when he would get comfortable, his foot would stumble over a misplaced step, or they would reach a platform and whip around the corner to continue.

Regal looked behind him, able to see Keir clearly in the dim light. It was obvious that the angel wasn't comfortable. He sighed and snapped his fingers, sparking a violet flame into life. The dark fire flickered in his palm, casting a purple glow along the walls.

"Better?"

"Much... thank you," Keir replied gratefully. However, he still felt claustrophobic and disoriented with the way Regal's magic light created shadows that danced along the walls. "How much longer until we're out of here?"

Regal stopped on the seventy-second floor. "As soon as we turn invisible."

Keir immediately cloaked himself, feeling his head grow light for a split second as he used more magic. Although it was a natural ability, using it frequently for long periods of time was draining. Regal shielded himself as well and then kicked at the door in front of him, letting the bright light of the main hallway shine into the stairwell. His flame went out with a puff of black smoke. Regal squinted his eyes as Keir happily greeted the artificial light with a soft sigh.

"Let's move fast. There are cameras in the halls, and although I enjoy making the other tenants think these apartments are haunted, I'd rather not have any mishaps happen," Regal grumbled as he walked into the hall, heading toward his apartment. He always stayed in the same place whenever he had an assignment in New York City, which was rather often.

Keir followed behind with a small bounce in his step, feeling better as his wings welcomed the warmth of the light. He observed the apartment complex as they walked. It had carpeted floors, bland wall colors, and flickering overhead lights. Just as Regal said, there were security cameras placed every few yards. Keir laughed a little at the thought of Regal causing playful mischief in his free time.

Soon they came up to apartment 72B. Regal touched the doorknob with his palm, and in moments the lock was picked. The door flew open, banging on the wall behind it. The apartment was completely dark. Regal moved aside to let Keir in first. "After you."

The angel was hesitant to step inside of the demon's lair, wishing he could stay out in the hall where it was light. Unfortunately for him, Regal would not have any part of this, and made a low grunting noise in the back of his throat to coax Keir to move.

The Art of Falling

The angel finally went inside, standing up straight to appear confident and unafraid. Regal closed the door behind them and sighed, kicking his shoes off before going to the bathroom.

Keir took the moment to explore his new home. The walls were bare; no decorations littered the walls. The furniture was old, although well-kept. The living room was a decent size and was connected to the kitchen and dining room. Down the hall were two doors. One led to the bathroom Regal just went into, and the other to a bedroom.

"Kind of boring, isn't it?" Keir said absentmindedly when Regal came back out of the bathroom, rubbing his wet hands on his pants.

"I don't see the point in wasting my time and energy decorating a place I don't call home," Regal replied tiredly. He felt exhausted, even though it was dark outside. Normally he would sleep during the day and be awake at night, but Keir's sudden appearance had disrupted his sleep schedule.

The demon didn't even bother to change into his pajamas as he walked into his bedroom, falling into the bed wearily. He stretched and rolled onto his side, yawning as he buried his face into his pillow.

Keir peeked around the door frame, curious to learn more about Regal. Would this room, the most personal one in the apartment, reveal something new about the demon's personality? His bedroom walls were for the most part bare, except for a small calendar and a "Too Weird to Live, Too Rare to Die" Panic! at the Disco album poster taped up haphazardly. His furniture was nothing special, most likely left behind by previous owners. He did, however, have a brand new stereo sitting on his dresser with a stack of CDs next to it. Despite what Regal said about not feeling like this apartment was his home, this bedroom seemed to be his comfort zone.

"I'm going to sleep," Regal mumbled as he heard Keir walk into his room. "You can sleep on the couch."

"Alone?" Keir asked with a sheepish smile as Regal shot a quick glare at him.

"Yes. Alone." The demon rolled back onto his side and faced the wall. He let his wings spill out, covering his body to protect him from the sunlight that would eventually flood through his window.

The angel watched him for a moment and sighed before heading to the bathroom to wash his face and get ready for bed. Just before he closed the door, he peeked back inside quickly and said, "Sleep well." Regal grunted in response and shook his wings slightly.

Keir walked into the bathroom and flicked on the light. The bathroom was clean, and much like the rest of Regal's apartment, bare. He stared at himself in the mirror above the sink. Part of him couldn't believe what he was getting himself into, but the other part knew that this was his only choice.

After washing up for the night, Keir searched the living room for a blanket. Of all the rooms in the apartment, this one was the messiest—and there wasn't much around to be messy. There was a stack of magazines several months old on the coffee table, unread and collecting dust. Beside that was a candle that was mostly burnt out. Keir picked it up and read the label: Autumn Leaves. He took a deep breath in, smelling the musty fragrance of maple leaves mixed with rosemary and pomegranate. It was the perfect scent for this time of the year.

Other than the candle and magazines, there was nothing else in the living room. Keir set the candle back down, noticing the ring of dust around where it once sat. It was clear that Regal hadn't stayed in this apartment for several months.

After searching, Keir couldn't find a blanket anywhere and

headed back to Regal's room. Slowly, he cracked the door and peered inside. The demon seemed to already be asleep. Rather than waking him up to ask him for a blanket, he went back to the living room. He knelt down beside the couch and recited a prayer before going to bed.

Meanwhile, Regal was not sleeping easily. His mind was reeling, trying to figure out what to do with Keir. He couldn't simply let him stay an angel. He had to make him fall, but how? He needed to be creative with his tactics.

He had seven sins to accomplish: greed, lust, envy, wrath, sloth, pride, and gluttony. Some would be easy, while others would be very difficult. Regal expected that his personal sin, lust, would be one of the harder to do. Keir was crafty and would avoid any sexual contact. He'd need to find another way around that issue.

Regal spent most of the night thinking to himself. He struggled to come up with a plan that would make Keir fall. It'd be best to start small, so Regal devised a plan to start with easy sins that humans committed daily. Once he had Keir's trust, he could focus on the bigger sins.

After hours of planning, Regal rested his mind and rolled onto his side. He pulled the covers over his head, shrouding himself in darkness. He stared at the clock on his dresser; only three more hours until sunrise. He sighed, wishing that he had the energy to stay up the rest of the night so his sleeping schedule wasn't completely ruined. However, he was far too tired to stay up any longer and decided to sleep. If he had to deal with a few extra hours of sunlight tomorrow, he'd manage. He just hoped that damned angel didn't wake him too early.

CHAPTER *Seven*

A VAGUE SENSE OF warmth washed over Keir's sleeping form, stirring him enough to wake him. He smiled, stretching his wings out. It felt so good to be in the heat of the sun, even if it was through a curtain.

With bleary eyes, Keir got off the couch, cracking his stiff back as he stood up. He trotted over to the window, opening up the curtains to let the sunlight shine through. He stretched and sighed, basking in the bright sun. It woke him, making him feel refreshed despite only a few hours of sleep.

He stared outside, watching all the people who walked to work, thinking they looked like ants beneath them. Keir found humans to be interesting. Most of them believed in Gloria. However, many didn't do as much as they should have. But that was okay; it gave angels something to do during the day. It was always a treat when a human, whether religious or not, did something good. Unfortunately, many humans didn't do much to help others, which caused problems up in Heaven.

Keir shook his head, forcing the thoughts from his mind. He couldn't think about Heaven. If he did, he'd start to get homesick and wouldn't be able to carry out his mission with Regal.

Regal.

The angel sighed dreamily when he thought of him. At first, he'd despised Regal for what he had done. But that all changed the moment Regal had kissed him. He had never wanted to have such strong feelings for something so sinister and evil, but something about that night made him long for something forbidden. Keir was still uncertain what had made him fall for the incubus: the effects of his sin, or his own heart betraying him.

The Art of Falling

After the night in Paris, he had tried to fight it, but he wasn't strong enough to overcome the lustful desires that coursed viciously through his veins. He felt dirty, broken, and empty. Keir had wept for days, begging Gloria to have it lifted from him, but She didn't respond to his prayers.

At first, he didn't understand why She would abandon him and leave him feeling so corrupt. He thought it was because he had failed Her, and that he was now worthless. However, Gloria was forgiving and surely wouldn't blame him for something he couldn't control.

After months of battling with his new internal demons, he decided to go to Gloria and confess what had happened. He was ashamed to admit that he had failed his assignment and was now tormented by the curse Regal had placed on him. However, Gloria wasn't upset with him. In fact, She seemed to be interested in his exchange with Regal.

"He kissed you and you've fallen for him?" She had asked wistfully, smiling a little as She sipped herbal tea from Her delicate china.

"Y-yes Ma'am," Keir had replied, lowering his head. *"I tried really hard to push him away, but I wasn't strong enough, and now I'm..."*

"Don't worry, darling," Gloria cooed, resting Her hand on Her angel's shoulder. *"That's what demons do. Even if Regal were one of my children, I think he would have still had the same effect on you."*

"Yeah... probably." Keir had blushed at the thought. He wasn't used to the aching need in his heart for someone else.

Gloria had leaned back in Her chair, a warm yet curious smile on Her lips. *"However, such a relationship isn't permitted. Angels and demons can't be together."*

"I know... that's why I'm so conflicted. My head is telling me it's wrong, but my heart is telling me something different. I don't know what to do."

"The way I see it, there are a few things you can do to solve your

problem. You can try to ignore it completely, or you can disobey the rules set in place by the gods..."

Keir's gaze fell to the floor with dismay. He would never break the heavenly laws, and he couldn't bear trying to ignore the feelings growing inside of him any longer. If those were his only options, he was doomed to fall from grace.

"...or you can try to save Regal."

Keir perked up at the suggestion. "Save Regal? That's something I can do?"

She smiled. "Of course. If angels can fall, why can't demons ascend?"

He then realized that Gloria's reasons to not cleanse him of his sins were not a punishment, but rather the start of a much larger mission. He smiled, understanding the task at hand. Maybe it was his destiny to save Regal and bring him to heaven. Only then would he be able to feel such intense love without feeling blasphemous. "I'm going to save him."

Gloria set Her cup down. "I believe that is the best choice. However, it is a big task for such a young angel." She folded Her hands together and laid them on white desk in front of her. "Do you believe you are ready for the task?"

"I may be young and inexperienced with Earth, but I have trained long and hard." The lustful urges inside of Keir transformed, turning into the desire to save the demon. He wanted to claim him, to be with him, to forever stay by his side in harmony. "I know I can do it."

"Then it's settled. You can have an unlimited amount of time to guide Regal to act on the Seven Heavenly Virtues. Once he has willingly committed Chastity, Temperance, Charity, Diligence, Patience, Kindness, and Humility, the ascension process will start."

"Chastity may be a difficult one..." Keir said, his face heating up at the thought of Regal's sexual hunger.

"To help you with your task, I'll ask Michaelangelo to go with you and—"

"No! I want to do it on my own."

Gloria blinked with surprise. "I don't believe that's a smart idea."

"If I came after Regal with reinforcements, he'd put up a fight," Keir explained. *"On my own, I may be able to save him without him knowing. I have to do this on my own."*

She smiled in return. "So be it."

Now a year later, Keir was finding himself in more of a pickle than he had anticipated. When he told Regal that he had no affiliation with Gloria anymore, it was a white lie. He wasn't in direct contact with Her anymore, determined to have Regal to himself. However, he was welcome back into Heaven whenever he wanted.

As Keir watched Regal's sleeping form through a crack in the door, he knew that saving him would take some time. It was obvious that Regal wasn't only an incubus, but he was prideful too. He wouldn't let himself ascend so easily. Keir had to be sneaky with his plans. He had to think like a demon. The angel's stomach churned at the realization that he would have to act like the mortal enemies of his people, but he forced it down. His determination to save Regal was stronger. He would do it. He had to.

Keir opened the door and walked into the bedroom, coming up to the side of the bed so he could look at the form under the blankets that was Regal's body. Gently, he ran his fingers over the thick fabric. He knew it protected Regal from the sunlight that unfortunately shone through his covered window in the morning.

The angel jumped when Regal yawned and rolled onto his side, grumbling softly as he slowly woke up. He stumbled back, holding his hand close to his chest as he saw Regal poke his disheveled head out from his shelter. He squinted and groaned, pulling his head back into his cocoon of blankets.

"Keir."

"Yes?"

"Close the curtains."

"They are closed..."

Regal hissed to himself. It had to be a clear sky for the sun to shine so strongly into his room. He grumbled and dragged himself out of bed, pulling the blanket close to him as the edges dragged on the floor. He walked past Keir into the hall. He slammed the doors shut as he walked until he was at the end of the hall, which was the darkest area of the apartment. Regal plopped down onto the floor and pulled the blankets around him, sighing in relief to finally be out of the sun. Keir followed like a lost puppy, already missing the sunlight.

"Regal, can I open the windows but keep the curtains pulled?"

"The wind will blow them open."

Keir sighed softly, frowning. Regal peeked out from the blankets, glaring at the angel who had a saddened look on his face. He couldn't tell which was worse—Keir's expression or the fact that open windows would let in sunlight.

"Fine," he said after a moment. "You can open the windows. But the curtains had better not move to let in the light, or so help me, I'll..." he paused, knowing any pain he'd cause Keir would reflect back to him. "...I'll be angry."

"Thank you!" Keir flitted across the apartment to draw open the window and let the breeze in. It was crisp and fresh, but there was lingering warmth from summer. The air helped clear the stuffiness of the apartment and made him feel like he was outside. However, dust kicked up and made him sneeze.

Keir went into the kitchen, looking around for cleaning supplies. All he was able to find was a dust rag that was covered in cobwebs. He took it out and shook it over the sink, then went about cleaning all the surfaces of the apartment.

As Keir cleaned, enjoying his daylight, Regal remained in

his dark corner and rubbed his temples. It didn't take much for him to get a headache. With his butt numb from sitting on the floor, he pulled his blanket off to make a nest to sit in. Regal's wings curled around him, trying to block out the light with no avail. Now that they were translucent, his wings did not help to protect him from the sun's rays.

After the living room and kitchen were dusted, Keir went to clean the bathroom and bedroom. He checked on Regal with mild interest for a minute, observing the way the demon's wings neglected to cast shadows onto his body as they would have before they were see-through. Keir frowned a little and walked over. His footsteps caused Regal to look out and narrow his eyes, silently scrutinizing him.

Without hesitation, Keir dropped onto his knees and pressed his body against Regal and wrapped his arms around the demon protectively. This immediately caused Regal to hiss and stiffen, squirming at the angel's touch.

"There," Keir murmured, his sweet voice making Regal's stomach flip. "I can protect you from the sun and you can use my shadow."

Regal was caught off-guard, surprised at the angel's strange reasoning. He wondered for a moment if he should push him away and move back under his blankets, but knew that would be less comfortable. He had to admit, the angel's embrace wasn't as horrible as he thought it'd be.

Regal relaxed into Keir's hold, his wings fluttering behind him as they welcomed the shadows cast by Keir's body. The demon sighed and leaned against the wall, sliding down so he was sitting comfortably in his nest. He let his eyes fall shut, and his sleepiness dragged him back under.

Keir was happy to see that Regal allowed him to do something productive for him. He adjusted his position so he could also be comfortable, wiggling himself until he was leaning against Regal's chest, his head resting on his shoulder. He couldn't help but run his hand through Regal's graying hair slowly, as though entranced by its beauty. Gloria was right; even if Regal were an angel, he'd still be too beautiful to stay away from.

No wonder he made a good incubus, Keir thought to himself quietly as Regal slept, happy to be so close to Regal without him running or fighting.

From this position, he could tell that even Regal wasn't perfect. He had a small scar on his eyebrow; most likely from a fight. He was starting to get gray stubble from not shaving, and his angular face was a bit too thin for Keir's tastes. He wondered what more flaws Regal had, not only physically, but mentally. Were there any fears or insecurities under that tough skin he had developed? Was there anything that made him softer and more relatable? Most importantly, was there anything that Keir would be able to use to help Regal ascend?

Keir was startled into consciousness when Regal began to stir. Somehow he had fallen asleep. Staying up all night tracking the demon had worn him out more than he expected. He scooted back, allowing Regal space as the demon rubbed his bleary eyes.

Regal sat up groggily, noticing that he was fully covered in shadows. The sun had shifted so it was no longer shining toward the hallway, so he knew that it was afternoon. He stretched and shook his wings, the translucent feathers falling to the floor.

"What time is it?" he grumbled softly, his voice hoarse from waking up. Keir stood up, his back stiff from the position he slept in and looked at the clock on the wall in the living room.

"Almost two in the afternoon."

Regal nodded, grunting as he stood up, cracked his back, and flapped his wings to loosen them up. He retracted them and shuffled into the kitchen, trying to avoid spots of light on the carpet in his path.

The white counter tops reflected the sun's rays at him as he walked around, opening cupboards to scavenge for food. He didn't feel like making an actual meal; not when he planned on going back to sleep until sunset. He found a bag of chips shoved in the back and grabbed that, slamming the cupboard shut as he pulled a can of soda from the fridge.

Keir watched quietly, trying to stay in between Regal and the sunlight, casting his shadow over him. He peered over Regal's shoulder curiously. Regal glanced back at him and scowled as he sat back down on his nest of blankets.

"What are you looking at?"

"I've never had chips before."

"Seriously?"

"I try to eat only organic foods while on Earth. Stuff I could find or grow myself."

Well isn't that pretentious? Regal thought to himself. He leaned back, resting against the wall as he ripped the bag open with his teeth and dug his hand in. "Well, you're missing out on one of the most delicious snacks mankind has ever invented."

Keir sat down on one of the barstools that were lined up against the kitchen counter. He back was turned toward the sun, his wings fluttering to soak up the warmth. "May I try one?"

Regal grinned, an idea forming in his mind. He handed the bag over to Keir. "We live together now; might as well share the spoils." He sipped on his cherry coke as he watched the angel tentatively try a chip.

Keir made a small sound of surprise as he let the chip melt on his tongue. "This is better than I expected." Regal merely nodded, teeth glistening as he smirked wider. Keir ate another chip, and soon another, finding they were too good to stop. He paused; face flushing. "I'm sorry. I'm eating all of your food."

"Don't worry. I try to keep them in stock since they don't spoil as quickly." Regal handed his drink over to Keir as well. "Would you like to try this? It's cherry."

Oblivious to the sugary and addictive substance in the can, Keir took a small sip, licking his lips as he smiled. "This is wonderful, too."

Regal hummed softly in reply. "Feel free to have as much as you like." He stood back up, grabbing his blanket and slinging it over his shoulder. "I'm going to head back to my room. Luckily my room faces east and the sun won't shine through my window for the rest of the day. I can get some more sleep before I have to go out."

"You're going out tonight?" Keir asked, nibbling on the snacks as he followed Regal back down the hall and into his bedroom.

"Of course. I'm a demon. That's what we do." Regal tossed his blankets on the bed, finally peeling off his sweater and pants to change into more comfortable clothes. He felt Keir's aura waver with a spike of desire. He chuckled to himself; of course the angel would get flustered from seeing someone changing. He sat down on the edge of the bed after pulling on a pair of sweatpants and watched Keir uncover his eyes.

"Oops, not used to having to shut my door while changing. Usually people like to see me undress," he purred, his tone mocking Keir lightly as the angel's cheeks turned red.

"It's all right..." he mumbled, playing with the hem of his shirt. He looked back up at Regal shyly. "Should I leave you to rest?"

Regal nodded, lying back on the bed and sighing. "I'll be up in a few hours. Feel free to explore the city. Take the spare key by the front door and my wallet to buy whatever you want. Just be back in before sunset."

CHAPTER *Eight*

KEIR TOOK REGAL'S advice to walk around the city while he rested. After eating a meager lunch consisting of a second bag of chips and a glass of water, he shrugged on a black leather jacket he found in Regal's hall closet and grabbed the demon's key and wallet. He left the apartment through the window, not wanting to get Regal into any unwanted trouble. He wasn't sure how often Regal used his powers with the camera all around.

He floated down to the alleyway and landed lightly on his feet. Before taking to the streets, he needed a moment of meditation to become visible to humans. Once he looked completely normal, he stepped out of the alley. In an instant he felt overwhelmed.

New York City was massive, much larger than the small town where he had found the demon. There, he had been surrounded by cozy establishments, and a forest was never out of sight. Here he was surrounded by tall buildings, a sea of people, and the occasional rat. Pulling the collar of his jacket closer to him, he walked down the sidewalks and began his exploration.

Regal's apartment wasn't too far from Times Square, only four blocks away. Keir made his way down Park Avenue, heading toward the center of the city. He passed by The Museum of Modern Art and Radio City Music Hall, carefully memorizing the landmarks as he walked, knowing if he didn't, he would get lost trying to come home. That was the good thing about the city; there was always a building that looked just a bit different to help you not get lost.

One that he definitely noticed was M&M World. The large sign featuring the iconic red and yellow M&Ms caught his eye from a mile away. He broke away from the crowd and walked up to the window, peering inside for a moment before he gasped with amazement and headed straight for the door.

He took a deep breath once he was inside. His mouth instantly began to water as he took in the sweet smell of chocolate. Flocks of people were crowding the large tubes filled with M&Ms. Being surrounded by a rainbow of candy was heavenly, to say the least. He couldn't imagine how one building could hold so much candy.

Deciding to join in on the fun, Keir hurried up to the tube chock-full of assorted chocolates and loaded up one of the small plastic baggies.

I hope Regal likes chocolate, Keir thought as he filled the bag to the brim. He knew he sure wasn't going to eat the whole bag himself—just a few to treat himself.

After paying for his candy, Keir continued to walk the streets. New York City truly was a concrete jungle. Although he could probably explore much faster with his wings, he wanted to experience it from the ground.

Soon enough, the flow of traffic led him to the center of the universe. The streets in Times Square were buzzing with life. Hundreds, if not thousands, of people crowded them. Tourists looked up at the tall buildings and flashing TV screens, pointing and laughing with their friends at the fantastic sights. The angel blended in perfectly with the tourists with the way he looked up at the buildings in wonder.

"I wonder if Regal ever took the time to—oomph!"

"Hey, watch it, kid!" a business man wearing a crisp suit and tie barked as he pushed past Keir, shouldering him out of the way. Keir stumbled and bumped into another group of people, apologizing quickly.

"All right, move around!" A voice yelled over the noise. Keir looked to see a few cops directing a mass of people. The crowd was forced to walk around a roped-off area where a new movie was going to be filmed. Someone bumped into him from behind as the group was pushed forward. He turned to apologize, but was met with a man wearing nothing but a cowboy hat holding a guitar to cover his privates.

Keir murmured a quick apology and skittered away from the man, his face flushing brightly. Maybe he wasn't cut out to live in this city like Regal was.

In desperate need to get away from the crowds, Keir ducked into the closest store and found a quiet place to turn invisible. He then flew away from the congestion and headed to a more peaceful area of the city.

Standing out amidst the bleak and architectural city was a large expanse of nature. Keir was drawn to it, landing just outside of the entrance. As he stepped inside, the hustle and bustle of taxis, people, and buses faded away. With wide eyes, Keir walked along the path through the park, looking at all the scenery in awe.

Everything was green and blooming with life. Large trees cast cool shadows onto the winding cobblestone paths; sunlight shone through the leaves, speckling the ground. He hopped from patch to patch, staying in the warmth of the sun as he continued his journey. This was a completely different world. It amazed Keir how such a beautiful and serene place could exist next to one of the biggest cities in America.

Soft music could be heard from the other side of Central Park. Keir made his way to the melodious sound, and saw a small acoustic band performing for some kids who were playing nearby. Keir walked up to the crowd that had formed and listened happily to the cheerful tunes.

That was what Keir loved most about Earth and humans.

It seemed that wherever he went, there were kind people who made others happy. It was these small moments that made living on Earth worthwhile.

He observed the people who were listening to the band with him. Most were teenaged kids and young adults who were captivated by the sweet sound of the guitar and harmonica. One elderly couple sat on a park bench a few yards away, listening to the beat of the bongo drums. They tapped their feet slowly, not trying to keep up with the quick rhythm of the drums.

A small girl ran by Keir, giggling and laughing as she danced by herself. She seemed to be in her own world, her dress twirling around as she spun. Watching her dance so carefree and happily, it warmed Keir's heart. He could imagine her with white wings and a small halo. She looked like she would make a good angel.

He noticed that the elderly couple sitting on the bench was smiling as they watched the girl dance. He could immediately sense that there was a bond between them and the child. One of the angel's special skills was to see the ties that brought people together, whether they were good or not. The link between these three was warm and loving, and it made Keir swell with joy.

The positive energy filling Keir was swept away as a dark presence came over him. He instantly knew it wasn't Regal's aura. He prepared for a demonic attack as he searched for the source of the negative energy.

It's strange to see your kind amongst the humans.

Keir whipped around, looking to see who had spoken to him, but no one was there. Flirtatious laughter echoed in his mind, as if taunting him.

It's fun to play with you angels. You all get so confused each time you hear someone else other than your mother in your head.

Keir spun again, catching sight of a person standing in the shadows of the trees. He couldn't see the person's face, but he could easily make out the voluptuous and curvy stature of a woman. Cautiously, he moved toward her.

That's right, sweetheart, keep coming closer. I don't bite.

Keir found it hard to deny her influence on him. He stepped closer, her voice enticing him until he could see her angular face. It was such a strange, yet beautiful contrast to her rounded, hourglass figure. She had a warm complexion without a single blemish, sharp cheekbones, and full, red lips that were pulled into a gorgeous smile. Her wide eyes looked brown in the dim light, but he could see the flash of vivid orange when the light hit just right. Her wavy, blonde hair fell to her mid back, and her bangs were dyed to match her irises.

"Speak aloud," Keir commanded, stopping once he could see her face more clearly.

She sighed, coming out from the shadows and walking toward him. He could see that she had a small freckle on her cheek near her right eye. She looked innocent, like someone he could trust; but he knew better than that. Keir narrowed his eyes as he watched her carefully.

"You're wearing his jacket," she said as she came closer, circling him. "I'm surprised he let you borrow it."

He narrowed his eyes and clenched his fist. "How do you know Regal?"

"He's an old colleague of mine." She stopped suddenly, turning to face him. "And he's now your... roommate?"

Keir narrowed his eyes. How did she know that he and Regal were living together? They had managed to keep the whole situation a secret. Who had filled her in? Had Gloria betrayed him? Why would She... no, it was impossible. She would never do that. It had to be Jackal. It was the only logical option.

His reaction made the demon throw her head back and burst into laughter, her low voice quickly turning into a scraping cackle. "This is simply hilarious, an angel falling in love with a demon!" She turned toward the humans who were walking by, and started to announce loudly, "Did you hear that? This angel—!"

Keir grabbed her quickly and covered her mouth, pulling her back into the shadows before she let the humans hear her voice. His eyes widened with disbelief at her insanity and risk. "Are you crazy?! Don't expose us like that!"

She simply giggled and pulled his hand away. "You're calling me crazy? You're the one who fell for a demon and became his *pet*."

The comments made Keir tense up. "Our situation is none of your business."

"Oh, but it is." She pulled away from Keir's grip, turning to face him as he leaned back against the tree. "You see, Regal is somewhat important to me, and I will not have some pathetic angel steal him away from his rightful place as the Prince of Lust."

Keir gasped. Regal was *the* Prince of Lust? That made him the most powerful incubus in Hell after the death of the first Prince of Lust, Asmodeus.

The demon chuckled. "Surprised? You shouldn't be. Trying to make an incubus fall in love is a waste of your time."

"How do you know it's a waste of time? Lust can easily turn into love," Keir challenged. He refused to let her get into his head and make him doubt his mission.

"Because he doesn't even fall in love with demons, that's why," she snapped in response. Her fangs were bared as she growled at him. They resembled shark's teeth, with serrated edges that were perfect for devouring the bodies and souls of her prey, no doubt. "His heart is as cold and solid as ice, and it will never thaw out; especially not for an angel like you."

"Or maybe an angel is exactly what he needs."

The demon growled lowly, standing up straighter. She curled

her lips in a snarl and raised her hands. Keir prepared to duck out of the way, expecting her to lash out at him. However, instead of something happening to him, something happened to her. A slit formed across her palm and ripped apart, exposing sets of razor-sharp teeth embedded within the skin. Keir sucked in a sharp breath as he watched the ichor drip from the lamprey-like jaws that manifested on her body. She seemed to take pleasure in his surprise.

"I am more powerful than you know. I suggest you don't test me, or I might have to take back what I said about not biting." She hissed, suddenly vicious, her voice echoed by the mouths that now spoke along with her. It was obvious now that she was one of the more persuasive and dangerous demons, especially if she had this ability. Apparently intimidation had been the only thing she'd wanted to accomplish at the moment, because she suddenly closed her palms, and the two extra mouths in her hands disappeared. Keir swallowed the lump in his throat, making a mental note to never forget her ability.

"Then what do you want? Why did you really come here?"

Her snarl turned into a delicate smile again. It was unnerving to Keir how quickly she could change expressions. "To persuade you into giving up this whole plan to make him ascend," she said as she walked toward Keir, reaching her hand out to rest against his shoulder. "Don't act like you don't know what I'm talking about. No angel in their right mind would honestly try to be with a demon without making him rise first."

Keir tried to hide his surprise and his abhorrence. He didn't like how easily she was reading him, as if picking through his mind.

She smiled again, moving to his side. She leaned against him, resting her head on his shoulder. "Don't feel bad; it's in your nature to want him to rise." She ran a hand down his arm, her claws gently scratching at his skin. "You don't have to feel guilty about that."

"Guilty...?" Keir asked quietly, glancing down at her as she smiled back up at him. He felt her hand wrap around his shoulder, her fingers toying with his hair.

"Yes, guilty. That's the one emotion that really eats away at a person." He could hear her voice in both ears, as if she was speaking to him with two mouths. He was almost afraid to look over to see if another mouth had formed on her palm as she continued to twirl his hair.

"I don't see how guilt would be a factor in this..."

"It's always a factor," she whispered, her lips brushing against his ear.

Keir could feel her influencing him, using her words to get into his mind to make him react in the way she preferred. She was far more powerful than he first expected. He shook his head and pulled away quickly, putting distance between them.

"You're like him."

She quirked a brow, her smile falling into a thin frown. "Excuse me?"

"You're strong enough to influence an angel. You're a prince."

She laughed. "I prefer the term *Princess*. After Beelzebub died, Jackal thought a woman could do a better job."

Keir easily recognized the name. Beelzebub was the old Prince of Gluttony. He died along with Asmodeus and the rest of the princes during the battle with Satan.

He tried to move away into the sunlight, hoping if he could get into the open, he could flee. She growled, her footsteps following him to force him back into the shadows. Keir flared his wings, trying to intimidate her, but it only made her mock him more with her echoing laugh.

"Don't bother fighting. You're hardly a threat now that you've been marked."

"I am still powerful regardless. I will fight you if you dare try to harm me."

"You're not worth the trouble of fighting," she hissed. "Let this meeting be a warning. Give up on Regal. Or else, you'll be seeing me again, and I won't hesitate to exterminate you."

"The Heavenly Laws prevent you from—"

"The laws can be broken. Both of our lords are guilty of that."

"Liar!" Keir screeched as he launched forward. How dare she accuse Gloria of such a thing. The demon dodged the attack, laughing shrilly as she formed another tooth-filled grin on her palm. A dark umbrella was spit out from the mouth before the gap closed again. She swung it at Keir, forcing him back as she opened it with a click. Keir could see the razor-sharp blades lining the edges of the top.

"Until next time," she giggled as she turned and began to walk away, shielding herself from the sunlight.

Keir spread his wings and flew back to the safety of Regal's apartment, her voice lingering in his mind.

CHAPTER *Nine*

*K*EIR HURRIED DOWN the flight of stairs that led from the roof. As soon as he was on the seventy-second floor, he sprinted down the hall and let himself back into Regal's apartment. He shut the door behind him and locked it, leaning against the heavy wood as he caught his breath.

Panting and heart racing, Keir headed back to Regal's bedroom. He knocked quickly to be polite, but didn't bother waiting to be invited. However, when he opened the bedroom door, he discovered that the demon was missing.

He heard water running in the bathroom and headed straight for the door, knocking on it impatiently. "Regal, are you in there?"

"Of course I'm in here, who else could it possibly be?" he heard Regal bark over the spray of water.

"Sorry, but I need to talk to you about something."

Regal, who was obviously in the shower and currently scrubbing the shampoo suds out of his hair, sighed. "Fine, just wait in the living room. Now isn't the best time to talk."

Keir groaned lightly and headed for the living room. He sat on the couch and waited as patiently as he could. He couldn't help but to look out the window nervously, watching the sun set behind the skyline of the city.

Taking his sweet time, Regal continued to scrub at his scalp. He was going to be out soon, but now he felt like taking a bit longer, just to mess with Keir. He shampooed his hair twice and stood in the spray of hot water long after the soap had been washed off his body. Once his skin was starting to prune, he got out of the shower and paced around the bathroom.

He stretched his wings, shaking out his damp feathers as he brushed his teeth.

After fifteen minutes, he couldn't stall any longer. He pulled a dark blue turtleneck sweater over his head and tugged on dark denim jeans. Just as he was leaving the bathroom, he caught a glimpse of himself in the mirror.

His wings were spread out behind him, looking dim and ashen. All of the life was drained out of them. Regal scowled, fury bubbling up inside of him. He could never return to Hell looking like this. The other demons would think of him as a joke. He was no joke. He was Jackal's son, the heir to the throne, the Prince of Lust.

I'll show them all I can conquer any angel.

Regal ripped the mirror off the wall with a loud grunt and threw it onto the floor. It crashed loudly, the glass shattering into sharp fragments. He stared at the broken mirror on the floor—seven years of bad luck if he cared, one for every sin he had to place on Keir—and looked at the blank space on the wall where the mirror was mounted.

"Regal! Are you okay?" Keir shouted from outside of the door.

"I'm fine," Regal said as he picked up the broken pieces of the mirror and opened the bathroom door. Keir was standing outside with a panicked look on his face.

"What happened?"

"Mirror fell," Regal lied as he took the remains of the mirror and threw them into the trashcan in the kitchen.

"How?" Keir asked as he bent down to pick up the remaining shards.

"Old nail, I suppose. It's fine. I wanted to replace it anyways." He grabbed a can of beef ravioli from the cabinet and cracked it open, dumping the contents into a bowl. "So, what did you want to talk about?"

Keir leapt up and rushed to the kitchen, careful not to cut himself on the glass as he threw them away. "A demon confronted me today while in the park."

Regal raised his brow silently as he punched in 2:30 on the microwave and heated his meal.

"She said she knew you and started talking about you."

"I get around," he said with a chuckle as he rinsed out the empty can under the sink.

Keir groaned and shook his head. "No, not like that! She said that you two were close."

"Like I said before." Regal tossed the can to Keir, who caught it with a somewhat unpleased expression. He set it on the counter as Regal drank straight from the tap.

"She had mouths on her hands..."

Regal coughed a bit and rubbed the back of his hand against his mouth, before turning off the sink again. "Did she have blonde hair, a curvy figure, and a voice that could make you go deaf?"

"Yeah, that's one way to describe her."

"I know who you're talking about."

"She knows about us, our situation," Keir continued.

"What? How?" Regal commanded, clearly upset at the revelation.

"She didn't say."

Regal growled, walking past Keir again to slip on his shoes. "I'll figure it out. For now, avoid her. She likes to get into your head and manipulate you."

"Like how you use unconsciousness and dreams?" Keir asked, somewhat curious.

Regal looked over his shoulder, eyes narrowed with suspicion at Keir's sudden interest. "Yes. Demons of my rank are able to manipulate humans a bit easier than lesser demons."

Keir played with the hem of his shirt nervously. "She said that you were Asmodeus' replacement."

"I'm not a replacement!" Regal barked, a low growl in his voice as he snarled. "I'm..." he sighed, shaking his head. "Never mind. How I came to be a Prince is not important."

"She mentioned something else that bothered me too," Keir continued as he leaned against the back of the couch.

"What was it?"

"That both our lords break the rules they enforce," Keir said. "That's not true, is it?"

Regal scowled. "No, it's not, and for her to claim such a thing is blasphemous. Jackal is noble and would not break any heavenly laws. I'm sure it is the same for Gloria."

The angel smiled, feeling comforted. "Yeah, I thought so." How silly of him to think that Gloria would ever break her own commandments.

"From now on, don't listen to her. Never trust a demon."

"Should I trust you?"

Regal smirked slightly. "Probably not. However, we're in a slightly different situation. It's your call in the end."

Keir pondered that thought. He knew better than to put any trust in demons, but Regal was different. Keir had managed to fall for him and mark him. He could possibly save him and make him ascend as well. Some form of trust had to be made for that to work.

Regal headed back down the hall, with Keir following behind him, and removed the screen from his window.

"What are you doing?" Keir asked, standing in the doorway.

"It's breakfast time for me. I'm off to hunt some souls." The look on Keir's face was that of disgust and horror; it made Regal laugh. "I'm just kidding. I don't eat souls like the Gluttons do. I feed on sex drives, but that doesn't cure my hunger. Demons need to eat real food too."

"So... you're going out for dinner?"

"No, breakfast. Keep up, angel."

"Right... breakfast." Keir rubbed the back of his neck, looking at the floor for a moment.

Regal could see that Keir wanted to go with him, but he wouldn't treat him to that just yet. He had a plan to stick to. "Don't worry, I'm just going to a restaurant. No souls today. I'll be back in an hour or so." He reached out to Keir expectantly. "My jacket?"

Keir shrugged off the coat and handed it to Regal. At that moment, the microwave beeped loudly from the kitchen, startling Keir. "Oh! Weren't you just making something to eat?"

"Yeah, for you," Regal said as he sipped on his jacket. "You must be hungry after flying around all day. I know I don't have much to eat right now, but I figured you'd like something other than chips."

"Is that stuff... healthy?" Keir wondered, leaning to look down the hall toward the kitchen. "It came from a can..."

"Just because something came out of a can doesn't mean it isn't healthy. Chef Boyardee's recipes are a national treasure. If you can trust anyone's food, it'd be his."

Keir could just make out the scent of tomato sauce and meat. "Is there beef in that?"

"Yeah, is that an issue?"

"I prefer not to eat meat except for fish."

So damned picky... Regal rolled his eyes. "Fine, I'll get something without meat for you to eat tonight."

As the demon crawled through the window to descend on the city below, Keir called out, "I would have imagined the Princess of Gluttony to be a bit pudgier!" The comment made Regal burst out into laughter; it was a genuine, heartfelt laughter that made Keir swell up with joy. He had never heard a more beautiful sound.

"I'd love to see the look on her face if she heard you say that," Regal replied with a chuckle as he turned invisible and leapt out through the window.

Keir headed back to the kitchen and took the bowl of ravioli out of the microwave. It slightly burned his hands, causing him to nearly drop it. He dug around the drawers until he found some plastic wrap, covered the bowl, and placed it in the fridge for Regal to eat later. He then grabbed a can of soda and walked into the living room to sit and watch TV. He was happy to stay indoors if that meant avoiding interacting with the female demon lurking the dark streets.

Meanwhile, Regal was scanning the city for the absolute worst food joint to go to. He flew over Little Italy and Chinatown, knowing he could find some grub that was delicious and terrible for the arteries.

His plan to expose Keir to one of the seven deadly sins was flawless: make him crave the very foods that humans ate without a care in the world. Gluttony was by far one of the easier sins. It was simple to fall into a pattern of bad eating habits, especially when the foods are made with addictive elements like sugar or caffeine.

Unfortunately for him, Regal found none of the Chinese or Italian restaurants... greasy enough. Although they were notorious for being unhealthy, he could do better. He smirked when he thought of the many fast food joints that littered America. It was no wonder that Americans were stereotyped as overweight.

After forty-five minutes of flying around the city and wasting time, he stopped at a McDonald's and ordered the absolute worst meals he could. Regal wasn't a big fan of fast food himself. He liked the fact it was fast and tasty, but the additives and fats made him feel lethargic. He hoped that it would do the same to Keir. Once he had his bagged food in hand, he headed out the back door, made himself invisible to humans, and took off into the sky. It was dark by this time, and couldn't see the stars as he flew through the cloud cover back to his apartment.

He lowered himself onto the roof, tucked in his wings and headed down the stairwell. He walked down the hall with his paper bag of junk under his arm, opening the door to his apartment with ease. "I'm back with food. You still hungry?" he called out to Keir.

Keir looked up from his spot on the couch, nodding as he stretched. "Yeah. Chips don't really fill you up much."

"I know. I went for the fast route to make sure I could get something back to you quick," he purred with an easy smile. "Don't want to keep you waiting."

"Fast food? Isn't that stuff bad for you?"

Regal groaned loudly. "Dammit, are you ever going to stop asking me that?"

"Sorry," Keir replied sheepishly. "I just want to make sure I'm making the best choices."

"When we get settled I'll stock up on healthier groceries. But for now, this is what we've got. Besides, it's better than waiting for a meal to be cooked or to do the work yourself."

Regal walked over and sat on the couch next to Keir, emptying the greasy bag onto the table. He pulled out a Filet-O-Fish to give to Keir.

"What's that?"

"A sandwich with breaded fish and tartar sauce."

"Tartar sauce?"

"Just try it. It's good."

Keir balanced the cardboard container on his lap as he carefully lifted the sandwich. He took a bite, grinning as he made a small, joyful sound. "This is great!"

"I told you." Regal handed Keir a large fry as well before tearing the paper off of his cheeseburger. He took a bite out of it and sipped at his large drink, kicking his feet up on the table.

"You know, I never would have thought to try this while on Earth," Keir explained with a laugh. "Whenever I wasn't looking for you, I was camping and catching my own food."

Regal raised an eyebrow. "You never thought to stop in a restaurant?"

"I didn't have any money, and I wasn't going to steal food. Sometimes a kind stranger would offer me something to eat, but I never begged or asked."

"Jesus, how did you survive for so long?"

"Luck?" Keir said with a sheepish laugh. "It was hard living off the land, and very lonely not interacting with others often. I always wanted to spend more time with the humans... to learn more about them, but I just kept my focus on you and didn't give up." He felt himself blushing, and in an attempt to change the subject, looked down at his Filet-O-Fish. "So, I can see why humans enjoy these so much."

"It's fast, cheap, and tasty as hell. Of course, I've never actually tasted Hell before, so maybe it's a figure of speech," Regal said through a chuckle. Keir laughed a little as well.

Both fell silent as they ate their dinner/breakfast, lost in their thoughts. Regal watched Keir from the corner of his eye, trying to figure out if Keir was slowly falling into his trap. However, the angel was also thinking hard about how long he should act oblivious to Regal's intentions. They both knew not to fully trust one another.

Regal took another sip of his drink, watching as Keir mimicked the action subconsciously. He smirked a little, knowing that this sin would be the easiest of the seven to complete. Crumpling up his wrappers and tossing it into the paper bag, Regal stood up to throw away the trash.

"All done?" Regal asked briefly, holding open the bag for Keir to toss his scraps away. The angel nodded and gingerly placed his leftovers into the greasy bag Regal held. Regal laughed and shook his head. "It's garbage. No need to treat it like it's made of gold."

"Sorry, habit..." Keir said sheepishly. Regal waved his hand in a nonchalant manner and threw away their trash. Keir looked up at Regal and twiddled his thumbs slightly. "So... are you going out tonight?"

"Out?" Regal asked as he turned. "Yeah. Why do you ask?"

"No reason. I just assumed that you'd go and do... demon things at night."

Regal snorted. "'Demon things'? It's much more specific than that."

"Like what?"

The demon shrugged, walking closer to him with a grin. "Oh you know, the usual: sucking the souls out of innocent humans, killing for sport, maybe stealing some cash from a local bank." Keir's expression of shock made him laugh even harder. "Damn you guys are so easy to fool!"

Keir ruffled his wings, some transparent feathers falling to his feet. "We aren't easy to fool! It's just appalling to hear such vile things, even from a demon. Just don't say stuff like that." This was why demons were so frustrating for angels. All they did was lie and joke around. It was this infuriating behavior that drove angels up the wall.

"That's like telling an angel to stop praying. You have to learn to live with it." Regal finished off his soda before dropping the cup in the trash and heading back for his bedroom window. "Anyways, I'm going to hunt down that demon you were talking about and make sure she knows this is my territory and not to meddle with what is mine."

The Art of Falling

He gave Keir a long glance, his eyes darkening slightly. Keir felt the soft marks on his cheeks chill, Regal's brand searing with power. He couldn't help but do the same to Regal in return, flaring his heavenly essence to make Regal feel the same sensation. It caused the demon to falter a moment before stalking into his room to leave once again.

"Don't bother waiting up."

Regal jumped back out of the window and dove down to the ground before pulling up to launch himself into the clouds. Keir hung out the window for a moment, watching his dark shadow fade away, before closing it shut and heading to bed. He needed a good night's rest to deal with what Regal had in store for him.

CHAPTER *Ten*

REGAL WASN'T ABLE to find the demon who had tormented Keir. He had searched for four days, and was unable to find any trace of her in the city. However, not finding her was the least of his problems. Regal had also been acting extremely nice and well-behaved toward Keir in an attempt to make the angel trust him and fall for his plan. After almost a week, his patience was growing thin.

Although he wanted to choke himself for having to give constant praises, heartwarming laughs, and pretending to become Keir's friend and potential lover, he didn't stop. His attempt at classical conditioning was working.

Regal knew that the psychological test could be used on Keir easily. If it worked for Pavlov's dogs, it could work for some dumb angel. As long as he kept ringing the bell whenever it was time to feed, Keir would be falling to gluttony in no time.

Although he did stock the fridge with fresh fruit and vegetables like he promised, he refilled his cabinets with processed canned goods, chips, and soda. Regal continued to return home every day with a new delicious dinner in hopes of getting the angel addicted. Veggie burgers, pizza, cakes, fish tacos, ice cream... nothing was off limits. The more food Keir tried, the more he would eat. At least, that was the plan.

When he would return home, Keir would be waiting, watching the same TV show that was always on at that time while he had a light snack. At first he started with the celery and apples, but started to integrate his more indulgent treats into the mix; a grab-bag of Lays sour cream and cheddar chips (which had quickly become his favorite), or M&Ms from the god awful tourist trap near Times Square. Regardless of what he ate, he always paired it with a can of soda.

They would eat their dinner and relax, talking about whatever was on their minds. They both avoided the obvious topic of their current living arrangements and instead focused on what was happening in the world around them. Regal would amuse Keir by seeming interested in Keir's little adventures out of the house. However, those were becoming rarer. Keir was fond of watching T.V. and seeing what shows the humans created.

Regal could barely contain his excitement. The angel was actually succumbing! This was easier than he would have thought. All he had to do was tough it out and stick with his plan.

However, on the seventh day, Regal accidentally slept in later than normal.

The sun had already set and the first quarter moon was sitting high in the sky. He cursed himself for being late on his schedule, hoping it wouldn't mess up his plans. He jumped out of bed and quickly changed into his clothes before running out of his room and straight into Keir.

The angel had been walking down the hall to wake up the demon. He chuckled as Regal blearily rubbed his eyes in an attempt to wake up faster. "Good evening! Or... should I say good morning?" Keir said cheerfully as he held up a McDonald's bag filled with food. It had become his favorite over the last few days.

Regal blinked, surprised that the angel had gone out and gotten dinner for himself. "Uh, either is fine. You... went out at night?"

Keir nodded, sitting down and pulling out their usual. "I figured you were still tired, so I went and got dinner for us. I hope you don't mind, but I used your wallet again."

Regal shook his head lightly. "It's fine... Father makes sure I have enough to get me by so I don't have to worry about trying to have a mundane job while working for him. Haunting the building also gets me a great deal from the landlord."

Keir laughed, the sound irritating Regal's nerves. Keir was laughing at everything Regal said lately.

He walked over, sitting down and murmuring a small thank you before taking a bite out of his burger. He glanced at Keir, who was eating happily his Filet-O-Fish while humming the theme song to Law and Order as the show began. Regal grinned.

It worked. All of the time and energy it took to win him over wasn't a waste! The angel had started a bad habit that would be hard to break, choosing to eat some of the worst foods for the human body—or in this case a heavenly body—all on his own. Not only that, but he chose to run out for food instead of make a dinner at home! Maybe he was killing two birds with one stone by making him commit sloth as well as gluttony. Regal's hands were shaking with excitement and he struggled to keep the smile off his face.

He was so curious to see if the sins were final, if his plan was enough to make the angel slip. He leaned closer for a moment, trying to see if there was a physical mark on him somewhere. Keir glanced over, causing Regal to reach out and grab a packet of ketchup he didn't really want.

Damn... he'll catch me if I stare.

It seemed like more patience was needed. He would wait until morning to see if it was worthwhile. If not, he'd have to think of another plan; unless... he could somehow convince Keir to reveal his body. Regal practically purred with delight at his idea. It would be difficult, but it might be the perfect time to try.

Regal casually scooted closer to Keir on the couch, draping his arm across his shoulders as he continued to eat. The angel next to him stiffened slightly, uneasy at Regal's movements. The demon simply looked at him and smiled as innocently and boyishly as he could.

Keir cautiously leaned into his touch. Regal remained still, laying his hand on Keir's shoulder affectionately. The angel seemed to not mind the touch, and in fact moved in closer to cuddle up to him.

Regal let his head fall on top of Keir's, taking the moment to breathe in his scent. Underneath the familiar smell of his shampoo was the crisp and clean smell of an angel's essence, although tainted with darkness. It wasn't as bad as he expected. He almost enjoyed it, knowing he was the cause of the impurity.

His stomach twisted at the thought. He was actually getting used to having the angel around. Was he becoming soft? He had to fix that. Now. He glanced down at Keir and decided now was the best time to try and seduce Keir.

Keir tried to peek up at Regal to examine his expression, but couldn't get a clear look at him without exposing himself. He wanted to trust Regal... to believe that maybe he was growing fond of him. Unfortunately, Keir knew that probably wasn't the case.

The demon began to gently rub circles into Keir's shoulder, trying to lull him to sleep. Slowly but surely, his actions began to work. Keir fell into a light slumber. Regal smiled deviously, waiting a full twenty minutes to make sure the angel was truly asleep before attempting to manipulate his way into his dreams.

He shifted, laying Keir down onto the couch so he was positioned comfortably on his back. The demon moved on top of Keir and took a deep breath as he expanded his wings to encase them in darkness; although his transparent wings did nothing. He gritted his teeth in annoyance and continued his ritual. On a normal hunt, he wouldn't dare try this without some sort of magical shield around them, but he was in the safety of his apartment and was certain no one would see.

Slowly, he closed his eyes and tapped into his special ability to dreamwalk. He used his mind to gently pry away the layers of Keir's subconscious like an onion. He couldn't move too fast, knowing it was easiest to make a mistake on the outer layers.

As soon as he was in the deepest depths of sleep, Regal would slowly climb his way back through the subconscious until he was back into the layer of dreaming. Now, his psyche was anchored to the bottom layer of delta, rather than the waking world. If something were to go wrong, he could slip back into the lower stages of sleep rather than being forced out into the open.

This was his major goal, to ease his way into his victim's dreams with a solid support system so he could influence them without them being suspicious. After an hour of working his way through Keir's mind, he was inside of his dreams.

He wasn't sure what he was expecting to see; perhaps a dream taking place in Heaven or about doing some sort of good deed. He couldn't imagine what types of dreams angels would have. Regal wasn't expecting it to be so... mundane.

He could see Keir, not finding it peculiar that the angel was the star of his own dream. The angel was sitting on the edge of a dock, seemingly staring out at the choppy water. Even in his mind, he was lost in his thoughts. Was there anything this angel did except think?

Regal walked forward slowly, not wanting to startle Keir into waking. He needed to pretend he was meant to be there. The angel didn't seem to hear him walking up, his footsteps quiet on the boardwalk. He stopped, standing behind Keir as he stared out at the water, expecting something amazing to happen.

"What are you looking at?"

Keir glanced over, not seeming surprised at Regal's presence. This was somewhat unexpected for the demon. It meant he was already a common subject in the angel's dreams.

"Nothing really... just thinking," Keir replied softly, his voice somewhat hollow. Regal sat down next to him, his feet dangling over the edge and barely brushing the water. He noticed he was barefoot. Keir was manipulating the dream to suit the scene.

"Thinking about what?" Regal prodded, hoping for more answers. Keir merely shrugged.

Regal knew that this was a dangerous situation to be in. He was already well established in Keir's subconscious mind; one mistake and it'd be obvious he was pushing through from the outside. He had to act how Keir imagined he would. The only problem was that he didn't know how he should act.

He could be completely normal, but would that be too obvious that it was really him trying to pry into Keir's dreams? If he acted more loving and gentle, would that be more accurate to Keir's imagination? Or does Keir dream about him being the same cruel and mocking demon he was? Would being too sweet be a red flag?

These questions swirled in Regal's mind, causing him to lose focus and fade out. He had to cling on tight and clear his mind for a moment to bring himself back into the present. Keir's dream self didn't seem to notice.

For a second, Regal panicked, and decided to be himself. He chuckled a little, leaning closer to Keir. "You know, with that dazed look on your face, I'd think you were daydreaming about something pretty important."

Keir glanced over at him, his face tingeing a bit as he looked away quickly. "Depends on what you mean by important."

Regal's shoulders shook slightly with amusement. Just like how he'd act in the waking world. His 50/50 chance had been correct when he decided to act normal. Of course, normal for him would be to try and seduce his victim while inside of their dreams.

It was dangerous to try and attempt such a thing with an angel. Incubi were taught early on that angels had extremely specific rituals they performed before they mated; an act similar to humans getting married. Angels never had affairs or had sex before "marriage." To attempt this in an angel's dreams was lunacy. However, Regal's curiosity to see if he could pull off such a feat was strong. He couldn't fight back the desire to give it a shot.

"Of course, I speak of myself when I say something important," he purred, sliding closer as he wrapped an arm around Keir's form. The angel's face turned redder, but he didn't move away from Regal's touch.

"You're important, but not *that* important."

"Oh, not *that* important?" Regal asked, a light and playful tone in his voice. "But I thought you loved me?"

"I do love you," Keir squeaked, turning to face Regal. The expression on his face was honest, but it shrouded something Regal couldn't decipher. The angel was hiding something...

"Really? I don't know if I can believe that with the way you're acting." Regal pulled Keir closer, smirking against his ear and he nuzzled his nose against his hair. "I thought lovers were supposed to be close and honest with each other."

"S-since when were you ever honest with me?" Keir asked, pulling away slightly.

Regal sneered, cursing himself for saying such a stupid thing. He had to remember that Keir knew his personality better than his other victims. "I just mean that if you want this whole bonding thing to work between us, we need to actually try to open up." He forced a sigh, trying to sound like he was having a hard time admitting what he was about to say; although that wasn't too far from the truth to begin with. "From now on I'll... try to be more honest and... trustworthy."

He practically choked on the word.

It was convincing enough for Keir's subconscious, which smiled in return. He rested his head against Regal's shoulder. "Alright. I think I can live with that. I'll try to be more open with you as well."

Regal held back the urge to smirk and instead smiled as sweetly as he could. He rubbed his hand against Keir's shoulder gently. "I'm glad. I don't want this to be harder than it should. I'm sure demons and angels can find a way to get along somehow."

"I think so too," Keir murmured, closing his dark blue eyes as Regal continued to hold him. Slowly, Regal began to become bolder in his actions; he kissed Keir's temple while his hands teasingly ran down his side to rest against his hip. Keir shivered slightly, aware of Regal's movements, but not speaking against them.

Regal moved his lips to Keir's neck, peppering kisses along the expanse of porcelain skin. Keir quivered again, a gentle sigh escaping his lips. His hands moved over to rub Keir's shoulders, trying to gently coax out his wings. They easily fell out from Keir's shoulders, a blinding white light shining around them.

The demon winced, trying to hide his face from the light. In Keir's dreams, he wasn't marked in a physical way; he still had his white wings. He let his own wings fall out, happy when they were his normal solid shade of black. He curled them around his body, protecting himself.

Doubt started to cloud his mind. If Keir's dream self was untainted, would any sin forced on him in the waking world transfer? If not, Regal was doing this all for nothing. If it did, he'd have to dig deeper.

His hands roamed lower, brushing over Keir's stomach to pull him into his lap. He crouched over him slightly, his face buried into the crook of Keir's neck as he continued to tease his throat with soft kisses. The gentle touches made Keir shiver, his wings shaking slightly.

"W-what are you doing to me?" the angel asked meekly, glancing back at Regal as he attempted to sit up straighter. Regal blinked, hiding his expression from Keir as best as he could. Was he catching onto his game?

Regal lifted his head and looked at Keir with innocent eyes. "What do you mean? I'm not hurting you, am I?" he asked, brushing his nose against Keir's jaw. He knew he was being too affectionate, but he hoped Keir would brush it off.

"No, you're not harming me..." he replied, slightly stuttering. "B-but... you're doing... something..."

Damn... he's catching on. Regal thought to himself bitterly as he continued to hold Keir close. "I'm not sure what I'm doing wrong."

"This... all of this," Keir murmured as Regal placed another gentle kiss along his jawline. "You're never this... this touchy."

Regal smiled sweetly. "This is how people show their love for one another." His hands moved, trailing up Keir's chest tenderly. Keir stuttered incoherently for a moment, his muscles tensing under Regal's tender touches.

"I..." he began, trying to get the words out. His eyes were half-lidded, his body beginning to accept the gestures of affection. Regal smiled as he used his wings to help push Keir over, looming over him as he lay against the dock.

"You?" he asked teasingly, his eyes dark. Keir didn't respond; his face flushed a deep scarlet as his mouth parted slightly. It was as if his words got caught in his throat. Regal took the moment to lean dangerously close to Keir's face, their lips barely touching. His right hand moved to caress Keir's cheek, his thumb brushing against his cheekbone delicately—tracing the spot where the mark of their bond should have been. "What's wrong? Demon got your tongue?"

Keir's lack of response made Regal more eager to possibly slip in another sin. With the gentlest smile he could make, he bent his head down and pressed his lips gently against Keir's.

The last time he had kissed Keir, it was when he marked him. Before that, it was just to make the angel weak enough so he could escape from him. Now, however, it was different.

The Art of Falling

It was always a new sensation when kissing someone in their dreams. It was often more sensual, if not "dreamy" and light. Most times it felt almost surreal and unnatural—almost too good to be true. In this case, Regal could still tell that this was Keir, and not a fantasy. There was a sense of delicateness and virginity that was familiar from the first time they kissed. However, something about the warmth of Keir's untainted angelic aura sent sparks own his spine. Kissing Keir in his dreams definitely felt better than in the waking world. In fact, it felt better than anyone else Regal had ever seduced. It was thrilling and terrifying, and that only aroused Regal more.

He was starting to get lost in the moment when Keir's hands moved up along Regal's back, weaving his fingers through his hair. Regal groaned, taking pleasure in the feeling. Keir's hands tightened into fists and yanked, pulling Regal's mouth off of his.

Regal hissed, his wings flaring angrily as Keir pushed him away. "What the hell?" His focus on Keir was turning fuzzy fast, and he realized almost too late that Keir was forcing himself awake. Regal let go of the anchors that kept him tied into Keir's dreams and let himself get pushed out by Keir's waking conscience.

CHAPTER *Eleven*

Regal's physical body loomed over Keir's sleeping form, in a trance of sorts as he worked inside of his mind. As Keir forced him away, he was pushed back into the coffee table. The sudden movement broke the connection between their minds. It knocked over their drinks and leftover food, spilling them both onto the carpet. He grunted and rubbed his head, lifting himself onto his feet as he saw Keir stirring.

Most times, he'd hide in the shadows and wait for his victim to fall back asleep. But this was Keir. He was dealing with an angel who could fight back. There was nowhere to run or hide. They were bound and unable to run away without the other knowing. So he tried to act like absolutely nothing had happened. He quickly ran and sat down in a chair across the room, trying to find something to pretend he was doing. However, Keir woke up before he could find something to hide his actions, so Regal just sat and stared at him.

Keir sat up dizzily as he came out of his dreams. His head rushed and his eyesight went fuzzy for a moment. For a moment he was confused, but then slowly remembered the dream he'd just had about Regal. Then, he saw the knocked-over table and spilled food, and lastly, Regal sitting in the chair silently with a stoic expression. It didn't take Keir long to realize what Regal had done.

"You were in my dreams!"

Regal shrugged. "Glad to know you're dreaming about me."

"You know what I mean," Keir said angrily, standing up to storm over to Regal. "You tried to seduce me!"

"That's quite an accusation to make."

"Don't try to act like you're innocent."

The angel had a point. Regal sighed. "Can you blame me? I am an incubus, after all. It's what I was bred to do."

Keir flared his wings, shaking them angrily as he stood face to face with Regal. "I can blame you. I thought we were trying to make this work."

Regal glared, his own wings slipping out to spread out behind him. "I am trying. You're just making it difficult for me."

"Bullshit!" Keir screamed, surprising himself and Regal. Angels were never ones to curse or swear. That was more natural for a demon. They stared at each other, wide-eyed and with wings fluttering in agitation, until Keir finally cracked and turned away.

That's when Regal caught sight of it; the small imperfection on Keir's wings. A dark spot had formed on the transparent feathers at the base of his wings, right between Keir's shoulder blades. They were becoming opaque and tainted. The more he sinned, the darker they would turn, unable to return to their pearly white complexion. It was proof that the past week hadn't been a complete waste of time.

He smirked, unable to hold back the devious joy that was welling up inside of him. It worked; it *actually* worked. The angel had succumbed to gluttony, and possibly sloth as well. His own wings tucked in as he shook off the laughter that bubbled up in his throat.

"What are you giggling at?" Keir growled, his eyes flashing a bright blue as he turned to glare at Regal. The demon merely shook his head, his shoulders shaking. "Answer me!"

"If I were to answer, you wouldn't believe me, would you? After all, demons only lie, right?" Regal bent down to set the table upright again. Keir hesitated for a moment before moving to pick up the items that had fallen to the floor. Dark stains where their sodas had spilled were left on the carpet.

106

"You're not giving me any reason to trust you, Regal." His voice was laced with anger.

Regal scoffed, laughing to himself, which only made the angel more frustrated. "I don't care if you trust me or not. I'm just doing my job. So kill me if I gave into my curiosity."

Regal's lack of caring made Keir's blood boil. *How dare a demon mock an angel by acting like his privacy was worth nothing?* Despite being in love with him, Keir couldn't help but be enraged. He lunged at the demon, shoving his shoulder into Regal's diaphragm. Keir tackled him to the floor as his wings beat heavily behind him to give him more power. Although the effects of holy light coming from the angel's wings were weakened from being transparent, Regal could still feel the residual glow.

"You should care!" Keir yelled. "If you didn't, why did you agree to this arrangement?"

The demon smirked. "Because you make a fantastic trophy."

Keir's fist slammed into Regal's face. His neck snapped backward and his head crashed into the carpeted floor. At the same instant, Keir cried out in pain as the force of his blow rebounded on him. He had completely forgotten that any pain Regal felt, he would also feel.

Fueled by rage, Regal grabbed Keir's wrists and dug his claws into his skin, ripping him off and throwing him away. Flapping his wings harshly, he lifted himself back up onto his feet. His vision was still swimming, but he could still see the angel rising opposite from him.

Regal darted at Keir and wrapped his hands around his neck. He strangled him, driving him back into the wall. The plaster cracked from the force of the impact, and drywall chipped away and fell to the ground. Regal felt a surge of pain in his back and shoulders, and his throat had a tingling, choking sensation. He ignored it completely, too overcome with anger to stop.

Keir reached up and gripped Regal's hair in his hands to hold him still. The angel jerked Regal's head forward, pressing his own neck against Regal's grip to slam his forehead into the bridge of Regal's nose in an attempt to break him away. However, his hold was too tight and he didn't let go.

The demon swung Keir around, throwing him over the couch, both sending objects flipping across the room.

Keir struggled to find his balance as he staggered to his feet, but was met with Regal's fist driving deep into his gut. He choked as the air was driven out of his lungs.

Regal buckled over and began coughing as well. He wrapped his arms around Keir's waist and flung him to the ground, pinning him down. "Foolish angel. You think you can overpower a demon?" he sneered, his voice resonating with dark energy. He sounded less like a human and more like a beast. Any other creature would cower in fear at the tone. However, the angel hardly flinched, a deeper part of him stimulated by the threat.

"What makes you think you can subdue an angel?" Keir returned, his voice also echoing with power as though he had a choir of angels around him talking in unison.

Keir grasped Regal's wrists and twisted his body suddenly, forcing the demon off. He threw Regal into the coffee table, and rose to his feet once more.

Both were lost in the moment, only vaguely aware of the dangers they were putting themselves in. Just as they were sharing pain, if one died during their battle, the other would, too.

They tumbled and rolled, throwing each other around the apartment. Regal reached for his pocket watch, but Keir smacked it out of his hand before he could activate it. The demon grasped Keir's pendant and ripped the chain off his neck and threw it across the room. With no weapons, they could only rely on their own strength.

Keir grabbed a lamp to use as a makeshift weapon as Regal leapt into the air. Before Keir could block Regal's attack, the demon delivered a powerful kick to the side of the angel's head and knocked him to the floor. Regal lunged at him, ready to rip out his throat. Keir rolled onto his back and kicked out at Regal. The weight of his desperate strike forced Regal up and over, his body crashing into the wall.

The demon cried out, screaming as a burning sensation exploded from where Keir had kicked him. He doubled over, gasping as the hot twinge of Heavenly flame licked his skin. His body was not really on fire, but the pain of it felt just as real. It took his breath away as he writhed in agony, his hand gripping at his side.

Keir gasped, feeling a strong burning sensation in his side as well. His hands went for the wound, but there was nothing there, just the lingering sensation of pain. However, it was already fading. Regal, on the other hand, was still in agony. No longer in a flurry of rage, Keir rushed over to Regal's side to check on him. "Regal! Are you okay?"

The demon's only response was profanities and curses that he spat out in anguish. Regal had heard about an angel's wrath being the most painful experience in existence—next to Gloria's wrath, of course. However, he never imagined he'd be alive to suffer through it.

Keir pushed Regal slowly onto his back, trying to soothe him through his pain. He lifted up Regal's sweater to see that the edges were singed. Once he pulled away, Keir could clearly see the white-hot burn that was on Regal's waist where his ankle had connected.

"Okay, don't panic! Don't panic!" Keir quickly ran into the bathroom and ran the faucet, collecting water in his hands. He hurried back to Regal's side and knelt beside him. The angel slipped into meditation, praying quietly to himself as he focused his healing energy into his palms. The water began to shimmer and purify, becoming holy. Keir began to let the water drip from his hands onto Regal's wound.

The demon cursed again loudly, lashing out to smack Keir's hands away from him, spilling the water onto the floor. "Are you out of your mind?"

"I... I figured holy water—"

"Just leave me alone." He didn't need Keir's help. Regal curled into a ball on the floor and waited for his own natural healing abilities to kick in. With time, the searing pain began to fade away, leaving just a white scar in its place.

"I think... I think my halo touched you," Keir murmured.

"No shit, Sherlock," he grumbled as he reached down to touch the scar. It was sore, but at least it wasn't burning anymore. "I forgot you wore yours around your ankle..." he mumbled to himself. How could he have forgotten the angel's only real weapon against damned creatures?

Keir smiled, a small ounce of pride welling inside of him. "The other angels said that was a silly place for a halo, but I knew it'd come in handy." He lifted the edge of his pants to show off the thin strand of metal around his ankle. It shone brightly, flecks of gold embedded in the angelic material. It was simple, not laced with thorns or serrated edges; just a dull metal band that seemed to heat up whenever Keir was enraged.

"I'll make sure I stay away from your ankles from now on..." Regal grunted as he stood up, wincing as his side ached.

Keir scrambled to his feet, ready to help him if he needed it. "I'm so sorry... Regal... I didn't mean to hurt you." Although he knew it was reflex to protect himself from an attack, he felt guilty. He honestly didn't want to hurt Regal, no matter how infuriating he was.

"It's natural to want to kill each other. We were bound to get into a fight eventually. So don't worry about it." Regal found Keir's pendant on the floor and picked it up, tossing it over to Keir before searching for his pocket watch. Once he found it, he brought it into his bedroom and set it on the dresser. He flopped onto his bed, closing his eyes immediately as his head hit the pillow. The halo had sapped away any strength he had left. He didn't hear Keir following after him, and assumed that the angel had decided it was best to leave him alone for the daylight hours.

He took this time to call on his father.

After a few moments of silent "praying," for lack of a better word, Jackal appeared in Regal's bedroom, seeming to materialize out of thin air, the smoke curling around him to form his physical body. He loomed over his son, smiling somewhat fondly. "You called?"

"He's more of a hassle than I expected," Regal groaned, rolling over onto his back to face his father. "Much more of a fighter."

"Angels were made to be warriors. Remember that." Jackal sensed a disturbance in Regal's normal energy field. He quirked a brow and waved his hand over Regal's body, locating the burned area on his son's skin. "You came into contact with his halo?"

Regal nodded, sneering, "He keeps it on his ankle. What a strange and useless place."

"Not so useless, is it? It managed to harm you," Jackal said with an easy smile. Regal huffed and sat up and threw his legs over the edge of his bed so his father could sit beside him. Jackal sat down, crossing his legs and folding his hands in his lap. "So, why have you called me? I'm assuming it wasn't to complain about your boo-boo."

"I managed to coerce a sin on him. Maybe even two. His wings are turning opaque again, but gray instead of white,"

Regal explained in an excited whisper. He wasn't certain if Keir was listening through his door, but doubted it. However, it was best to not underestimate Keir's sneaky nature and play it safe.

Jackal chuckled, patting his hand on Regal's back. "Good job."

Regal smiled, his pride boosting as his father praised him. His wings fluttered happily behind him, although Jackal scowled at that. He quickly tucked them back in, hiding his blatant sign of being marked by an angel.

"However, only one sin—maybe two—after a full week? Your odds of squeezing the rest in three weeks aren't too good," Jackal remarked. "Especially with that extra assignment you have in the city. Or have you completely forgotten your duties?"

Regal's smile fell. "I'm doing the best I can," he replied shortly, bristling with annoyance. He hated when his father would praise him, only to kick him back down.

"And your best isn't enough, it seems," Jackal said sharply as he stood up from the bed. "You're wasting too much time. He'll have you wrapped around his finger long before you lay another sin on him if you keep this up."

"Then what do you suggest I do?" Regal hissed, growing more frustrated.

Jackal's eyes turned black, the irises beginning to glow red in anger like molten iron. Regal flinched, preparing for another furious strike. However, Jackal held back.

"Punish him," Jackal commanded. "Make him realize what he did was a mistake, and make him suffer for it."

"And what does that mean exactly? I can't just whip him like we do at home. That'll hurt me just as much as it hurts him."

Jackal stroked his chin for moment, contemplating Regal's options. "Deny him comfort. Make him sleep on the floor. Force him to live without sunlight. Lock him in the house during the day and force him to join you at night. If he fights back, take away his luxuries until he begs for mercy. I want you to *break him*. Treat him like a pet until he behaves like one."

Regal nodded and bowed with his hand over his chest. He knew that he was lucky to get that much advice. "Of course, Father. I hope I do not disappoint you."

Jackal gave him a quick pat on the head before stepping back, breaking the contact. "Now, I must be heading off. Do try and get some rest. I would hate if you didn't perform horrible deeds in your best condition." He winked, a grin spreading across his features before he disappeared in another cloud of smoke.

CHAPTER *Twelve*

*R*EGAL AWOKE WITH the sunrise the next morning. Despite the sun in his window, he forced himself to get up and trudge out of his room and down the hall. He went from room to room, braving the lights as he locked the doors and windows with a wave of his hand. The edges of the windows and doors glowed violet, magically sealed shut.

He glanced over his shoulder and saw Keir sleeping on the couch, his limbs dangling off the edge. Regal sneered and took the angel's blanket as he walked past. When he walked back into his room, he hooked the blanket up in front of his window to block out the sunlight that would eventually fall in.

The demon curled back up in bed, burying himself into the blankets and hiding his head under the pillow. As he drifted back to sleep, he wondered how easily the angel would handle being kept inside for the day. He knew that forcing Keir to follow his orders would be a challenge, but Regal was excited by the idea. Although he desired obedience, Keir's stubbornness made his task much more exciting.

When Keir woke up a few hours later, he was greeted with the sunlight trying to break through the closed curtains. With a large yawn, he got up and walked over to the living room window and pulled the fabric back. He smiled, feeling warmer as the sunlight shined on him. He tried to unlock the window to get some fresh air, but found that it wouldn't budge.

That's odd... he thought as he went to the front door. He twisted the knob but it wouldn't turn. The door was also locked.

Unease began to creep into his senses. He went to the bathroom window: locked. He hurried to the kitchen window:

also locked. Keir's heart was racing as he realized he was trapped. His wings unfurled, trying to open to full wingspan to help ease the sense of claustrophobia that was clawing at him. Keir rushed into Regal's room, knowing the last window that led outside was above his bed.

The demon glanced over at him nonchalantly, not at all surprised to find the angel in a panic. "Good morning," he said easily, stretching as he curled back up into his pillows.

Keir ignored him and bounded forward, jumping onto Regal's bed and stumbling over his body in an attempt to reach his window.

Regal growled as he was bounced around by Keir's movements. "Hey! Get off!"

The angel tried to throw it open, but it was locked as well. He jumped up, using the bed as a springboard, and kicked his foot at the window. The halo around his ankle burned brightly before it smashed into the glass, shattering it.

"What the hell?" Regal yelled as he shielded his face from the glass that fell around him. He growled, gritting his teeth as he grabbed Keir's thigh and yanked him hard to the floor. "You broke my window!"

"Why are all the windows and doors locked? Why can't I leave?" Keir asked, his blue eyes wide with confusion as he sat himself upright on the floor.

Regal sneered. "Who would have guessed that you would be so desperate to leave me?"

Keir bristled, his wings shaking. "I don't want to leave you. I just want to get out and stretch my wings."

"Should have thought about that yesterday," Regal said sternly, sitting up as he ran a hand through his tousled hair. Fragments of glass fell out onto the bed.

"W-what?" Keir asked shakily.

The Art of Falling

"This is your punishment for burning me with that damned halo," Regal grunted, standing up with a grimace. His side was terribly sore and his back was stiff. "You're forbidden to leave the apartment during the day." He looked over at his now-broken window and frowned. The wind was blowing the blanket and allowing the daylight to filter in. "I was going to let you to fly at night with me when I leave, but now that you've gone and broken my property, I'm going to take that luxury away as well."

"You can't keep me locked up here."

"Watch me," Regal hissed.

"I didn't mean to hurt you. It was an accident," Keir said lowly, his anger dissipating.

Regal sighed. "I know, but there are still consequences. Even your Lord punishes those who break commandments."

"Yes, but Gloria forgives them once they repent."

"Then repent. Once you behave, you'll have your privileges back. That seems fair."

The angel huffed and stalked out of Regal's room. He paced the hall, shaking his hands in an attempt to get rid of his nerves. Keir scowled as he stared down the hall toward the kitchen.

He should have thought about the halo before attacking me, Keir thought bitterly. He should punish Regal in some way for his behavior, as well. However, Keir knew that he was the one who started the fight. He had punched Regal first, and therefore, being punished was fair... even if Regal invading Keir's dreams caused the angel to lash out.

Groaning at his own ethics, he turned and walked back to Regal's room. As he turned into the doorway, his eyes caught Regal getting dressed. He couldn't help but stare for a moment in awe, desire, and curiosity.

His back and shoulders were well-defined, the muscles toned to perfection. Thin white scars adorned his skin, an almost elegant pattern of lashes that looked like lace covered his back. On his shoulder blades, two light patches—similar to birth marks—showed where his black wings emerged. It was somewhat surprising to Keir that the marks on his back were not dark like his wings. They were similar to the patches angels had on their own shoulders.

Perhaps angels and demons aren't all that different.

As Regal pulled on a dark sweater, he turned and saw Keir's stare. "Something on your mind?" he asked gruffly, his gray eyes narrowing slightly.

Keir flushed and rubbed the back of his neck, clearing his throat. He wasn't going to admit that he was fond of staring at Regal. He didn't want the demon getting any ideas. "I was just wondering what I should do while I'm... detained."

Regal shrugged. "I don't care. You can do whatever you want here as long as you keep the curtains drawn shut. I want it to stay dark. The residual energy from the sun gives me a migraine."

Keir nodded and headed back to the living room. Regal eyed him as he left, sighing as he continued to get dressed. It was still far too early to be waking up, but that damned angel ruined those plans. He needed to get away from Keir. Regal walked over to his dresser and pulled out a small mirror. He groaned when he saw the bags forming under his eyes, and his five-o'clock shadow. He doubted that he'd be able to pick up anyone looking like this.

After going through his morning routine, Regal locked his bedroom door and went to the kitchen to look for something to eat. Keir was already there, rummaging through the cupboards. "Are we out of food?" he asked briefly as he grabbed a can of soda. Keir nodded and sighed, grabbing the last bag of chips they had. "I'll run out and shop," Regal said before chugging down his drink.

"You're going out? Now?" Keir asked, his voice rising in surprise. Regal nodded, grabbing his leather jacket off the coat rack. "During the day?"

"I'm not some vampire. I won't burst into flames," Regal snapped, still somewhat cranky from his lack of sleep.

"I thought vampires only felt slight irritation when in direct sunlight?"

Regal sighed heavily. "It's a figure of speech... shit, you're so clueless."

Keir ignored the comment. "Won't you get tired?"

It's your damned fault for waking me up so early in the first place... The demon walked over and rested his hand on the angel's shoulder. "Listen, I'm not a child. I can handle a few rays of sunshine. So don't worry so much."

"Alright. Just don't get completely drained," Keir replied with a small smile.

Regal blinked, caught off guard again. *Keir is wishing me well?* Even after everything that had happened in the last week, he was honestly looking out for Regal's well-being? He murmured a short, confused thanks and unlocked the front door so he could leave. He closed it behind him and locked it once more before heading out.

After walking several blocks, the light gave him a headache. Regal rubbed his temples, gritting his teeth as he wove his way through the crowds. He wasn't accustomed to the lingering warmth of the autumn weather on his shoulders. He preferred the nighttime climate. Tugging on the collar of his sweater, he continued to walk to a local market.

He stepped inside, the smells of fresh-baked goods washing over him. He sighed, his mouth already watering. Regal loved sweets more than he'd normally let on. He enjoyed cookies and cupcakes, but he had a soft spot for éclairs. He grabbed a small basket and strolled through the bakery section, placing various treats inside before continuing to buy the essentials.

Mundane tasks such as these were his least favorite thing to do. He didn't want to be bothered shopping for food he could easily steal under the darkness of night. However, he had a roommate to care for now, and Keir probably wouldn't like it if Regal stole... he shook his head and growled, moving through the self-pay line before leaving. *What the hell am I thinking? Like I would ever show compassion for that angel.*

Regal ducked into an alleyway and turned invisible. He concentrated on his baked goods, and soon they, too, became invisible. He quickly headed back into the streets and ducked into a nearby drug store, walking in alongside another person so the front doors didn't seem to open by themselves.

He moved along the aisles until he found the rack of sunglasses. After checking for security cameras, he pulled a random pair off the rack and put them on, looking at himself in the small mirror.

Handsome as ever, he thought with a grin.

Regal turned to leave, when he noticed someone at the counter paying for their items. A tiny, wicked idea surfaced in his mind. He grabbed a second pair of sunglasses, turned them invisible, and walked up behind the woman at the counter. Just as she approached the exit door, he slipped the sunglasses into her purse and slipped out of the store ahead of her. The alarms started sounding, and the woman seemed extremely confused to find the sunglasses—now no longer invisible—in her purse. The manager came up and started accusing her of shoplifting, causing a scene.

Regal laughed, patting himself on the back for the small prank that would most likely ruin the woman's day. He felt good about himself committing a bad deed; even if it was simply stealing a pair of sunglasses and framing a human for theft.

As Regal soared high above the city, he felt his energy draining. Although his new sunglasses helped him see better in the bright sunlight, they did nothing to protect his body. The sun drained him of energy, making him far more tired than he normally would be at this time of day. He felt himself dropping lower as it became harder and harder to keep his wings beating, until eventually he was forced to find shelter.

He landed heavily, stumbling a bit as he leaned against the brick wall. The demon panted, feeling worn down from the sun. *No more flying around during the day,* Regal reminded himself. He slid to the floor, reaching into his bag of food to grab a cookie to eat to try and regain energy. He sat in the shadows, soaking up the darkness as best as he could. After almost an hour of recuperating, he got up and slowly headed back to his apartment. He didn't feel strong enough to fly, so instead he walked back home through the alleys. When he had to travel in the open, he made himself visible and used the humans around him as shelter from the sun. For once, he ignored the needy stares of strangers as he passed, not feeling up to flirting.

He walked into the apartment complex and took the elevator, leaning his head back against the wall as it shot him up seventy floors. He hated elevators. The closed space and sensation of flight without having to move made him uncomfortable. He let out a tense breath as the doors opened to his floor. He walked down the hall to his apartment, letting himself inside. Kicking off his shoes and shrugging off his jacket, he set his sunglasses on top of his head and looked over at Keir, who was sitting on the couch, flipping through TV channels with a bored expression on his face. He looked lethargic and tired; the constant darkness was sucking away any energy he had left.

When Regal walked in, Keir looked up over his shoulder

and smiled. "Welcome home."

"Nn..." Regal grumbled, locking the door behind him as he went to put away his groceries. It would be enough to get them through the day until he went properly shopping at night.

Keir got up from his spot on the couch and walked over to the kitchen, leaning on the counter as Regal slid a cinnamon sugar bagel over to Keir. He smiled happily, murmuring a quick thank you before taking a bite out of it. The demon yawned and went to sit down on the couch, flipping through the TV guide unenthusiastically. A familiar movie title caught his eye, sparking an evil idea in his mind. It wouldn't mark Keir with a sin, but it would scare him into obedience.

"Hey, Keir," he called, glancing back over to the angel. Keir looked up as he put away the groceries. "Feel like watching a movie?"

"I thought I was being punished?" Keir warily glanced at the TV.

Regal shrugged, patting the seat next to him. "Yeah, well, I don't want you dying of boredom. That would suck for the both of us. Besides, I think you'll enjoy this. It shows you about the life of humans more in depth. You are curious about humans and their lives, aren't you?"

Keir nodded, chuckling a little. "Yeah, even after all this time, they still don't make sense to me sometimes..." he admitted, smiling softly. He walked over and took a seat next to Regal, easily sliding into his arms. It was strange for both of them, how easily they were able to sit next to each other. Although after only knowing each other for a year, and being stuck together for little over a week, they were comfortable with each other—for the most part.

Regal smiled down at him. "The movie that's on will help you understand how their minds work—especially under extreme or stressing situations."

"Oh... that sounds interesting. I know that humans can

suffer from stress, while some thrive on it," Keir murmured as he pulled a blanket over them. He cuddled up to the demon. Regal stiffened, somewhat uncomfortable by Keir being so close. He brushed it off and focused on the movie as it started.

Regal could barely contain his excitement as Keir was sucked into the movie. The angel's eyes were glued to the screen, and Regal's were glued on Keir. Fifteen minutes into the film, the deceivingly cheery beginning faded away and the generic slasher plotline began to unfold.

Keir tensed up, completely horrified as the characters on the screen started being traumatized and killed off by some lunatic axe-murderer. "Regal, what are we watching?"

"Not sure exactly. Some random movie."

The woman's scream made Keir jump. "I don't want to watch this anymore." Keir stood up to turn off the TV, but Regal firmly grabbed Keir's wrist and tugged him back into the sofa. He wrapped an arm around Keir, holding him close.

"You wanted to see what humans were like, right?" Regal asked with a smile. "Maybe this will help you understand me more, too." Regal reclined in his seat, completely unaffected by the sight. Bloodshed and death was normal for a demon. After watching the gore-filled film for another ten minutes, he felt something wet on his shoulder.

He glanced down and saw that Keir was crying silently as he hid his face from the movie. Even though it wasn't real, Keir could imagine the pain and horrors of the people in the film, and it was too much for the gentle angel to deal with. Regal reflexively tried to comfort him, holding him closer, but he didn't know why he did. Although he was trying to punish Keir, something inside of him didn't want the angel to cry. When Keir looked up at Regal with pitiful expression in his eyes, Regal sighed and turned off the TV. He couldn't seem to stand seeing him like that.

Keir whimpered and wrapped his arms around himself, seeking comfort. When Regal didn't pull away, he curled closer and buried his head into the demon's chest to try and block out the images replaying in his mind.

Why do I feel like I'm suffocating? Regal thought anxiously. Everything around him felt humid and sticky, and this growing feeling refused to let go. Something was bubbling up inside of him, and he wasn't sure what. The urge was starting to grow at an immense rate, and he couldn't bear the feeling any longer.

The angel could feel Regal's growing anxiety and looked back up again. The pained expression on Regal's features snapped Keir out of his own fears and helped him focus. He sat up slightly, brushing Regal's bangs from his face. "Regal... are you okay?"

"I... don't know," he murmured, trying to take deep breaths to relax. But he couldn't, not when he could clearly see Keir's face; the angel's cheeks puffy and red from crying, his eyes shining with fresh tears. The demon grimaced, forcing himself to look away.

"Tell me what's wrong," Keir said quickly, already prepared to heal Regal if he needed to. The demon shoved the angel away, pushing him into the cushions. He stormed to the bathroom, locking the door behind him. Panting, he stripped down and turned on the shower. He blasted the water, making it freezing cold and jumping inside to try and clear his head and cool down the hot suffocation he was feeling.

Regal stretched his wings and rested his forehead against the tile, letting the icy water drip down his back and onto his feathers. They shook softly behind him, splattering the excess water against the walls. By the time the feeling in his chest passed, he was shivering and ready to get out. He turned off the water, but remained in the shower, running a hand through his bangs to slick them back.

He desperately wanted to call his father to ask him what he had just experienced, but decided against it. If he continued to ask for help, he would look weak. The demon needed to cope on his own, and find something that would help ease his anxiety.

Flying in the moonlight was his first thought, but he didn't have that option available to him at the moment. Going back to Hell was his second choice, but he didn't have enough energy to create a portal. Plus, if his father saw him returning home and leaving Keir at the apartment, he would have lots of questions that Regal didn't want to answer. His only other option was sleeping around. Hunting down sinners always helped him relax and distract his mind.

Regal stepped out of the shower, shaking out his hair and wrapping a towel around his waist. He quickly moved to his bedroom, ignoring the worried glances Keir gave him. He changed into fresh clothes, this time a loose-fitting tee and dark denim jeans. He took a step toward his window before remembering that it was broken.

"Dammit," he grumbled as he stormed out of his room and sealed the door shut behind him. He didn't want Keir slipping out. He walked into the living room and opened the front window, unfurling his wings so they could catch the cool air.

Keir, who was still worried about Regal despite the horrors the demon had tricked him into seeing, glanced over at Regal. He was just as curious and distraught over what had come over the demon as much as Regal was. He doubted that it was the movie that bothered him, so what could it have been?

"Regal, where are you going?"

"I'm off to do *demon things*," he mocked shortly, his voice gruff and angry. Regal looked up at the sky. Large clouds were beginning to gather, blocking out the sun. It should be easier for him to do his job without draining his energy more than it already was. He could smell the essence of innocents roaming the streets; it soothed his nerves somewhat.

"Are you sure? It's still daylight..." Keir asked, walking up to the window. Regal ruffled his wings, shaking off some wet feathers that hadn't completely dried.

"I'm certain," he barked, glaring back at the angel. He leaped out the window, waving his hand to slam it shut and lock it before heading toward the outskirts of the city, leaving Keir confused and slightly traumatized.

Keir watched him silently for a moment before turning to rest on the couch. With a sigh, he plopped onto his makeshift bed and stared at the closed window. He sat there for a long while, eyes drifting closed as he relaxed; but as soon as was about to completely calm down, images would flash in front of his eyes and startle him.

"Oh, Gloria... give me strength," he whimpered softly. Although She did not directly answer him, he did feel a sense of peace come over him. It was not enough to completely erase the horrifying pictures that replayed in his mind, but it was enough to help him focus on something more important: Regal. He wanted to follow after him and make sure he was okay, as well as protect whomever Regal might hunt down. Most of all, he needed to get out of the house.

Keir heard a loud click. He sat up and stared at the window, narrowing his eyes. Slowly, Keir rose to his feet and walked over to the window. He lifted it, surprised when it opened easily. Had Regal left it unlocked, or did Gloria open it for him? He did not question it. He merely thanked Her for Her blessings and headed out in search of his companion.

CHAPTER *Thirteen*

REGAL NORMALLY HUNTED at night, but he was desperate for sustenance. He hated to admit it, but he had completely forgotten about his original assignment. His target was a man named Jeremy Zales. He lived in Chinatown, only a few minutes away via flight. However, Regal was too exhausted to fly. Trying to focus on his mission and not on the brutal headache he was developing, Regal ran through the streets toward the subway. It would only be about a 20-minute trip underground, and he would have time to recover from the sun exposure.

He bounded down the steps and over the gate where people swiped their subway passed to enter the station. Regal waited impatiently for the train to zoom past and slow down to a stop. He shoved his way past those who were coming out, knocking strangers to the side, ignoring their confused expressions. He stood in the center and allowed for himself to be lost in the crowd before dropping his invisibility and sitting down in a chair. He closed his eyes and rubbed his temples as he tried to prepare himself for his mission.

Though he didn't have much of a physical description to work with, other than the fact that Zales was short middle-aged man who was balding, Jackal had told Regal that his target had a clear, red aura with lemon yellow along the edges. What made him stand out were the flecks of black that tainted his energy fields. Personality-wise, Zales wasn't going to be hard to manipulate. He had a nasty habit of cheating on his wife with male prostitutes, a role that Regal could easily fill. Regal would have finished this assignment and moved onto the next weeks ago if he hadn't run into Keir and got into this mess.

Don't think about Keir.

Regal concentrated on meditating, welcoming the moments of darkness on the subway when the fluorescent lights would flicker. He was going to need all of the strength he could get to capture Zales' soul. No matter how willing a victim was, he couldn't be sloppy.

When the subway finally arrived at the proper station, Regal filed out with the crowd up to the surface streets. As he began to walk in the general direction of where he believed Zales lived, he let himself become receptive to the thousands of auras around him.

The rush of lust, desire, and competition hit Regal hard, drawing him like a moth to the flame. However, muddled in with the tantalizing auras were feelings of rage, envy, deceit, panic, joy, awe, and stress—mainly stress.

He let himself become bombarded for almost a half hour until it became too much. He rubbed his temples as he slowed to a stop, leaning against the wall of a restaurant. His head was pounding and felt nauseous, the bursts of color and energy only making it worse. He was on the verge of giving up when he caught Zales' aura on the fringe of his vision.

He turned and saw Zales' bald head shining among the sea of people. He was walking home from work with a briefcase in hand. Regal jumped at the opportunity to shadow him. He kept several feet behind him, not wanting him to get the sense that he was being followed—not that he would see Regal, who had turned invisible. They walked several blocks through the streets before heading into the apartment complex where Zales lived. Regal rushed to follow him in, barely slipping through the door before it closed behind him.

Zales' wife didn't seem to be there. Regal remembered learning that their work schedules clashed, and they often had several hours where they were apart. No wonder he was able to get away with his infidelity for so long.

When Zales went into the shower to get ready for his night, Regal made himself visible, unable to keep his shields up any longer. Carefully, he searched the house for any tips on what type of men he liked. He knew he had limited time to rifle through Zales' belongings, so he dug through drawers quickly and carefully, making sure to put everything back in its place. After ten minutes, he found no leads. Regal's only other choice was to check Jeremy's e-mail. He found the laptop and tried to break into it by guessing possible passwords and hacking into the mainframe, but nothing worked. Jeremy was cautious.

Regal slammed his fist on the table and cringed. He looked over toward the bathroom door in silence. The water didn't stop running, and Regal let out a breath. He needed to calm down and not get frustrated. He couldn't turn invisible again in an emergency.

The demon groaned and pulled at his hair. He wished a demon of envy was here to help him. They were masters at gathering information from all sources, regardless of what security measures were in place. It was useful for knowing what seeds of doubt and jealousy to plant into their victims.

The water turned off with a squeak, and Regal jumped up from the chair. He shut the laptop and looked around for a place to hide. Zale's house was spotless and tidy, and the open-concept layout only made Regal's frantic search for a hiding spot more difficult.

Having no other place to go, he ran as quietly as he could into the nearest room, which happened to be the bedroom. He shut the bedroom door behind him just as he heard the bathroom door open. He scrambled under the bed, bumping his head on the wooden slats that held the mattress above him.

Look at yourself. Hiding under a bed like a mundane thief. Have you no dignity? Never in his life had he stooped so low—literally—to get a job done. At least no one was here to see his humiliation.

Zales walked into the bedroom, whistling as he dropped his towel to the floor. Regal watched his feet pad across the carpeted floor toward the closet. Regal held his breath, not wanting to have Zales look under the bed for any reason. The demon glanced to his right and noticed shoes tucked away beside him. He carefully pushed them out into the open so Zales could find them easily.

Regal bit his lip and held back a grunt of annoyance as Zales sat down on the bed. The mattress creaked and squished down on the incubus. Regal felt his wings pressing against the mattress in an attempt to give him more space. He hated feeling this trapped. Shivering, he waited as patiently as he could for Zales to get up and leave.

The phone rang, causing Regal to jump, hitting his head on the wood again. He froze in place, but Zales didn't seem to notice. He was already making his way for the phone on the night stand. Regal listened in closely, hoping that it wasn't going to be a long business call.

"Hello, Jeremy Zales speaking." He was silent for a moment. "Oh, hey Nick... yeah, I'm just getting back home from work. I just have a few errands I have to run before we meet up... no, my wife doesn't come home until later tonight, she has some press event and thinks I'm working late... yeah, we'll have plenty of time... Wyndham Garden at five? Perfect, I'll see you then..."

Regal watched as his victim put on his shoes before leaving the bedroom for a moment. He crawled out from under the bed, grabbed the cell phone Zales had left behind, and checked the caller ID. Nicholas Hunt was the last name on the list of recent calls. Regal couldn't be 100% certain that this rendezvous wasn't for business, but his years of experience had him feeling like it was a solid lead.

Regal left the phone behind as he slipped out from the bedroom and looked around. He spotted Zales in the kitchen and dropped to his knees. He crawled behind the couch, peering underneath to watch Zales head back into the bedroom. When the coast was clear, Regal made a dash for the exit, not bothering to be silent as he opened the door and closed it behind him before he ran from the apartment.

All I have to do is beat him there, Regal thought as he sprinted to the hotel. *I've got two hours. It should be easy.*

But Regal was exhausted, and he had to slow his pace to a staggering jog. By the time he reached the hotel, his legs felt like jelly, his chest ached, and his lungs burned. He fell against the wall, catching himself with his arm as he tried to catch his breath and fight back his cramping muscles. He didn't wait until he was fully recovered before going in and walking to the front desk. Time was running out.

"Excuse me," he said breathlessly, leaning against the desk as he cocked his head to the side. He hid his exhaustion by running a hand through his hair as he smiled politely. "I was wondering if a Mr. Nicholas Hunt had checked in yet. He's my dad. He just flew into town and called me up to tell me to meet him here." Regal chuckled, trying to lay on as much charm as he possibly could. "I ran here as fast as I could once I heard he had arrived. I haven't seen him in so long, and I'm really excited to get to spend time with him."

"Let me see," the clerk said as she looked through the records. Regal watched her fingers fly across the keyboard. "I do see that he is in room 413. Would you like me to call his room and let him know you're here?"

Regal shook his head. "No, thanks. He knows I'm coming. Thank you for all your help, miss. I truly appreciate it." He left with a wink to seal the deal, and headed for the elevators. However, he didn't take one up. Instead, he went for the stairwell. There were no cameras there. He climbed up to the second floor, and mustering all of the magic he had left, he turned invisible and sprinted into the hallway until he found the maintenance room. He slipped inside and shut the door behind him, dropping his guise. He turned on the light and dug around the cabinets until he found a bellhop's uniform that fit him. It was snug, but it would be a good enough disguise. Once he was dressed, he left and walked to room 254 and looked around.

He cleared his throat before knocking and saying "room service." He waited for a few seconds with no response. He knocked again. "Room service!"

"I'm coming!" he heard from the other side of the door. Hunt opened it roughly, ready to yell at someone for disrupting him. He didn't get his complaint out before Regal rammed his elbow up into Hunt's face and knocked him backward. He hurried inside, pushed the door shut, and kicked Hunt in the side. Hunt groaned and tried to sit back up, disoriented by being mugged. Regal finished the job quickly by grabbing Hunt by the hair and slamming his head into the wall.

The force knocked him out, as well as leaving a decent sized hole in the drywall. Regal slumped against the bed. This was not at all what he had hoped to happen, but he had reacted too quickly to think before acting. Now he had an unconscious man in a heap on the floor, another one coming to cheat on his wife, and property damage he wasn't going to pay for.

Regal looked at the clock. One more hour until Zales arrived. "We've got quite the wait," he said to Hunt's unconscious body.

He knew that Hunt would wake up before then. Regal needed to get rid of him.

Killing him was the easy way to handle the situation. However, slipping into his unconsciousness and stealing his soul seemed more enticing. It was a risky choice with Regal's powers so drained, but he craved being inside Hunt's sinful dreams.

Regal picked up Hunt's body and dragged him onto the bed before forcing his way into Hunt's dreams. It was completely dark, except for blurs of color that swept past him. The scenery of a home Regal didn't recognize was painted around him. Orange-colored walls and cream carpet, brown leather couches and oak furniture filled the space. Regal recognized it as a dream forming. His impatience had gotten the best of him. He had jumped in too soon.

The dangers of heading into a dream as it was forming created the risk of becoming attached to the subconscious. At full strength, Regal could pull himself out with ease, but he was weak from being out in the sun and he could feel himself getting stuck. He could possibly be trapped in Nicholas's subconscious until he woke up, which would expose him to anyone who may walk into the room.

Dammit, dammit... how did I let myself mess up this bad? Regal thought as he tried to find a crack of the unformed dream. He could still escape through the darkness, but the rooms were developing too quickly. His legs felt like lead, sucking him deep down into the viscous subconscious. He wouldn't make it out in time.

His cognitive self was forced out, pulled from the dream by an outside presence. It was like being dragged out of tar. The moment he broke free, he felt his mind and body reconnect. He fell to the ground and gasped for air as something pushed down on his physical form. His vision was cloudy and his head spun as he tried to regain composure. Had Zales come early?

Room service? Whoever it was, they were dragging him across the floor. He blinked to clear his vision and saw Keir forcing him toward the open window.

"What do you think you're doing here?" Regal barked. "You are still being punished!" He was thankful to be free, but angry that the angel had come to mess with his plans. Again.

"I know I am, but the window was open and I was worried about you," Keir said as he yanked on Regal's legs, pulling him across the dingy carpet.

"Liar. I left all the windows and doors locked."

"Well, one was open and I took my chance. Good thing I did, too, or else you would have hurt him."

"You idiot," Regal growled as he struggled to break free. But he was tired and weak, and Keir was growing stronger from the sunlight streaming into the window. Keir managed to pull Regal out the window by using his wings to lift him up into the air. Regal unfurled his wings as Keir dropped him and hovered in place. "I was doing my job."

"And protecting humans is mine," Keir argued.

"Stay out of my business."

"This is my business, too. If you think you can keep going out and hurting the innocent without my interference, then you're wrong." Keir flew closer to Regal, closing the distance so they were face to face. "I will find you and stop you every time you try to hurt someone."

Regal hissed in rage and lashed out at Keir, swiping his clawed hand at the angel. Keir jerked back, but not soon enough to completely dodge the attack. His skin turned red from the scratch, and tiny pinpricks of blood welled up on the surface. Regal felt a flare of pain on his cheek as well, but there was no mark. Keir was shocked. He lifted his hand to his cheek, feeling the minor wound healing over.

The Art of Falling

The demon growled and took off, sluggishly riding the wind toward Central Park. He needed space from Keir, but he could feel the angel's aura trailing behind him. Regal groaned. He couldn't stand that the angel could make him feel... guilty.

Regal's wings finally gave out. He fell into the treetops, his feathers tugging on stray twigs as he managed to perch himself onto a branch safely. It bent under his weight, creaking softly as he remained still.

Keir carefully maneuvered himself around the branches to avoid getting his feathers caught before landing gracefully onto a nearby branch. Unlike the demon's, it did not shift from his soft landing. Keir could sense Regal's annoyance. It seemed to radiate off him as he hunched over, his wings bristling behind him.

"What is it?" he asked. Regal didn't respond. Keir sighed. "If this is about your job, I get it. You're a demon. But you have to understand that I am an angel."

Regal twitched and spun to look at Keir fiercely. "Don't make me..." he growled, his claws digging into the branch, splintering the wood. His wings fluffed up and fluttered as Regal maintained eye contact with Keir.

The angel flinched in reply, his face full of fear and confusion as the demon poured his anger on him. He couldn't understand what Regal was feeling. He looked completely exhausted, like he would pass out if he had to take another step. Keir wanted to help him, but he didn't know how. "Don't make you what?" he asked, uncertain of what Regal would do.

Regal growled and clenched his fist. The feeling from earlier was coming back stronger than ever. His chest was tightening, as if he was about to get sick. He closed his eyes, his shoulders shaking as he tried to push down the feeling. It came back in waves, making his head spin.

Regret. That's what he was feeling. It came to him so suddenly, the answer to the problem he had faced today. Demons weren't made to feel regret or remorse. They were coldhearted and deadly. To feel this emotion was unnatural. Yet no matter how hard he tried, it refused to stay down. He couldn't fight back what was coming up.

Swallowing his pride, he let out a shaky breath and gave into the pressure, his voice barely above a whisper. "I'm... sorry."

Keir blinked, taken aback by the softly grumbled response. "W-what?"

He growled, not wanting to say it again. "God damn it, I'm sorry I hurt you, okay? Now just stop making that face; you look like you're about to cry again!" Regal shouted, wincing at the fire that rose up in his throat.

Keir's eyes widened with shock as Regal said Gloria's name in vain. He was frozen in his place, watching as the demon coughed and choked. Regal held his hand against his throat as the burning sensation of blasphemy refused to fade away.

Why he burst out at Keir in apology was beyond Regal. Normally, he wouldn't have the urge to apologize to anyone except his father, let alone an angel. Yet it came out of him without warning. He was vaguely aware of Keir finally breaking out of his stunned state to hover from his tree branch over to Regal's.

"It's okay. I forgive you," he cooed as he laid a comforting hand on Regal's back, rubbing it softly as he soothed Regal with his own healing abilities. "I still love you."

He closed his eyes and kept his head low, trying to focus on Keir's hand and the gentle, cooling sensation of Keir's healing ability spreading through him until the fire finally subsided. His body visibly relaxed, as if released from suffering.

Keir continued to rub his back. "Are you feeling better?"

Regal grunted softly in response and let his wings droop

slightly. He did feel better. The weight in his chest was gone, and the ache in his throat had faded. He lifted his head, looking toward Keir with dark eyes. Again, the angel had protected him from being harmed. He even said he still loved him after everything Regal had put him through. It was another act of kindness and forgiveness he couldn't quite understand. Angels were so odd.

With a soft sigh, he pulled his wings in tight and slipped down off the branch, landing heavily on his feet. His legs almost gave out under him, but Regal refused to stumble. "I'm heading home..." he mumbled, shoving his hands into his pockets as he headed back in the general direction of his apartment.

Keir jumped down after him, using his wings to slow his descent so he didn't make a sound. "I'll follow you, then."

Regal shrugged, trying to brush off the fact that Keir had just healed him for a second time. Although his final destination was the apartment, he wandered for hours, walking aimlessly through the city.

They walked around the city well into the evening. Regal watched as the moon rose into the sky; its face growing rounder each day. Soon, it would be a full moon out, and he would be at his weakest. The angel was extremely good at tracking him down, and if his plan was to weaken him by forcing him to go out in the daylight, then Keir was much cleverer than Regal had anticipated. He knew he needed to focus on making Keir fall before the end of the month.

As night fell, Regal let the darkness energize him. The angel followed him diligently in silence, ignoring how the darkness made his skin crawl and made him feel more tired. Keir could feel his own headache coming on as his body grew fatigued. His feet and legs were aching, and he was shivering from lack of heat. He walked closer to Regal, so their arms were brushing as they traveled from Brooklyn to Manhattan and back again. Regal's wings were expanded fully, soaking up every droplet of moonlight. Keir kept his wings in tight, not wanting to lose the warmth of daylight that they held.

The sun was beginning to rise by the time Regal decided he was tired of walking. He could feel the warmth already giving him discomfort.

Keir, however, smiled when he felt the sunlight coming over the horizon. He casually made his way between the rising sun and the demon, casting his shadow upon Regal to protect him from the sun's rays.

Regal decided to relax and let down his guard as he basked in the darkness. It was actions like these that made him wonder if Keir truly did love him unconditionally, like he said so boldly before. By the time they were back to the apartment complex, Regal felt energized enough to fly up to his broken bedroom window. He cleared out the rest of the glass with his foot, careful to not cut himself, before slipping inside and landing on his bed in a heap.

Keir flew in steadily, hovering over his body as he watched Regal reach tiredly for the blankets. He closed the curtains, shrouding the room in darkness.

Regal curled up into the corner and closed his eyes, pulling the blanket tight around him. "I hate the sun..." he muttered under his breath, exhaustion hitting him.

Keir chuckled slightly, a soft and loving smile on his face. "No kidding," he said as he sat down in front of Regal and pulled his knees up to his chest, his arms wrapped around his legs tightly. "Are you going to be okay?"

His concerns fell on deaf ears. The demon was already asleep; the angel's plans to wear him out so he could get a full day's sleep worked. Keir smiled, examining his sleeping face.

The Art of Falling

Regal looked at peace like this, as if he were an ordinary human. No malice or mischief in his expression. No dastardly plans or evil intentions. He looked, dare he say, innocent. Keir wished that maybe Regal was innocent at heart, that if he wasn't born and raised a demon, maybe he would have turned out differently.

He closed his weary eyes and drifted off to sleep as the sun warmed his back, protecting Regal from the dangers of the sunlight that crept into the bedroom with every gentle breeze.

CHAPTER *Fourteen*

REGAL HUFFED AS he checked off another day on the calendar. Another four days wasted. Two weeks into his assignment, and he had only managed to place one sin on the angel. He felt like a failure. He needed to step up his game, start taking bigger risks. If he kept playing it safe and tried to win Keir's trust, he'd never make it in time.

He ran a hand over his chin and felt stubble. He was certain his still had bags under his eyes as well. Even after a few nights of rest, he was still drained. He sighed, turning on the faucet to splash cold water onto his face before beginning to shave. Once again, mundane tasks he wished he didn't have to deal with. It was the sin of sloth awakening inside of him.

Sloth. Regal still wasn't certain if Keir had actually committed sloth when he fell for gluttony. After all, he did come rushing to stop Regal from harming Hunt. That was the opposite of laziness. However, Regal had a back-up plan to ensure that the angel did fall for sloth. It was a bold move, and much less passive and sneaky than his other attempts, but it was worth a shot.

Regal walked over to the living room where Keir was laying down and watching TV. He sat down on the arm of the couch, startling Keir out of his daze.

"We need to have a talk."

Keir glanced toward the demon.

"I know you're an angel and that it's your job to protect the humans and all," Regal continued, "But I'm a demon and I have to, you know..."

"Kill them."

Regal shrugged. "I prefer to say 'relocate their soul', but we

139

can go with kill if that pleases you. But it is something I have to do. It's a part of my DNA."

"No, it's a choice," Keir stated.

Damn him for being so stubborn, Regal thought as he rubbed his temples. "Whether or not it's a choice, it's my *job*. So how about you let me finish my job so I can focus on more important matters. Like, making this whole thing work between us."

Keir seemed unfazed. "You're honestly asking me to not save a human's life so you can do your own dirty work?" The angel looked away and glared at the TV. "I'm not stupid. I know you would love to steal another soul."

"Asking is better than going off and doing it on my own, yeah?" Regal stood up and walked in front of the couch, sitting on the coffee table to block Keir's vision and to face the angel directly. "Keir, just this once. That guy I was targeting isn't worth saving—"

"All lives are worth saving," Keir argued.

"Not all of them. In your ideal world they are, but even you know that not everyone can go to Heaven. Jeremy Zales is one of those men," Regal said, growing more frustrated.

"Humans aren't perfect. Humans make mistakes."

"He cheats on his wife. Isn't that one of Her rules? *Thou shalt not commit adultery.*"

"You actually know the Ten Commandments?" Keir asked, somewhat surprised.

Regal shrugged. "It's like a demon's code of conduct. We try to break those rules as best as we can." He was surprised to hear Keir chuckle in amusement. "Anyways, he's already breaking that commandment, and he's on the path to commit more."

"Which means we angels should work harder to stop them from taking the wrong path." Keir crossed his arms defiantly. "With time, he can be saved."

"He's been at it for years, Keir," Regal explained. He was straining to convince the angel to give up on Zales. "Adultery is a drug for him. Even if you did manage to save him, he'll end up slipping back into the old routine. Besides, his wife deserves better than someone like him, right?" Keir didn't respond right away. "He's my last assignment. Let me just do this one final job, and then I can put my focus on you... on us." Regal reached forward and took Keir's hands in his own, squeezing the palms tenderly.

Keir stared at his hands in Regal's. It went against his morals to not try and save a human. However, Regal had a strong point. There are many stories of failed attempts to save a soul. Some people were just unable to get into Heaven. On top of that, Keir was too tired to want to try and save him. Being locked inside and kept away from the sun had drained him of his diligence. If Regal's assignment was so corrupt, would it be worth the trouble to try and undo everything Jeremy Zales had done? A flash of warning spurred inside of Keir, but he didn't pay attention to it. He looked up at Regal. The demon's gray eyes were clear; there were no hints of lies in his gaze. With an exhausted sigh, he nodded.

Regal held back his gloating. He leaned forward and placed a kiss on Keir's forehead, knowing it would please the angel. His stomach flipped at the sensation of his cool lips pressed against Keir's warm skin. "I'll be quick, and I won't make him suffer, if that helps."

"Promise that this will be the last human soul you covet."

"I promise."

"Promise on your life."

"My life?" Regal asked, confused.

"That way you can't break it." Keir smiled. "It'll be like our bond."

Regal narrowed his eyes. "Sure thing."

The Art of Falling

"Say the words."

The demon resisted the urge to growl and cleared his throat. "I promise... on my life." Regal got up and walked to the front door, unlocking it. He pulled out a spare key, one that he never used himself, and set it on the table next to the door. "As a thank you for being so understanding, your punishment is lifted. You're free to come and go whenever you want."

He left out the front door, practically jumping with excitement. He did it! He actually convinced the angel to consent to not saving a human soul that was in danger, thus technically falling for the sin of sloth. Of course, he had to make the oath to stop hunting humans after Zales, but he was betting on the chance that it could be broken, much like his bond with Keir. He decided to worry about that later. Right now, he had to keep up the momentum and continue placing sins; another idea was already forming in his mind.

As Regal flew away from the apartment, he fished his cell phone out of his pocket and speed-dialed the number five. His call went directly to voicemail, as it always did. It didn't matter. The mythos he was calling would get the message. "It's Regal. I'm in need of your services."

The moment Keir was given his freedom, he took off into the sky. Keir soared over the city for hours. He soaked up the warmth of the sun shining down on his feathers. The cool spring breeze tugged at his wings and lifted him weightlessly as he spread out his arms. The angel closed his eyes, taking a deep breath. The higher atmosphere was cleaner than the dense, smog-filled air closer to the ground.

Aimlessly he flew, gazing down at the numerous landmarks that made up New York City. Central Park stood out amidst the bleak gray, the green square of nature thriving in the concrete jungle. The Statue of Liberty stood tall and proud, raising her torch of enlightenment up toward the heavens. Keir circled around her, marveling at her beauty, before continuing toward Manhattan. He watched as hundreds of people walked and rode their bikes across the bridge that connected the two boroughs.

Humans were so fascinating to him, and part of him wondered if he had made a mistake in allowing Regal to steal one of their souls. The demon had a point saying that some humans were simply doomed from the start; Keir had witnessed several angels spending months, or even years, trying to guide and save a single human soul, only for all of their hard work to end in vain.

However, by forcing Regal to make the oath to stop hunting humans after Jeremy Zales, he knew that he had saved the innocent souls of Regal's prey in the future. Surely that could justify his decision to not stop Regal.

Conflicted about his feelings, Keir headed back home. It was too late to do anything about his choice. Regal had surely completed his task by now, and if Keir had made a mistake, he was prepared to accept the consequences.

Keir snuck into the apartment building through the rooftop door, much like Regal did when he first brought Keir to the city. He walked up to the apartment and pulled out the key that Regal had left for him, letting himself inside.

Standing in the center of the living room was the female demon he had encountered in Central Park.

"Surprised to see you here, angel," she purred. In her hand, she twirled a silver-tipped umbrella. Occasionally, she tapped it against the hardwood floor. Each clack it made sent shivers down Keir's spine. "Where's Regal?"

"Out," he said sharply.

"Then I hope you don't mind me waiting here for his return," she replied sweetly with a toothy grin.

Keir narrowed his eyes, his blue irises flashing dangerously. "Maybe you should come by another time."

"Maybe I should corrupt you with my sin like Regal did way back when?"

"I wasn't expecting you to drop by, Viraine," Regal said as he walked through the front door, closing it behind him. "What a pleasant surprise."

Keir spun around as Regal came up to stand beside him. The angel could sense an array of emotions ebbing from Regal: stress, confusion, caution, revulsion.

"I thought I'd pay a visit to my favorite incubus." Viraine walked around the couch to stand across from the two men. "Though I didn't realize you already had a guest."

Regal stepped in front of Keir, putting himself between him and Viraine. "He'll be leaving. Keir, go to my room."

"Protective, aren't we?" Viraine grinned, resting her hand on her hip.

Keir scowled. "I don't need protection."

Viraine laughed shrilly. "Foolish angel!"

"Keir, go. Now," Regal ordered.

"She doesn't scare me."

Viraine's eyes flashed a bright orange as she snapped her umbrella open, the serrated edges gleaming as she spun the weapon in her hand. The silver tips whizzed as she growled and took an offensive step forward, threatening to slash Keir open.

Keir took a step backward, suffocated by the sudden explosion of demonic energy that ballooned from inside her until it invaded the entire apartment. He severely underestimated the power Viraine had as a Prince of Gluttony. He had assumed she would match Regal, but she surpassed him immensely. He knew fighting her would be a death wish.

Before Viraine could come any closer, Regal stepped forward, blocking Keir from Viraine's silver-tipped weapon.

"One misstep and you can consider our alliance destroyed," Regal growled.

Viraine huffed and withdrew her weapon. She tossed the umbrella into the air and let it drop into one of the open mouths on her palm, vanishing into the infinite caverns of her soul.

Regal looked over his shoulder at Keir and flicked his gaze to the bedroom. Keir nodded in silence and followed Regal's orders, heading to the bedroom and locking the door.

"Now, why have you decided to pay me a visit?" Regal asked as he grazed his eyes over Viraine's voluptuous figure. Old habits were hard to break, but he knew that the longer she stayed here, the more dangerous the situation became. Viraine was never one to be trusted. Her wit was sharp, and her tongue even sharper. She was a dangerous enemy to have, and Regal didn't like her barging into his private life and threatening him or Keir.

"No need to be hasty. Let's enjoy each other's company." Viraine walked over to the kitchen and opened up one of the cupboards, finding a bottle of red wine that Regal had bought for a special occasion. She uncorked it with her teeth and took a big swig out of the bottle.

Regal held back a growl of annoyance. Just like her to take what was his and spoil it. "I don't have the time to sit around and chat. I've got important business to attend to."

"Like making that angel fall?"

"That was certainly the plan," he said lowly, walking around so he could move to sit on the couch. "But hasn't your source already told you that?"

"Source?" Viraine asked as she walked over to the couch. "I have no idea what you're talking about."

"Someone spilled the beans. I'd appreciate if you could fill me in on who."

"No can do, Reggie."

Regal scowled. "I told you not to call me that."

"I must have forgotten." Viraine stopped by the couch and wrinkled her nose in disgust. "That reeks of his scent," she hissed. Regal lifted a brow, somewhat confused at her statement. She waved a hand at the couch. "That. It smells like the angel."

"Oh, yes. He sleeps here during the night while I'm out." Regal had grown so used to Keir's presence; he didn't notice the smell anymore.

"You let him *sleep* here?" She laughed. "You treat him as if he were a roommate."

Her laughter was beginning to get on his nerves, just as it did in the past. "I treat him as if he were a pet. If he were my roommate, we would have already shared a bed," Regal said tersely. He smirked, the corner of his mouth turning upward. "You would know that well, Viraine."

She grinned, her already wide mouth growing bigger to show off her rows of shark teeth. "Indeed I do. Would you like to reminisce?"

"Best to leave it in the past." Memories of their past came back to him in quick flashes: playing in the tunnels under the castle, fighting each other outside of training, courting her in an attempt to gain more power, and the numerous times she gave herself up to him and let himself gorge on his own sin. He was foolish to think mating with a Glutton would make him more powerful. It was always take and never give with them. *If she's here to try and get me back, she's sorely mistaken,* he thought grimly.

The two stared each other down, summing each other up. It had been years since they last saw one another. They had both gotten much stronger, and much more experienced in their field.

Viraine snarled, her eyes turning to slits as she glared at Regal. "I am here for answers."

"Such as?"

She thrust her hand out, pointing down the hall. "Why didn't you kill him off yet?"

"That's suicide, and I enjoy being alive," Regal replied.

"You would rather be that angel's property for the rest of your life over your freedom?"

"I'll have my freedom back in due time."

Viraine set the wine bottle down and walked over to Regal. She reached out to brush her fingertips against his cheeks, tracing the faded mark that he and the angel shared. She made a soft *tsk* sound as if she pitied him. The gesture would have once sparked desire in his gut, but now it made him seethe.

His hostile energy made her bristle with annoyance. "Tell me, did you mark him the same way you do all your victims?" Viraine came closer to Regal until her body was pressed up against his, her lips barely brushing against his. "Or was he special?"

Regal let his eyes close for a moment, controlling himself before he shoved her away from him. "Step that close to me again and I will rip out your throat."

She hissed in response, her hands flexing as her secondary mouths opened and screeched. The sound grated Regal's ears, and he knew that Keir must be suffering from the sound as well. She got up from the couch and headed for the hall.

Regal rushed forward and blocked her path. "You will not harm him."

"Earlier I thought you just didn't want me damaging your goods, but you're actually protecting him!" she yelled, her eyes wide with rage.

Regal growled lowly, not letting his wrath consume him. He needed to have complete control in this situation. "He is my property. I will not let any other demon touch him," he warned, his voice bellowing with sincerity. "I will fight anyone who tries to lay a finger on him."

"Tell me, how will you keep protecting him if your plan is to make him fall? That's not very caring of you," Viraine mocked.

Regal's eyes darkened in response.

She grinned, her lips pulling back to show off her fangs. "That's what I thought."

"Once he falls, I'll abandon him, just like I did to you," he spat in a hushed tone. "Mark my words, Viraine. I will succeed, and I don't need anyone else to interfere."

Viraine stood up straighter, willing her extra mouths to seal shut. She took a deep breath, calming herself for a moment before stepping back. "It'll be fun seeing you try." She pulled off her necklace; the black gem attached began to glow a deep violet before a small portal opened before her feet. "Try not to bleach those wings while I'm gone."

She hopped through, the seal closing behind her. Regal watched as the portal dissolved from view, releasing a breath he didn't know he was holding.

CHAPTER *Fifteen*

*K*EIR WAITED UNTIL everything was silent before opening the bedroom door and poking his head out. He hadn't been able to hear most of the conversation, but he could feel the aggressive energy filling the room and seeping into the hallway and under the crack of the bedroom door. Keir peered down the hall and saw Regal's back facing him. The light from the living room cast long shadows that reached down the corridor. "Regal?" he called.

Regal turned, glancing over his shoulder toward Keir. The shadows masked his face, but the angel could see Regal's eyes glowing. "She's gone. For now."

The angel came out from his hiding place and walked up to Regal. The demon's body language seemed relaxed, but his eyes were blazing with mixed emotions Keir couldn't identify. Keir walked up to Regal and wrapped his arms around him tightly.

Regal went rigid, caught off guard by Keir's action. "What are you doing?"

"Hugging you."

The demon sighed and let Keir hug him for a few moments before lifting his hand to pat Keir's head. "Alright, alright, you can let go now. It's not like I got hurt again," he grumbled, shrugging Keir's arms off of him.

The angel chuckled softly and smiled up at him. His blue eyes showed nothing but concern and adoration.

Regal cleared his throat and glanced at the clock on the wall. "I know it's late, and you're probably tired, but I don't want to stay here tonight. In fact, I want to leave the city."

"Right now?" Keir asked.

"I don't like the fact Viraine found my apartment, and I don't

149

like that she is making you a target," Regal said. "Knowing her, she'll break in one night and I don't want to be here when she does. I want us to be off her radar."

Keir nodded quickly. He wanted that, too. "Okay, yeah, we should leave. Where do you want to go?"

Regal thought for a moment. Although he loved city life, he needed to get away from the noise. The memory of Keir's dream flashed in his mind. "A beach or a lake front?"

"Wonderful!"

"Great." Regal grinned. He was pleased at himself for being able to remember something Keir was fond of. "But first, I'd like to feed if that's okay."

"What?"

"Don't worry, not on humans."

Regal went into his bedroom and began to change into a new outfit consisting of his leather jacket, dark jeans, and a black and blue baseball tee.

Keir stood in the doorway of the bedroom, staring at the ground to avoid seeing Regal undress. "Then who?"

Regal shrugged. "Whoever I can find. Vampires, were-folk, fairies. I'm not picky. Any Mythos will do."

"I don't know..." Keir murmured. Although it was an angel's job to focus on saving the lives of humans, Mythos were occasionally included, despite many of them harboring negative feelings toward ethereal beings like angels and demons. Keir preferred protecting Gloria's chosen species over the others, but it still upset Keir to think that Regal would prey on them.

"I need to feed," Regal insisted. "If I don't, I won't be strong enough to protect you from Viraine or other demons that might want a piece of you. Besides, you protect humans, right? What's a missing Mythos going to do?"

The incubus had a point. "Fine," Keir sighed. "But do not

kill them. Absorb only as much energy as you need."

Regal nodded. "Deal. Now change into something dark. Better yet, grab something of mine. Where we're going, you'll need to fit in."

"Wait," Keir said as he pulled on one of Regal's dark blue turtleneck sweaters. "What about all our stuff?"

"Leave it. We can get new things later."

Keir frowned. He didn't like the idea of spending extra money when they had perfectly good clothes lying around here. He went to pack up a small bag, but Regal called his name and told him to come over. He went to Regal and stood beside him.

Regal took his sunglasses and put them on. He then pulled out his watch and opened the compartment to retrieve his demonic nomad stone. Regal created the portal and reached out to take Keir's hand in his own. He laced their fingers together and squeezed Keir's hand gently.

Together they turned invisible and jumped through the portal, landing on top of the Louis Tussaud's Wax Museum in Niagara Falls, Canada. Keir was bombarded with the sounds of a carnival. He walked to the edge of the building and saw crowds of people lined up at various tourist attractions along the hill.

"Why are we here?" Keir asked.

"There's an underground club for Mythos just outside of the city," Regal explained before he jumped off the building to fly over the crowds. Keir trailed behind him, gazing down at the sights below.

The two soared down the hill that led them to the pier. A huge two-story boat sat waiting to pick up a mob of humans wearing blue smocks. They forced their way onto the ferry, crowding on until it was at full capacity. As the boat pulled away for its final voyage of the day, Keir looked up to see that it was heading toward two enormous waterfalls that sprayed with water as they came closer. Keir followed Regal as they headed over the falls. Keir lowered himself so he could brush his hands against the raging waters and feel the mist on his face. The sun was just beginning to set, reflecting on the water's surface.

Soon, they left the hustle and bustle of Niagara Falls behind them and arrived at a vacant building on the outskirts of town. It looked like an old home that was now forgotten. The siding was beginning to peel away and the windows were boarded up. The door hinges were rusted and squeaked when Regal forced them to open, leading them into a dark foyer. Keir timidly followed Regal as he walked inside, jumping when the door slammed shut.

He huddled close to Regal, practically walking on his heels as they walked through the hall toward the cellar. Regal could see easily in the darkness, his pupils dilated until his eyes were completely black. His hand reached out to take Keir's, directing the angel to the stairwell. As they began to descend down the stairs, Keir's hand squeezed Regal's tightly, his wings pulling out slightly in anxiety.

"Keep those in. Your kind isn't exactly welcome here," Regal warned.

"Then why did you make me come with you?"

"You're safer if you stay near me."

Keir nodded with understanding and tucked his wings back in completely. He could now hear the thrum of music beating from inside the cellar. The stairwell seemed to descend impossibly deep, never coming to an end.

As they descended, Keir felt something brush past his leg. He yelped and stumbled into Regal, who nearly lost his own balance and fell forward. "Something touched me!"

"Ignore it," Regal instructed as they continued.

Keir strained to look at the ground where he felt whatever it was touch him, then saw a black shape slither across the ground toward his feet. He yelped and jumped up, his wings fluttering briefly before he landed again, watching as the figure escaped into the wall. That's when he saw dozens of other shadow-like figures moving in and out of the walls, pulsing with the beat of the rumbling music beneath them. Another ominous shape danced along the wall, following them, before reaching out to grab at Keir. This one was clearly in the shape of a hand, and its spindly fingers dug firmly into the cuff of his pant leg.

"What are those?!" Keir cringed and pressed himself as close to Regal as possible, trying to keep out of reach of the grabby shadows. They were fixated on Keir, completely ignoring Regal's presence.

"Sentient Shadows. They're a defense mechanism to protect this place from unwanted guests. If I weren't with you, they'd probably be more aggressive."

"Great..." Keir whined, his eyes shifting from one dark corner to the next.

They reached the bottom of the stairwell and Regal pressed his hand against the wall. It pushed under his weight and caused the wall to move to the side and lead them down another corridor. It was just as dark, but small torchlights lit the way. The music was much louder now, and strobe lights could be seen at the end of the tunnel. The shadows retreated into the darkness, screeching as the brightly colored lights bounced off the walls. Keir sighed and held onto Regal's arm tightly as they walked to the end of the hall and stopped.

Regal drew back the black and purple curtain hanging in the doorway to reveal a large cove where flashing lights dangled from the ceiling and artificial smoke clouded the room. The smell of witch-brew, an intoxicating drink common among places like this, overwhelmed Keir and caused him to cringe slightly. Regal didn't seem to mind the scent, and in fact embraced it as he took in a deep breath and smiled.

Dozens of Mythos were dancing to the pumping bass music that echoed in the small cavern. Vampires and werewolves danced against each other without any hint of rivalry. Keir even saw a lesser demon serving a warlock a sparkling drink at the makeshift bar. Regal looked around the room for a moment and caught sight of a beautiful young vixen toward the edge of the crowd. His instincts flared and his mouth began to water.

"Okay, I'm off to do my job. You stay here and try not to draw too much attention."

"What about staying close to you?" Keir asked, his voice drowned out by the music as the demon headed straight into the mass of dancing bodies.

This was Regal's element. He was bred to thrive in places where alcohol destroyed inhibitions and the mind was clouded by carnal urges. Although he was dying to dive into the hunt, he took his time to scour the crowd and find the perfect prey.

In the corner of the room, a drunken half-human, half-manticore was standing alone. The lion-like creature was swishing his barbed tail fervently as he looked for a potential mate. An easy target. He began to make his way over when he caught the scent of another demon prowling among the mythos—a succubus. Regal's eyes latched onto his female counterpart as she made her way through the crowd. She hissed as she stretched her small, dragon-like wings at him to display her dominance. Regal stopped, not wanting to fight a greedy succubus over one meager meal. He watched as she glided past him and claimed the manticore for herself. Within seconds they were making out.

Absolutely no class, he thought as he watched his fellow demon of lust gorge on the manticore's naturally high sex drive. It took no time for the two to make their way toward the private rooms at the back of the club.

Regal turned to focus on his own hunt. He soon chose a well-dressed vampire who had her eye on him. Soon, they were dancing up against one another, flashing fangs and eyeing each other with dark gazes. He had to admit, the idea of biting was a turn on for him. He flashed his own fangs, albeit not nearly as impressive as hers, and got a chuckle out of her. They never spoke a word to each other, communicating solely with eye contact and body language. He made a mental note to come back to her for a full meal before moving onto the next potential victim.

He felt a surge of demonic energy and looked over the vampire's shoulder. The succubus from earlier came out of the back room, overflowing with rejuvenated power. Even in the dark, Regal could make out the blood stains on her clothes. There was no way the manticore survived the encounter. She looked at him and blinked slowly to acknowledge Regal's presence before moving onto a second victim.

Fuck, feed, repeat.

Keir had witnessed the entire exchange, and he felt his heart rise into his throat as the succubus lured one victim after another into her lair. She never seemed satisfied, and the thought was disturbing. Even Regal had limits, or at least the courtesy to stop when he had his fill.

The angel stepped backward against the wall to hide among the shadows. He knew that it did nothing to protect him from this dark world. He was certain they could sense he wasn't like them by the way they glanced over warily. They could tell he was an ethereal being like Regal, but they couldn't tell he was an angel; the Mythos were more accepting of demons interacting with them. He kept his wings pulled painfully tight, afraid to let one feather show.

The Art of Falling

He tried his best to ignore the stares and instead focused on keeping an eye on Regal. He watched him flirt with the many different Mythos, trying to choose his best victim. It made his stomach churn seeing Regal getting so close to someone else. He wanted to rush over and force Regal into leaving. His heart burned with jealousy.

He felt something brush up next to him and squeaked, shying away when he realized that a female werewolf stood close to him. She growled lightly, her tail swishing against Keir's leg. "You look a little lost, Hun," she purred, her voice low and gravely. To Keir, it made her just a little less attractive; one of the things he most enjoyed about Regal was how smooth and rich his voice was.

"I'm with a friend..." he said timidly, his arms circling around himself.

"You have poor judgment in friends if they leave you alone in a place like this."

Keir narrowed his eyes in annoyance. "I don't need Regal to babysit me."

"Oh, your friend is Regal?" she said with surprise.

"Yes." Keir grinned, feeling satisfied at the she-wolf's astonishment.

"Well then, I take back what I said. You have horrendous judgment."

"Excuse me?" Keir shouted.

The she-wolf chuckled hoarsely. "Don't get so offended. All the regulars here have been under his spell at some point or another."

"I'm not under some spell." Keir dug his fingers into his arms to contain his aggravation.

"That's what you think. He's very good at deceiving those who underestimate him."

Keir glued his eyes on Regal, watching as he used his body language to flirt with the vampire. He was too good at his trade, and it ticked Keir off. "I don't underestimate him. He's just doing his job." He wasn't sure if he was saying it to convince the werewolf, or himself.

The she-wolf scoffed at the idea. "Yet you sit and wait for him to notice you like some whipped bitch," she barked.

The words stung him, sparking a feeling inside of him that made him want to yell at her and prove her wrong. His eyes flashed a bright white, causing her to step back. She growled, her lupine ears falling back aggressively. Keir felt his wings threatening to flare out, his shoulder blades itching to show off his wide wingspan. That would show her to back off.

He was on the verge of revealing his identity—a potentially fatal mistake.

CHAPTER *Sixteen*

FEEDING ON SOULS was like drinking electricity. It recharged Regal like a battery as he let his hands brush along the vampire's waist and his lips graze her neck. Although he preferred a direct connection with a person's soul via their dreams, soaking in the build-up of emotion in this way worked well enough.

He had barely started feeding when a flare of angelic energy caught Regal's attention, distracting him. He looked over at Keir and saw the angel arguing with a werewolf and could tell that he was about to let all heaven break loose.

A death sentence in a place like this.

Regal broke away from the vampire abruptly, pushing his way through the crowd until he was in between Keir and the she-wolf.

"Step away from my property," he said lowly, adrenaline running through his veins. He boldly flared his wings, unafraid to display them. In the dark, they looked solid again, massive and as black as tar.

"Your property?" she snarled, her eyes turning to slits as she eyed Regal up and down. Her gaze flickered to Keir, staring at him harshly before laughing—her voice shrill and sharp like a hyena. "You telling me that guy is your pet?"

"Of course not. He's my subordinate," Regal replied smoothly. "Don't confuse him for your kind," he snapped back, his voice laced with malice.

She seemed to bristle at the remark, a low growl forming deep in her chest.

Regal smirked and took Keir's arm to lead him away from the she-wolf. As soon as they were out of her sight, he scowled at Keir. "Careful. This is not the place to reveal your identity."

"People seem to know you well enough," Keir snapped back.

"They know I'm a demon, but they don't know how powerful I am," Regal hissed. "Some things aren't meant to be shared."

"You're not meant to be shared."

"What?"

"You heard me," Keir continued. "I don't like seeing you flirt with other people."

"Wow, I didn't expect you to become so possessive," Regal said with a lighthearted chuckle. "I have to admit, I'm pleasantly surprised." He stopped walking, tugging on Keir's arm. The angel stopped and looked at Keir, his eyes still glowing menacingly in the dark. "I'll try to ease up on the flirting."

"Really?"

"Yeah. It'll be tough, but... I'll work on it. I don't want you to believe a word she said about you being a pet. You're not a pet. You're my..." Regal paused, closing his eyes. "I'm not sure yet. But you're not that."

Keir smiled just a little, his gaze softening. Regal looked somewhat vulnerable with the way his peppered hair fell over his eyes. Keir's hand reached up, his fingertips brushing away his bangs softly. Regal's eyes caught Keir's for a brief moment before he pulled away.

"I need to feed some more," Regal murmured, his voice nearly drowned out by the music. "I barely got anything out of the vampire."

All of the strength he had shown earlier while defending Keir vanished, leaving Regal looking exhausted. He had bags under his eyes, and his posture was limp. Even his wings, which he had not retracted, were drooping. It was obvious he was running on no fuel.

"Go on," Keir said. "I know you need it."

Regal blinked tiredly as a silent thank you before turning

to go back into the crowd. He didn't feel up to hunting, but if he wanted to keep up with Keir's seemingly endless energy, he needed to steal some souls. He looked around the crowd and noticed a witch standing alone by the wall. Not very exciting, but she'd have to do.

Keir watched as Regal straightened his posture, put on his best mask, and strode over to the witch. The angel hated the way Regal wrapped his arms around her shoulder murmured in her ear, causing her to giggle. "So much for cutting back on the flirting."

Keir walked over to the bar on the other side of the room and sat down on one of the stools. He watched as Regal coerced her into a more private area located in the shadows where Regal could chip away at her soul. Keir didn't know what Regal did to feed or if his victims were aware of his actions, but it made Keir sick to his stomach. Masochistically, Keir stared as Regal moved from one target to another, growing strong with each passing Mythos.

A cold sensation washed over him, his wingtips tingling as it spread up to his shoulder blades and over his chest. A large weight was forming and causing his stomach to twist into a knot. The feeling was overpowering, eating away at him from the inside.

Instinctively, Keir got up from his seat and walked over to Regal's side just as he was starting to flirt with two women, another vampire and faerie. The faerie stood up on her tip toes to brush her lips against Regal's cheek just as Keir pushed himself between them, earning a hiss from the women.

"Excuse me, I was talking!" the faerie said shrilly, her voice much higher in pitch than he first expected. The vampire snarled as Keir took a step closer to her. Regal raised his brow and watched Keir silently, studying the scene that was unfolding.

"You're allowed to talk, but not so close to him," Keir barked with authority in his voice. "In fact, I think it's best you don't get near him at all!"

"What makes you think you can tell us what to do?" The vampire snarled, her blood red lips curling to show off her fangs. Keir didn't flinch, too overwhelmed with the feeling of vigor.

"Because he is mine and mine alone," Keir stated. "No one else is allowed to get close to him without my permission."

"Keir," Regal growled angrily, "we talked about this."

"I don't want you fooling around with others," Keir said, turning around to face Regal.

The faerie laughed. "Sounds like the demon is in trouble."

The vampire leaned in close to her friend and snickered. "Now we know who the sub in the relationship is."

Normally, Regal would defend his dominance in a situation like this. However, he decided to let Keir take control. It was all according to his plan.

Keir clenched his fists in anger. "I suggest you keep your mouths shut before I shut them for you!"

"In all my life, I never thought I'd hear one of Her children say such a thing," a sultry voice said from behind them. Regal and Keir turned to see a man walking toward them from a hidden staircase. He had short black hair that was slicked back with gel. It was streaked with violet, and in the dim lighting it seemed to shimmer like gasoline. He was well-dressed in a suit, and he wore white gloves that matched his tie. Keir could see black tribal tattoos poking out from beneath the collar of his shirt. His skin was a deep tan, reminding Keir of Indians, and his golden eyes seemed to bore into the angel. Keir shivered and stepped closer to Regal, who stiffened beside him.

The crowd around them backed away, not wanting to get anywhere near the angel. Keir turned, watching as they kept their distance. Even the faerie and vampire who were trying to confront him stepped back.

"It's a surprise to see you out of your office, Pythos," Regal replied, moving to step in front of Keir slightly as he put himself between the angel and the warlock.

Pythos shrugged and sighed. "I felt like seeing the wildlife." His remark caused a ripple of anger to resonate through the crowd. Even Keir felt somewhat offended by the statement, his compassion and empathy causing him to sense the crowd's resentment.

Regal laughed. "I'm impressed that you were able to find out what my partner was." His chuckle sounded strained to Keir's ears.

"I would be a terrible warlock if I couldn't identify all of Earth's inhabitants," Pythos stated with a grin.

Regal sneered in response as he glared at Pythos. Keir, however, sucked in a sharp breath. He had never encountered a warlock before. They were the most powerful of the Mythos when it came to magic and spell crafting, with elves being their only rivals. Keir's eyes locked onto Pythos' tattoos and saw how complicated and intricate they were, reflecting the amount of magic and skill he possessed. He was definitely someone who shouldn't be messed with.

"What's the matter, Regal? Aren't you glad to see an old friend?"

Keir felt Regal tense up beside him, his aura flaring with unease. He could sense the stress that was building inside of the demon. He hated seeing Regal uncomfortable or upset.

A wave of anger hit Keir again. The feeling that stirred inside of him was foreign to him, yet felt completely natural. Caught up in the moment, Keir pushed himself away from Regal and stormed up to the warlock, his eyes flashing a bright white as his wings spread out. "Friend or not, he does not want to see you."

"Oh? Aren't you bold?" Pythos mocked, moving to come closer to Keir. "Has his mark affected you in some way?" Keir remained grounded in his spot, although his eyes widened slightly by the warlock's words.

"Affected me?" he asked, his fists clenching beside him as he tried to keep control of the resentment that was growing inside of him.

Pythos laughed, his shoulders shaking with amusement. "You truly are naïve!" He stepped toward Keir, daring to close the distance between them. "Aren't you aware of his plans?"

"Of course I'm aware," Keir said. "He's trying to make me fall." He felt Regal become rigid next to him. *Did he really think I wouldn't know? I'm not that dimwitted. He won't be able to make me commit sins. Not before I make him commit virtues.*

"So tell me, do you think he's succeeding?" Pythos challenged, bending down to stare at Keir with narrow eyes.

Keir bit his tongue. He wanted to punch Pythos in the face and make him be quiet. The angel had never felt such anger and hatred toward a person before. His wings bristled threateningly as he held his temper back.

Regal growled lowly under his breath. Although he had asked for Pythos to help with making Keir fall, the warlock was already getting on his nerves. He had enough of Pythos' attitude and flippant habits of revealing too much information just for the sake of getting under people's skin. If Keir found out that he was already tainted, Regal would never succeed. He strode forward, grasping Keir's arm.

"Obviously not. If my plans were working, he would have already attacked you without thinking twice." Regal brushed past Pythos, taking Keir along with him. "Now if you'll excuse us, we'll be on our way."

Regal led them toward the door to leave. Before heading into the tunnel, Regal looked over his shoulder. He saw a gleam in Pythos' eyes as the warlock winked and gave the she-wolf who had confronted Keir her payment for her services. Although Regal didn't exactly like Pythos, the warlock was always helpful.

Once they were concealed in the darkness, Regal returned his focus on Keir. He had to make sure that the angel believed his stunt about his plans failing. He rubbed Keir's back, soothing him from the experience they had. He could see each feather on Keir's wings as he slid them back in. What was once a small spot near the base had now bled out to the edges. Every feather was completely gray, now tainted with pride and envy. Buried within the dull plumage was a single pitch black feather. Only three more to go until those once-pure white wings were polluted completely. Regal was so close he could almost taste it.

"He won't make me fall," Keir grumbled quietly to himself, but Regal was able to hear the determined angel's soft voice. He had to hold back his own laughter.

Oh, if only he knew how much he has fallen.

Keir looked back, but was unable to see the club once they were climbing the stairs. The smell of witch-brew and fog faded away. He sighed, relieved to be out of the cave and back out in the open.

He spread out his wings, stretching them as far as they could. Regal did the same, flapping them so he could hover above the rotted floors. The demon pushed himself forward, gliding up next to Keir as they headed out a back door.

"Who was that guy?" Keir asked, rubbing his hands over his arms to get rid of the tingling feeling of the shadow figures clawing at him.

"Pythos. He's the owner of that club and one of the more powerful warlocks in Canada. He's helped me out a few times in the past, but I can't stand being around him for long periods of time," Regal explained.

"I don't like him."

"Most people don't."

Keir rubbed the back of his neck anxiously, staring at Regal. Pythos' words swirled in his head. The warlock had brought up Regal's intentions to make him fall. Keir wasn't bothered by that. He was more upset over the fact that he mentioned Regal's successes. He hadn't noticed any changes in himself. It was true that he was starting to adopt Regal's mannerisms and way of speaking, but Regal was doing the same. Was that a sign of him falling, or Regal ascending?

"Are you okay?" Regal asked, taking Keir's hand in his.

"What? Oh, yeah I'm fine." Keir decided he'd have to watch Regal more closely from now on. "Were you able to get enough energy?"

"Plenty."

"Then where are we going next?"

"Someplace you'll love," Regal promised. He opened a new portal, and with Keir's hand in his, led them through. Keir was no longer frightened by the black and violet swirls.

The two were transported to a new destination. They landed in a rural area with hardly any people. The dirt road was barren, not a single car in sight. All of the shops were closed, and they were surrounded by dense woods. The only place that was open was a single hotel standing seemingly in the middle of nowhere.

"Welcome to Paradise," Regal said as he closed the portal behind him. "This place is far from New York and civilization. Michigan's upper peninsula is just what we need for a vacation."

The two walked through the front doors of the hotel. They were greeted with burgundy carpeting and hardwood floors, high ceilings, and pristine white walls. A pool could be seen through the glass doorways, and leather couches and chairs filled the seating area. To the right was a check-in desk made of oak where a young man greeted them.

"Good evening," the man behind the counter said. "How may I help you?"

"I'd like to check out a room."

"Not a problem, sir. Can I just have your name and ID?"

"Ryan Mattel," Regal replied without skipping a beat. He handed a fake ID to the clerk.

The clerk barely looked at it before finding a room for them on the computer. "We have a single bedroom available."

"That's fine." That made his job much easier in the long run.

"All right Mr. Mattel, your room is number 204. It's down the first hallway on the right, and your room is on the left. Thank you for staying with us."

After a quick thank you, they headed to their room. It was clean and tidy; white walls and a nice king-sized bed sat in front of an older-model television. The room was decorated with green-themed curtains and comforters. Outside of their room was a balcony that looked out at the lake, although Keir was uncertain of which one.

Keir headed straight for the balcony, sighing happily as he watched the dark water ripple against the sandy beach. The nearly full moon was hanging low in the sky, making the waves of the lake shimmer. "It's beautiful here."

Regal walked up behind Keir, looking out toward the bleak horizon. "You're looking at Lake Superior."

The two squeezed onto the tiny balcony and barely fit next to the white plastic lawn furniture. Their shoulders touched as they stood in the dark. Keir looked up at Regal. He loved how the moonlight made his already-pale features more intense. The darkness suited him well.

"Go get some rest," Regal told Keir. "It's been a long day."

"What will you do?" Keir asked.

"Relax and enjoy the dark." Regal sat down on one of the

creaky chairs and leaned back, staring up at the sky.

Keir paused before sitting down in the chair beside Regal. "I think I'll stay and enjoy the dark too."

"What?" Regal asked in confusion.

"I might not like it, but that doesn't mean it shouldn't be appreciated," Keir explained with a yawn.

"You're odd," Regal mumbled as they settled into a comfortable silence, watching the waters of Lake Superior wash upon the beach.

CHAPTER *Seventeen*

KEIR WOKE UP groggy the next morning, his face buried in the pillows. He sat up and rubbed his eyes. Memories of the previous day came back to him slowly.

Right... we're in Michigan now, he thought as he stretched and yawned. *I don't remember falling asleep... did Regal tuck me in?*

Keir glanced around the hotel room, but Regal wasn't there. He got up and looked out onto the balcony. Regal wasn't there, either. He headed to the bathroom and knocked on the door. "Regal, are you in there?"

Regal opened the door, an oddly warm smile gracing his lips. Steam from the shower he just finished rose around him and drifted out into the hallway, warming Keir's chilled skin. Regal had a glow to him that made him look lively—more than he should in the morning.

"You're up early," Keir said with surprise.

"So are you." Regal turned off the bathroom light and stepped out, closing the door behind him. "I've been waiting for you to get up. I want to show you something."

"Pardon?" Keir asked, somewhat confused.

"You heard me. I've got a surprise for you," Regal continued as he ran a hand through his slightly damp hair.

"What kind of surprise?" Keir asked carefully.

"Not the bad kind, I swear," Regal assured. "No tricks. Just something I think you would honestly enjoy."

"You want to go out during the day?"

Regal paused. It was a strange thing for him to request. However, what Keir had said the previous evening had struck a chord with him. "Well, you stayed up to appreciate the night.

I figured I might as well do the same favor."

The angel beamed. "Really? You'd do that?"

"Yeah, why not?" the demon said with a shrug.

"Well then, I'd better get ready!" Keir hurried around the room in circles. He then remembered that they left their belongings behind.

Regal chuckled and picked up a shopping bag filled with clothes from the closet. "I grabbed a few necessities last night while I was exploring. It was a challenge finding a place that was open so late around here." He tossed the bag to Keir, who sheepishly caught it and went into the bathroom to change.

Most of the clothes were dark, but he was happy to notice that Regal had thought of him while shopping. There was a light green t-shirt, a gray and white hoodie, and a pair of jeans that were his size. He dressed, rinsed his mouth with the mouthwash the hotel provided, and went into the main room to put on his shoes. "Are you ready?"

Regal put on his sunglasses. "Yeah, as ready as I'll ever be. But first, let's get breakfast."

The two left the hotel room and headed down the hall to the continental breakfast the hotel served. They were the first ones to arrive. The delicious smells of freshly made breakfast wafted into Keir's nose, making his mouth water. Waffles, sausages, eggs, muffins, and cereal greeted him, along with orange juice and coffee. He didn't know what he wanted to have first. Regal was already heading straight for the bacon and eggs, but Keir decided to have a cup of yogurt and a giant Belgian waffle.

"So, where are we going?" Keir asked as he drenched his waffle with maple syrup.

"I can't spoil the surprise," Regal said as he ravenously shoveled his breakfast into his mouth. "Just some place I discovered while exploring last night," he yawned.

"Were you up all night?" Now Keir was confused as to why the demon would want to go out during the day after spending the night out.

"No, just for a few hours."

Keir paused to eat his yogurt. "Did you put me to bed?" he asked quietly, his voice barely audible. His heart was racing at the thought of Regal taking care of him. When Regal nodded, his mouth filled with eggs, Keir could hardly contain his joy.

"Calm down there," Regal said with a soft chuckle, "It's no big deal."

"It is to me."

Regal's eyes stayed fixed on Keir for a lingering moment. "Try not to let it get to your head," he mumbled before he switched his focus to his food. Keir laughed softly at Regal's suddenly shy behavior. The demon always seemed to surprise Keir with his shifts in mood, especially when he wasn't being a pervert, or a wrathful monster, or a general asshole. Keir liked seeing Regal's softer side, and he relished every time Regal let his guard down.

The two finished their meal in comfortable silence, tossed out their trash, and headed back to their hotel room. Keir walked closely beside Regal. The demon didn't flinch or try to move away. In fact, he let his hand brush against Keir's for a fleeting moment—a sign of comfort and acceptance. Regal was finally getting used to Keir's company, and the thought of it made Keir swell with bliss.

He'll ascend in no time, and then we can be together.

The moment they stepped inside their room, Regal locked the door and turned invisible. Keir followed suit and went to the balcony. They leapt off and flew down toward the beach. The clean, white sand was littered with large pieces of driftwood and polished rocks that washed up onto shore from the lake.

Tiny footprints from seagulls faded as the waves rolled up and smoothed them away.

In Regal's opinion, the cooler air of the Upper Peninsula felt much better than the warmer weather in New York City. He could see Canada across the lake and a large freighter traveling north. The choppy waves sent up icy sprays of mist. He continued to lower himself until he was able to skim the water with his fingertips.

Keir followed behind him, keeping up with Regal's swift pace easily. It was still early in the morning, the sun hovering close to the horizon. The mixed sensations of the sun's heat and the water's cool mist gave Keir goosebumps.

"It's so peaceful here," Keir sighed as he flew by Regal, their wingtips brushing.

Regal's eyes locked on Keir's tainted feathers and he smiled. "It really is." The demon looked down at the water. He couldn't see his reflection in the rippling waves. That meant Keir couldn't see his either.

The demon reached out to grab the angel's hand, pulling him slightly as he began to fly back toward the forests. Keir smiled and turned with him. Their movements were fluid and relaxed, with Regal leading the way and Keir trailing beside him. They flew over the forest, grazing against the treetops as they sped past. The tops of the trees swayed, causing the birds to fly out from hiding in front of them. The birds sensed the beings of power and scattered. Those that were closest to Keir flew beside him, but the ones who were near Regal fled.

"Animals don't usually like me."

"That's too bad," Keir replied as his bird companions left to follow the others. "It's strange they don't like you, since demons are a lot like wild animals," he teased.

Regal grinned. "You'd think that, wouldn't you?"

The Art of Falling

They continued to fly north, eventually passing over a small town. There were people stirring below, heading to the small fishing shop for bait. Near the lakeshore, a large white house with a red roof was connected to a lighthouse. The light inside the tower flashed as it turned rhythmically, guiding ships and freighters away from shore.

"Race you to the lighthouse," Regal said.

"You're on," Keir replied as he shot forward, flying as fast as he could toward the bright light. Regal zoomed above Keir, diving in front of him. The angel jerked to the side to avoid colliding with him, and then made a sharp arc to slingshot himself back on track. He copied Regal's tactics, shooting in front of him to force him off track.

The two continued to perform this dance until Keir clipped Regal's head with the tips of his wings. The demon was startled by the playful smack, which gave Keir the extra boost to get ahead and reach the lighthouse.

"I win!" Keir laughed, landing heavily on the observation deck. The sound that used to grate Regal's ears was welcoming as he landed beside the angel.

"Good job," he panted as he sat down beside Keir, letting his feet dangle off the edge. Together they sat and looked toward the horizon to watch the sunrise. Regal could feel the tendrils of sunlight warming his skin. For the first time in his life, it felt comforting. Something about being in this place, at this time of day, with this angel made him feel safe.

"Are you doing okay?" Keir asked as he looked over at Regal, who was starting to look fatigued. His eyelids were drooping as he crossed his arms and rested them on the metal railing.

"Yeah. Just a bit tired."

"Do you want to go back and rest?"

Regal shook his head slowly. "I promised I was going to

show you around. I'll be fine as long as we take a few moments to rest in the shadows."

"There's more?" Keir asked. "I figured this was it."

"This is only the first part. What I really want to show you is coming up." Regal stood up, reaching down to help Keir to his feet. The angel's hand felt cool in his palm; possibly a sign that Keir was falling. He smiled at Keir, who beamed back up at him. Holding hands, they leapt off the light house and headed west.

It was about an hour's flight. Every twenty minutes or so, they had to stop to let Regal rest among the shadows of the woods and regain his strength. Each time they stopped, Keir would ask if Regal was okay.

"I appreciate the concern, but for the love of Jackal, please stop asking," Regal said after the sixth time.

Soon, Regal began to descend into the woods. Keir followed behind him as they headed for a clearing not too far from a river. They landed lightly, barely rustling the dead leaves that were beginning to fall from the trees.

"Alright, now it's just a bit of a hike up through some trails," Regal explained as he headed through a path he had marked the previous night. Broken branches and claw marks in tree bark led them through the dense woods.

Soon, Keir could hear the sound of water and wondered if they were heading toward the river. "Regal, where are we going?"

"You'll see; we're almost there."

The pleasure in Regal's voice made Keir fill up with excitement as he jogged behind him. After another fifteen minutes of hiking, they could hear the rush of water splashing against rocks. They stepped out from the woods and onto the paved path that led up to the edge of a large waterfall. Keir gasped with surprise and walked up to the end of the walkway, leaning on the wooden railing that allowed him to feel the spray of the falls. The water was clear, but tinged brown like rust. Giant rocks jutted out from the river, and the white caps smacked against them and coated the ground with mist.

"This is Tahquamenon Falls," Regal explained as he walked up next to him, resting his hands on the railing. "One of the more well-known waterfalls in this region. Others simply don't compare to this beauty."

Regal was right. This waterfall was gorgeous and made Keir feel extremely happy. During the time he spent tracking down Regal, he hadn't taken the time to stop and enjoy the nature that Earth offered. "I can't believe you found this place."

"It's a tourist site. It's advertised all over the place." Regal nudged Keir's shoulder and pointed down a trail. "This is only the upper falls. There are the lower falls too, but I didn't explore that far last night. I thought we could see it for the first time together if you'd like."

"I'd love to!"

"We can take the trail or fly. It's about four miles away."

"Let's take the trail," Keir suggested. "Besides, the trail is in the woods. You'll be sheltered from the sun there."

"You're right," Regal agreed. "Then we might as well relax." He let his invisibility fall away like a heavy sheet. He needed to conserve his energy. Keir followed suit, happy to fully bask in the sunlight.

After staring at the upper falls for another lingering moment, the two headed down the trail that led down to the lower falls. It was a long hike, but they didn't mind. They walked at a leisurely pace, stopping to look at the river or into the woods. From time to time they would stretch their wings and fly a short distance before walking again. As the day continued and the weather warmed up, tourists would cross paths with them on the trail.

"Stay here," Regal said quietly as he turned invisible and jogged over to a tourist who had taken a break on one of the benches.

Keir watched as the demon crouched down behind the bench, digging in the soft dirt for a moment before finding a beetle that had been burrowing. He picked it up and gently placed it on the jogger's arm. He then ran his finger along her skin to grab her attention. He backed away and watched gleefully as the jogger looked at her arm and immediately jumped off from the bench in fright. She shouted and shook her arm, flinging the beetle away.

Regal held back his laughter, covering his mouth as the jogger shook off her nerves and continued on her way down the path past Keir. He smiled and waved before running over to where Regal was bent over laughing.

"Regal! That wasn't nice."

"I could have done a lot worse," he replied with a playful grin.

Keir looked at Regal with confusion. Regal was acting like a carefree child. Where did the lustful incubus go? "Do you have sun stroke?" he asked as Regal became visible once again.

"No. Why do you ask?"

"You're just... acting weird."

Regal shrugged. "Can't demons have some innocent fun?"

"I never thought to associate innocence with your kind."

"Never underestimate the depth of a demon. We may seem shallow, but we do have personalities and morals."

"You just choose to ignore those morals and act like jerks."

"Do you think I'm a jerk?"

Keir smiled. "Most of the time."

Regal smiled back. "Good. I have a reputation to keep."

They continued their hike to the lower falls. As more tourists passed by, Keir held onto Regal's hand to keep him from causing more invisible mischief. Instead, they kept to themselves and appreciated the natural beauty around them.

"This is my favorite time of the year," Regal said suddenly as they watched two squirrels chase each other through the treetops.

"Really? I would have never guessed for you to be a fan of autumn," Keir replied.

"Well, winter isn't a good time for a demon. The days may be shorter, but the snow reflects the sunlight, and there are no leaves on the trees to create shade."

"I can't imagine you'd like summer either."

"Too hot. I like wearing sweaters, and the sun is out the longest."

"So, what knocked out spring from your top two?"

Regal grinned. "Persephone."

Keir frowned.

"Don't worry. I don't love her, if that's what you're worried about," Regal said. "I don't even want to marry her when I inherit the throne. She's more of a mother figure to me."

"Oh." Keir's cheeks turned pink with embarrassment. Had his disdain for Persephone been that obvious? He didn't have anything against her personally, but he didn't like the idea of her marrying Regal. "So, she's not your mother?"

Regal shook his head. "I don't know who gave birth to me. Father doesn't say. He says it doesn't matter. Persephone is the closest thing I have."

They fell silent for a moment, weighed down by the intimacy of the conversation.

"What is she like?" Keir asked.

"You know when it's technically autumn, but it's still too warm for the trees to completely lose their leaves?"

Keir nodded in reply.

"When she first comes back to Hell, she's like that: still filled with summer," Regal explained as he stared out at the forest. "She's beautiful like autumn, but she's still gentle and loving.

But as autumn continues and turns into winter, she grows cold and bitter. If you saw her then, you'd never believe she had the capability of being nice. When spring comes, she starts to warm up again, and then she leaves until summer is over."

Keir listened in awe as Regal talked about Persephone. The way he talked about her was soft and kind. It was clear he looked up to her and regarded her as royalty. The angel wondered if there would ever be a day where Regal talked about him with compassion, tenderness, and respect.

"That's wonderful," Keir replied softly, afraid that if he spoke too loudly it would disrupt Regal's peace.

"What's your mother like?"

"My mother?" Keir asked in surprise. He hadn't expected Regal to ask about his personal life. Normally, Regal didn't care much about Keir's past. "Oh, well, both my parents are angels."

"Obviously."

Keir laughed shyly. "Yeah. Well, my mother is a Guardian Angel. So she's assigned to specific humans to watch over, care, protect, and guide them down the righteous path."

"That's great," Regal said with a sigh. "But what is she *like?*"

"She's beautiful." Keir closed his eyes, picturing his mom in his mind. "She has dark skin and hazel eyes. She has long brown hair that falls to the dip of her back. She's welcoming to everyone she meets. She's loving, gentle, understanding, supportive... it kind of comes with her line of work. She was always there for me growing up, giving me all of the support I needed to have a happy childhood."

"So, she's the perfect mom?"

"I'd think so."

"Hmm." Regal thought about that for a moment as they walked down a small hill. In the distance, the sound of the waterfall could be heard. "Well, what about your father?"

The Art of Falling

"He's a Dominion, which is in the second sphere of the angelic hierarchy. They're Archangels who have moved up in ranks to become the captains of Gloria's army," Keir explained, in case Regal wasn't familiar with angelic ranks. "We used to be close when I was little, and he always reminded me that I was capable of being something great. But then he was appointed as Chief Dominion and he became really invested in his work. Now all he does is train the Archangels and their Deputies. I rarely see him, and when I do, we clash. I'm the spitting image of him, just not as strong or as big."

"Gotcha," Regal said.

"My favorite season is spring."

Regal chuckled. It wasn't surprising to hear. "How come?"

"Persephone," Keir answered with a grin. Regal looked at him with slight confusion. "When she comes back to earth, everything starts to warm up and become more colorful. The snow melts away, and the trees begin to bud and blossom. The world is filled with warmth and energy. It's all thanks to her."

Regal hated to admit it, but spending time with Keir wasn't as horrible as he would have thought. His original intention was to get Keir to think he was "changing for the better," but the angel wasn't getting on his nerves. Instead, Keir was pleasant to be around, and Regal found himself opening up and relaxing around him. Being nice toward Keir felt completely natural, and Regal knew that was dangerous.

The two continued their hike to the waterfalls. The trails were becoming more crowded with people as they got closer.

"It's amazing!" Keir jogged up to a crowd of people who were looking out at the falls. Four miniature waterfalls branched out from one large river and cascaded down the hillside before meeting again at the bottom. In the center was a small island. They could see a deer crossing the river despite how deadly the falls could be. The rocks that lurked under the rusty water would surely kill a human who was dragged under.

"Follow me," Regal whispered as he took Keir's hand and led him away from the crowd of people. Keir followed easily without any worry of mistrust. He believed that Regal would care for him as they made their way down a path through the woods. Once they were away from the tourists, Regal unfurled his wings and propelled himself into the air. Keir followed suit, trailing behind him as they flew higher.

They crossed over the river and waterfall, gliding over the island and circling it slowly. Keir sighed with happiness as he saw all of the small falls that surrounded the small piece of land. There were at least five in all, each equally beautiful.

"I thought this would be the best way to see everything," Regal said as he flew next to Keir. As they beat their wings in unison, their feathers brushed against one another. "We can land on the island and walk around if you'd like."

"If you don't mind," Keir said with an eager smile. Regal paused mid-flight and gestured for Keir to lead. The angel dove down quickly. Regal was hot on his heels as they landed in the thickest part of the forest.

They walked around the island slowly, stopping at each fall to watch the water roll over the edge. Keir crossed his arms and rested them on the fence. Regal watched him with amusement from one of the various benches that were on the path.

"Thank you, Regal," Keir said as he looked back over toward him.

"It was no big deal." He opened his arms, beckoning Keir. The angel walked over and wrapped his arms around him, hugging him as he sat beside him. "Unfortunately, I'm already feeling drained."

"That's okay. We can head back and you can get your rest. I'm happy to keep exploring on my own."

Regal chuckled. "We've had such a busy morning. I'm surprised you have the energy to keep going."

"Well, I do have a bit of a headache..."

"You're probably getting hungry. I'm sure a lunch break and a brief nap will help. Let's head back and rest up."

They got up and took off toward the sky. Flying back to the hotel was much faster than trying to walk. By the time they were back, Regal was exhausted. He barely had enough energy to keep himself invisible to unlock the balcony door. Once they were inside, he dropped his illusion and collapsed into the bed, sighing with comfort as the down comforter and feather pillows cushioned him.

"Thank you again," Keir said as he sat on the edge of the bed.

"You're welcome. Now let me sleep," Regal mumbled.

The angel merely laughed. "Rest well."

Keir left Regal and went into the bathroom to wash off before getting something to eat. He hopped in the shower to wash off the sand and lake mist that had clung to his body. The warm water soothed his tired muscles after such a long day of hiking, flying, and exploring. It even helped ease his headache a bit.

He had never felt so happy in his life. Regal was finally treating him well, and for the first time he truly believed that Regal might ascend! At heart, Regal wasn't that bad, and Keir planned on tapping into that and using it to save the demon.

Once he was done, Keir stepped out and dried himself off, slipping into a fresh pair of clothes. He shook out his hair and his wings to get any extra water off.

That was when he saw his reflection in the mirror and his entire world seemed to crash around him.

CHAPTER *Eighteen*

*K*EIR STARED AT his reflection for a minute as though he were staring at a stranger. He fluttered his wings and gasped at the sight of the gray feathers as they moved behind him. He felt like they didn't belong to him, even though they still moved at his command. He reached back and plucked a feather to look at it more closely. He held it in his fingers gently, turning it to stare at the dark plumage. It was real. It wasn't a trick of the mirror.

He was tainted.

Keir began to shake. Tears welled up in his eyes and fell down his cheeks. He tried to be strong and not show weakness, like Michaelangelo advised him to do in battle. After all, this truly was a battle of good and evil. But he was losing.

The angel couldn't hold back the sobs that wracked his body. His wings curled around him. Normally they would be a source of comfort, but all they did was remind him of his foolishness. *How stupid of me to trust him,* he thought as he covered his face with the towel to muffle his pain-stricken sobs. His body heaved with each ragged cry, his gasps for air making his throat raw.

Pythos' words burned in his memory: *Do you think he's succeeding?*

At the time, Keir's answer would have been no. He hadn't noticed any change in himself. However, he had noticed changes in Regal that made it seem like he was the one unraveling.

I should have known better. I should have expected this.

Regal had tricked him, lied to him, and used him. Keir felt betrayed, and anger began to seep into him. He was mad at himself, at Regal, and the entire situation.

"Keir, what's wrong?" Regal asked from the other side of the door.

Keir couldn't respond. His voice was raw and choked up from crying. He just shook his head and buried his face into the towel more.

Regal knocked on the door again. "Let me in." It was a command, but it was laced with mild concern.

The angel forced himself up to his feet and threw open the door. He was glaring at Regal, although his eyes were glossy and red from crying.

At first Regal was confused, and the sight of Keir's sadness made his stomach flip. He tried to remind himself that he wanted to see the angel weak and hurt, but something deep inside was telling him that it was a lie. Then he saw Keir's wings hanging limply and their reflection in the mirror, and knew Keir had found out.

"Oh, shit."

"That's all you have to say?" Keir shouted, throwing the towel at Regal, who caught it before it smacked him in the face.

"Well... I could say that I was only doing what came naturally."

How dare that demon try to justify his actions. Keir clenched his fists and shoved past Regal. His sadness was overwhelmed by a sudden resentment.

"You're definitely right to be angry," Regal said as his own wings spread out in defense. If he needed to flee, he would. "But I really don't have any other choice."

"You have free will. You can *choose* to make this relationship work," Keir argued, his voice cracking sharply.

"Free will? If I had any free will, I would have chosen to not be in this mess!" Regal yelled, his own wings itching to spread out in a display of dominance.

Keir charged at him, shoving Regal up against the wall. The

sudden action made the demon lose his breath. He growled and pushed at Keir to shove him away, but he wasn't strong enough. The combination of being awake during the day and the moon being full that night worked against him. Regal was at his weakest. Keir held him down, despite how hard he pushed back with his wings. Keir's eyes were glowing bright white, completely consumed by holy energy that only drained Regal more. He knew he was in trouble.

"You lying, selfish, son of a *bitch*." Keir hissed, his voice hollow with rage. "I trusted you. I actually believed that you were starting to change. That you were starting to see me like an equal, not some toy you can play with. I can see now, all the steps you took to drag me down. The food, the movies, the bathroom mirror—ha! As if you really wanted to do some remodeling. You probably even dragged Viraine into your plans."

"First of all, I admit to everything except Viraine," Regal yelled. "I would never compromise our situation by getting her involved."

"Like I should believe you?" Keir barked.

"Second of all, I told you not to trust a demon. I gave you a fair warning. And third of all, you're such a hypocrite!"

"Excuse me?"

Regal ruffled his feathers with anger. "You heard me. Look at yourself! You're standing over me like some righteous victim who deserves to be comforted and praised for being so *pure* and *innocent*. But this is all happening because you wanted it to! You're the one who stalked me down for a year, you're the one who called my bluff about this deal that should have never been accepted, and you're the one who decided to trust in a demon who never wanted to be in this mess. You had a plan all along: to save me from my sins. Well, I don't want to be saved!"

Keir's anger slowly began to dissipate as the weight of his own mistakes bombarded him. Regal had a point. This wasn't completely his fault. Keir had to take some of the blame too. He was the one to track him, yes, but it was because Regal had instilled love into him that night. He was the one who took the deal, yes, but that was because Regal had offered and it was Keir's only chance. He was the one who decided to trust in a demon, yes, but trust is the foundation of love. He had a plan to save Regal, yes, but isn't that the right thing to do?

The angel's eyes returned back to their normal blue as he came down from his anger. He focused on Regal, and then a confused look manifested on his face, his brows knit together as he stared past Regal. He let go of the demon and stepped back, putting distance between them, all without saying a word.

The absolute silence was unnerving.

"Keir..." Regal said as he stood up slowly.

"I don't know why I didn't notice earlier..."

"Notice what?"

"Maybe you need to take a look in the mirror for once," Keir barked.

A wave of panic flooded Regal. He hurried past Keir, practically shoving him out of his way as he ran into the bathroom. He spread his wings open and saw that they matched the shade of Keir's perfectly. The only difference was that he lacked a solid black feather. His eyes scanned anxiously for a white one, and he sighed with slight relief when he couldn't find one. However, he was devastated. He had been marked with virtues.

His wings shook as he stepped out of the bathroom, glaring at Keir. "What did you do?"

Keir smirked. "I guess I did what came naturally."

"Don't mess with me," Regal barked. "What virtues did you place?" He lashed out, grabbing Keir's wrist tightly.

The angel winced, yanking his arm back in an attempt to free it. However, he wasn't afraid of Regal hurting him, aware that the demon must feel the same aching pain in his own wrist from the tight grip he had. "Honestly, I'm not sure. Angels don't have to plan which virtues to place. They just happen," Keir explained. "But I can sense which ones are stirring inside of you."

"Tell me."

Keir closed his eyes, focusing on the positive energies resting inside of Regal's soul; the same ones he had been noticing this whole time, but hadn't realized were the cause of Regal's change in mood. "I mostly sense patience."

"I figured as much," Regal snapped. Of course he had succumbed to patience. It was the biggest hole in his plot to make Keir fall. "What else?"

"Kindness and charity."

Regal squeezed Keir's wrist tighter. Both of them flinched from the pain. "You're lying."

"No, I'm not," Keir argued.

"Then when? When did I—?" Regal was in an enraged panic.

Keir thought for a moment. "When you decided to take me here and show me the waterfalls, because you knew it would make me happy. That was an act of kindness, not a deed with ill intent. When you chose to go out during the day to get food or supplies, even though it hurt you, you showed charity. Those were all your own decisions. I did nothing to influence you." The angel winced as he felt Regal's nails digging into his wrist. "Regal, I didn't—"

The demon let go and headed back toward the bathroom. He slammed the door shut behind him and locked it. He needed to be away from Keir.

He stared at his reflection in the dingy mirror. *I can't believe it*, Regal thought as he looked at his gray wings. In less than a month they had gone from a perfect, pitch black and turned into this... horrid color that reminded him of dirty snow. "There's no way I fell for kindness and charity," he groaned as he held his head in his hand.

You're slipping.

Regal looked up at the sound of his father's voice in his head. "Why can't you just come here instead of using telepathy?"

I'm busy in a meeting, Jackal said. *But just because I am preoccupied doesn't mean I'm not watching. And I do not like what I'm seeing.*

"I couldn't control it!" Regal argued. "How was I supposed to know he would—?"

You should expect it. I have taught you better. Jackal's voice was filled with anger, and it made Regal cower. The young demon was ashamed.

"At least I managed to get him a black feather," Regal grumbled, sliding down the back wall until he was sitting on the bathroom floor. "I'm still one step ahead of him."

The light that is growing inside of you will purify your wings long before you taint his if you don't get your shit together and make him fall.

"I will never ascend," Regal vowed under his breath grimly. "I am forever your son and your servant."

I'm pleased to hear your loyalty. However, Gloria and Her angels are cunning. They are not much different from you and me when it comes to influencing others. Watch yourself, Jackal warned. *You don't have much time left.*

"I can do it."

Don't fail me.

Regal didn't respond. He stood up, walked out of the bathroom and looked for Keir. He found the angel sitting on the edge of the bed, staring out the window at the setting sun. The entire room was glowing orange and red from the light.

The demon walked up to Keir, sitting down on the edge of the bed next to him.

"Keir."

The angel didn't respond.

"Listen, I'm—"

"Don't apologize. You don't mean it."

Regal didn't listen to Keir. "But I am sorry," he continued. "I know I haven't been very trustworthy. But I felt like I didn't have any other choice."

"There's always a choice."

Regal sighed. "Okay, you're right. I didn't make the correct choice before. I wanted to take the easy way out instead of trying to make this work. But can you give me another chance?"

Keir looked over at him. His eyes were filled with hurt and anger. He didn't respond.

"I promise that I will try to make our situation work."

"Empty promises." His words no longer held anger. They only sounded sad and dejected.

"Then on my life," Regal said. He knew the dangers of swearing on his life, but he *had* to get Keir to trust him. It was the only way he could ever complete his goal to make him fall. "I promise on my life."

Keir glanced at him and sniffled, rubbing his eyes with the heel of his palm. "You know that you can't break that promise," Keir said, turning slightly toward Regal. "If you break it, you'll be judged by Gloria and your father. They'll..."

"Forcibly break the bond between us so they can punish me as severely as they see fit without the risk of harming you."

They sat in silence, burdened by the weight of the situation. Keir knew that Regal valued his life too much to risk losing it over a broken promise. It was probably why he hadn't done it to try and break their bond in the first place. In a strange way, it kept them together. Although Regal's promise didn't fix everything that had gone wrong, it did make Keir better... slightly.

The angel leaned forward and hugged the demon, holding him close. Regal wrapped his arms around Keir and rested his head on his shoulder. Regal's only option to try and make Keir fall was to rebuild trust and make a promise he could never break. To him, the only way to make this relationship work was to make the angel fall.

Keir was aware of this. He knew very well that he should not trust Regal, should not give him a second chance. But the demon promised, and Keir knew that the vow would make Keir's goal easier to accomplish. He was certain if he kept at it, he could save Regal. That was all Keir cared about. He wanted to save Regal, and he wanted the demon to love him.

"I'm sorry I hurt you," Regal apologized. "I didn't know of any other way in the past. I'll do better next time." He pulled away from Keir to look at him, and then bent down to give him a gentle kiss. "I promise."

The angel didn't flinch, but he was caught off guard by the gesture. He narrowed his eyes skeptically as Regal laid down on the bed, patting the empty space beside him.

"I don't know about you, but I'm exhausted."

"You want me to sleep next to you?" Keir asked.

The demon nodded.

"In a minute," Keir said as he knelt in front of the bed and clasped his hands together. He rested his forehead against his hands and let out a shaky sigh. Regal watched Keir as he began to recite a scripture from the bible—a prayer that he hoped would help him achieve his goal, and perhaps teach Regal a lesson about love.

"Love is patient, love is kind. It does not envy, it does not boast, it is not proud," Keir started, the prayer rolling off his tongue with ease. Regal listened to his soft voice continue on. "It does not dishonor others, it is not self-seeking, it is not easily angered, it keeps no record of wrongs. Love does not delight in evil but rejoices with the truth. It always protects, always trusts, always hopes, always perseveres.

"Love never fails. But where there are prophecies, they will cease; where there are tongues, they will be stilled; where there is knowledge, it will pass away. For we know in part and we prophesy in part, but when completeness comes, what is in part disappears. When I was a child, I talked like a child, I thought like a child, I reasoned like a child. When I became a man, I put the ways of childhood behind me. For now we see only a reflection as in a mirror; then we shall see face to face. Now I know in part; then I shall know fully, even as I am fully known.

"And now these three remain: faith, hope, and love. But the greatest of these is love."

When Keir was finished, he laid down next to Regal, facing toward him to stare at his back. He trailed his hands along the tangle of scars before scooting closer and wrapping his arms around the demon's waist.

Regal stared at the wall, his chest aching and his body cold as Keir's psalm about love revolved in his mind. He didn't flinch or move away when he felt Keir's fingertips tracing along his back and when he held him from behind. They had grown used to each other's company. The thought satisfied Keir, and terrified Regal.

PART *Two*

CHAPTER *Nineteen*

"WE NEED TO leave," Regal said the next morning as he took a bottle of Lysol and sprayed the entire room.

"Why?" Keir asked, coughing as a plume of disinfectant swept past him.

"This place isn't good for us. Not enough people."

"To hunt?" The tone of Keir's voice was bitter with lingering anger toward the demon.

Regal shook his head. "No. To hide among. Any angel or demon could sense us from a mile away."

"Do you think Viraine is following us?" Keir asked, trying to mask his nervousness by seeming apathetic.

"Maybe. It's best to keep on the move," Regal explained. "We'll keep heading west. I have a place in Chicago that I rent out. We can stay there."

The two checked out of the hotel, not bothering to pack any belongings with them, and headed to the new apartment.

Upon arriving, Keir could tell that Regal didn't stay there often, if at all. At least in the New York City home, there were traces of life in every room. This apartment was spotless and brand new. It was an open concept, with sky lights and large windows. Lush carpets covered the living space and stretched into the bedrooms, the bathroom floors were tiled, and the kitchen had dark hardwood floors. The walls were painted a soft moss green, which complimented the tan carpet. The kitchen appliances were stainless steel, and the cupboards were made from the same dark wood as the floor. The single bedroom the two would share was painted a dark gray, suited for Regal's tastes.

The Art of Falling

Keir walked up to the large window on the far wall to look out over the city he was dying to explore. He wanted to see everything. It was like being in New York City for the first time all over again. This was the perfect chance to get away from Regal for a while.

"I'm going to go out," Keir said. He didn't bother asking for permission.

"That's fine. Take some money and have fun."

Keir took Regal's wallet and turned invisible. He jumped out the window and began to soar over the city. The first thing to catch his eye was a strangely-shaped metallic sculpture located in the center of a plaza. Carefully, he flew down close to it. The bean-shaped sculpture was stunning to say the least; it was simple, yet beautifully crafted. It looked like it was made of mercury; malleable and metallic. He watched as people walked underneath the curve of it, disappearing for a moment before appearing on the other side.

After hiding behind a nearby building to turn visible again, he walked up to the sculpture to see his own reflection. He ran his hands across the cool surface, chuckling at the way his body seemed to look smaller and distorted in the curves of the monument. He turned and saw a group of high school students lying in a circle in the center. They were staring up at the middle of the bean, taking photographs of their reflections and laughing at how they turned out. Keir couldn't help but smile at their creativity and amusement.

"What is this sculpture called?" he asked a young woman next to him.

"It's called Cloud Gate," she said as he adjusted her glasses and looked at the brochure in her hand. "But everyone here calls it The Bean."

Keir preferred Cloud Gate. It reminded him of home.

He left Cloud Gate and moved with the light crowd down the street. He passed by a beautiful garden with a large pool in the center. Connected to that pool was another sculpture that also acted as a fountain. It was of five women made from bronze; however, they were a dull turquoise in color. The water flowed from the top of the fountain and made its way down through each woman until it reached the large pool at the bottom. Keir read a plaque next to them and learned that they represented the Great Lakes.

Maybe Regal would like to visit all of the Great Lakes, he thought as he watched the water flow through the fountain. Keir shook his head quickly. "No! Stop thinking about him! You're still mad at him!"

Keir left the fountain, sprinting down the street until he couldn't run anymore. Three blocks later, he walked into a store to distract his worried mind with clothes shopping and souvenirs. No matter how much he tried to ignore his thoughts, they kept creeping back to the forefront of his mind. Every piece of clothing and trinket reminded him of Regal. He couldn't push the demon out of his mind.

He dropped his items onto the counter and looked out the shop window. As the cashier rang him up, he rubbed his fingers along the bridge of his nose to ease the headache that was building.

"That'll be $48.34."

Keir absentmindedly handed him a fifty. "Is there anything fun to do around here?"

"Well, Navy Pier is a pretty fun place," the cashier said as he handed back Keir his change. "It's only a few blocks north of here."

"Thanks." Keir gathered his bags and shoved his extra money into his pocket.

"Have a great day!"

"You too."

Keir headed toward Navy Pier, trying to shove Regal from his thoughts. But the damned demon was persistent, and his plagued Keir's mind without relent.

It reminded of him of how he felt when he first fell for Regal.

He sighed, rubbing his temples, feeling a headache forming. Why did the demon have to make him feel this way? Some days he wished he could go back in time and avoid ever having to face him. However, Keir couldn't imagine where he would be if he didn't meet Regal. It was because of the incubus that his life had purpose and meaning.

He was certain this was his destiny, and he had to do anything to follow it through, no matter how tough it was.

Feeling a new surge of confidence, Keir walked up to the pier and took in the wondrous sights. In the center of the wooden boardwalk was a large Ferris Wheel. He watched the children riding to the top, waving over the side down to their parents. He could hear their laughter over the music. The smiles on their faces were infectious.

Maybe this would be a good step to mending their fracturing relationship.

Toward the end of the pier was the Museum of Stained Glass. Although Keir preferred observing human interaction more than paintings or sculptures, he always felt drawn toward artwork. He walked inside and felt a chill wash over him. Many of the fragile pieces of stained glass depicted religious images such as Jesus and Gloria herself—although She was depicted in different forms.

Keir's chest ached and his eyes stung with tears. He missed home. He longed to return back to Heaven, to see his friends and family, and to be in the safety and care of Gloria's presence. However, a part of him wondered if he had already destroyed any chance of returning. He was so close to falling, would

Gloria even want him back?

He stared solemnly into the colored glass, his reflection muted out by purples, reds, and blues. Gloria's painted image looked back at him, unwavering. All of his confidence fell away at Her presence.

"Was I wrong to try and do this on my own?" he asked quietly. "Was I wrong about my purpose in life? Is my destiny to fail?"

Gloria did not respond, not in the glass and not in Keir's mind. All connection to Her was cut off. That was part of the deal that was made. He wanted to save Regal on his own, and the only way to do that was to ensure that he would get no outside help from Gloria.

"I won't give up," Keir vowed. "I may not be an Angel of Diligence, but I won't stop until I save him." He continued to tell himself this, refusing to think about what would happen if he did not succeed.

Keir stayed in the museum for a long time, looking for peace among the religious images. However, he was unable to find any. He had never noticed it before, but the expressions of the people were always in pain. Their eyes seemed to follow him, accusing him of his sinful deeds. He could almost hear his friends and family in Heaven scolding him, damning him, praying that he falls. As the sun set, and the stained glass turned dark, he left and headed back to the closest thing he had to home.

He flew in through Regal's window, thankful that the demon hadn't woken up and locked it. He began to unpack his new belongings when the tired incubus came out from the bedroom.

"What did you get?" he asked as he rubbed his bleary eyes.

"Some clothes and souvenirs," Keir explained. He took out a small box and handed it to Regal. The demon turned it over in his hands, shaking out the shiny bean magnet into his palm. He raised his eyebrow and looked back over at Keir.

"Why?"

"I figured we would get bored of the same old outfits, and that it'd be nice to have something small to remember where we've been," Keir explained. "I didn't think to get anything from New York or Paradise, though."

Regal set the magnet on the counter and headed to the kitchen to get something to eat. "We can also stop back and buy something if you'd like." He rummaged through the cupboards, but found nothing. It had been months since he was last here. "I'm going to get food. Want anything?"

"Not fast food," Keir said. He now knew that was how he had fallen for the first sin. He wasn't going to keep succumbing to those habits. "I'm going to start eating healthier now, if that's all right by you."

The two stared at each other, as if sizing up one another. Regal knew Keir didn't care if Regal approved of his decision to change his eating habits. It was a power play, a way for Keir to show that he still had free will to make his own decisions. Although, they both knew that changing their habits now would not remove the marks of the sins and virtues placed.

"Yeah, I'll bring home organic stuff," Regal said after a long moment of silence. "Feel free to get some rest." He headed to the bedroom, leaving Keir alone in the living room.

Regal got himself ready for the night and headed out the window once the sun was set over the horizon. The moon, now starting to creep closer to its third quarter, gleamed in the sky. The city was colorful at night, shining with the lights of the buildings and streets. Night owls roamed the sidewalks, oblivious that a hungry demon was hovering above them. Regal was starving for souls, and Chicago was crawling with sinners.

He longed to hunt down the most desperate, most sexually deprived, most pathetic human soul the Windy City had to offer, but he knew that he couldn't. He had made an unbreakable vow to never harm another human.

Fear struck Regal hard like lightning: if he couldn't break his bond with Keir, then he may never be able to break his vow to give up hunting. If he couldn't hunt souls, what sort of demon would he be?

The scent of a demon interrupted his paranoid thoughts.

Viraine.

Regal froze, hovering in midair. He ignored his nerves as he tried to find the source. The scent was bitter, metallic, and filled with selfishness. He grinned as he recognized it. It wasn't the scent of gluttony.

It was greed.

He changed his direction to follow the familiar aura. It was strangely comforting, far more than Viraine's gluttonous stench was. If his hunches were correct, he was going to be seeing a good friend soon—one whom he would honestly call a friend.

Regal was guided to an electronics store. He furrowed his brow with curiosity as he landed behind the store. He walked around the edge and stepped inside only to be instantly hit with a strong smell of metal.

He shook his head a little to clear his mind and headed down one of the aisles. It was hard to pinpoint the source when he was surrounded by nothing but technology. For an untrained demon, the greedy aura would get lost in the environment, but Regal was very familiar with this demon and followed the trail deeper into the store. He walked past the cellphones and CDs, his eyes searching over the racks of merchandise. He caught sight of someone turning to look at him, and smiled when he recognized their face.

The greed demon looked Asian in appearance, with styled black hair that fell to his shoulders; however, his bangs were bleached white. He was well-groomed, which matched his meticulous personality. His eyes widened at the sight of Regal. He beamed as he walked over to the incubus, holding out his hand toward his comrade.

"Regal, what a surprise to see you here," he said cheerily, clasping his hand around Regal's in a firm handshake. The green and gold gaze behind the thin rimmed glasses was always friendly when aimed at Regal. Regal smiled back and shook his hand just as vigorously.

"Etoile, it's been too long," Regal said. He looked down at Etoile and noticed the blue collared employee shirt and khaki pants that the demon was wearing. "Don't tell me you have a mundane job. What happened to training fledglings?"

Etoile laughed and clasped Regal on the shoulder. "You know my fascination with the development of technology. So much has changed since the fifteenth century. Young demons simply don't hold my interest."

Regal laughed, shaking his head. "Fifteenth century? You're older than that."

"There was nothing fascinating about my childhood. It only started to get good once the automobile was created. Ahh, what a beautiful piece of machinery it was—and look how far it has advanced. They even make cars that talk, automatically park, and even avoid accidents! It's all so fascinating! In the 1800's such features would have been considered witchcraft! Now it's something everyone wants."

"You know, as much as your passion-filled rants drive me nuts, I sure did miss you," Regal said with a warm smile. "I'm happy to see you haven't gotten yourself killed."

"I appreciate the sentiment." Etoile looked around for a moment and grinned, his eyes gleaming mischievously. "But we shouldn't talk about that stuff out here. Let's catch up somewhere more private."

CHAPTER *Twenty*

*E*TOILE LED REGAL toward an unmonitored corner of the store and pulled out a fountain pen from his breast pocket. He tapped the end, and black ink immediately flowed to the top, defying gravity as it beaded at the point. Pressing the tip against the wall, he drew a thick line in a circle large enough for a man to fit through. Once he completed the drawing, he stepped back and placed the pen back into his pocket. The white wall inside the ink drawing began to darken and swirl until it was a solid mass of darkness.

Regal stood up and walked over to the portal, looking into it for a moment before grinning a little at Etoile. "Still using the fountain pen... you know, I figured you would have upgraded your methods of transportation to something more technologically advanced by now."

"Trust me, I am still researching a way to jump right into the thicket of the internet, but it still remains out of my reach. Not only do I have to make a portal, but I have to turn myself into binary code. Much harder than it seems; that's the work of a warlock," Etoile said. Regal had no doubts that he was already contacting warlocks to help him.

The incubus stepped into the portal, falling down into the pit of ink. His wings unfurled, catching the air to slow his descent. His feet touched cobblestone—or what felt like cobblestone—after several feet of falling. He looked up and saw the silhouette of Etoile jumping through the ink portal before it sucked shut behind him, blocking out any remaining light. Even this darkness was too much for Regal. He couldn't see a thing in front of him.

201

The Art of Falling

He felt Etoile land beside him, his own wings brushing up against Regal's. They were coarse and synthetic. Greed demons normally did not have wings; however, they possessed the ability to mimic and take from other demons. He was certain Etoile liked a demon's wings and decided to "borrow" them to build his own unique mechanical pair.

"This way." Etoile began to walk forward. Regal followed blindly after him, his wingtips brushing against the walls so he could map out the pathways in his mind.

"I'm amazed you know where you're going in this darkness," he commented as he walked behind him. He heard Etoile's short chuckle echo.

"If it weren't for the eye Jackal gave me, I'd be just as lost as you. I've even tweaked it to give me perfect night vision."

Regal remembered when Etoile first told him the story of his unusual gift from Jackal. He had lost his left eye in the war against Satan. Shortly after he was named a Prince, Jackal gave him a new eye. It took several months for the wound to heal, and he was amazed when it was a bright green instead of golden.

"Wow, you must be one of Jackal's favorites," Regal teased.

The greed demon scoffed. "Oh, hardly. His favorites are given wings, which is why you're so special and why I had to synthesize mine." Regal smiled a little at that. He held great pride in the fact his father held some favoritism toward him.

A light appeared at the end of the tunnel, and soon Regal was able to see clearly in the passage. The two walked out and into a well-furnished cavern with tables, chairs, and a fireplace. The walls were made from stone and dirt, and all the lighting was artificial, obviously built under the ground.

"Please, take a seat," Etoile said as he motioned toward the chairs near the fireplace. Regal sat down, the green light illuminating from the magic-induced flames casting long shadows on the floor. He leaned into the plush chair with a sigh and looked around.

"This place brings back memories," he murmured as he ran his hands against the arms of the chair. Etoile grinned and poured them each a glass of wine.

"Yes, you were quite fond of my home as a child; you were always digging your own secret passages from your bedroom to here." Etoile handed Regal his drink and they gently clinked the glasses together before taking a sip. "Do you have any idea how many holes you've made in my walls?"

Regal grinned. "Far too many to count."

"To be fair, it was smart to tunnel your way here. Flying to the caves is too dangerous. Even Jackal avoids visiting me."

Etoile choosing to live in the caverns near Tartarus' mouth was yet another reason why Regal looked up to him so much. He was a total badass who wasn't afraid of anything, except perhaps his reputation being tainted.

It was his reputation of being a level-headed and wise demon that got him his title as Prince of Greed. When Hades died, along with four of the original princes, the remaining council members demanded that Etoile lead the demons of greed after showing bravery and wit in battle.

However, Etoile rarely took his title seriously. This lack of responsibility is what drew Regal to Etoile in the first place as a child. The Prince of Greed had a knack for balancing work and play, and whenever Regal was scolded by his father, Etoile was there to bail him out.

Despite being of a completely different sin, Etoile cared for Regal when Jackal couldn't. He became an adviser for the young incubus, showing him how to properly place sins on humans and telling him which incubus elders could teach him how to dreamwalk best. He even made sure Regal knew how to sneak out of the city limits and how to taunt Tartarus by flying close to the mouths without getting caught.

Regal never knew why he was one of Etoile's favorites; he never bothered to ask. All that mattered was that someone other than his father was fond of him, and Regal trusted Etoile with his life. Etoile was his best friend.

"The last time you came to visit you were still a child. How old are you now?" Etoile said as he crossed his legs, bouncing his foot up and down lazily.

"Ninety-four," Regal replied with a small frown. He hated getting older. It would eventually make his job harder. He took a sip of his wine, trying hard not to grimace. Demon wine was made with just a drop of human blood. This one was laced with greed; it was far too bitter for his tastes. He preferred a muskier flavor.

"You grew up so fast," Etoile sighed. "But at least you'll get stronger as you age." A beep was heard in the room, and Etoile immediately reached for a bag lying behind the table. He reached in and pulled out various phones, beepers, and iPods until he found the one that made the sound.

"Seriously? You hoard those?" Regal asked incredulously.

Etoile pouted. "Regal, all demons hoard. It's in our nature to take what we like and to be possessive. I love technology, and being a demon associated with greed does not help."

Regal raised his hands and chuckled. "Whatever you say. Don't blame your genetics for your lack of control."

"Hush."

They laughed with ease. It felt as if nearly half a decade hadn't passed between them.

Etoile eyed the silver chain dangling from Regal's pants pocket. "Are you still using that old pocket watch I gave you as your primary weapon?"

Regal smiled and tapped his fingers against it. "I never go anywhere without it."

"I could upgrade it for you if you'd like."

"What else can you do with it? It's already pretty well equipped."

A childish glimmer shone in Etoile's eyes. "Never doubt my creativity. There is a lot I can do with a simple weapon. In fact... let me show you the most successful upgrade I've ever done."

He stood up, rummaged around his piles of toys, and pulled out a bronze and silver revolver. It looked like any regular gun, but the cylinder, which held seven chambers, had runes carved into the metal. A scope with crosshairs was welded onto the end of the barrel. It was designed to mimic the technology in Etoile's eye, allowing crystal-clear precision in total darkness.

"When my fountain pen is inserted into the slot, this beauty concentrates the energy into a bullet," Etoile explained as Regal whistled with awe.

"I've got to admit, you're got a real talent for building some pretty cool shit. How does it work?" Regal asked.

"Let me demonstrate!" Etoile took his pen and slipped it into one of the chambers. The runes on the chamber glowed as the revolver recognized the energy source. Etoile cocked his gun, aimed at the wall where a target was posted, and fired. A flash of yellow exploded from the barrel, and a bullet made out of black ink shot out. It embedded itself into the wall, cutting through it easily. There was a slight rumble beneath their feet as Tartarus felt the prick of the bullet in his flesh. Etoile turned and looked at Regal, who could barely hide his own excitement. "Because this gun has seven chambers, theoretically it can carry the auras of seven different demons and respond accordingly."

"Damn, you really outdid yourself this time," Regal said. "Have you tried it out with other demons? To actually see if it works?"

The Art of Falling

"I have in the past, with inconclusive results." Etoile turned the revolver in his hands for a moment, looking it over with a careful gaze.

"If you can make this thing work, you could sell it to the Marquis and make a fortune!"

Etoile's smile wavered for a moment, a sign of his own inability to take a compliment when it was due. "Perhaps you're right. However, this is a very dangerous design, and could cause a lot of damage if given to the wrong hands. I would much rather keep it to myself." He looked up briefly at his companion and held the gun out for Regal. "However, it would be nice to see if my recent adjustments worked."

"You want me to?" Regal asked, taking the weapon. It was cool in his hands, and not as heavy as he expected.

"I wouldn't trust anyone else to try it."

Regal smiled, a warm sense of importance and pride coursing through him. "How do I make it recognize my energy?"

"Press the button on the top to load a new chamber with your aura."

The incubus, excited and giddy like he was a child with a new toy, cut the tip of his thumb with his nail and let the blood seep into the second chamber. It began to glow, this time a dark blue. Regal aimed again and fired. This time, there was a flash of blue before a bullet shot out and hit the wall. He grinned wickedly, feeling a rush of adrenaline burst in his system. "I need one of these."

The demon of greed laughed as he took the gun from Regal and sat back down. "No way, but I can upgrade your pocket watch to be locked against another demon's aura next time you're in the area. However, I don't think you're here just to talk about getting an upgrade."

"I wasn't trying to seek you out, but I'm glad I ran into you,"

Regal replied, getting serious again. "I've gotten myself into a bit of trouble."

"Did you get a girl pregnant?"

"Worse. Viraine decided to stop by my place."

Etoile grimaced. "I'm sorry to hear that. She's such a pain. Always getting in the way and causing problems while I'm trying to work. She makes fun of me and my day job. She doesn't seem to see the importance in technology," he grumbled as he flicked through his files on his phone. "Ignorant little thing she is."

"Yeah, you can say that again," Regal chuckled. "However, she's also pretty sly. She managed to talk to an angel a while ago."

"Oh..."

"That's all you have to say?"

Etoile flicked his thumb over the screen of his phone absentmindedly. Regal's eyes widened in realization.

"You're the one who told Viraine about Keir, aren't you?"

The greed demon sighed. "I'm sorry, Regal, I really am, but can you blame me? You know how she is. She always manages to loosen my lips with strong demon wine, then the next thing I know she's pulling information out of me like a child of envy. Persephone really shouldn't confide in me so much..."

Regal stood up and growled. His wings flared and began to shake. "I can blame you! Your low alcohol tolerance does not excuse you from sharing that type of information!"

"Calm down, Regal."

"Calm down? With the way she runs her mouths, soon all of Hell will know!"

Etoile lazily aimed his gun at Regal. "No they won't. It may be hard to believe, but she is protective of you and wouldn't slander your name. She may gossip about a demon who was marked by an angel, but she would never say it's you. Your reputation is safe."

"Keir's isn't. Don't you see how much danger she can put him in?"

Etoile stared at Regal dumbfounded, blinking slowly.

"Argh!" Regal cried out as he tugged at his hair with frustration. "This is what I meant by trouble. The damned angel is rubbing off on me!"

Etoile pointed the gun at Regal's seat, beckoning him to sit. "I'm honestly surprised it's you. I never thought you'd be one to slip up."

"I didn't either..." Regal admitted. "He's a real pain, and..." he paused, wondering if he should confide his fears in someone. He didn't want to admit that he was making mistakes. Although, he knew that if he had to confess to anyone, he'd want it to be Etoile. Jackal would scold him, but Etoile would help him, like he always did. Regal sighed and his wings drooped. "I think he's starting to make me ascend."

The green-and-gold-eyed demon looked at him in silent shock. He leaned forward and whispered, "Really? You think he's making you ascend?"

"Yeah... I'm certain of it. I'm trying to make him fall, too, but we're kind of at a stalemate right now."

Etoile leaned back and sighed. "At least a stalemate is better than a checkmate. Keep your guard up and start working harder. This is no time to play around."

"I know, I know," Regal grumbled. "I am working hard. I'm doing everything I can to get him to sin. He's just so damned intuitive at that kind of stuff."

The greed demon cocked a brow slightly, although he was now back to staring at his phone and flicking through the apps. "Intuitive? How so?"

"No idea. He just has a knack for avoiding my attempts." It was extremely aggravating. What made it worse was that Regal couldn't seem to dodge Keir's attempts to make him ascend. He groaned and leaned back, running his hands through his hair. "I'm at my wits end. I've been wasting time trying to make him happy while thinking about what to do for the last two weeks."

"Ahh, that's your problem," Etoile said as he stood up. "You're trying to make him happy. Angels thrive on happiness. You need to make him suffer and grow weak."

"I... can't do that."

"Can't?" Etoile furrowed his brow as he stared hard at his young pupil. "What in Jackal's name are you saying?"

Regal played with his hands nervously, looking up briefly at Etoile before staring at his slightly chewed cuticles. "I... made a promise to him."

"On?"

"My life."

Etoile groaned and rubbed his temples. "What did you promise him?"

"To make this work."

"Dammit, Regal, what did I teach you as a fledgling?" Etoile paced in circles, his lecture beginning. Normally Regal hated when Etoile would start up a rant, but this time he couldn't complain. "Never make a promise you can't keep. Especially one on your life."

"I know, but I couldn't avoid it. It was the only way to get him to trust me after he found out I was making him fall," Regal said with exasperation as he threw up his hands.

"Then learn to handle the consequences!" Etoile snarled. "You've made your promise, so keep it. Make your relationship work."

"The only way it could ever work is if I make him fall."

"Is that the only way you see it could ever work?"

"Yes."

Etoile sighed with relief. "Good, then you're not breaking

any pacts by going against his wishes and attempting to make him fall. The real question now is do you know what you're going to do?"

"No idea. He's more work than I would have expected. I'm kind of lost at this point..." He was ashamed to admit his failures.

Etoile stood silent for a moment, his fingertips brushing against his lips as he pressed his hands together. He closed his eyes, thinking deeply for a moment before snapping his fingers with an idea. "Just to confirm the data, you are admitting to me in confidence that you are trying to make an angel fall, you've formed an unbreakable contract, and you are at the end of your rope and need guidance?"

Regal nodded, shoulders sagging. "Unfortunately, yes."

"Then, I may be able to help you with your endeavors." Etoile leaned forward, resting his elbows on his knees and his chin on his hands as he stared at Regal. "Now... I'll let you in on a little secret on how I make humans succumb to greed. I don't get my hands dirty whatsoever. I let them do all the work themselves by building up the thing they want until they can't resist it. If you plant a seed of desire into a person's mind, soon they'll be doing everything in their power to obtain it."

Regal furrowed his brow slightly and shook his head. "There isn't anything materialistic Keir really wants. He usually just buys clothes, and that's a necessity, not a luxury."

"Then get creative," Etoile said with an almost eager tone. It was higher in pitch and rushed, almost a complete change from his normally suave and deep tone. "That's the best part about our job!"

"It's harder than it sounds," Regal murmured with tediousness. This was not exactly the advice he was hoping to hear. "I only have two weeks to make him fall. Trying to make him succumb to another sin after I promised to stop may backfire."

"That could work to your benefit. Get him pissed enough and he may fall to wrath."

"Well, it's not like I have many options left anyways," the incubus sighed as he slumped in his chair. There have been several instances of Keir's temper flaring up. Instigating a fight may be his only possibility to make him feel true wrath.

Etoile got up to pace the room, his mind turning as he chugged out ideas like a machine. "Now, the best form of greed is burglary. You say he likes clothes, hmm? It's not my forte, but I could probably think of something. What if you took him to one of the most expensive clothing stores in Chicago? Perhaps something would catch his fancy. Maybe jewelry? No, no... he would be too keen to not pocket something that expensive... "

Regal groaned inwardly as Etoile continued to ramble on about possible scenarios where Keir could succumb to greed. He always got wrapped up in his schemes to the point that it was almost obsessive.

"Why not make him want something more abstract?" Regal suggested mildly as he took Etoile's phone and played around with it, skimming through the contacts. "Maybe make him desire time, not money."

The suggestion caught Etoile's attention immediately. His eyes dilated and his grin grew until it looked like it would tear his face apart.

"Now you're talking!"

CHAPTER *Twenty-One*

REGAL WALKED BACK into his apartment the next morning beaming. The happy glow of energy surrounding him made Keir wary. The angel watched as he whistled and rummaged through the kitchen, pausing when there wasn't any food.

"You never did go shopping like you said," Keir mentioned, leaning against the counter.

"I must have gotten distracted last night," Regal replied with a laugh.

"Distracted by what?"

Regal turned quickly to face Keir, his eyes bright with joy. The image startled Keir. "I ran into an old friend!"

"The last friend you ran into was Viraine."

The incubus laughed. "Oh, no! No, no, he's not anything like her. I'd actually call him my friend," Regal joked. "I haven't seen him in forty years."

Keir warmed up a little, smiling as Regal prepared tea for Keir. "That's quite a long time to go without seeing a friend."

"We've had different paths," Regal said. "I was training to take my father's place, and he was living among the humans instead of training young fledglings like myself."

Keir sat down at the table as Regal brought him a steaming cup of tea. "So he was your teacher?" he asked as he took a sip.

Regal nodded. "One of the best. I learned everything I know from him."

"So he's an incubus."

"No, just a demon of sloth," Regal corrected. "Which is why I'm not surprised he stopped training me, and went to laze around humans all day. Anyways, he's one of the more

212

trustworthy demons in Hell. Unlike Viraine, you can actually count on him to do the right thing. His judgment isn't clouded."

"Well, that's good."

"We're going to hang out together tonight," Regal said happily. "I haven't been in this area in a long time, so it'll be fun to explore the city together."

Keir frowned. He had wanted to show Regal around, to make up for when Regal took him on their tour in Paradise. He wanted to speak up, but held his tongue.

"That'll be nice," he said flatly.

Regal didn't seem to notice his unease. "I have to catch some rest first," he yawned. He walked past Keir, brushing his hand through Keir's hair as he passed. "Good morning."

Keir sat quietly at the kitchen table, drinking his tea slowly as the morning sun began to rise over the cityscape. He weighed his thoughts, trying to decide how to feel about the situation. He was happy Regal had reunited with his friend, but he was worried of the dangers it brought.

"As long as he's happy," Keir murmured—although part of him didn't believe it.

———

That night, when Keir returned to the apartment after a day of idle exploring, Regal was ready to race out and meet with Etoile. Keir was surprised at how nice he looked. The demon appeared to ditch his "unruly, bad-boy" look for a more "well-groomed, proper" appearance. Instead of turtleneck sweaters and jeans, he was wearing slacks and a dress shirt. He was freshly shaven, and his hair was neatly combed and partially styled with gel.

He never dressed this nice when we went out, Keir thought, scowling. "You look nice."

"Thanks," Regal replied. "You don't think it's too much? I know we're just two friends going out for a night on the town, but I didn't want to look like I've lost my touch. He doesn't know of our situation, after all. I need to look like I'm still the hottest incubus Hell has ever seen."

"Well, that's not hard to achieve," Keir commented with a chuckle. "I'm sure he won't suspect anything."

Regal walked over to Keir and gave him a soft kiss on the forehead. A silent thank you. The gesture made Keir glow with joy, but also with a hint of pride.

"I'll be home in the morning, and then maybe you and I can do something."

"I'd really like that."

"Then it's a date."

The next morning, Regal was too tired to go out, and apologized profusely to Keir for having to cancel. He promised that he'd make up for it the next time.

The cycle continued, though. Regal would hurry out to spend time with Etoile, leaving Keir alone in the apartment, and would come home too exhausted to spend time with Keir. At first, the angel let it slide, but after a week, he was growing frustrated.

"Regal," he said sternly as the demon flew in from another late-night adventure.

"Keir!" he exclaimed. "You will not believe what Etoile and I saw last night."

"Can I talk to you about something first?"

"Did you know there is a pier to the north of here?" Regal continued. "The place sure is hopping as soon as the sun starts to go down."

"Yes, Regal, I did know that."

"They have a Ferris Wheel there! It's crazy."

"I know, I—"

"It might seem kind of childish, but Etoile and I decided to ride it."

Keir gasped with dismay. That was what he wanted to do with Regal. Now some other demon was stealing not only their time, but also Keir's plans. "You what?"

"I know!" Regal laughed. "It's not nearly as fun as flying, but it sure is relaxing on the wings. You've got to—"

Keir interrupted Regal by slamming his hands on the table. The demon paused, looking at Keir with surprise.

"Keir, are you okay?"

"No. I'm not," Keir said sharply.

"What's wrong?"

"You haven't been around as much," Keir explained, his voice low.

"Our schedules don't match up that well to begin with."

"But you used to at least put time into trying to spend time with me. Granted, it was to try and make me fall—"

"I apologized for that," Regal interrupted. "I'm trying to make up for it."

"You're dropping the ball." Keir crossed his arms over his chest. "I don't want to be like this, but you're not spending *any* time with me, and I don't like it. If you want to make this relationship work, then you're going to have to put more effort into it."

"Keir, I'm sorry... I didn't realize that I was hurting you," Regal said sadly. He walked over to Keir and hugged him. "Really, I didn't."

The angel sighed. He couldn't tell if Regal was being honest, or lying through his teeth.

"I'll do better."

Empty promises, Keir reminded himself.

"Let's go out this evening," Regal suggested. "I need a little time to recover from last night, but after a couple of hours, we can go and have time for ourselves. Just us, okay?"

The Art of Falling

Keir didn't expect Regal to keep his promise. However, the demon pulled through in the end. Regal was awake and ready, dressed up in his best attire, when Keir returned from flying. The two headed out, holding hands as they flew over the city. They made their way toward Navy Pier to ride the Ferris Wheel. They stepped into line and looked up at the gondolas as they rose into the sky. The sight of it filled the angel with mixed emotions: joy, bitterness, envy, and hurt.

They slowly made their way to the front of the line. Regal paid the attendant and held open the door for Keir to step inside. The gondola swung as they took their seat. Keir gripped the metal pole that stuck out from the center as the Ferris Wheel began to move. He wasn't used to the sensation of being in the air without having to use his wings. The vertigo made him uneasy, and he wanted to slip his wings out to balance himself.

"It's okay, you won't fall out," Regal said as he leaned back in his seat. Keir watched him with anxious eyes, wondering how the demon could be so calm. However, he could see the incubus shuddering when the gondola would swing to a halt. It comforted Keir to know that Regal was also on edge.

When they slowed to a stop at the top of the Ferris Wheel, they felt calmer and were able to relax. Regal slid over to the side where Keir was sitting. The movement caused the gondola to swing, leaning to the side where all the weight had shifted. Regal rested his arm around Keir's shoulders, keeping him close as the angel tensed up.

"Looks like you guys are in need of some extra weight," Etoile said as he flew over to their gondola and landed lightly inside. Keir jumped at the sudden company, pressing himself against Regal. The incubus was also startled, but seemed overjoyed.

"Etoile! What are you doing here? I thought you said you had plans tonight," Regal asked, leaning forward to clasp Etoile's hand.

"Plans change." Etoile shook his synthetic feathers, folding them against his back. He then dropped his invisibility charm. "So, who's your friend?"

"This is Keir." Regal rested his hands along Keir's shoulder blades to coax him into keeping his wings hidden. "He's a fledgling demon."

Keir looked at Regal with wide eyes, holding his breath with anxiety. *He's thinks I can pull off being a demon?*

"So you're taking on that job now?" Etoile said with surprise. "Man, you've grown up."

"Well somebody had to after you left," Regal joked.

Keir sat silently next to Regal, stiff and uncertain that this ruse would work. He tried to sense Etoile's motives, but the demon wasn't putting off any negative vibes. He seemed to believe that Keir was a fledgling.

"So, what sin are you?" Etoile asked, looking over to Keir.

"Uh..." Keir hesitated, looking over at Regal out of the corner of his eyes. Regal glanced over at him, a flash of worry in his eyes. "I'm an incubus," Keir lied, coughing as the words caught in his throat. "I mean, why else would Regal be my mentor?"

"Well, I trained Regal when he was little even though we didn't share sins."

"I'm not that generous." Regal laughed. Etoile laughed in response as well. Keir chuckled nervously. Everyone sounded tense.

"Well, I'm happy to hear you think that." Etoile stretched and looked out toward the shore of Lake Michigan. "So, do you guys mind a third wheel?"

"Yes," Keir said at the same time Regal said, "not at all."

The three sat in uncomfortable silence, their eyes flitting back and forth between them.

"I mean... give us a moment." Regal leaned in close to Keir as Etoile turned to face away from them. "What's the matter?"

"I don't want him around," Keir whispered sharply.

"I know you want to spend quality time together, with just us, but he's not all that bad. I think you'd grow to like him if you took the time to get to know him."

"I don't doubt that he is a great person," Keir replied. "But I don't feel comfortable with him being around."

Regal knit his brow in confusion. "Are you afraid of him influencing you? You don't have to, you've already combatted sloth before. Being around him won't make you... you know. It won't hurt you."

"It's not that," Keir said loudly, causing Etoile to glance over at them for a moment before looking away.

"Then what is it?"

"I want your undivided attention," Keir said firmly.

Etoile stretched as the Ferris Wheel began to move again. Regal glanced over at him, a worried look on his face. Keir narrowed his eyes, wary of their relationship. He faced Etoile, steeling himself. "Etoile, you need to leave."

The demon's green and gold eyes widened in surprise. "What's the big deal?"

"You and Regal have had all week to hang out and catch up. It's my turn now to spend time with him."

"Do you know how long it's been since I've seen him?" Etoile challenged, his eyes flashing as his metallic wings shuddered. "Nearly half a century. I think I deserve some quality time with my old apprentice."

"It's your fault you let your sin get the best of you," Keir barked. "I bet you stopped training him because you simply got too lazy. Well, you had your chance and blew it. I will not blow mine."

Regal sat stiffly between the two of them, his gray eyes flitting back and forth as he watched the two forces clash. The corners of his lips twitched as he held his tongue, his gaze shifting to look at the humans who were curiously peeking over the edge of their gondolas to listen to the argument.

"So you think you can just have him all to yourself?"

"Yes, and I will."

Regal stood up, his eyes gleaming as the gondola tilted from the shift in weight. Etoile looked up at him and sighed, standing up as well.

"I get it. It's over," Etoile said as he turned invisible and launched himself from the Ferris Wheel, causing the gondola to shake and rock. Regal fell into his seat beside Keir, his wings flaring out to balance him.

"I'm sorry," Regal apologized as the Ferris Wheel began to move again. "I know I've been saying that a lot lately, but I didn't realize he'd cause so much trouble."

Keir didn't reply, still bristling from the encounter. The two climbed out of their seat and headed back down the pier. Regal brushed his hand against Keir's, trying to comfort him, but the angel pulled away.

"Do you still want to have quality time?"

"Let's just go home."

Keir and Regal were silent once they returned to the apartment. Keir went off to the bathroom to shower and wash away all of the negativity that was building up within him, leaving Regal alone in the living room. He stood under the spray of the shower, not feeling the energy to go through the motions of washing.

Damned sloth, he thought to himself as he turned off the shower after only ten minutes. He dried himself off and changed back into his clothes, leaving to go lay down on the couch. As he passed the bedroom, he heard Regal's voice laughing and murmuring through the wall.

The angel paused, eavesdropping on Regal's conversation. He couldn't make out any words, but he could definitely hear the chipper tone in his voice. Keir walked up to the door and pressed his ear against it, straining to make sense of Regal's conversation.

"That was so ridiculously easy," he said gleefully. "I don't think he ever caught on."

Keir's stomach dropped. Etoile's voice lingered in his mind. They had tricked him.

Regal lied.

Again.

Keir squeezed his eyes shut, biting back the pain. *Fool me twice...*

"I'll be in trouble when he does find out," Regal continued.

You're damned right!

Keir kicked the door open, his halo glowing through his jeans. The door slammed back and bounced off the wall, leaving a hole where the doorknob hit. Regal jumped off his bed as Keir stormed in. He grabbed the cellphone from Regal's hand and threw it across the room, smashing it against the wall and cracking the screen.

"Keir! I thought you were showering!" It was the first time Regal looked genuinely surprised in a long time.

"You lying bastard," Keir hissed, his wings flaring behind him. Regal could clearly see the black feathers littered among the gray.

The incubus' look of shock melted away as a grin of ecstasy and pride grew on his face. "No kidding."

Keir shoved him back down onto the bed. "What is he?"

"Guess!" Regal laughed, unable to contain the glee that he had been holding inside the entire night. "What do you think he was?"

The vicious mocking tone of Regal's voice grated Keir's ears. The sins he had accumulated rapidly cycled through his mind: gluttony, sloth, envy, pride...

"Do you need a hint?" Regal taunted. "He barely had to influence you. You were already so needy to spend time with me."

Keir's eyes glowed a vivid blue as he let out a guttural hiss as he realized the sin he fell to so willingly.

"It was so easy to make you jealous enough to act on your greedy thoughts," Regal gloated. "It was a nice change. I barely had to lift a finger."

He raised his fist to slam it into the demon's face, but Regal was prepared and was able to grab Keir's wrist to hold his attack back. He dug his claws into Keir's hand as he felt his own rage building up inside of him.

Then more gray feathers started to turn black before Regal's very eyes. He stopped struggling, watching in awe as the black seemed to blossom from the base of the feathers and drip down to the tip until it was completely black. Etoile was right: Keir was succumbing to wrath.

Keir broke free from Regal's grip and socked him in the face. This time, he didn't flinch as he felt the wave of pain hit him as well. Instead, he continued to wail on Regal; he let out all his anger, his hurt, his sorrow. Every negative feeling fueled his attacks. Keir had never felt so angry before. Even when he first learned he was having sins placed on him, he had not felt any anger or resentment. He had only felt pain and betrayal. Now he was blind with rage, determined to make the demon pay for what he had done.

Regal sat back and took each hit. He didn't want to risk interrupting Keir's anger. The more wrathful and hateful the angel felt, the more tainted he would become. Despite the pain, knowing that he was so close to breaking his bond made it worth it.

The Art of Falling

Until Keir stood up and decided to give Regal one good kick for good measure. Regal saw the glowing halo seconds before it smashed into his chest and he was able to block it with his arm. However, it burned him and caused him to hiss in pain and finally push Keir off of him.

This time, it didn't burn as much. He wondered dazedly if the sins were affecting the power of the halo, or if he was becoming more pure with every blessing placed on him. It was a terrifyingly pleasurable thought.

Keir stood up and stared at Regal. He was panting and trying to regain his composure. He held back the urge to continue to beat Regal to a pulp. Keir knew that the demon had learned his lesson—or did he? Regal didn't show any sort of reaction except silence. Keir wondered if he needed to keep hurting Regal.

Keir, stop.

The angel paused and jerked back, stepping away from the bed. It was the first time he had heard Gloria's voice in a long time. The shock of it made him realize what had happened, and shame and despair overwhelmed him. This time he had allowed a sin to overtake him without Regal's involvement. It was starting to become natural for him.

He fell to his knees, holding his head in his hands. His stomach twisted in knots and bile began to rise in his throat. He curled into a ball and buried his head in between his knees, trying to will back the growing nausea. Keir was barely hanging onto grace, and knowing that one misstep would send him tumbling into Hell terrified him.

"I'm sorry," he murmured, hoping that Gloria would forgive him. He knew that he could never forgive himself.

Regal looked over at the angel and frowned. Although he was only one sin away from completing his goal, the suffocating weight of guilt was pressing on him again. "Well, I deserved it, didn't I?"

"I'm not apologizing to you."

"You don't have to," Regal murmured as he sat on the edge of the bed, looking at the burn on his arm. It matched the permanent mark on his side. They complimented the lashes that laced his back from his father whipping him into submission and obedience. His purifying wings made them stand out.

He was riddled with scars, and it made him sick. He could handle mental or emotional trauma, but physical wounds were a sign of weakness and inexperience. They were a brand that screamed, *I am imperfect, I am flawed, and I cannot be in control.*

And for the first time, Regal wondered if Keir was feeling the same. Was Keir losing control? Was he traumatized by the sullying of his wings? Or was he more upset by the emotional trauma the demon had forced him upon: the kiss that made him fall in love, the seemingly endless sins that were dragging him down, the emotional rollercoaster he was being subjected to as he tried to save Regal from his own biology.

They were both damaged, unable to cope with their mistakes and the consequences that they'd brought. They were too broken to be fixed, brittle shards of glass that could never be glued back together into their original shape.

The only way they could heal was to create something new with the pieces they had left.

CHAPTER *Twenty-Two*

KEIR LEFT REGAL sitting on the bed, unable to forgive him for all of the pain he had caused. He flew straight to the nearest holy ground he could find. It didn't matter if it was a Catholic Church, a Jewish Temple, or a Muslim Mosque. He could contact Gloria regardless of where he prayed. He just needed the comfort of religion to soothe his him.

He settled for a Baptist church. Keir gently landed in front of the large wooden doors and let himself inside. He was instantly hit with a throbbing headache. The angel was shocked. All angels could step foot into a holy place without trouble. Only demons ever felt afflictions. Had Regal tainted him so much with sins that he no longer could feel comfortable?

Startled, he turned away from the church and took back off into the air. He was trembling and nauseated. The last place he thought he could feel connected to home was no longer safe.

Keir was alone.

Tears stung his eyes as he propelled himself up into the atmosphere. Higher and higher he flew, desperate to get away from earth. He wanted to go home.

"Gloria!" he cried, his voice rasping as he screamed. "I can't do this!" He hovered in the air as high as he could go without his chest feeling like it was going to burst from the altitude. His head continued to pound, intensified from the intense sun exposure; so that had been the cause of his chronic headaches. He sobbed, holding his arms tightly around him to try and hold everything inside. "He's changing me... I'll never be able to go home," he moaned in sorrow. He looked up, hoping he could find some comfort in the heavens above. "I need guidance. I need strength. I need..." he trailed off.

He needed Regal.

Keir hated that he loved the demon so much, how Regal was becoming more important than being loyal to Gloria, how much he had changed.

Maybe he had misunderstood his destiny. Maybe he wasn't meant to save Regal.

Maybe he was meant to fall.

A gentle breeze swept past him, tickling his skin. Although he was still confused about his path, he felt comforted knowing that Gloria hadn't abandoned him.

Meanwhile, Regal felt lost. He needed to figure out how to get Keir's trust back. Lust was the final sin. It should have been the easiest, with Keir's undying love for him and all. But would the angel really let him get close enough to commit such a deed after what had happened? He doubted it.

Soon after Keir left the apartment, the demon cleaned himself up and headed out on his own. He craved to feel the wind in his feathers. The sun didn't upset him as much as it used to. He knew to blame the light growing inside of him. He soared west, opposite of the direction he figured Keir would fly. The angel loved nature and would naturally gravitate to the lake. Regal needed the commotion of the inner city to distract his mind.

Below him, he could sense the energy of a hundred sinners walking the streets. He could gorge himself on gluttony, make himself drunk on lust, and drown his anxieties in wrath. The temptation was enormous, but even still Regal couldn't bring himself to hunt. The weight on his conscience was too much to bear.

Regal sensed an angelic presence coming near. He wondered if Keir had come to talk to him, or possibly beat him up one more time. He hovered mid-flight and searched for the angel, but could not see him. The sensation grew stronger, and Regal soon recognized it as a stranger's aura. Keir's was soft and kind. This angel radiated determination and strength.

Something heavy hit him hard in the back and sent him spiraling forward. He spun rapidly, his wings stretching to try and catch himself. The air tugged harshly at his joints as he was pulled back from falling. He spun and saw the blurred form of an angel diving straight back at him, a large golden sword gleaming in the sun.

Regal dove out of the way, gasping as the angel expertly angled his white and gold wings to boomerang back around to attack once again.

Who the hell is this? Regal thought tensely as he dodged another rapid attack. He felt the wind rush past him as the blade of the sword narrowly missed his wings. *Whoever he is, he's* much *stronger than Keir.* He fled from the scene, knowing that fighting an angel clearly above his rank was a death wish. All he could do was fly as fast as he could to safety, but where could he ever be safe?

Regal wove between buildings, attempting to lose the angel on his trail. However, his enemy sliced through the air with ease and was inching closer and closer. The angel swung his blade down to chop off Regal's wings. The demon was able to spin around just enough to avoid the full force of the attack. However, the tip had cut through his sweater and into his skin.

The demon cried out as a searing sensation overwhelmed him. His body froze in shock, his wings unable to move as he tried to breathe through the pain. He dropped like a stone for several feet until he was able to will his wings to catch him before he hit the ground. He looked up and saw the angel dive bombing at him. Regal hastily grabbed his pocket watch, opening up the side compartment to release black smog.

The angel burst through the cloud, swinging himself around

in a wide arc to adjust his position and attack again. However, Regal had used this cover to open a portal to the apartment.

He rushed through the gateway, landing hard on the ground as it closed shut behind him. He limped slightly as he looked around the apartment after nearly twisting his ankle from the force of his landing.

"Keir! Keir, where are you?" he called out, hoping the angel was home.

No response.

"Dammit!" In a panic, Regal turned to leap out the window to search for Keir, but he saw the glistening armor of his assailant mere moments before he could surge through the glass. Regal sprinted out the front door, racing for the stairwell that led to the rooftops. He broke the lock and let himself inside, slamming the door shut behind him as he ran up the stairs. He couldn't spread his wings and fly up; his wingspan was too large. It would slow him down, but it would slow the angel down, too.

Once he reached the top, he kicked open the door with his uninjured foot and limped out onto the roof. He looked behind him and saw that the angel wasn't following him.

Instead, the angel flew up around the side of the building and dove back at him from above, his sword armed and ready to run him through. Regal stumbled back and stretched his wings. He leapt up as the angel drove his weapon forward. The gilded blade drove into the concrete, cutting through it easily. Regal flew upward, watching as his attacker yanked his sword from the ground without any struggle. The angel threw his sword, and midair it transformed into a spear. The demon surged upward to avoid being skewered, but the spear pierced cleanly through Regal's thigh and embedded itself into the ground behind him.

The Art of Falling

Regal screamed as he dropped onto the rooftop, gripping the bloody wound as he tried to stand. Tears welled in his eyes as his body shook in pain. He looked up to see the angel snapping his fingers to summon his weapon. It returned in a shimmering mass of golden metal that reformed into the large sword.

This is it... Regal staggered onto one knee as he faced his attacker.

A gust of wind blew past them, kicking up dirt and gravel. For a brief moment, there was a sense of calm. Both were still, staring each other down. Regal took the moment to take a long look at the angel who was about to kill him.

He was dressed in golden armor decorated with white swirls and symbols. His halo floated above his head, defying all laws of physics as it stayed perfectly in place. His skin was as pale as his wings, and along his right arm were faded white tattoos. His platinum blond hair was cut incredibly short—not quite a military cut, for it was too choppy. His teal eyes were locked on Regal and were burning with retribution. This angel was a soldier of Heaven and was ready to exterminate him. Regal could see the resolve in the archangel's gaze, and he knew that this time he wouldn't miss.

"I'm going to die," Regal breathed softly. "But not without a fight." His hands trembled as he faced death, but he prepared his weapon regardless. He wrapped the chain around his hand as the pocket watch dangled beside him. Razor-sharp blades sliced out of the sides of the watch. The angel blinked slowly, accepting the challenge. He charged forward, his already-stained sword hungry for more ichor.

"Stop!"

Keir dove down and landed between them, his shield already drawn. Regal fell back as a wave of relief crashed over him. All of the blood that had seemed to drain from him came rushing back with a flood of adrenaline.

"Keir!" he called out, his voice drowned out by the sound of the heavenly sword colliding with the shield. Sparks flew off the metal from the impact, and both angels rebounded backward from the force. The young angel stumbled, panting as he protected Regal behind him. The demon could see that Keir was putting less pressure on his left leg. It matched Regal's injury.

"Don't hurt him!" Keir commanded.

"Keir," the other angel said. His voice was gentle but filled with power. It was more feminine than Regal would have first expected to come from such a strong warrior. The archangel's eyes were filled with sadness. "Your wings..."

Keir flinched slightly, his fingers twitching. "Are none of your concern."

"Of course they are. It is my job to diligently protect all of Gloria's archangels in training." He pointed the tip of his blade at Regal, scowling. "That demon is making you fall!"

"That demon is doing only what he thinks is right!" Keir argued. He swallowed the lump in his throat and tried to ignore his racing heart. *Wasn't that one of Her instructions? Forgive them, for they know not what they do.*

"Keir, you cannot use that to explain the motives of demons."

"Gabriel, you should understand that instruction most of all."

"Gabriel?" Regal gasped in shock, unable to hold back his surprise. He was facing one of Gloria's strongest archangels—only second to Michaelangelo. He was the perfect equivalent to Belphegor, the Prince of Sloth.

"Do not bring my family into this," Gabriel warned.

"Then don't meddle in my affairs!" Keir shouted.

Gabriel lowered his sword, but did not sheath it. "Keir, I heard your pleas. I can save you and bring you back home."

"I prayed to Gloria, not you," Keir snapped.

Regal looked over at Keir. The angel didn't glance in his

direction at all. For once, Keir was in complete control. It was a side of the angel he hadn't seen ever since Paris. The determination and confidence were astounding.

"If you hurt him, I will never come home," Keir threatened, his voice lower than Regal had ever heard it before. He sounded more like a fallen angel.

More like a demon.

"I know you may think that saving him is your only option," Gabriel said as he pulled a large serrated dagger from the belt around his waist. It was made of dark obsidian flaked with gold, with a dark leather-wrapped handle. "But this blessed blade was designed to cut the bond between two souls. It will free you without causing any harm."

"You won't stop at severing the tie. You will kill him."

"And you will be saved."

"I don't want that!" Keir stepped away from Gabriel, moving closer toward Regal. "I may long to come back home, and I may fear falling, but I need Regal more than I need Heaven." He narrowed his eyes, his mostly-black wings pumping behind him strongly. "And if you try to take him away from me, I will fight back."

The three of them stood in silence. Regal got to his feet, limping to stand beside Keir. Both of them gripped their weapons tighter, preparing to fight. Another breeze blew by them, breaking the crackling tension.

Gabriel sighed and sheathed the blade and his sword. "So be it. Your fate is your own decision, and I have to accept that. Just keep in mind everything, and everyone, you are giving up for that demon." The archangel frowned, his eyes sad. He reached into his pocket and pulled out an angelic nomad stone and disappeared in a swirling vortex of golden light.

Regal was bedridden for several days while his body healed from his encounter with Gabriel. Keir tended to him, but he often left the apartment to clear his muddled and confused thoughts. He was a mixed bag of emotions that constantly shifted from frustration to fear to determination—all of them stemming from his desire for Regal.

He could sense the demon had another virtue placed on him. Keir knew that Regal had succumbed to temperance when he allowed Keir to continue punching him during their fight.

Three more virtues and Regal was saved, but Keir had no idea how to accomplish that.

The angel decided to ask for some advice from his mentor. Regal was getting outside help; therefore, he should be allowed guidance as well. It was only fair.

One day when Regal was sleeping, Keir went out in the city. He flew over the water, trying to meditate and relax before seeing his mentor. After being gone for so long, he was nervous about what his mentor would think of him.

"Michaelangelo, I need your wisdom," he prayed as he watched the waves ripple across Lake Michigan and into the shoreline. He flew against the dense clouds that were threatening to release their rain at any moment. Dreary days like these always made him feel down, but at least he wasn't feeling any ailments from sunlight.

Across the water, in the center of the city, Keir saw a bright, twinkling light on the roof of the Art Institute. It was a familiar glow, one that he had learned to trust over many years of training. He quickly turned to head in its direction. As he came closer, he could feel the overwhelming warmth and comfort that came from the light. It surged with power and wisdom, and it made Keir feel somewhat uncomfortable. He knew it was something he should cherish, but a part of him was repelled from it, most likely due to his tainted soul.

He landed lightly, keeping his wings out as he looked for Michaelangelo. However, he was not there. Keir waited patiently, walking toward the edge of the building to watch the humans walking through the garden with their umbrellas. The clouds above began to drizzle, causing them to hurry for shelter. The light was gone. However, he could feel that he wasn't alone.

The angel looked up at the dark clouds that hung above him. The feel of the rain hitting his face was soothing, and his wings outstretched slightly to catch the droplets. He wished that the rain could wash away his sins. He would happily watch the black and gray melt away and leave him with sparkling white feathers.

"I don't think baptism is the answer you're looking for."

Keir turned and saw Michaelangelo standing a few feet behind him. Keir, who stood at five-foot-nine, seemed short compared to Michaelangelo. The archangel was dark-skinned, unlike his wings, which were a brilliant white with golden tips. The wing span was larger than most angels, and they radiated light like a beacon in the dark. His hair was a deep chocolate brown that was long and pulled back into a tight, low ponytail; it was a fairly formal way of styling hair. His bangs hung in his face, covering his eyes, which were an authoritative brown color. He had a strong jaw that was covered in stubble, and he wore old-fashioned formal clothes that didn't quite match the modern-looking platinum halo around his left wrist.

Keir kneeled instinctively, bowing his head. It was only proper to show submission to an archangel, even if the archangel in question was your mentor. "Thank you for coming," he said with a giddy smile before jumping up to hug him. "I've missed you."

"I've missed you, too," Michaelangelo replied with a chuckle as he hugged Keir back. "Heaven isn't quite the same without you there. Now how can I be of assistance?"

Keir wanted to blurt out all of his problems to his Michaelangelo, but fear held him back. Michaelangelo didn't know much—if anything—about Keir's mission to Earth. What would he possibly think of him now that he had fallen so far?

"I would never think poorly of you," Michaelangelo said, reading Keir's anxious thoughts. "It will be easier if you just tell me the truth."

"How much do you know about why I'm here?"

"Enough to know, but not enough to understand."

"Then you know about my feelings for Regal..." Keir said sadly.

"Yes. How you care for him and are doing everything in your power to save him."

"And I'm so close! I've been able to place virtues on him, but he's making me sin faster. I can't keep up. I'm afraid I'm going to..." Keir paused, unable to say the inevitable.

The archangel reached out and ran his fingertips along Keir's wings, brushing the tips of his feathers gently. "Don't lose hope, Keir. You have not fallen yet."

"But I can feel that I'm right on the edge. If I make a mistake, I will have failed."

Michaelangelo rested his hand on Keir's shoulder and bent slightly to look at him in the eye. "Everyone slips up from time to time. Humans, angels, demons... they all make mistakes."

"Not archangels."

"Even archangels," Michaelangelo corrected. "I've made plenty during my lifetime. The wonderful thing is that Gloria forgives them and welcomes us back. She will do the same for you once you save Regal."

Keir looked up at the sky as it began to pour. They remained silent for a while, enjoying the cool rain that drenched them.

Keir stepped closer to Michaelangelo, thriving in his presence. He wanted to ask his mentor how many sins were placed on him. He knew he was close, but having a definitive answer terrified him.

Michaelangelo answered Keir's thoughts. "Six."

Keir felt like he was punched in the gut. Six sins. He didn't realize he had fallen so far. He trembled, goose bumps covering his entire body.

Michaelangelo tried to soothe him by rubbing his back. "Do not be afraid, Keir. Everything will work to your benefit," Michaelangelo explained smoothly.

"To my benefit? How is this to my benefit?" Keir asked sharply, annoyance resonating inside of him as his panic continued to grow.

"You are influencing him as much as he is influencing you. It may be a close match, but I'm certain you will succeed."

"Lust is the final sin he has to place. That's his specialty."

"I am aware. But that is why I know you will not fall."

"Why do you have so much faith in me?"

"Because you have an advantage over him." Keir furrowed his brow, causing Michaelangelo to grin. "I haven't trained an idiot. Figure it out."

Keir groaned. That was one thing that Michaelangelo always did to bug him: hold back secrets and force Keir to figure them out on his own.

"It'll come to you in time. Perhaps you should forgive Regal and try to work things out with him."

"Last time I tried that, he pissed me off."

"Do you love him?"

"Yes?" Keir said with slight confusion. "At least, I think I do."

Michaelangelo laughed as he patted Keir's head with his hand. "Then don't give up. Love is a special thing to have. Just be patient with him. He'll come around eventually."

Keir smiled and wrapped his arms around Michelangelo's waist tightly. "Thank you for understanding," he said as he hugged his mentor. Michaelangelo hugged him back.

"I'm always on your side." The archangel stepped back and rested his hand on Keir's shoulder. "Now, go fulfill your duties as an Angel of Kindness and save him."

CHAPTER *Twenty-Three*

EGAL STRETCHED HIS legs. It took a full week for his wounds to heal, but he was now back on his feet and ready to finish his mission. He had ten days to make Keir fall for lust. A piece of cake for a skilled incubus, but he wasn't feeling as excited as he thought he should. His chest felt heavy with the guilt of knowing that he would be condemning Keir to Hell. His stomach twisted as his mind imagined the last of the angel's gray feathers turning darker until they were as black as the ichor that would course through his veins.

"Stop thinking about it," he mumbled to himself as he continued to stretch, shaking off the chills that consumed him. "You have to. You have no choice." If he didn't make Keir fall, the angel would make him ascend, and Regal would be the one ripped from his home.

Before he could make Keir fall, he knew he needed to mend whatever was broken between the two of them. He would never get Keir to fall to lust unless the angel forgave him.

It was sunrise. Keir had just woken up, and Regal had come back from roaming the city. He sat patiently on the couch, watching as Keir left the bedroom and headed into the kitchen. Keir made coffee for the both of them, and walked over to hand Regal a steaming mug. The angel had refused to change his normal sleep schedule, refusing to admit that the daylight made him uncomfortable. Regal couldn't blame him. He had been doing the same, forcing himself to go out at night even though it weakened him.

"We need to talk," Regal said.

"I think so, too," Keir replied. He sat down on the table across from Regal and sipped his sweetened coffee. For a while they sat in silence, neither of them knowing how to start the conversation. Regal cleared his throat and Keir twiddled his thumbs.

"Okay, so—"

"I forgive—"

They both paused.

"You go first."

"No, you go."

Neither spoke for another few seconds. Keir finally sighed and frowned. "I forgive you, for everything you've done."

Regal blinked in surprise. He wasn't expecting that statement in the slightest. "You do?"

"Yeah. I mean..." Keir took a sip of his coffee, trying to not burn his tongue as he organized his thoughts. "I just do, because I guess I understand why you acted that way."

"Do you really?"

"No, not at all."

They both got a chuckle out of Keir's response. Regal smiled, but it didn't linger long.

"Why did you continue to mark me? I understand why in the beginning, but why break that promise you made?" Keir asked.

Regal bit his lip. His fingers drummed along the side of the warm mug in his hands. "It was the only way I knew how."

Keir leaned forward, resting his elbows on his knees. "There's always other options."

"I don't get other options," Regal snapped. He saw Keir's face and apologized. "What I mean is... I have a lot to live up to. Jackal is my father. I could be one of the next leaders of Hell. I have to prove that I'm strong enough to do that."

The angel was surprised to hear Regal opening up to him. The demon seemed to deflate, his shoulders dropping as he stared down into his black coffee. It was hard for him to say such things; Keir was certain of that.

"I have similar pressures, too," Keir said. "I train under Michaelangelo. He's the leader of the Archangels."

"Yes, but Gloria will still accept you, even if you don't follow in Michaelangelo's footsteps. Jackal isn't as forgiving." Regal took another drink. Keir didn't respond, allowing Regal to keep talking. The demon leaned forward and set his mug down on the table beside Keir's leg. "Jackal... he's not like Hades," he continued. "Hades was similar to Gloria: forgiving, understanding, kind, even. Yeah, he ruled over Hell, but that was what he was created to do. Jackal is a combination of Satan and Erebos, and although Erebos is a lot like Hades was..."

"Satan is nothing like that," Keir finished.

Regal nodded. "Jackal loves me, but sometimes his affection comes out in strange ways."

"What do you mean?"

"You've seen me without a shirt on. You know."

Keir paled and frowned, nodding with understanding.

"I deserved the tough love treatment," Regal added. "I was a brat of a child that never listened to directions."

"So now you always listen?"

The demon shrugged. "For the most part, yeah. I mean sometimes I feel the desire to go against what he says, but if I do I risk being hit... or worse, being demoted from one of Jackal's favored demons and being just like all the other incubi in Hell."

Keir noticed Regal flinch as he mentioned the other incubi. Was he different from the rest of them? Did they not like him because of his status? "Would they not accept you?" Keir asked, no longer feeling timid about trying to learn more about Regal's past.

238

"I'm different from them. Mentally and physically," Regal said after being quiet for a minute. "First of all, I don't look like them. The other incubi have scaled wings that are similar to dragons, if they're lucky enough to even have wings. Mine are feathered, like my father's. I'm also not just some sex-hungry monster. I actually think about what I'm doing."

The statement surprised Keir. So Regal was aware of the humans he was hurting when he preyed on their souls. For some strange reason, Keir wasn't very surprised to learn that.

"That's why you don't target people who are... uh... easy?"

"My father wanted me to be a Prince from the moment I was born, so I've trained my entire life to become one," Regal explained, his voice becoming tense with resentment. "The other incubi go for anything they can sink their claws into. They focus on one thing, and that's to collect any desperate, lustful souls they can find. They put no work, no passion into it! I hunt the souls that will be challenging. I want to make my prey *think* they want me, not just cloud their judgment to *force* them to want me."

"Like the woman in Paris..."

Regal nodded. "I feel like I have to constantly work hard and prove that I deserve my title. I'm the youngest Prince in Hell's history, and I don't want any other incubi to look down on me because of my age."

"I never realized all the pressure you had," Keir said solemnly.

"That was why I kept trying to make you fall," Regal confessed, his tone softening. "It was the only way I knew how to make our relationship work while still pleasing my father."

Keir reached across and took Regal's hand in his own. The demon's skin was warmer now that his blood pumped a mixture of virtues and sins. Keir's hand, however, was extremely cold despite his sunny appearance.

"Do you want to make me fall?"

Regal stared hard into Keir's eyes. That was the hardest question he had ever been asked before. He didn't really know anymore. Yes, he wanted to make Keir fall and break the bond between them; but... he didn't want to hurt Keir anymore. "I..." he started before his voice quieted. Keir squeezed his hand reassuringly. "I'm not sure."

The angel felt a surge of relief wash over him. Keir's virtues were changing Regal, making him listen to his conscience and reconsider his actions. Perhaps all hope wasn't lost!

"Regal," Keir started. "Even if you wanted to make me fall, I would still love you."

"Seriously?" Regal asked, his voice laced with skepticism.

Keir nodded. "You're more important to me than falling or ascending."

Regal knew that this was his chance. He held back the rising urge to take advantage of the situation. Keir was doing all of the work for him. "I'm starting to feel that way, too," he lied.

They stared at each other in the eyes, letting the world around them vanish. Keir was on cloud nine, and Regal was teetering on the edge of victory. Just one more nudge, and he'd have Keir. *I'll be free.*

"Do you love me?"

"What?"

Keir asked again, "Do you love me?"

His first instinct was to deny such an accusation, but he knew what Keir wanted to hear. He smiled softly. "Yeah, I do."

Keir smiled in return. He was expecting that answer. He knew that's what Regal would say regardless of if he loved him or not. Keir wanted the undeniable truth. "Do you love me with all of your heart?"

"If you can call it one, yeah," Regal said with a chuckle.

"Do you love me with all of your soul?" Keir asked. He could see that he was making Regal uncomfortable. *Good. He needs a bit of a push.*

"Yes." He expected the lie to hurt, but it felt... comfortable—almost natural. He was able to admit it with ease. *Am I telling the truth?* Regal wondered. He didn't know what his heart felt toward the angel anymore.

Keir beamed, his smile spreading across his entire face. He hadn't looked this happy since Regal had marked him. The angel leaned over and kissed Regal, wrapping his arms around the demon's shoulders.

The demon stiffened, but let Keir continue. His hands naturally went to rest on Keir's waist, and he was surprised to feel Keir ease into the gesture. *Is he... .enjoying the contact?* he wondered. If that were the case, now was the perfect chance to mark him.

Grinning, he pulled Keir closer. To hell with slipping into Keir's dreams. He was confident he could get the job done in the physical realm. He expertly moved his hands up under Keir's shirt. He felt the angel shiver and paused. He pulled from the kiss and looked at Keir. The angel's face was flushed, and his lips were parted as he caught his breath.

"I'm fine," Keir said. Regal nodded and drew the angel back in for another passionate kiss. He continued to run his hands up Keir's waist, across his back to run his fingers over the patches where his wings fell out, sliding back down to his hips to pull him closer.

The angel practically melted from the affection he'd been unjustly denied. In fact, he coaxed Regal on by moving his hands along the demon's shoulders and down his arms. His hands rested on top of Regal's, holding his hands in place on his hips. Keir wanted to be closer.

Regal stood up, guiding Keir to stand with him. The angel wobbled slightly, but never pulled away from Regal's embrace. The demon guided him backward toward the bedroom, allowing himself to give in to the emotions rising within.

CHAPTER *Twenty-Four*

THE BLINDING SUN woke Regal up the next morning. He sat up, rubbing his eyes tiredly. Ever since he had virtues placed on him, he hadn't woken up with headaches. The sun didn't affect him nearly as much. He hated that.

Beside him, Keir stirred, rolling from his side onto his stomach to bury his face in the pillows. Was he hiding from the light? That's what Regal hoped.

Memories from the night before sent a surge of excitement through him. He lifted the blanket and scanned his eyes over the angel's body in search for a sign. His fingertips brushed against the now dark patches on Keir's shoulder blades, trying to coax his wings out. If they were black, he won.

They slid out from Keir's back, unfurling slightly. Black feathers welcomed Regal, but they were no different from the day before.

What? Regal thought in horror. He sat up, jostling the angel as he examined Keir's wings. *That's impossible... I placed lust on him! Why aren't his wings black?*

Keir woke up, rolling back onto his side to look up at Regal. He smiled. "Good morning. I'm surprised you're—"

"How are you feeling?" Regal interrupted quickly.

"I'm... feeling great, actually."

"No headache? No grogginess? No sense of feeling heavy or worn down?"

"No, none of that. Is that what I'm supposed to feel after that?"

Regal was appalled at the sight of Keir practically glowing with happiness. There was no way this was happening. He stood up and walked to the dresser. His hands were trembling as he

242

opened the drawers and dug through the clothes. Normally he was comfortable in his own skin—literally—but now he just felt exposed and scared.

"It didn't work," Keir said. He could sense Regal's anxiety, and he knew exactly what was on the demon's mind. His heart fell as he wondered if everything they had shared was a lie.

"Impossible," Regal growled as he turned to face Keir who was still in bed. "We had sex."

"No, we made love."

"Oh, what's the difference?" Regal barked. "You should have succumbed!"

Keir narrowed his eyes. "The difference is the emotion." His wings fluttered behind him, showing off the fact that the sin hadn't stuck. "What I did was out of love and devotion. Lust doesn't include those qualities. Nothing can change that."

Dread overwhelmed Regal. He could feel every ounce of hope and pride draining away from him. Was Keir right? Was lust completely absent from love and devotion? Would the angel's intense feelings cancel out the effects of the sin?

"And, I'd even bet that the emotions behind your actions had those qualities, too."

It can't be true... Regal thought. But even he knew that it had to be. Keir hadn't fallen from grace.

Regal turned and headed to the bathroom, locking the door behind him as he shakily sat on the tile floor. He was trembling and felt clammy. His thoughts whirled and scrambled in his brain: *the last sin... he hadn't fallen... Keir was unaffected... love conquered over lust... a waste of time... lust could never work... I was doomed from the start.*

The horrifying realization hit him hard and it caused him to double over. Everything he had done was for naught. He would have never made the angel fall, because Keir *loved* him—honestly and truly loved him. Worst of all, Keir had managed to make Regal—

Keir knocked on the door. "Regal, are you okay?"

"Not now, Keir," he replied hoarsely.

"Are you sure?"

"Not now!" Regal screamed.

The angel didn't speak up, and the demon heard him walk away quietly. He rose to his feet shakily, gripping the porcelain sink. He stared hard at his reflection in the mirror hanging on the wall. He tilted his head to get a better look at his jaw and cheekbones. The soft tendrils from Keir's mark were fading. Unfortunately, he knew it was from his slow ascension and not Keir's rapid but plateaued fall. He snapped out his wings, examining the dingy gray feathers that were horribly littered with white. There were more white feathers today than there were yesterday.

I'm still changing... he thought miserably. He glanced over toward the closed door, knowing that Keir would be waiting for him in the hall. The desperate need to flee was overwhelming, and his anxious thoughts kept telling him that running away might be his only chance to avoid ascending—and Jackal's wrath.

He reached for his pocket watch and froze. If he utilized it, Keir would sense the surge in demonic energy and force himself in. He would have to fly. But Keir may sense that as well.

Regal took out his watch and left it on the counter. He was betting on the chance that their bond was weakening as they grew farther apart. Maybe it would keep Keir oblivious for a while—long enough for Regal to escape. He turned and threw open the window. He welcomed the morning air, a thought that terrified him. As Regal fled, he looked back and tried to ignore the pangs of loneliness and regret that stung his heart.

He shook his head, attempting to clear his thoughts. *Distraction, I need a distraction.* Getting his bearings, he headed west in a frantic desire to surround himself with sinners.

Only fifteen minutes had passed before Keir suspected that something was off. After getting dressed, he walked to the bathroom and knocked on the door again. "Regal."

There was no answer. Keir knocked again and called out to him. He focused on the energy he felt coming through the door. It was Regal's, but it felt different—mechanic. Keir knocked on the door one more time and shouted, "Regal! Open the door now!" When Regal still failed to respond, Keir kicked the door open.

The bathroom was empty, except for the pocket watch ticking on the counter. Keir recognized that as the source of the demonic presence he felt. Panic surged through him.

Keir rushed to the window and pushed himself out, trying to sense which direction Regal had went. It was a windy day in Chicago, and the strong breeze masked any trail Regal could have left. He knew he had to start somewhere, so he went to the first place he could think of. Keir grabbed Regal's pocket watch, jumped out the window, and flew toward Navy Pier.

Halfway to the Pier, Keir crossed the familiar scent of greed. He immediately turned and followed the trail until it ended near an electronics store. He landed heavily in an alley way, and immediately broke into a sprint the moment his sneakers hit the concrete. Keir ran straight for the store, nearly bumping into a couple walking out as he rushed in. He was hit with a strong demonic scent and followed it through the aisles until he found Etoile stocking one of the shelves. The demon turned toward Keir the moment the angel stepped into the aisle.

"Where's Regal?" Keir demanded.

Etoile seemed surprised, his eyes widening behind his glasses. "He's not with you?

"If he was, I wouldn't be coming here for your help!" Keir shouted.

"Shh, shh. Don't yell," Etoile whispered as he lifted his palms to quiet Keir. People around the store glanced toward them briefly. "Why don't we talk about it outside?"

"No way. As long as we're in public, you can't do anything to hurt me," Keir said sternly. "Now tell me, where's Regal?"

"I don't know," Etoile said sharply as he went back to work. "I haven't seen him since the Ferris Wheel ride. I promise."

Keir cursed under his breath and left the store. Etoile was no help to him, and he wasn't wasting his time stalling when Regal was on the run. He only made it about a block away when he sensed Etoile's energy following him. He whipped around, his eyes flashing with anger. "Don't follow me."

"Listen, I don't want to hurt you. I just want to help Regal."

"Then help me find him."

"I can't do that."

"Why not?"

Etoile crossed his arms. "You think I'm going to help you, the person who is making him ascend, find him? At this rate, you getting closer to him would only speed up the process."

"I don't want to find him to make him ascend!" Keir shouted with frustration. "I want to find him to—"

"To what?" Etoile interrupted. "To save him? From what? Himself?" The demon of greed grew angrier by the minute. "Regal never needed saving. He was never broken. He was loved and cared for before you ever wedged yourself into the equation."

"I didn't want this, either." The angel's eyes filled with tears as he thought about his past with Regal. "Do you think I wanted to fall in love with a demon? That I wanted to lose my first solo mission on earth? That I wanted to be burdened with such strong feelings of lust that I thought I would never feel whole again?" Keir held back a sob as he launched himself into the air, his wings lifting him high into the air. Etoile chased after him, worried that someone noticed them taking flight. The two spiraled into the air until they were above the clouds. Keir stopped and sobbed into his hands as Etoile came up beside him.

"This situation was forced upon me, too," Keir continued, his voice cracking as the pressure of being bonded to Regal crashed onto him. "Before him, I had a future. He ripped that away from me, and now I have to try and find a new future for myself... so I redirected the pain and transformed the lust into love until I believed it."

"Did you believe it?" Etoile asked. "When the bond was first placed?"

"At first, no," Keir replied. He rubbed his eyes, trying to stop them from tearing up. "At first, Regal was awful, and I tried to trick myself into thinking he could change. I tried to tell myself that if I could save him, I could save myself."

"What about now?"

"Now I see... he's not that bad. He's got a good heart underneath his pride and stubbornness. He's smart and cunning, almost to a fault, but he's caring and protective, too. He tried to make me fall, and he tried to hurt me, but he also made sure no one else hurt me. He said I was his property... but I think I was more to him than that. I like to think that he started to care for me in the end."

Keir realized then that he didn't want Regal to change. If Regal was an angel, he wouldn't be the person Keir had fallen in love with. Of course, he first fell in love thanks to a curse; but it had evolved and grown into a true love that he didn't want to live without. This realization fueled his desire to find Regal and to save him—not from demonhood, but from ascending. Regal was meant to be a demon, and Keir would help him stay that way.

"Can you sense where he is?" Etoile asked.

Keir shook his head. "I can't feel him anymore... I can tell he's safe and that he's scared, but that's it. I think our bond is weakening and making it harder to stay connected."

"I'll help you."

The young angel looked up at Etoile with red, bleary eyes. "Really?"

"I can tell you honestly care about him. You don't want to hurt him. I think that's noble." Etoile hummed in thought. "It's not my forté, but I could probably track him. It will take a long time to do..."

"I have a week. Or else Jackal..."

"Jackal will interfere," Etoile finished. "Okay, new idea. Hire a warlock or witch. They specialize in spells and could probably track him much faster than I could."

"I know a warlock in Niagara Falls."

"Pythos?" Etoile asked with disbelief. "I'm surprised you know him."

"Regal introduced me to him."

"That makes more sense," Etoile replied. "Pythos is a neutral being, but he normally doesn't work with angels. He wouldn't be my first suggestion, but he is powerful and has the resources to do the job. His prices can be high, though. Do you have anything of worth?"

"I can figure something out. I'm resourceful."

"Good. Do you have an angelic nomad stone to travel?"

Keir shook his head. Only archangels were given angelic nomad stones to travel. Keir chose to go after Regal instead of finishing his training.

"I can get you there, but I can't get you back." Etoile pulled out his fountain pen and began to draw a portal in the air. The ink clung to the air particles and created a portal stable enough for Keir to travel through.

"Thank you for your help," Keir said as he hovered in front of the jet black gateway.

"Before you go, can I know what sin he couldn't place on you?" Etoile asked.

Keir smirked. "You're smart. I'm sure you can figure it out." The angel dove into the portal. He swore he heard Etoile make a comment about him being a smart ass before the portal closed behind him.

CHAPTER *Twenty-Five*

REGAL LANDED ON top of the Luxor hotel, balancing on the tip of the pyramid delicately as he looked around. It was approximately six in the evening. The Las Vegas Strip was everything he expected it to be; nothing but resorts and casinos. He could feel the thrum of sinners breeding here, feeding off of their vices. It was delicious, and it made him feel normal again to be surrounded by such terrible influences. This was definitely the place to be for a demon. He wanted to bury himself deep in this city and rid himself of these virtues.

Carefully, he scaled his way down the sides of the Luxor before leaping off to glide down behind one of the many buildings. Once on the ground, he pulled his wings in and slipped into the streets, taking in a deep breath. He could smell the sins brewing as tourists and locals alike began to stir from the depths, eager for the night life that would be coming in a few hours. He wanted to hunt, but with his promise to Keir still in effect, he would have to focus on stopping the virtues within him from spreading the old-fashioned way.

Getting laid would do the trick. He just had to find some slutty girl or horny guy to hook up with. It was still too early to do that, so he decided to bide his time doing other devious activities.

Regal walked into the nearest casino, flashing his ID at the door before going inside. The sounds of roulette tables spinning, coins jingling, and slot machines dinging greeted him. His eyes adjusted quickly to the dim lighting as he tried to decide where to start his evening. He wasn't one to gamble, but it was never too late to try something new; especially when he was so close to ascending.

Anything to stop the virtues.

There were many games to choose from: Slots, Texas Hold'em, Blackjack, and Craps... he didn't know where to start. He had always been decent at poker, thanks to Etoile teaching him how to play when he was a child. As he made his way over to the table, he noticed that the dealer was a handsome, blue eyed blond. Regal felt a knot form in his stomach, and he instantly changed direction. Across the room he saw a group of people standing around the iconic black and red Roulette wheel.

Regal reached into his wallet and pulled out a one hundred dollar bill and handed it to the roulette dealer. After he was given his chips, Regal placed a twenty dollar bet on the number six. He crossed his arms and leaned against the table, watching with narrow eyes as other gamblers placed their bets.

"No more bets," the croupier called out before spinning the wheel and dropping the ivory ball. Regal watched as it spun round and round. He felt his heart race as the wheel began to slow. The ball landed on seventeen.

Regal sneered as the dealer collected all of the chips. No one had won that round. Almost immediately, people were placing more bets. Regal joined in, placing another twenty on six again.

"You sure you want to do that, kid?" an older gentleman grunted. Regal looked over to see him placing his chips in between the twenty nine and thirty two.

"It's my lucky number. I'll hit sometime," Regal replied confidently.

The dealer called off bets and spun the wheel again. Everyone's eyes flickered as they watched the ball bounce and fly around the wheel. When it slowed, it landed on four.

"Not so lucky, is it?" the man beside him said. Regal watched as the man placed another bet in a new spot. Regal decided to stick with his gut feeling and stayed with six.

The Art of Falling

The croupier spun the wheel as Regal watched with anxious eyes. The thought of wasting all his money on one number made him feel sick. The ball began to slow down. Regal sucked in a sharp breath.

It landed on six.

"Hell yeah!" Regal shouted as he pumped his fist. He collected his winnings and grinned, looking over to the man beside him. "Lucky six. Third time's the charm, isn't it?" The gentleman merely grumbled under his breath and placed another bet.

If Etoile were here, we could make a fortune, Regal thought as he counted his chips. He had almost made double what he started with, but he didn't want to push his luck with Roulette. Unlike some demons of greed, he couldn't manipulate the odds to work in his favor.

However, he didn't feel completely satisfied with what he had won. He cashed out, exchanging his roulette chips for regular casino chips before leaving the table to play a different game. He headed to the casino cage to trade in his chips for slot tokens. He had a feeling he could hit the jackpot. Once he had a cup filled with coins, he headed to the slot machines.

A group of boys passed by him. They were joking around, slapping each other on the backs as they made their way to the bar. One boy bust out into joyful laughter that made Regal's heart speed up.

Don't think about him.

Regal went over to the slot machines and sat down in the plastic seat. He put in the proper amount of tokens needed and pulled the lever. He watched the images spin until they landed in a mismatched pattern. No win this round. Regal repeated the process slowly, not wanting to waste all of his winnings.

The lack of windows and clocks helped the time move

by fast, and Regal soon found himself almost out of money. "That's impossible," he grumbled as he held the last token in his hand. He didn't even remember going through it all. He flipped the coin, watching as it spun in the air and landed back in his palm. He didn't want to push his luck. However, this measly token wasn't going to buy him any drinks. It was worth the risk of losing to take the chance at winning the jackpot.

A sudden, shrill scream made Regal jump out of his seat.

Keir.

He turned and looked around with wide and panicked eyes, searching for the angel. But was it in fear of being found, or to run to Keir's aid? He wasn't sure which. Instead of finding Keir, he caught sight of a woman winning a game of craps from across the room.

Regal shuddered. No matter how hard he tried to ignore it, the angel's presence—or lack thereof—was still getting to him. *Get him out of your head!*

He slid his last token into the machine with shaking hands and pulled the lever.

"I don't need a jackpot," he bargained, although he wasn't sure who he was bargaining with. "Just give me a cherry. One cherry and I can earn a few extra bucks."

The images spun, a blur of color that teased Regal with the chance of winning. They landed on a mix of images. Not a single cherry landed.

Regal hissed and slammed his fist on the machine, creating a small dent in the metal. Etoile's advice from when he was a young teen echoed in his head. *Don't ever use a credit card to gamble. That's the fastest way to lose everything.*

"He never said anything about buying drinks with it." Regal left the casino cage and headed to the bar. He reached into his back pocket to grab his wallet, but it was missing.

Regal stopped and searched for his wallet. It wasn't in the back or front pockets. He hurried back to the slot machines and then the Roulette table to see if he had left if, but it was nowhere to be found.

"Are you kidding me?" he shouted, startling a few bystanders next to him. He scoured each corner of the casino, searching for his wallet to no avail. If he had left it somewhere, it was taken by now. *How could I be so stupid to lose my wallet?*

Regal left the casino and walked the streets. He took slow, deep breaths to try and calm himself down. "What the hell are you so worried about? You're in Vegas. This is a demon's playground. Take advantage of it."

After his small pep talk, he switched gears from greed to lust. Now that the sun was setting, there were sure to be drunk people ready to be seduced by a handsome young man like Regal. He walked inside one of the bars lining the street, breathing in the mixed scents of flavored liquor, beer, and lowered inhibitions.

He chose the first person he saw: a young woman sitting alone at the bar. She had red hair that lay straight against her back, and tanned skin hiding underneath her tight-fitting black dress. He preferred blonde, but she was good enough for his tastes. He walked up and sat at the barstool beside her.

"Is this seat taken?" he asked.

"No, go ahead," she replied stiffly.

She's going to be a challenge. Just what I need. He sat in silence as he looked over the small menu of drinks at the bar. Should he play the gentleman, or the stud? The shy introvert, or the confident comedian? So many roles he could choose, but only one would truly win her over.

"What's a beautiful woman like you doing sitting all alone?" he asked without looking up from the menu. His eyes flickered over toward her to see if she had any reaction. Normally many girls would blush at the simplest compliment, but this red head had a fantastic poker face.

"Waiting for friends to come back from the hotel," she replied. She looked over at him, her gray eyes staring at him dully from behind her glasses.

Regal smiled and set his menu down. He leaned his elbow on the counter and rested his chin in his open palm. "Oh? What's taking them so long?"

The woman frowned. "One caught a stomach bug and the other went to take her back. I'm holding our seats."

"I see." Regal paused. He couldn't read her to figure out if his ploys were working. Her lack of expression made him uneasy. Sighing, he decided to dive right in. To hell with being subtle. "Well, it would be more fun to pass the time with someone."

"Yes, it would." She didn't move away as he leaned closer to her.

"How about you and I—?"

"Not interested."

He was taken aback. "I'm... I'm sorry?"

"I said, I'm not interested," she replied firmly.

Regal had to force himself not to freeze up. She wasn't interested? No woman ever said that to him before, except when he was a young fledgling attempting to seduce his first victim. It had been nearly seven decades since his last failed attempt.

It was time to pull out all the stops. He cleared his throat and ran a hand through his hair, pushing his bangs out of his face. He made sure he did this while he flexed his muscle—human women seemed to love men with muscles. He chuckled huskily, smiling as seductively as possible. Regal's gray eyes were hooded and stared directly into the woman's. He could feel that he was practically oozing with unworldly sexiness that seemed to draw the attention of other women, even the male bartender.

"Don't you think I'm worth a chance, beautiful?"

"No."

Regal couldn't believe what he was hearing. *Damn this woman.* Biting his lower lip, he tried to suppress the frustration welling inside of him. "How come?"

"I'm into chicks, not dicks. Now get out of my face before I kick your ass."

Strike three. Game over. Regal sat in silence for a moment and stared at her. He stood up and left without a word, his entire body numb from shock.

"She was a lesbian," he mumbled numbly. How could he have not sensed it? He had never failed to catch a human's sexuality before making a move on them. Why now? Was it because of the virtues? That was the only reason why he failed to accomplish the one thing he was born and bred to do.

A flare of anger welled up inside of him. "A lesbian!" he shouted as he picked up a discarded beer bottle off the street and threw it at a wall. It shattered and littered the ground with green glass. A man walked past him and he was certain he heard the stranger mutter "poor luck" under his breath. A human pitied him? How much lower could he fall?

I just have to try again... he thought as he stood at the crosswalk, waiting for the light to turn green. *That's all... just try again.* He tapped his foot impatiently, trying to ignore how rattled he felt from his unsuccessful first attempt.

Out of the corner of his eye he noticed movement. A young man, no older than twenty, was staring down at his phone. His hair, which was dyed a striking blue, covered his eyes, and green headphones were covering his ears and blocking out the noise of traffic. He walked past Regal, stepping into the crosswalk. Regal glanced over to the right and noticed a car speeding down the main road.

He's going to get hit, Regal thought suddenly as he was pulled out of his daze. He launched himself forward, reaching out to grab the collar of the man's shirt. He yanked back, forcing them both to stumble onto the sidewalk. The car sped by, its horn wailing as it passed.

Regal released the man's shirt from his grip. "Idiot!" he shouted, although he was unsure if the man could hear him over the music. His heart was hammering in his chest just as much as the young man's must have been.

The stranger turned and pulled his headphones off. His brown eyes were full of shock. "Oh my god," he said breathily. "I almost got hit!"

"Next time pay attention to the road," Regal continued to shout. His hands were shaking, and he wasn't sure why.

"You saved me," the man continued. "Holy shit, you just saved my life!"

Regal grimaced. "Yeah... whatever."

"Is there any way I can—?"

"No. I don't need repayment," Regal cut him off. "Just... just go and be more careful."

The young man nodded. The light turned green and he crossed the road with his headphones dangling around his neck. Regal sighed and crossed as well, pinching the bridge of his nose between his thumb and his forefinger.

"Idiots... all humans are idiots," Regal grumbled. "Always needing protection." He came up to the other side of the road and froze. He went rigid when he realized he had just saved a human's life. "No... no, no..." Regal sprinted down an alley way and hid in the shadows. He spread out his wings and curled them around himself to stare at the feathers.

The demon watched in despair as his wings turned whiter before his eyes. Humility, a virtue of selflessness and modesty, washed over him and bleached his wings. He stumbled back and leaned against the wall of a building.

He had committed a virtue on his own free will. Keir wasn't anywhere near him and he still did it. Distance wouldn't change the fact that Keir was still influencing him.

"What's happening to me?" he groaned pathetically as he tried to get a grip on the reality of his inevitable ascension.

CHAPTER *Twenty-Six*

KEIR LANDED ON the rooftop of the abandoned Niagara Falls home. Underneath its floorboards was the nightclub where Pythos lived.

Swallowing back his anxiety, Keir lowered himself to the ground. He walked around the porch to the front door and pushed on it. It was locked. Not wanting to cause any excess damage to the property, he made his way around the building and looked for another entrance. He noticed a partially broken window on the second story and flew up to it. Shards of glass were still intact and jutting out at different angles. Keir used his foot to kick out the rest before slipping inside.

The glass cut his hands and tugged at his wings as he wiggled in, pulling out a few feathers in the process. He landed heavily, picking out the shards from his palms. The skin began to heal over the minor wounds easily. He walked down the staircase and toward the basement. Slowly, Keir walked down, his hands reaching out to hold onto the railing as he descended deeper. He felt the familiar sensation of shadowy hands tugging at his ankles, trying to trip him, but he continued to walk steadily down the stairwell.

The last time Keir was here, he had to rely on Regal to guide him. This time, his eyesight adjusted quickly. His body was becoming more attuned to the darkness the closer he came to falling from grace.

As he made it to the last step, he could hear music playing, but not as loudly as the first time he came. It was different, too. Instead of electronic pop, it was classical. Slowly, he walked down the corridor and entered the empty club. No one was there, not even the bartenders.

The Art of Falling

"Hello? Is anyone here?" he called out as he walked across the dance floor. The space was a lot larger when it wasn't crowded with bodies. He looked around, searching for someone—anyone—who could possibly help him.

"Why hello there, angel," a familiar voice purred from behind. Keir's wrist was grabbed and he was pulled back into the arms of a familiar looking face.

"Pythos!" Keir said, startled.

The warlock smiled. "Indeed. And you are the angel that Regal marked. I could never forget such a face." Pythos began to sway along to the changing music, pulling Keir into a waltz.

The angel shivered as he was forced to dance. Although he wanted to back away, he didn't want to get on the warlock's bad side. He would play along, for now. Keir distracted his discomfort by looking at Pythos' arms. He was dressed more casually than the first time Keir met him. Instead of a full suit, he wore black slacks and a white dress shirt with the sleeves rolled up so Keir could see the black runes and symbols hidden within the tribal tattoos that decorated the warlock's flesh. The angel could feel the power and magic coursing through the marks on Pythos' hands.

After a few more moments of idle dancing, Keir decided to speak up. "Regal is actually the reason I'm here."

Pythos quirked a brow and chuckled, spinning them in wide circles. "I figured as much. I can't imagine why an angel would ever come to a place like this. Speaking of which, how did you get inside? The club isn't open until sunset."

"One of your windows was broken," Keir replied, stiffening in response as Pythos held him closer. His skin crawled as he felt Pythos' hands brush against him. He hated be so close to him. The only person he wanted to be close to was Regal.

The warlock smirked. "Sneaky. You were also able to get past my wards."

"I've been around demons long enough, I suppose," Keir replied as he resisted being dipped backwards.

Pythos let go of Keir and stepped back. "Where is Regal, anyways? I'm surprised you're not with him."

"He ran off. I'm trying to find him, and I thought..."

"You need someone to track him, hmm?" Pythos' eyes glistened with excitement. He clapped his hands, turning off the music before crossing his arms. "I rarely get the opportunity to work for your kind, and believe me I am thrilled to be of assistance to one of Gloria's children, but I can't give you special treatment. My help comes at a price."

"What do you want?" Keir asked eagerly, ready to give anything.

"It's not what I want. It's what I think will be worth the service." Pythos lifted his hand and dangled Regal's pocket watch between his fingers. Keir widened his eyes and the light bounced off the surface. The warlock had pick-pocketed him while they were dancing.

"This can be sold for a very large price, so this will be good enough," Pythos said as he slipped it into his coat pocket.

"I can't give you that. It doesn't belong to me."

"I know who it belongs to and what it does. I think it's a fair deal, especially since you're looking for its owner."

"Isn't there anything else you could take?"

"That pretty pendant around your neck, perhaps."

"That's not for sale, either."

"If you're not willing to pay for my services, then leave," Pythos snapped.

Keir groaned. Pythos' price was too high, but Keir *had* to find Regal and the warlock was his only option. "Fine... keep the watch," Keir forced out, hating himself for giving Pythos the pocket watch. Regal wouldn't be happy about it, but Keir wasn't going to give up his shield.

The Art of Falling

"Interesting decision," Pythos said as he held out his hand for Keir to shake. He grinned as gold and blue sparks danced around their hands, sealing the deal. "Let's get to work." He took Keir toward a back room that was shrouded from sight behind a thick, black drape.

Keir felt nervous following him, but he knew that warlocks were neutral and he wouldn't harm him. His wings fluttered beside him anxiously as he looked around the room. It was small, but spacious. The walls were made of brick, and glowing lanterns hung from the ceiling, casting shadows along the floor. Gold and violet drapes hung from the walls, seemingly covering useless windows. In the center of the room was a circular rug with silver markings scrawled across it. At the far end was a large oak desk. Behind it was a wardrobe and an apothecary's table.

Pythos pointed over to the plush chair in front of the desk. "Please, sit down and make yourself comfortable."

Keir followed his orders and sat down. His knee bounced impatiently while he watched Pythos rummage through the many drawers of the apothecary's table. Pythos pulled out a small box and headed back over, taking a seat behind the desk. He set it down and opened it, pulling out a sharpened obsidian knife, a small bottle of a liquid that looked like water, and an old piece of wood that resembled an Ouija Board.

Out of all the materials that were brought out, the board was the most intricate. It was made of dark wood with different symbols burned in. There was a large oval in the center, with various numbers and letters surrounding it. However, the oval was filled with horizontal and vertical lines that created a map of Earth.

Keir watched attentively as the warlock took his time setting up the board, putting everything in their right place and murmuring under his breath some incantations. As he spoke, the hidden runes and symbols glowed white against the black ink of his tattoos. He opened the bottle and sprinkled some of the liquid over the table. It started to sizzle and smoke as it hit the board, making Keir jump slightly.

"All right, it's ready. Now we just need a source to track from." Pythos looked up at Keir with a gleam in his eye.

"What about the watch?"

"I don't want to damage the goods I just received as payment." Pythos lifted the dagger and handed it over to the angel. Keir lifted the heavy blade up to his hair to cut off a lock, but Pythos stopped him. "It needs to be something much more potent." His golden eyes flicked to Keir's cut-up hands.

"You want my blood," Keir said, his mouth going dry from nervousness.

"It's the strongest thing to work with. Even though you're still an angel, your blood is tainted with his sins."

Keir swallowed and glanced up at Pythos. He nervously took the blade and gripped the handle tightly, his fingers twitching. The knife gleamed in the low lighting of the back room. He pressed the tip against the meat of his palm and bit his lip. Before he could chicken out, he sliced a shallow cut into his flesh and hissed in discomfort.

The dingy golden blood beaded up at the seam. Pythos made a soft humming sound, obviously pleased at seeing it despite the fact it was heavily tainted. It almost didn't look like angelic blood due to how dark it was. He took Keir's hand and squeezed, making the blood well up faster until it dripped down his wrist and onto the board.

The liquid that was sprinkled on the board instantly began to affect the blood, causing it to bubble and split into two separate beads of color; one bead was a bright gold—much brighter than it was before it was cleansed from demonic influence—

and the other a dark black. The ichor began to run quickly toward the center of the board, coagulating into a ball the size of a marble. The angelic blood headed toward the compass in the left corner of the board and formed a ball there.

Pythos took two small glass thimbles from his coat pocket and placed one over each ball. He reached into his breast pocket and pulled out a handkerchief, handing it to Keir. "You can wipe yourself off now. It's all set for tracking."

Keir took the cloth and wiped off his hand. The cut was already healing over and hardly hurt anymore, but the cloth was still stained with his heavenly blood.

"Now what?" he asked as he handed the handkerchief back to Pythos. The warlock cracked his knuckles and his neck and waved his hands over the board for a moment with his eyes closed, trying to get a feel for the energy that each glass-encased bead held.

"I need you to focus. Think of his face. Think of his essence. The stronger the image in your mind, the more accurate the tracking will be." Pythos tapped the top of the glass encasing Regal's blood. "This will move to the location of where he is."

"And what about my vial?" Keir looked at the container holding his blood.

"We could do this without it; however, it does help make the process faster. It's more personal," Pythos mumbled shortly. "Now, no more questions. Focus."

Keir nodded, closed his eyes and tried to think about Regal: how they had first met, their first kiss, their bond, the first sin Regal had placed on him, when Regal took him to Paradise, how Regal would hide from the sun under blankets, how Regal always ate his burger before his fries at dinner, the way the Demon's feathers seemed to molt 24/7 and cause a mess, how peaceful Regal looked when he slept...

As Keir thought in silence, Pythos watched the golden vial begin to grow brighter, which in turn caused the black vial to begin to glow. It shimmered with violet, but golden light flickered from within as it vibrated on the board. The warlock was intrigued by the reaction, but didn't stop murmuring incantations.

It didn't take long for the vial to move. Keir's memories were strong and vivid. The ichor bead pushed against the glass wall of the thimble sized container, forcing it to head toward the west side of the board. At the sound of it scraping against the wood, Keir opened his eyes. He didn't stop thinking about Regal, where he might be, and what he must be feeling. He watched it slide a few inches before coming to a halt.

Pythos pulled out two caps, swiftly flipping the vials and trapping the blood samples inside. He wiped off his hands briskly before looking up at Keir. "There you go."

Keir looked down at the map with a frown. The black trail left by the ichor didn't tell him much of anything other than Regal had headed west and was still in the United States.

"This is it?" Keir asked sharply. "The best you can do is tell me the general area? It will take me days to search the western states for him.

The warlock grinned. "I can always tell you the exact location. However..."

"It comes at a price?"

"Of course."

Keir stood up and grabbed Pythos by the front of his shirt, dragging him closer. His wings spread out behind him, their feathers casting a dark shadow over them. His eyes were glowing a bright blue with irritation.

"I'm tired of your games," Keir hissed. "Tell me exactly where he is, or I will make you pay for *my* services." He held up the obsidian dagger he had snatched against Pythos' throat.

The warlock laughed as he looked down at the weapon. "My, you are bold. Regal really is rubbing off on you." He looked back up at Keir and sighed. "All right, my friend, I know when to back down from a threat. I'll tell you."

Keir released Pythos and watched him closely as the warlock fixed his wrinkled shirt and sat back down.

"He's in Las Vegas, Nevada," Pythos said quickly as he read the board. "Most likely stealing away another young woman's drunken virginity—"

Pythos barely had time to finish his statement before Keir was running out of the nightclub. He stood up from the table and took his prizes to lock away, wondering if Keir would be successful in his goal to find his beloved demon before it was too late.

CHAPTER *Twenty-Seven*

THE SOUND OF music over the speakers and loud laughter and chatter filled the tavern. Terrible karaoke was being held near the bar area, which is where the demon of greed lazily swirled his tall glass of beer. Etoile sighed and watched the humans laugh and drink as they ate, sang, and bowled. The occasional sound of pins falling down, followed by loud laughter, made Etoile rub his temples. He really wasn't the type to be in this kind of crowd.

However, he was on a date of sorts. He would have never decided to choose a random bowling alley/tavern in the middle of Kansas of all places, but his partner had asked to meet up here. Etoile took a large swallow of his drink, hoping it would help his headache just a bit. Unfortunately, it did nothing to soothe his ears against a familiar, shrill laugh behind him.

"Ettie, you actually showed up?"

Etoile grimaced at the pet name and turned to look over his shoulder at Viraine. "I may be a demon, but I do have manners."

The glutton rolled her eyes and sat beside him, waving over for the bartender. "Who needs manners when you're as old as Jackal himself?"

Etoile growled lowly at that and took another drink, guzzling down the last few drops. He silently pleaded for the alcohol to kick in. He knew he would need something stronger. He ordered himself a cocktail while Viraine ordered a dirty martini and a plate of cheese fries for herself.

"You should lay off the carbs," Etoile said. "They'll go straight to your thighs." He knew that the glutton was self-conscious of her figure, despite her sin. It was a low blow, but she mocked his age, so she deserved it.

The Art of Falling

She growled lowly and ate another fry before pushing the plate away. "You're probably wondering why I wanted to meet you here."

"Certainly not to make yourself fat."

"If you make one more comment about my body, I will rip your throat out."

Etoile took another drink of his cocktail. "Well, you gluttons do thrive here." He drummed his fingers on the bar. Taverns were not the place for greedy people.

"You've got that right," she said with a grin, her shark teeth glistening. "Plus I thought it'd be fun. Grab a few drinks, bowl for a while, and catch up on old times?"

Etoile couldn't stand the way she would try to suck up to him and make him like her. "Fun for you," he grumbled as he took his cocktail and drank a bit.

"More fun than sitting around playing video games all the time," Viraine snickered as she ate the olive of her martini first.

Etoile sighed and turned to watch the humans. They were far more entertaining than Viraine. Her sense of humor—if her sarcastic attitude could be considered humor—did not match his own; he was far more sophisticated than that.

"Ettie—"

"Don't call me that."

"Want to bowl?"

He lazily rolled his head to look over at Viraine. Her orange eyes glittered playfully, and her grin seemed innocent. Etoile knew better not to trust that smile.

"I'm not the athletic type," Etoile said simply, sipping his drink again as he kept his gaze locked on her.

Viraine groaned and rolled her eyes. "It's just bowling. I'm not asking you to play football or run a marathon," she complained, getting out of her seat to go grab one of the bowling balls off the rack. "You used to be so much fun, Ettie."

"That was when you and Regal were children and I could entertain you with a game of checkers," Etoile grumbled as he set his drink down and followed after her.

She grabbed a bowling ball and tossed it toward him, laughing when he scrambled to catch it and made a grunt as it hit him in the stomach. He glared at her, but kept his cool as she rented out bowling shoes for the both of them.

"You go first, Ettie," she purred as she rolled her ball between her hands.

Etoile sighed and stepped into the alley, nearly losing his balance as the bowling shoes slipped on the waxed floor. He stood at the front of his lane, a frown locked on his face. He aimed the ball before swinging his arm back and practically throwing it down the lane. It made a loud bang as it connected to the floor and crashed into the bowling pins.

"Wow! You've got some game! I thought I'd be a shoo-in to win," she chortled as she watched his first set go down in a strike.

The comment made him grin just a bit. "I'm not completely uncoordinated." Etoile walked back to his seat and took another sip of his cocktail as he watched Viraine bowl her first set. She, too, managed to get a strike, and beamed at him coyly as she sauntered back.

This continued on, back and forth, for the entire game. Etoile would get a strike, and Viraine would match it. They ordered more drinks—although Etoile switched to soda once he felt that he had met his limit.

It was this mature and responsible attitude that was driving Viraine insane. One of her favorite pastimes was to irritate Etoile. She adored seeing the geezer's synthetic feathers ruffled. However, she didn't ask him to meet her at the bar just to play tricks on him; she had more serious goals to accomplish.

The Art of Falling

Viraine wanted information. She had been keeping an eye on Regal ever since she last saw him in New York City. The moment she sensed his essence had left, she was tracking him. She was able to follow him from Niagara Falls, to the Upper Peninsula, to Chicago with the help of some demonic informants that had noticed his presence. By the time she arrived in Chicago, he had been on the move again, and this time the trail had faded too much for her to trace on her own.

She planned on her next informant being Etoile. She was 95% positive that the two demons would have caught up during Regal's stay there. She had questions, and she hoped to get him drunk enough to spill the beans; just like when he first told her about Regal's affair with the angel.

So the moment she realized that their boring game of bowling was not getting him to loosen up and that he was done drinking human alcohol, she knew that it was time to kick her antics up a notch.

As Etoile aimed his final bowl for their game, Viraine opened up one of the mouths in her hand. The teeth ripped open the flesh and stretched the meat of her palm. A black tongue slithered out of the mouth, carrying a small vial of demon liquor laced with heavy amounts of gluttony. It was extremely sweet in taste, and she knew the syrupy flavor of Etoile's soda would block it. Her liquor of choice wasn't very alcoholic. It was the equivalent of a shot glass filled with beer. However, she was not looking for potency. She was looking for addiction.

The glutton swished the cup around as Etoile aimed and put all of his focus on winning. Once she was finished, she dropped the vial back into her palm, sealed up the opening in her palm, and smiled innocently as Etoile came back to the table.

"My turn!" Viraine grabbed her ball, skipped down to the

lane, and let herself miss the strike and the spare. The moment the ball left her hand, she turned to look back over at Etoile, who was taking another drink of his now-laced beverage. "Aww, you won. I want a rematch."

Etoile groaned and shook his head, rubbing his eyes with his fingertips to soothe his irritation toward her. "I'll pass on that," he said quietly as his bi-colored eyes flickered up to her.

She smiled and walked over to pat the top of his head. "You're so old you can't even handle playing another round," she harassed, snickering when Etoile flashed a cold glare in her direction. She hurried off to order another round of drinks and some appetizers to snack on. She walked back and slid into her seat, sliding the drink over toward him.

Etoile pushed it back. "I don't want any more alcohol." However, Viraine wouldn't take no for an answer.

"Oh come on, we're *demons*. We can hold our alcohol better than any of these humans. One more won't hurt," she persuaded. Etoile sighed, his eyes moving between the drink and Viraine for a moment before he took it. Viraine drank as well, grinning behind her glass as she watched him guzzle it down easily.

The glutton-based alcohol she had slipped in was doing its job. Soon, he would crave and desire more and more, and "one more" would soon turn into two, then three, and eventually he wouldn't be able to count the rest.

It only took about an hour of drinking to get Etoile drunk. Viraine had nursed her drink and was barely even buzzed in the end.

"How are you feeling, Ettie?"

"Pretty damned good," he chuckled, leaning against the table. "Probably a bit too tipsy for my liking, but like you said, I'm a demon and I can handle it. How're you holding up?"

She smiled, teeth flashing dangerously. "Absolutely wonderful! Although... I've been a bit worried lately." She pouted, allowing her voice to fade away as if she were nervous. It seemed to convince Etoile enough.

"Worried? You rarely like... ever get worried about anything," he said with a pause, seemingly trying to get his words to work together. His mind was a bit fuzzy, but he was certain that he could help Viraine enough to soothe her.

"Well..." she started, her eyes peeking up to glance at Etoile. "I saw Reggie about a month ago."

Etoile laughed and shook his head. "If he heard you calling him that, he would tear your tongue out."

"That angel you told me about was still with him."

"Oh Viraine, hon, don't worry about that. It's *all* under control. He's making him fall. He even asked me to help him out when I saw him in Chicago," he bragged.

"Oh, really? How is that going along?" she asked, trying to coax more information out the greed demon.

"It was going pretty good. The angel didn't even suspect that something funny was going on. He soaked up that sin easily," Etoile murmured as he took another sip of his drink. "But he is a slippery one. When he came to see me—"

"Why would that good-for-nothing angel go see you?"

"He was trying to find Regal."

"Regal isn't with Keir?"

Etoile shook his head. "Nope. He ran off once he realized that lust wouldn't stick."

"What?" Viraine asked in genuine shock. "Regal couldn't make him succumb to lust? How is that possible?"

Etoile shrugged. "The fact the two are in love probably cancelled it out."

"In love?" Viraine screeched, ignoring when some customers

looked in her direction. "That's impossible. There is no way that Regal would *ever* fall in love with an angel."

"With the rate he's ascending, it's not a big surprise," Etoile said sadly.

Viraine hissed and gripped the edge of the table angrily, her polished nails chipping at the wood as the mouths on her palms ate away at the table. *How dare that angel place virtues on Regal, especially after I had threatened him. Didn't that pest know who he was dealing with?* She felt anger and vengeance bubbling up within her. She would make that angel pay.

"V, this is genuine oak."

"I won't let Regal ascend."

"Why are you taking your anger out on this innocent table?"

"Not while I'm alive and breathing."

"I can't imagine wood being good for your health either."

Viraine growled and stood up. She reached over and grabbed Etoile's wrist, yanking him from his seat and out of the tavern.

"Wh-whoa, V! Where are we going?" he asked in shock as he stumbled behind her. Even wearing those insane high heels, she was quick and agile enough to move too fast for Etoile to keep up—at least when he was drunk and had no balance.

"That angel won't get away with making Regal ascend," she barked as she led them out of the tavern and onto the street. "We're going to find him and kill him if it's the last thing we do."

That made Etoile sober up a bit more. "Wait, wait! Kill him? Kill the angel? V, are you out of your mind? Do you realize what you're suggesting?"

She whipped around and growled at him, her orange eyes shining brightly in the twilight. "I am perfectly aware of what I'm saying. I will kill him, and I will save Regal."

Etoile dug his heels into the ground and pulled Viraine over so they were hidden from the crowd in an alleyway. "V, listen to me," he said as he held onto her shoulders.

"Don't touch me," she growled as she shrugged herself out of his grip.

"Plotting to murder an angel is against the Ethereal Kingdoms. It will get you executed, or even sent to Chaos."

"As princes of Hell, we have every right to protect our kind, especially other princes!"

Etoile laughed. "Are you kidding me? Being a prince means nothing."

The princess seethed in anger. "Excuse me?"

"Having this title is a joke," Etoile growled. "Look at the court, at what we've become. The only original princes still alive are Sloth, Envy, and Pride. Belphegor never did anything to begin with, Leviathan refuses to leave the Sea of Chaos, and Lucifer left Hell altogether because he thought Jackal wasn't capable to rule."

"Lucifer is a blasphemer."

"No, he's the only one who really gets it."

The two stared at each other. Viraine couldn't believe what she was hearing coming out of Etoile's mouth.

"Are you saying you're going to abandon the court?"

"I'm only saying that I understand why Lucifer left."

Viraine slammed her fist into the wall, cracking the bricks. "You traitor, turning against Jackal like this. What would Regal think?"

"Regal is the only one who should be concerned about his title. He's the one who will inherit Hell. Not us."

"I will inherit Hell," Viraine hissed. "Once I kill that angel and save Regal, he will see that I should be his companion. And you're going to help me."

"You're crazy," Etoile barked as he turned away.

"I wouldn't walk away if I were you, Ettie!" she yelled. "I have information on you that I know you'd never want to slip out."

Etoile scoffed at the idea. "What makes you think you've got dirt on me?" he challenged.

"Well first off, I know your true age..."

The greed demon scoffed, shaking his head. "No one knows my real age. Even I forget from time to time."

"...and I know you were honorably discharged from the Marquis..."

"I was severely wounded in the war against Satan. They wanted me to focus on therapy rather than continue training in the army."

"...and I know your *deadly* involvement in Hades' death."

He stopped and turned to face her. She had struck a nerve. "I wasn't *involved* in his death."

"Oh, that's not what I heard!" She could barely contain her excitement as she watched Etoile's eyes widen slightly. She could feel the panic rising up within him. "You know, elder demons are really bad at keeping secrets. Especially Envy's children. They may believe they're the queens of gossip and blackmail, but they've got nothing on me."

She paused, waiting for Etoile to get annoyed with her rambling, demanding that she get back on topic. However, he was silent, clearly dreading the idea of what she may have heard. It was satisfying to see the almighty Prince get knocked off his high horse.

"Let's just say that most of them were praising you for saving the Underworld from Satan," she teased, suppressing a giggle. "Some even believed you should have been named the new Ruler instead of Jackal."

"Is that all?" Etoile said with a nervous laugh. Viraine grinned at the sight of his own bitter curiosity getting the best of him. "Everyone knows I never wanted to rule the Underworld."

"Others think you were working alongside Satan all along."

"What?" Etoile snapped, his natural eye turning black with anger, while his green eye seemed to light up brighter. "How dare they? I would *never* side with someone who was threatening my home!"

"I don't know, Ettie, you sure were loyal to your Prince at the time, and he was one of Satan's followers. It wouldn't be too much of a stretch to think—"

"You don't know *anything* about what happened that day," Etoile growled. "Unless you were there, you don't understand the horrors I saw." He was trembling, hinting to the psychological damage he had to work past over the last several thousand years. Viraine found it satisfying to see him crack.

"Maybe not the details, but you are a threat to the throne by default. Either you betrayed your Prince and took his place, or you are a follower of Satan and working to overthrow Jackal." Viraine stepped back and opened her hand to release her umbrella. "I could easily portal back to Jackal and let him know that you've been plotting against your leaders long before he was created. Hell, I'll even throw in that you helped Regal with his mission despite orders to leave him be." She swung the umbrella in her hand and giggled softly as she watched him. "I wonder what Jackal would do if he found out..."

"You know that is all bullshit," Etoile argued defensively, his voice higher pitched than normal. He cursed her silently for getting under his skin. "I'm not going to let you blackmail me with lies to get what you want!"

"Do you really want to play this game, Etoile?" she dared. "Because all of the odds are in my favor."

It was now or never. She would need his help to take down the angel. Tension was high as they stared each other down, trying to size each other up.

After a moment, the eldest finally broke and gave in. He

pulled out his pen from his pocket and knelt down, drawing a portal to help them locate a warlock who could track down Regal. He was completely silent, but his aura was raging.

"Don't worry, Regal," Viraine murmured as she knelt beside Etoile. "We'll protect you."

CHAPTER *Twenty-Eight*

*I*T TOOK KEIR three days of flying non-stop through wind, rain, and sunshine to get to Las Vegas. His plan was to get there within 24 hours, but his body couldn't keep up with his determination. After he dropped out of the sky for the fifth time, he let himself land and rest. He had stayed at the first motel he found and crashed for only a few hours before checking out and starting his journey again. He repeated this two more times, effectively spending all of his money. Now he was tired, hungry, and broke on the Vegas strip.

He arrived late in the evening. The buildings were beginning to shine their multicolored lights, and the sun set over the horizon. The angel yawned and landed behind one of the many casinos and started to walk the streets despite his body's desire to rest. Now that he was here, he wasn't going to stop until he found Regal.

Luckily for him, the night didn't drain him of energy anymore. Instead, it recharged him enough to continue his search. The sinners that surrounded him didn't make his head ache or distract him, either. In fact, they seemed to draw him in. He found himself searching the bars, the casinos, and even the love hotels. He searched for the lustful essence that Regal always gave off, but any senses of lust that he felt were not the result of his gray-eyed demon; they were only humans or mythos who were struggling to pay the bills, or were lonely and in need of some physical attention.

For being Sin City, there didn't seem to be any demons here.

"Some hot spot," Keir muttered as he continued his search. He spent hours flying over the city, scanning every place he could think of. Although the darkness of the moonless night kept him awake—and how strange it was to feel comfortable in this environment—he was too fatigued to go any further.

He flew over a hotel and circled the building as he tried to find an entrance. He noticed a back door and landed, stumbling over his feet from exhaustion. He peered inside, searching for anyone or any security cameras who might notice the door opening. He wasn't as good as Regal when it came to sneaking into buildings, but he had learned quite a bit during their month together.

The angel heard footsteps coming toward him, but he wasn't concerned. He was invisible, and any human or Mythos who was cutting through the alley wouldn't see him. The footsteps stopped, and the breeze carried a dangerous and aggressive scent. *A demon,* Keir thought. Silently, the angel turned to look behind him.

At the end of the alley, he could see the silhouette of a person. The glowing lights of the main strip flashed behind him. Even with his improved night vision, Keir found it was hard to see the stranger's face. What Keir could make out was that he was very short, probably only five-foot-four at most. The demon's build was small and lean, though his shoulders were broad. He walked with a heavy gait, as if frustrated and lost. Keir's nose wrinkled as the demon's stench grew stronger. It was hot and spicy, like pepper spray. It made his eyes sting and his nose itch.

As the man came closer, Keir noticed his attire consisted of a dark brown hoodie that covered unruly ginger hair, and ripped and faded jeans that had holes in the pockets. His eyes were a deep auburn with golden flecks in his irises, and he wore a scowl on his face.

Keir was surprised at how young the demon looked. He looked like a fourteen-year-old human; however, he knew that a demon's appearance could be deceiving. After all, Regal looked to be around the age of twenty-six. Even Keir, who appeared to be in his early twenties, was already eighty-six. The only way to determine an angel or demon's age would be to gauge their power.

"What are you doing in my city, angel?" the demon growled. He was ready to attack anything that crossed him. He reminded Keir of a wild animal in a cage.

Keir raised his hands as a sign of peace. "Looking for a friend. Maybe you've seen him."

"Maybe I have, maybe I haven't. Either way, you should leave."

"I will, once I find who I'm looking for," Keir snapped. He could feel the demon's aggression growing, but he was too tired and too frantic to be polite. "If you have any information on his location, it'd be appreciated."

"What makes you think I'd help an angel?"

"Your desire for me to leave?"

The demon growled. "What do you want to know?"

Keir grinned triumphantly. "I'm searching for an incubus."

"An incubus?" the demon asked. His interest seemed to grow, but his hostile aura didn't waver. "Why would..." he paused and then hissed, his eyes flashing a deep garnet. "You're the angel everyone is talking about. The one who marked a demon."

Keir paled. Word was spreading fast through the levels of Hell. "Yes... I'm trying to—"

"You're trying to make him ascend!" the demon barked.

"I suppose I was—" Keir was cut off as the demon hunched forward with a guttural snarl. The sin of wrath exploded from the demon's aura. The scent gagged Keir, forcing him to stumble back and watch as the demon transformed before his eyes.

Long talons grew from the demon's hands. His face elongated into a lizard-like muzzle, and his eyes began to glow with an internal fire of rage. His flawless skin hardened and became scaly and green in color. His clothes ripped around him as he grew to the size of a full-grown lion. Spiked frills grew along his spine and crested on the top of his head and shook, as a shrilled growl escaped his fang-filled mouth.

Keir turned and bolted. The demon chased him down, its tail whipping and smashing against the garbage cans and boxes that littered the alley.

The angel spread his wings, pumping them as best as he could. His wingspan was too large to fit in the tight quarters, and he couldn't lift off. He jumped up onto a dumpster and tried to get into the air, but the demon's claws latched onto his leg and dragged him back down, throwing him into the cement.

Keir cried out as he hit the ground, the concrete scraping his body as he tried to crawl away. There was a gash on his leg that was bleeding profusely. The demon crawled over him, his jaws dripping with saliva as he stared down at his trapped prey. He opened his mouth and bared his fangs. Rows of sharp, angled teeth made for ripping flesh glistened in the dim light of the alley. The demon lunged forward to finish his murder when Keir twisted himself around and used his arm to protect his face.

He felt the demon's teeth clamp down on his arm and he screamed in pain. His hand gripped his pendant, and the shield instantly expanded. The edge of the golden disc hit the demon in the face and forced him to let go. Keir swung his shield upward and smashed it into the demon's head.

The demon of wrath hissed in pain. He slithered back, shaking his head as he snapped his jaws. He crouched and leapt as Keir stumbled back and leaned against the wall.

Keir met the demon's attack with full force, ramming

his shield up into the demon's face. He lifted his shield up, attempting to throw the demon over his body, but he couldn't support his weight with his wounded leg, and it gave way under him. They fell, rolling onto the ground. Keir tried to get to his feet, but the demon was faster and was upon him. Keir swung his body around, flinging his wounded leg into a large arc. His halo glowed brightly as it lodged itself in the demon's gaping mouth.

The effect of the halo was weak, but it left a decent-sized burn in the demon's jaws. He reared back and screeched in pain, stumbling and falling onto his side as he shook his head to try and soothe the blisters that were forming in his mouth.

Keir knew it would only make the demon angrier, and he needed to escape. The angel shrunk his shield to a pendant again. He forced himself to his feet and limped into the open streets. Pumping his wings, he hopped on his good foot to try and get airborne. Luck was on his side, because the demon's talons missed him as he flew up into the air.

Panting and weak, the angel flew to the nearest rooftop and landed heavily onto his knees. He groaned and rolled onto his back. His leg was throbbing and his arm was beginning to fester. Keir knew that the demon's jaws were most likely filled with bacteria or laced with poison.

He needed holy water to counteract the infection. He squeezed his eyes shut as he tried to remember all of his training. If he couldn't heal immediately, he had to stop it from spreading. He sat up and began to rip his hoodie to shreds. He took the strips of fabric and began to make a tourniquet around his leg and arm to try and stop any infection or poison from spreading. Keir cried out in pain as he tied a tight knot in the fabric.

How on earth was he supposed to find Regal when he was hurt this badly? He needed to find Regal, and fast. The incubus was in more danger now that Keir was wounded. *Can he feel this?* Keir wondered as he laid back and stared up at the night sky.

"Gloria, help me," he prayed, squeezing his eyes shut in agony. "Please heal me." He began to feel the pain ebb away, and although it didn't completely disappear, he felt the strength to continue. The longer he remained out in the open, the more likely the demon of wrath would hunt him down. He had to continue.

He had to save Regal.

Keir forced himself back up onto his feet and began to limp away toward the edge of the building. Luckily his wings weren't damaged, so he was able to lift himself up and into the sky after some slight struggling. He left the rooftop to try and find a safer place to recover.

Meanwhile, Regal awoke in his hotel bed. Numbly, he got up and stretched. He walked into the bathroom and got himself ready for the night. It had been a long time since he had spent an entire night out and about, and he was determined to get back to his normal sleep schedule. Once he was showered, clean-shaven, and dressed in a simple white t-shirt, black jeans, and a black blazer, he walked to the window. He couldn't see the moon or stars. The sky was polluted with light. With a sigh, Regal wished that he felt at ease in the dark.

Wait, there's no moon? Regal thought with surprise. Was the month already over? "Impossible! There's no way I could have wasted that much time doing nothing!" He turned and flared his wings, staring at his reflection in the T.V. screen. His wings were almost entirely white, except for a few light gray feathers.

He seemed to have committed another virtue.

"How the hell?" Regal yelled in anger. He paced as he tried to think of what virtues were left. Diligence and chastity. He cursed under his breath and threw the coffeemaker into the wall. He should have noticed he was committing chastity. He hadn't hunted or slept with anyone after the woman at the bar shot him down, but he knew it was probably growing within him ever since he met Keir. He had tried to avoid hunting for sport, and instead focused on Keir. Now it was coming back to bite him in the ass.

He groaned and sat on the edge of the bed. He closed his eyes wearily. He wasn't an incubus anymore; or at the very least, he didn't consider himself one. What sort incubus chose to avoid slipping into humans' dreams and courting them?

"The fight isn't over," he said bitterly. "So what if I have six virtues? I will never be an angel. I still have time to fix this." His vow felt hollow, and he knew he was probably in too deep to stop it. However, he was stubborn and prideful. It was those traits that got him in this mess in the first place. He would never give up, even if it killed him.

Regal left the hotel and began to fly over the city. He was determined to commit a few sins. However, not too determined, in fear of committing diligence. Unfortunately, after only an hour of flying, he had a headache. He couldn't stand how the night was actually working against him; it was demonic blasphemy.

He paused, hovering in the air as he looked down at the city. He didn't know where to start. He had already lost his touch in seducing women, and he couldn't gamble without losing everything he had. Regal felt lost, but he was too scared to ask Jackal for assistance. Was Jackal even watching? Would he really intervene once the night was over and his deadline was over?

A sharp pain shot through Regal. He screamed as dropped several feet in the air as his entire body went into shock. He managed to land on a casino's rooftop, but his legs gave out from beneath him. Regal felt like the wind had been knocked out of him as his arm began to twitch and burn. He looked at his skin, expecting a gaping wound to appear, but his arm looked completely normal. It only meant one thing.

Keir was hurt.

Regal stumbled to his feet, limping as he leapt back into the air. He could sense that the angel was in the city. The pain was too strong to be long distance. Regal had no idea where to start searching, but he knew he had to find him. Keir was in trouble and needed to be protected.

He started heading east toward Chicago. Regal knew that Keir would have tried to track him. He was certain he could catch his trail at some point.

It wasn't long before the scent of angel blood in the wind caught his attention. His stomach dropped as he swooped down to head straight for the source. He was afraid of finding Keir almost dead, but he knew that if the angel died, he would die as well. Regal's head still felt clear, so he knew he wasn't close to death just yet. That meant Keir was safe for the time being.

As he came closer to the rooftop where Keir had been, the stench of blood grew stronger. It didn't have the same aura as it did when it was coursing through Keir's veins. This smelled pungent: sickly-sweet and rotten. It made Regal's stomach churn. He saw the dull gold blood pooled on the rooftop. He landed and knelt down, running his fingers through the puddle. He rubbed it between his fingertips and frowned. It was stale, but still fresh enough to be wet. It was dull gold color that was tainted almost black, and it smelled heavily of Keir.

He got up and ran in the direction of the trail of blood Keir had left when he fled from the roof top. It hurt to walk on his tingling leg, but he ignored the pain. He didn't have time for pain. He had to save Keir.

Regal leapt off the building and soared across the city. His wings pumped strongly, forcing him to fly faster than he ever had before. His chest ached and his heart pounded. Was this what love felt like? Demonic love was violent and aggressive, a game of power. This was warm, kind, and determined. It caused Regal to put his own life on the line to try and save Keir.

He circled over the city, keeping his eyes peeled for any trace of Keir as he followed the trail. As he flew over the Bellagio Fountains, a strong scent of wrath hit him. He noticed the demon of wrath huddled in the shadows behind the water feature. Regal landed heavily and stormed up beside him. The unfamiliar demon looked up and growled. His face was swelled from Keir's halo.

"What do you want?" the demon asked as Regal came up in front of him.

"I'm looking for an angel, and you reek of him," Regal said authoritatively. "So you had better explain yourself."

The demon of wrath laughed and washed the black blood off his hands in the fountain. It mixed with the water and made it shimmer with flecks of gold. "I warned him to get out of my city, and he didn't listen. He was *so* invested in finding you. So I taught him a lesson about messing with a demon of wrath."

Regal's eyes widened slightly. So Keir really was looking for him. It made him swell up with pride and joy, but it also bothered him. He should have known better; of course the angel would search for him.

"So you let your anger take control and you harmed him?" Regal asked aggressively.

"You sound like one of 'em. 'Let it control me,' ha! I *am* Wrath! How can I control what I am?" the demon said indignantly. He grinned, his monstrous fangs gleaming. "But you wouldn't know, would you, incubus? There isn't a single hint of lust on your skin. What a pity."

"Do not pity me. Once I find my angel and treat him, I will hunt you down and be sure to maim you twice as badly as you've done to him," Regal hissed, his wings shaking with hostility.

"I'd like to see you try."

Regal lunged forward. He tackled him and pinned him down, flaring his wings. The demon of wrath growled and pushed up against him, trembling as he prepared to shape-shift, but Regal slashed his claws into the demon's scarred cheek, causing him to screech in pain. "Don't test me," Regal warned. "Now tell me where he went, or I'll rip out your throat."

The demon snarled. "He ran off. I don't know where."

Regal nodded and pushed himself off. He flew up into the air and continued his search. The demon of wrath had proven to be of no help. He vowed to get his revenge on the demon once Keir was safe. He turned sharply, heading back toward the center of the city where he had found the puddle of Keir's blood. The angel couldn't have gotten too far, so he decided the best place to search would be near there again.

CHAPTER Twenty-Nine

*T*IME WAS TICKING away quickly for the both Regal and Keir. As the demon searched frantically across the city for his angel, Keir was breaking open the window to an empty hotel suite farther away from the Las Vegas Strip.

He fell into the room heavily, gasping for air. For a moment, he was concerned about his blood staining the carpet. However, he ignored the trail he was leaving behind and focused on tending to his wounds.

The healing Gloria had given him didn't last long. The pain had begun to intensify again. Thankfully, the venom was slow to kill him—a perk for being so close to falling, but Keir knew that it would only be a matter of time until his body succumbed.

He crawled his way to the bathroom and turned on the bathtub. The water gushed out of the faucet, quickly filling up the basin. Keir pulled himself up and fell into the tub, submerging himself in the cold water. It immediately became filthy with blood, sweat, and dirt. He turned off the water and let himself soak as he purified the water.

Or so he thought. Keir stared at the water as it continued to become a mixture of black, brown, and gold. It wasn't purifying. He closed his eyes shut and focused harder on healing, but the water wasn't clearing.

"I can't make holy water," Keir gasped with frustration. He shouted in anger and slammed his fist into the wall, cracking the tile.

He couldn't heal himself.

With despair, Keir pulled himself out of the tub, shivering as he grabbed a towel to dry off as best as he could. Tears stung his eyes as he caught a glimpse of himself in the mirror.

He looked like a complete mess. His wings were black, except for a few gray patches that marked his inability to succumb to lust. He was coated in a layer of blood and dirt. His hair was tangled and matted. He looked nothing like an angel.

"I can't do this anymore," Keir moaned as he stared at himself. "I can't keep fighting. I can't win. I can't save him."

Yet even in that moment of surrender, all he could think about was how he wanted Regal to be there, to comfort him and show him affection. To remind him of what he was fighting for. To bring him the strength he needed to continue. To fix what they had broken.

Keir knew the demon could feel his pain. He knew that Regal sensed he was in trouble. But he still didn't come for him—and why would he? Keir had caused nothing but problems for Regal. The angel wouldn't be surprised if Regal waited for someone else to finish the job. To release him from his prison.

Regal wouldn't come to help him.

Only Keir could help himself.

There was movement outside of the hotel room. Keir snapped out of his depression and back into fight-or-flight mode, as if a switch in his brain had gone off.

I can't be caught here!

He tried to put weight on his injured leg, but it couldn't withstand the pressure for long. He would have to crawl, hop, or slowly limp his way to freedom.

Keir opened the bathroom door just as the front door's handle began to jiggle. Someone was coming in, and he had no time to escape the way he came. He reeled backward, closing the bathroom door before turning off the lights. He carefully stepped back into the tub and hid behind the curtain.

Keir listened as the front door opened and two people

stepped inside. He hoped they didn't notice the large blood stains on the dingy carpeting. Their voices were muffled, but it was obvious that it was a man and woman. He wondered if the demon of wrath had found him and had brought a friend along. He couldn't smell the identities of the strangers over the scent of his own blood. It was only a matter of time until whoever they were found him.

The bathroom door knob jingled, and Keir felt a cold shudder run down his spine as he heard the woman speaking a bit clearer now. He would recognize that sinister voice anywhere. The door opened and the lights flicked on. A moment later the shower curtain was yanked to the side. Keir struck out with his fist, his knuckles contacting the bridge of Etoile's nose.

The demon stumbled backward, grunting as his glasses shattered. Viraine laughed shrilly beside him as she lunged forward and grabbed Keir's arm, yanking him off balance and onto the bathroom floor.

"I had a feeling he would do that," she mocked, her eyes blazing. She stood in the doorway and cocked her head to the side, a venomous grin on her blood-red lips. "Ooh, you smell divine," she purred. Etoile, his hand covering his broken nose, moved beside her.

Of all people, Keir wasn't expecting to see them. They must have been searching for Regal as well. "Regal isn't here," Keir said.

"I'm well aware of that," Viraine replied sharply. "We're here for you."

"Why?"

"You didn't listen to my warning the first time," Viraine sneered.

Keir was in panic mode. His pain vanished as adrenaline pumped through his veins. There was no way he could fight them off or defend himself when it was two against one. Even if he wasn't wounded, he doubted he could fend off two older and more experienced demons. His eyes moved around quickly, trying to find any sort of escape, but Viraine stood in front of the door and blocked any attempt at fleeing.

"Quit looking so scared. It's not like we're going to do anything bad to you," she teased with a laugh. "Unless you count killing you as a bad thing." The comment made Keir go pale and his eyes widened.

"Viraine, do you really have to traumatize the boy?" Etoile asked as he tried to fix his cracked glasses.

"After what he did to Regal? Of course I do."

Keir tensed up and looked at her with astonishment. "He... he already...?"

The glutton smirked and crossed her arms. "Yep. Already ascended and out of Jackal's grasp. Aren't you *proud* of yourself?"

Keir's hands trembled as he tried to soak up what she was telling him. *No... it couldn't be true.* Regal wouldn't let himself rise so easily. There was no way he could already be an angel. Viraine had to be lying, but... the look on her face was so genuinely upset and vengeful. *"She wouldn't be this angry if he had managed to stay a demon, right?*

"What do you have to say for yourself?" Viraine barked.

Keir steeled himself. He got back onto his feet, wincing as his leg threatened to give out under him. "I didn't want this to happen, but what's done is done. I won't apologize to you."

"Damned brat," she growled. She opened her left palm, the jagged mouth stretching so she could slide her right hand into the opening. The teeth cut at her hand and wrist as she forced it inside, pulling out her umbrella slowly. "Repent for what you've done before I run you through!"

"Easy, Viraine," Etoile chided as he reached out to grab her shoulder.

"Don't *touch* me," she snapped as she smacked Etoile's hand away from her.

"You'll kill me whether I apologize or not. I will die with honor. I will not grovel to the likes of you."

Viraine hissed and stepped forward, preparing to use the silver tip of her umbrella to draw the final blow.

All of Keir's training came flooding back to him. He could practically hear Michaelangelo guiding him. He took a deep breath and prepared himself to fight.

A gleam of silver and bronze behind Viraine caught Keir's attention. Etoile withdrew his gun from his jacket, and with an effortless motion, cocked it and pulled the trigger.

Bright yellow light flashed from within the barrel of the gun, and a jet black bullet shot out just as Viraine spun her umbrella behind her and opened it. The bullet hit the canopy and ricocheted into the ceiling. She spun and closed her umbrella, lunging forward to stab at Etoile as he reloaded his gun. He jumped back, dodging her attack.

"You think I wasn't prepared for you to turn on me?"

"You didn't give me any other choice."

The gun charged with the energy from Etoile's fountain pen before he shot off another round. It grazed Viraine's shoulder as she spun out of the way, attacking with her umbrella. Keir ducked as the bullet flew over his head, bursting through the plaster wall behind him.

He tried to save me, Keir thought as he watched Etoile face Viraine. He launched himself forward with his good leg, flinging himself into battle. He tackled Viraine, wrapping his arms around her waist to force her to the ground. She hissed and writhed, rolling over him.

Etoile rushed toward them, reaching out to grab Viraine and hold her still, but any time he had an opening to do so,

Keir would flip back on top. The greed demon didn't want to touch Keir. He backed away and paced around the two, wanting to shoot at Viraine, but he couldn't get a clear shot. Keir was always in the way.

"Get out of here!" Etoile shouted as Keir pinned Viraine and socked her in the face with his unwounded arm. "I can handle her."

"I'm not abandoning you," Keir said as he punched Viraine again. On the third strike, she whipped her umbrella around and blocked the attack. She smacked Keir in the eyes with the handle, pushing him off of her.

With Keir off of her, Etoile fired. Viraine backflipped out of the way, the bullet barely missing her. Etoile shot off another rapid round, hitting the glutton in the waist. She landed heavily and summoned a dagger out of her palm. She threw it with deadly precision, and it embedded itself in Etoile's chest.

He stumbled back from the force, gasping from surprise. He growled, his eyes glowing with anger. "First my glasses, and now my shirt," he grumbled as he yanked out the dagger. It was glowing with a sickly orange color.

While he was distracted, Viraine set her eyes on Keir again. She charged at him, flipping over one of the couches. Keir rolled out of the way, watching as the tip of her umbrella stabbed into the carpeting. He used this moment to attack. He steadied himself on his strong leg and kicked out with the other. His foot connected with Viraine and both of them cried out in pain. Keir's halo had connected with her flesh.

She dropped to the floor, hissing as her skin seared. Keir regained his balance, biting his lip until it bled. His body was shaking from the stress, but he ignored it and continued to fight. He swung his body around for a low kick, but Viraine jumped out of the way. Her umbrella sprung open. She spun it rapidly and swung it down at Keir. The razor edges shone in the darkness as her makeshift circular saw came down.

Keir summoned his shield. The umbrella's blades bounced off, cutting a gash into the dense metal. Sparks flew as she pressed on him, forcing him back. Her eyes focused on Keir's wounded leg, and she advanced on him quickly to make him put more weight on it. Her tactic worked, and his leg gave out. He fell to one knee and dropped his shield. Viraine snapped the umbrella closed and swung it at Keir, clubbing him in the temple and knocking him to the ground.

"I thought fighting an angel would be more difficult. I keep forgetting that you aren't one anymore," Viraine taunted.

Etoile shot two more ink bullets at Viraine, but missed his target by an inch. Without his glasses, his vision wasn't perfect anymore. He reloaded as Viraine unlocked the handle from her umbrella and pulled out the rapier hidden within. Her umbrella now split into two pieces; she was wielding a sword and shield. She charged at Etoile, using the canopy to protect her from the bullets as she struck out with her rapier. Etoile blocked her attack with the dagger, trying to force an opening. He couldn't shoot her this close. Her shield would deflect the bullet and possibly hit him.

"You've never been good in close combat, Ettie," she mocked as she spun away before coming back in to strike. "Especially when your hands are full."

"And you've never been good at fighting unless you cheat," Etoile barked back as he dodged another attack. "A poison dagger. Really? I taught you better than that."

"You taught me to be prepared for everything. Even betrayal."

"If you weren't such a psycho, I wouldn't have felt the need to betray you!"

Etoile struck out with his foot, tripping Viraine just enough to use the dagger to knock the shield out of her hand. He kicked it out of the way and spun back around, but he was too slow. The poison was starting to affect him, and he couldn't block the opening he had left.

Viraine stabbed Etoile through the stomach. She withdrew the blade as he stumbled back, and then kicked him onto the floor. As Etoile lay on the ground, sweating and panting, Viraine grabbed Etoile's gun and aimed it between his eyes.

"I could kill you right this second," she gloated as she cocked the weapon. "But that would be letting you off too easily. I would much rather let you take the fall for this massacre."

There was movement in the mirror on the wall. Her eyes flashed up to see Keir getting to his feet to flee. She spun around and fired as Keir dove back to the ground, scrambling behind the bed to avoid being shot. However, the gun only clicked. She tried again, but it refused to react to her energy. "Custom designed piece of shit," she hissed as she threw it against the wall, far from Etoile's reach. She wiped the blood off her rapier and began to walk to Keir's hiding spot. "Come out, come out, wherever you are, you worthless excuse for an angel."

She's making a game out of this, Keir thought as he tried to catch his breath. His head was swimming from the adrenaline and blood loss. He was certain he had a concussion from the blow to the head. He couldn't feel his leg anymore, and he felt like he was on the verge of passing out. But he had to keep fighting. He couldn't give up.

"Keir, look out!" Etoile shouted as Viraine jumped onto the bed. He sat up with the rest of his strength and threw the dagger, hitting Viraine in the back. She pitched forward, losing balance for a moment before a mouth formed on her back to swallow the dagger. It took enough time for Keir to ready his shield and launch forward.

The angel crashed into her, pushing her backward. She twisted in the air, slamming on her side as Keir wrestled her to the ground, pinning her with his shield. Viraine pulled her arm free and smacked Keir on the back of the head with the hilt of her rapier repeatedly. He winced and drew back, allowing her to slip away from him.

The two stood panting, eyeing each other viciously as they regained their composure. Keir prepared for Viraine to attack, but she stood still.

"You know, Keir, we're not all that different from one another," Viraine said. Her voice was cold, but her amber eyes burned with the intensity of a forest fire.

"We're nothing alike."

"Of course we are," she continued. She moved to the side and Keir mirrored her. The two began to circle each other slowly. "We both love Regal, and we would do anything to keep him safe. But he never loved us. He just used us for his own personal gain."

"Don't you dare speak about him like that," Keir barked.

Viraine grinned. "I'm only telling the truth. The only reason he ever bonded with you was to make you his slave. He never cared for you. If he did, don't you think he would be running to your rescue by now?"

Keir shook his head, trying to clear his thoughts. He couldn't let her get under his skin. "You don't know anything about our relationship."

"I know that if you truly loved Regal, you never would have pursued it. When he dumped me, I let him go because that's what real lovers do for one another." Viraine grinned, her sharp, shark-like teeth gleaming. "But what you two share isn't love. The bond forged between the two of you is toxic, forbidden. You're a parasite. No, you're a monster."

"If anyone is the monster, it's you, you crazy bitch!" Keir countered.

"Why me?" Viraine questioned. "I'm not the one who turned on my god to pursue something so illicit. I'm not the one who stalked him to trap him in a bond. I'm not the one that forced him to become an angel and leave everything he knew behind. That was all you. You were more than happy to ruin his life to fulfill your own fantasy. You destroyed everything that made him perfect."

"Shut up!"

"Is it hard to hear the truth? Is it hard to know that you angels are just as despicable as the very creatures you hate?" Viraine stepped forward, lowering her rapier as jagged toothed mouths formed all over her body, amplifying her voice. "You are selfish. You are weak. You are a burden. You are filled with Chaos. You are not worthy of being an angel or a demon. You are not worthy of Regal."

Keir shook as he held back his anger. He couldn't ignore her. She was suffocating him with her voice, echoing all around him. He couldn't breathe.

"Now stand still and die, so Regal can be free from you."

Viraine's aura pulsated with vengeance and anger, and it fed into Keir's. His patience snapped, and suddenly Viraine was nothing but a red target.

He hurled himself forward and slammed her against the wall. He pulled his shield back and then rammed it against her again. He repeated the process, the rhythmic drum of her head crashing against the plaster in time with the blood pumping in his ears.

She stabbed Keir through his wounded leg with her rapier, causing him to scream and arc his shield down on her sharply. The edge cut into her shoulder, knocking her to the floor and forcing her to drop her weapon. The shield bounced out of Keir's hands from the force of the hit. He fell on top of her, straddling her waist as he pinned her down. He balled his hands into fists and began to punch her repeatedly.

The Art of Falling

Each punch was for Regal, for himself, for the pain she caused the both of them. She deserved every single hit. She needed to be punished. She needed to die.

Keir froze, his fist pulled back as his weaker arm held down Viraine by the throat. This wasn't what he wanted. He didn't want to kill her.

Viraine coughed, blood splattering against Keir's shirt. He leaned back, his eyes welling with tears as he saw Viraine reflected within himself.

She was doing this out of love for Regal.

They were the same.

But he was the monster.

Viraine struck out with her hand, her palm slammed up into Keir's nose. The teeth on her palm's mouth cut into his face as she pushed him off. He rolled to the side, tears welling in his eyes from the impact. He blearily watched Viraine get to her feet. She was wobbly, but still strong enough to kill him.

Keir tried to scramble back, dragging his body with his arms. If he could just escape through the window, he could fly to safety. She wouldn't be able to follow him. She jumped on him, pinning him to the floor before he could flee.

"Stop!" Etoile yelled, trying to drag himself closer to them. "There's been enough bloodshed. You've had your revenge."

"It's not over until his heart stops beating."

"Regal!" Keir screamed. His voice was hoarse and shrill as panic and terror overtook him. He knew he wouldn't last much longer on his own. He prayed that his demon was near to save him. *But... if Regal really is an angel... then the bond is broken and my bond won't kill him. He won't feel any of my pain. He'll be safe.* The thought comforted Keir... but only a little. Keir wasn't ready to die.

"Yes, this is all for Regal," Viraine hissed lowly as she summoned the dagger back from deep within the caverns of her body and into her hand. She brought the blade down repeatedly in wide arcs, cutting into Keir's flesh over and over. Keir never stopped screaming and thrashing as he tried to defend himself with his arms. He tried to kick her with his halo, but couldn't make his leg move. It was too numb to respond and instead twitched helplessly as the poisoned dagger and demon venom in his system brought him closer to death.

Viraine looked back and saw the halo glowing dimly in an attempt to protect Keir. She laughed and looked back at Keir, who was bleeding and crying in front of her.

"Since you're so close to becoming a demon, you really don't need your halo anymore," she cooed as she ran the tip of the blade along the jugular of Keir's throat. He shivered with fear, swallowing thickly as she stood back up. She stood up and fetched her rapier, not worried about Keir trying to escape. It gleamed in the darkness as she walked back to the gruesome scene. Keir lay limp on the floor, covered in cuts and gashes that oozed tainted blood.

The demon of gluttony looked over at Etoile. "There's no harm in playing butcher, is there? I don't care if he has a missing limb or two."

"No!" Keir croaked, trying to sit up to stop her, but he was too weak. The world around him was growing fuzzy and dark around the edges. All he could see was the glistening blade that hung over his body. It swung down swiftly to chop off his ankle, and he screamed.

CHAPTER *Thirty*

A FLASH OF WHITE flew overhead and rammed into Viraine before her blade could touch Keir's ankle. She tumbled to the ground, screeching as she tried to throw off her attacker. Keir could see the glimmer of Viraine's sword cutting through the air, and the pearly white and gold of blood-stained feathers dropping to the floor.

Michaelangelo? Keir wondered dazedly. Had Gloria sent reinforcements to save him?

For a moment, he thought that he had blacked out or died. The world went dark around him and he could only hear the rush of blood in his ears, but soon a bright white light lit up the room and blinded him. He tried to pull himself to safety, but the room was a war zone and he couldn't flee from the battle.

Keir looked up, his vision swimming as he tried to focus. He could see Viraine struggling with the new angel. She had dropped her rapier, which was lying partially under the bed. She and the angel were rolling over one another, pummeling each other with their fists. Keir propped himself up against the wall under the window, pressing himself as close to it as possible to stay away from the fight.

Viraine was pinned underneath the angel, whose wings were glowing with purity and casting the room in a heavenly light. It stung Keir's eyes—a feeling he thought he would never have to sense. *So this is what demons felt around an angel's aura.*

The demon of gluttony screeched and slashed with her hands, the mouths trying to bite at her assailant, but the angel held her wrists down. His dark hair covered his face, but Keir could see the white glow of his eyes through the peppered bangs.

The aura radiating off the angel was familiar, but different. Did Gloria send in a stranger to save him? He noticed the angel's lack of a halo, which was odd for an adult angel. Even newborns were given halos shortly after birth for protection.

Unless this angel was a newborn.

A low growl came from the newcomer. Keir gasped, choking on his breath as he lurched forward. His heart swelled as he recognized the aura. How could he have ever forgotten? Keir's heart swelled.

"Regal!"

The angel looked up, his white eyes locking on Keir's. The angel blinked, and the white faded away to light gray.

"Keir."

Viraine hissed and ripped her hands out of Regal's grasp. She thrust her hands upward and screamed, releasing a surge of energy into Regal. The swell was enormous, enough to fling him off of her. She rolled back to kick Regal in the gut and sent him flying across the room.

She got up to her feet, using the bed as leverage. Her eye was clawed and bleeding heavily. She spun around, shifting her focus to Keir. She lunged at him, screaming as the mouths on her palms opened wide.

Keir scrambled to hide behind the bed. He reached to grab his halo, and as Viraine came upon him, he ripped it off his ankle. The metal cut into his flesh as it unhinged itself. He swung his arm up, slicing upward at Viraine. She screeched as the angelic weapon tore into her cheek. She seized up and howled in pain, clutching her face. Although it wasn't nearly as powerful as it used to be, it still held enough power to harm her.

"Don't move," Regal commanded as he stood up from the corner of the room, aiming Etoile's gun directly at Viraine.

The demon stared at him for a moment before shrieking

with laughter. She doubled over, unable to contain the bubbling mania inside of her. She looked absolutely mad, driven insane from her desire to kill the angel. "We're on your side!"

"The moment you thought of harming him, you were against me." Regal growled.

"You're crazy," Viraine spat, her voice growling like a feral animal. "That angel made you soft. You used to be one of the strongest incubi of this century!"

"I am still one of the strongest," Regal barked back.

Viraine laughed bitterly. "You're a filthy angel."

Regal knew this. His diligence to save Keir was enough to push him over the edge. He could feel the tugging on his entire being trying to pull him up so he could change completely, but he refused to budge until Keir was safe.

"You act like he's your property," Viraine hissed as she stood up a bit straighter. "He was never your property!"

"He's more than property. He's a part of me."

"I was only trying to save you, Reggie..." Viraine said, her voice wavering between manic desperation and sickly sweet concern.

"Why won't you people understand that I don't need saving?"

Viraine shook her head as she held her cut cheek with her hand. Blood seeped through her fingers and dripped onto the floor. "I won't lose you," she muttered as she turned to face Keir, who was cowering behind the bed. "Not to the likes of him."

"Make one step toward Keir, and I'll kill you," Regal warned as he cocked Etoile's gun.

Viraine began to giggle maniacally. "You can't shoot me. It only registers Etoile's aura." She headed back for Keir.

Keir held up his halo to protect himself.

Regal fired.

A bolt of blue energy fired out, bursting through Viraine's back. It exploded through her chest, exiting right below her diaphragm. She fell forward onto her knees, ichor spewing out of the wound as she crumpled to the floor.

Regal dropped the gun and ran over to Keir's side. He knelt down beside Keir, who was starting to tremble and lose consciousness.

"I know this is overwhelming, but you can't die on me. I've gone through too much shit this past month for you to die on me," Regal said as he pulled Keir into his arms. The angel shuddered and closed his eyes, too tired to keep them open. Regal held him tighter, wishing he could heal Keir the same way the angel did for him whenever he was hurt. Regal brushed a lock of hair away from Keir's face. *I wish I could save him...*

He then realized that wishing was for fools. Angels had better tools at their disposal.

"Our Father," Regal whispered, grimacing as he tried to remember the prayers Keir used to say before bed. "Who art in Heaven. Hallowed be Thy... be Thy... dammit!"

He looked up to the ceiling, glaring with frustration. "Gloria!" he shouted in desperation. "Listen, I've never done the whole praying thing before, and I don't really know what the hell I'm doing. I don't know your prayers, but people just talk to you and you listen, right?" He looked back down at Keir. The angel's breathing was growing short. "Do something to keep him alive... please don't take him away from me."

He felt warmth growing under his skin, like he was burning from the inside, yet it didn't hurt. Instead, it felt comforting. Regal watched with quiet awe as the light glowed from his fingertips and washed over Keir's body. The thin film of energy seeped into Keir's wounds, causing them to shimmer. The angel's heartbeat began to steady, and his trembling stopped. For a moment, Regal thought it was too late, but Keir opened his eyes slowly and looked up at him.

"It worked," Regal murmured as he smiled, tears welling in his eyes. "It really worked!"

"Don't be mad at Etoile," Keir whimpered weakly. "He tried to save me."

Regal laughed, relief and joy washing over him. He held onto his angel tighter, hugging him as he let the natural healing abilities work their miracles.

Keir held onto him as well, feeling strength flowing through his veins. The infection was healing slowly. He wouldn't die.

That's when he noticed something off about the energy in the room. Keir looked to where Viraine's body had fallen.

Except it wasn't there anymore.

She was standing behind Regal with the poison dagger in her hand, swaying on her feet as she conquered death.

"Look out!" Keir shouted as he pulled away from Regal's grasp. The newborn angel turned, blocking Keir with his body as Viraine took a jerking step toward them.

Keir reached for the rapier from under the bed and rammed it into Viraine's gut.

She stumbled and dropped the dagger. Black ichor bubbled up from her mouth and spilled to the floor. Keir whimpered and pulled the blade back out, dropping it immediately, distressed, as her blood splattered against him and the carpet. Regal pulled Keir away from Viraine as she fell into a motionless pile.

She was dead.

"Regal... I... I..." Keir wept, his entire body trembling.

"Shh, it's okay. Keep quiet." Regal hesitantly took the halo from Keir, in awe at how it was cool to the touch and didn't cause him any harm. Keir's hand was slightly scarred from holding it tightly in his grip. Regal hooked it around Keir's ankle, watching as the ends melded together to create a solid circle of metal once more. He then picked up his wounded angel and stepped over Viraine's body as he headed over to where Etoile was lying. He was unconscious. The poison had taken hold of him.

"Oh no..." Keir moaned as Regal knelt down beside Etoile.

Silently, the newborn angel rested his hand on Etoile's wound and began to pray. It came easier to him now. In moments, the greed demon's eyes fluttered open, widening when he recognized Regal.

"She blackmailed me."

"Save your breath."

"Please believe me, I would have never—"

"Etoile," Regal interrupted, his voice softer than ever before. "I forgive you."

The three of them remained silent as Regal finished healing Etoile. The demon was still wounded and would need to recover, but he had enough strength restored to get home.

"She was a lot faster than I remembered," Etoile said with a frown. "I couldn't get a solid hold on her."

"If I had to face you, I wouldn't let you touch me either," Regal said as he looked over at Viraine's body.

Etoile followed Regal's gaze. "Is she dead?"

"Yes."

"Good. She was becoming chaotic." Etoile summoned his weapon, removed the fountain pen from the cartridge inside the gun, and made a portal to go home. "I'm going to lay low for a while. If anyone asks—"

"You weren't involved," Regal replied.

Etoile nodded and reached out to clasp Regal on the back of the neck in a thankful gesture. Regal didn't flinch away, knowing that Etoile would never steal his power. After Etoile fled through the gateway to Tartarus, Regal and Keir left Sin City behind them with the wounded angel cradled in the ex-demon's arms.

"I didn't want to kill her," Keir choked out after a long moment of silence. "I was just protecting you."

"I know," Regal murmured. "It'll be alright in the end."

Although they both knew that Keir would be facing severe ramifications for committing such a deed.

Keir nodded, closing his eyes. He could hear Regal's heart racing, but the lull of Regal's steady breathing made Keir feel even more tired.

Regal gently shook Keir, forcing him to open his eyes again and look back up at Regal. "Do me a favor and don't fall asleep." It was easier said than done, but Keir understood why. There was no guarantee he would wake up if he were to succumb to the dark.

They landed in the middle of a golf course at a nearby country club. The sun was just starting to rise and lighten up the sky. Regal set Keir down gently onto the ground up against a tree and began to heal Keir's wounds again. He didn't want to take any chances.

"Are you hurt?" Keir asked.

Regal shook his head.

"But, our bond..."

"At first, I could feel your pain," Regal explained. "But once I performed diligence, I couldn't feel it anymore. It's a good thing I did too; otherwise I wouldn't have had the strength to save you."

Keir chuckled. *Save him.* He had been the one who wanted to save the demon to begin with, and in the end it was the opposite. He sighed and frowned as he stared at Regal's wings. "I'm so sorry..."

Regal glanced over his shoulder to see his now fully white wings spread out behind him. "Yeah, I guess I'm an angel now, or almost an angel. I don't know how the process works, really," he murmured. Regal noticed Keir's look of guilt and despair and cupped his tear-stained cheek in his hand. "Don't feel bad. I'm... okay with this."

"I don't understand," Keir murmured as he bit his split lip.

Regal ran his thumb over it and frowned. He didn't like seeing Keir so wounded. "The moment I heard you screaming, I knew I was going to ascend. I couldn't ignore it. How could I?" Regal explained as comfortingly as he could.

"You're not yourself like this..."

"I'm still me... just different," Regal said. "I think that this was my fate, to meet you and go through this change. This is something I should do."

Keir sat back, looking at Regal sternly. "You don't have to change if you don't want to. You have free will."

"Don't you want me to stay with you?" Regal asked with slight confusion. He chuckled a bit, a small grin forming on his face. "Can't you be a bit selfish for once?"

The angel laughed. "Not at all." He held Regal's hand in his own tightly, rubbing his thumb over Regal's fingers.

Regal leaned forward to kiss Keir softly, his lips brushing against Keir's. He could taste the hint of blood from Keir's split lip, and their mouths were chapped and rough, but it felt right. There were no lies or tricks. Just pure, misunderstood love. The sense of the archangels coming for them forced the lovers to pull away. Although the kiss didn't last long, it brought them both comfort for the time being.

The newborn angel sighed and stood up, waiting for someone to take him away. He was terrified of what laid before him. He had never been to Heaven, never witnessed Gloria or Her judgment. What if She didn't accept him into Heaven? Jackal would never take him back, he was certain. Where would he go? If She did accept him, would the process of ascending be painful? Would the other angels accept him? Would he be allowed to continue his relationship with Keir?

"Do what makes you feel right to you," Keir said softly as he looked up at him. His voice had cracked, betraying his attempts to sound strong. "Don't change for me."

Regal stared down at him silently for a moment, trying to figure out what truly made him happy in the world. Being a demon certainly did; he enjoyed the power and the mischief that came with it. Living the life of a goody-two-shoes would be a bore, but being beside Keir and knowing he was safe made him happy as well. Regal had grown to care for the angel in spite of how his annoying righteousness got in the way or how worried he was over simple things. Regal knew now that he did love the angel, and he didn't want to part from him. But in the end, Regal knew he had to be true to himself. After all, that's what Keir had fallen for.

"I love you," Keir said, tears welling in his eyes. He knew this could very well be the last time they saw each other, and it broke his already mangled heart.

Regal's chest ached. He knelt down and hugged Keir tightly. "I know you do..."

"That's not what you're supposed to say," Keir whispered with a small chuckle.

"Just give me time. I'm not used to feeling this way..." Regal could feel Keir clinging to him weakly, his fingertips digging into his shoulder blades. "Just know it's mutual." Regal wanted to hold Keir tighter, but feared hurting him. Instead he buried his face into Keir's shoulder, breathing in the angelic scent he had grown to crave and adore. He didn't want to leave his side. "I'll see you later, no matter what happens," he promised, his voice choked with tears.

Their goodbye was cut short when two bright portals materialized out of thin air. Gabriel appeared beside Keir.

He was glaring hard at Regal, knowing that he had been the cause of Keir's pain and suffering. Without hesitation, Gabriel touched Keir's shoulder gently, and in a flash of burning white light, they were gone.

Regal was left holding nothing. His last moment with Keir had been cut short. The lack of the angel's warmth made him feel empty and he questioned his choice. Could he ever truly be happy as a demon if it meant never seeing Keir again?

A different archangel appeared beside Regal. She was a shorter woman who had a long face and neck. Her eyes were as black as bricks of coal, and her skin was almost as dark. At first her head looked shaved, but then Regal was able to make out the short, coarse curls of hair disappearing into the darkness of her skin. She reached out and touched Regal's shoulder, and he felt a strong pull toward the portal. He was surrounded by the light and was sucked in.

CHAPTER *Thirty-One*

*T*HE INFIRMARY WAS similar to those on Earth. All of the walls, beds, and sheets were clean and white. It reeked of sanitizer and bleach. Although the beds were comfortable and the saints took care of those wounded, no angel wanted to end up there. It was one of the loneliest places in Heaven if you had to visit the quarantine sector.

This is where Gabriel took Keir the moment they were back through Heaven's Gates. Keir was on the brink of death, and he was only vaguely aware of the saints that swarmed around him and began to give him anesthetics. In seconds, they began to take effect, and he could barely feel his own chest rising and falling. He watched the saints clean and stitch his wounds. He groaned and looked away, unable to see himself being sewn up.

"Gabriel?" he wheezed past the strange feeling—or lack thereof—that was choking him. The archangel was by his side, silently smiling at him. Keir felt the strong pull of sleep and tried to fight it.

"Sleep," Gabriel commanded gently, laying his hand over Keir's eyes. The comfort of Gabriel's presence and influence was enough to make him fall asleep and forget the fear of never waking up.

———

When Keir finally came to, he was welcomed to the warmth of blankets tucked around him. He blinked, rubbing his eyes till his vision cleared. He looked at his hands to see that they were wrapped and no longer covered in blood. He pushed himself up and winced from pain. After settling back into the bed, he pulled the blankets away to look at his wounds. He was naked except for his underwear; the rest of his body was swathed in bandages.

"Look who's awake!" Gabriel said as he walked into the infirmary with his arm wrapped tightly around Michelangelo's shoulder. He balanced a tray of cookies in his free hand. "I hope you're hungry, we made cookies."

"Uh... cookies?" Keir murmured as he sat up straighter in bed.

"Gabe baked them. I thought something warm and comforting like soup would be better to eat. I made broccoli cheddar, your favorite," Michaelangelo explained as he carried a tray with a glass of water, and a steaming bowl of soup. He set it down on the table beside Keir's bed.

"Cookies always make people feel better, Michael," Gabriel added defensively as he sat down on the bed beside Keir. The young angel noticed that they were no longer in military gear and were dressed in casual clothes.

"Thank you..." Keir said tentatively. He felt honored that two archangels were coming to him, but it also made him wary. Most angels were lucky if one archangel visits when they were ill. The fact that they were both here put Keir on edge.

Gabriel grabbed a cookie from the plate and began to eat it. He took another and handed it to Keir. "Don't feel shy to eat. You're going to need something to help you with your blood sugar."

"That's why he should eat something that won't make him crash," Michaelangelo argued as he took it from Gabriel and set it down. The Archangel of Diligence rolled his eyes and continued to eat his cookie.

"I'm not really feeling up to eating," Keir said, ignoring the growl of his empty stomach.

"How are you feeling?" Michaelangelo asked.

"I'm okay. I'm a little dizzy, and my wounds ache..."

"We can ask Saint Rita to come and tend to your wounds. She's specialized in that field."

"We might need to ask Saint Martha to come in as well," Gabriel murmured as he took a bite of Michelangelo's soup. "She'll have to teach you a better recipe."

"My cooking is just fine," Michaelangelo argued, trying to hide his red face.

Keir observed the playful banter between the two best friends. It seemed genuine, yet forced. After everything they had been though, the two shouldn't be acting like all was well. There was tension in the way they acted.

Something was wrong.

"Why are you here?" Keir asked abruptly, his tone becoming serious. It caught the archangels off guard. "It can't be just to bring me treats."

Michaelangelo cleared his throat uncomfortably and glanced at Gabriel.

"Well... we have the issue of Regal to discuss," Gabriel replied.

"Then spit it out," Keir said.

Gabriel's eyes glanced over toward Michaelangelo. The Archangel of Kindness rested his hand on Keir's shoulder.

"Keir... I know it's been awhile since you've been home, but please try to remember your manners."

"Right, sorry Michaelangelo." Keir lay back against the pillows. "I guess I'm just restless to know what's happening to Regal... to us. So just lay it on me. What's the issue?"

"Well, there is the problem that you had allowed yourself to become attached to a demon," Gabriel started, crossing his arms across his chest. "Not to mention that you let yourself succumb to his tricks and almost fall from grace in the process."

"And putting yourself in harm's way on multiple occasions," Michaelangelo added, his face fraught with concern.

"You can't blame that on Regal though," Keir reasoned, looking over at Gabriel. "My mistakes aren't his fault."

"We know they aren't his fault, but he is directly involved," Gabriel said sternly. "He was the one who you were bound to, and he is the one who was trying to make you fall."

Panic flooded through Keir. "You didn't break our bond, did you?"

"He doesn't have the power to do that," Michaelangelo said, glancing over at his friend. "Unless he..."

Keir could practically sense their silent conversation. He noticed the subtle body language between the two: the raise of the eyebrow, the twitch of the lip. Michaelangelo wanted to scold Gabriel, who in turn wanted to defend himself.

"Gabe should have never brought that blade outside of Heaven."

"But I had a good reason to do so."

"So we're still bound?" Keir asked, hope in his voice. The two archangels stopped bickering and focused on Keir once more.

Michaelangelo sighed. "When Sauda took him to Purgatory, his soul was wiped clean. There shouldn't be a link between you anymore."

"Oh..." Keir said sadly. He had grown so used to feeling Regal's presence tugging at his heart. He felt empty now.

"Now all that is left to do is wait for the outcome of Regal's judgment," Gabriel added.

"He doesn't want to ascend."

"We understand that. Demons naturally don't want to. However, we're hoping that Regal may be the exception."

"Why? Why would he be the exception?" Keir asked harshly, his voice becoming more aggressive and defensive. "Just because he gave in to the virtues doesn't mean he has to become an angel. What ever happened to free will? Don't demons have that right, too?"

Michelangelo's eyes widened with worry as he hurried over to Keir's side. "Calm down, don't get yourself worked up. You still have traces of the demon venom in your system. We don't want your heart rate to pump it through any faster."

"Let it spread!" Keir demanded in hysteria. "I don't care if it makes me a demon or if it kills me! I'd rather fall from grace than force Regal to do anything he doesn't want to!"

"Think before you speak," Gabriel barked as he lost his temper.

"Gabe!" Michaelangelo shouted as he looked sternly at his best friend.

Keir felt the power coming off the archangels in waves. It instantly shut him up, and at the same time calmed him down enough to relax.

Gabriel sighed and rubbed the bridge of his nose. "Pardon my outburst…"

Michaelangelo shifted his harsh glare back to Keir and softened his expression. "What he means is to not think so irrationally. The amount of venom in your system isn't enough to kill you, but it is still toxic. It's best just to rest and let your body naturally get rid of it."

Keir nodded in obedience. "Still… if he doesn't want to be an angel, why do you think he'll give in?"

Michaelangelo smiled. "Well, because of you."

Gabriel nodded. "I could sense the shift in his aura when I retrieved you. As strange as it is, you were able to change something inside of him. Perhaps something he can't ignore."

Keir couldn't tell if that was a good thing or not.

The Archangel of Diligence looked down at his watch and nodded. "We should get going. There is still a lot to do to prepare for Regal's decision."

"Just one more question before you go," Keir said quickly, remembering Viraine's vengeance with a shudder.

"What is it?"

"What about the incident with Viraine? I... I didn't mean to kill her."

Michaelangelo sighed. "Normally, serious consequences would be made. However, you didn't hunt her down first. Your murder was out of self-defense. I'm sure you will be judged accordingly and will be found innocent."

Gabriel turned toward Michaelangelo, murmuring in his ear quietly so Keir couldn't hear. Michaelangelo nodded and murmured something back. The Archangel of Kindness sat on the bed beside Keir while the Archangel of Diligence left the infirmary.

Keir and Michaelangelo were silent, mulling over their thoughts silently. Keir wanted to ask more questions about Regal. He wanted to know if Regal was hurt. Even though Regal seemed unharmed during the battle against Viraine, Keir knew that the demon could have been hiding it.

"You're wondering if Regal is still injured." Michaelangelo stated. Keir nodded quietly. "He's fine. A part of the ascension process, whether he wants it or not, is cleansing of any wounds or impurities. His choice to be an angel or demon does not affect whether or not he is healed."

"Oh, that's good," Keir said softly. "I really don't want him to be hurt."

"Is this why you are so adamant on Regal staying a demon?" Michaelangelo asked.

Keir nodded again. "I just want him to be happy." Even if it meant being unable to see Regal ever again, as long as the demon was content, Keir would feel that he completed his job. He learned to love Regal in the end for who he was, not for what Keir wanted him to become, and he would give up anything to ensure that Regal stayed true to himself. From the gentle smile on Michelangelo's face, he could tell that the archangel could understand.

"That's very strong of you to do," Michaelangelo murmured with fascination. "Angels are not perfect. There are a good number that aren't so willing to give up the thing that pleases them for another's benefit. Although, love can do that to someone, can't it?" He sighed and leaned back on his hands. "Perhaps I am not fit to be your patron archangel," the Archangel of Kindness mused thoughtfully. "Surely Humility or Charity would have suited you more."

"I think you're a perfect patron and mentor," Keir said with a smile. "I've learned a lot from your teachings over the years."

Michaelangelo beamed. "I'm glad for that. It's all I ever ask for of my understudies." He stood up and rested his hand atop Keir's head. "I must go now, but do get some rest and trust that Regal will make the best choice for himself."

Keir nodded and watched as his mentor left him alone to his thoughts. He closed his eyes and prayed that Regal would find the outcome that suited him best.

CHAPTER *Thirty-Two*

SAUDA AND REGAL landed steadily inside a small, bleak room. It was boring and gray, with a simple table in the middle. On the table was a white bowl filled with apples, peaches, and grapes. Located on the walls of the room were four doors: to the north was a blue door; to the east, a golden door; to the south, a bronze door; to the west, a silver door.

"Have a seat," Sauda said. A chair appeared closest to Regal. A purple door materialized underneath it.

"What is this place?"

"This is one of Purgatory's judgment chambers. Here, we determine where souls will be sorted," Sauda explained, sitting down in her own summoned chair.

"The doors?"

"Earth, Heaven, Purgatory, Hell, and Chaos. I'm sure you can figure out which one is which. You're a smart guy."

"I'm not sitting down," Regal argued.

"This may take a long time, so it'd be best for you to relax. The door to Chaos won't open unless you're Chaotic. I doubt that will happen. You're safe here."

She watched him with gentle eyes. They looked like black holes, a void where he could shout all his secrets and know that no one will ever hear. Of all people to talk to, he had the sense that she would keep his secrets and protect him. She was a better angel to be around than Gabriel, that's for sure. He felt compelled to trust her, for now.

Hesitantly, Regal sat down across from her. The trap door remained shut. "I don't want to be here," he said as he sat on the edge of his seat, prepared to jump up if the door beneath him opened. He didn't want to go to Chaos.

"I know that," Sauda replied simply. She gestured toward the bowl of fruit. "Hungry?"

"No."

She leaned back and crossed her legs, bouncing her foot up and down. She smiled at him. "I know you don't want to be an angel. No demon ever wants it."

"Then what's the point in all of this? Let me go back home."

"We do this because we don't want anyone to make hasty decisions."

"So you're here to convince me to become an angel."

"I'm here to help you figure out what choice is best for you."

"By hyping up Heaven."

Sauda sighed. "If you want to think of it that way, then yes."

"Then where's the representative for Hell? This isn't a fair trial," Regal argued.

"You already know all about Hell. There's no need to try and sell it to you." Sauda sighed with frustration, letting out a deep breath to regain focus. "I know that you want to go back to Hell right now, but only a few moments ago you were considering ascension."

Regal tensed and glared at her. It was true that he was ready to give in and become an angel, but that was before he was reassured that he still had free will. Now he was certain he wanted to stay a demon. "That was then and this is now," he argued irritably.

The archangel chuckled. "Let's take our time and try to learn more about ourselves in the process. After all, you're gone through a lot of changes recently."

"I don't need a therapist or counselor!" Regal yelled. The more she talked to him, the more aggravated he got.

"I'm hardly a therapist," she said with a smirk. She leaned

forward and rested her hand on her cheek. "But I do know how you feel right now."

"You have no idea what I'm going through."

"Try me."

Regal stared at Sauda for long time. The way she stared back at him made his skin crawl. It was like she could read right through him. Why was she challenging him? What was the point of all of this? Did she think that talking about their feelings would make him decide he wanted to be an angel after all? *She's an idiot if she thinks that.* But the nagging urge to confide in her was overwhelming.

"Well?" she urged, trying to get him to talk.

He sighed with defeat and leaned back in his chair. "Well, first off, I'm Jackal's son," he started, staring down at his hands. "And not in the way that all demons are in a way related to Jackal because he owns our souls. We're related by blood. I'm one of four children. Each of us have some 'destiny' that we are meant to fulfill, but he hasn't told me what mine is yet."

"That sounds troublesome. Do you have any clue as to what it could be?"

"No. And I can't ask him about it either..." Regal doubted he'd ever be able to speak with him again after this.

"He is stingy in that regard. Very cryptic, very volatile."

Regal found her response odd. She talked with an air of certainty as if she knew Jackal personally. He narrowed his eyes, staring hard at Sauda, who simply looked back at him with a mirroring gaze. Then he saw the narrow slits for pupils hidden within her dark irises.

"You're a demon."

Sauda smiled. "I told you I understood how you were feeling."

He shook his head. "How did you ascend? Why didn't you fight to stay home?"

"You assume I didn't fight?" She shook her head and frowned. "Of course I fought. I was changing into an angel due to my own mistakes, just like you. I was terrified at the idea of ascending. However, as I sat in this room with the Archangel of Patience, I realized that this was truly my home. I was never meant to be a demon. I was too soft, with compassion and understanding. I'm sure your father had always felt that way about me as well."

"So you walked through the golden door..." Regal said as he looked over her shoulder toward the door in question.

"That's exactly what I did. I must say, I'm glad I chose it."

"So, what virtue did you end up being assigned to?"

"Patience, just like you will be if you choose to ascend."

Regal furrowed his brow. "There are two Archangels of Patience?"

Sauda frowned. "No. I had to take her place after she..."

"After she what?"

The archangel shook her head. "I can't tell you that."

"You just said you were here to tell me anything I wanted to know!"

"Needed to know," Sauda corrected.

"Come on, I'm telling you all my deepest secrets. The least you can do it tell me your story," Regal bargained, grinning a little with his old charm.

Sauda sighed and leaned forward, resting her chin on her knuckles. "Alright. I'll take you up on your offer. She succumbed to Chaos."

"How is that possible? Heaven is as far from Chaos as you can get."

"She faced a lot of heartbreak in her life. Her husband grew distant and withdrew into his work. She got involved in a relationship with a mythos on Earth. Her sons were taken

320

away from her. She suffered so much grief and eventually gave into Chaos' influence. As her deputy, I was moved up into her position after she fell to the Sea of Discord"

"I'm sorry to hear that. But I guess ascending worked out well for you, huh?"

"If I were going back to my demonic roots, then yes. It could work out well for you, too."

Regal scoffed. "I was a Prince, and heir to Hell's throne. What does Heaven have that I would possibly want?"

"Keir?"

All of the breath was knocked out of Regal. The angel was the only reason he would ever choose to go to Heaven. Doubt began to stir in him again. Sitting here in this room wiped away all sins and virtues. He was completely free of influence except of his own free will and desires. He wanted to go back home, but he also wanted to be with Keir. Knowing that the Angel was in Heaven made it tempting to ascend. After all, Jackal had been ignoring him. Would he really want a failure of a son to return home?

"People do crazy things for love," Sauda said.

He laughed softly. "You make a damned good argument. I'm... not sure what the right choice for me is."

"Tell me what you're thinking."

Regal looked up at her for a moment, his brow furrowing with worry and confusion. "I want to be where Keir is." He squeezed his eyes shut with frustration and curled his hands into fists on the table. "But I've been a demon all my life and I don't know anything else except that."

Sauda reached forward and rested her hands on Regal's, squeezing gently. "Make the right choice for you. Your fate is your decision."

This was by far the hardest choice he would ever have to

make. Growing up as a demon, he had only known sin. There, he trained and worked hard to become Prince of Lust. There, he was destined to become the ruler of Hell. In Heaven, he had no future, no destiny. Yet Keir had opened his eyes and allowed him to see a different way of viewing the world. The angel had shown him that kindness wasn't a flaw, but instead a great strength that overcame the very sin Regal was born into. Being here wiped him clean of any sinful or virtuous influence, allowing only raw emotion to remain. How could anyone expect him to make this choice?

"Do you need more time to decide?" Sauda asked.

"How about I make it for him? That'll speed up the process."

Sauda jolted up and pulled out a pair of daggers from around her waist and held them out defensively. Regal jolted up from his seat and whipped around, staring at the silver door behind him as it forced itself open.

"Father," Regal said in surprise as Jackal came through. The ruler of Hell looked completely enraged, his eyes pitch black from Satan's influence on his soul. Regal looked over toward Sauda and noticed she looked conflicted; her old master was in front of her and she had to fight him if he tried to interfere.

"You're forbidden from entering!" Sauda commanded, raising her blades to attack if necessary. She stepped in front of Regal protectively. "Only representatives of the Ethereal Kingdoms and judged souls are allowed to be here. Those are the rules Hades and Gloria made."

"Rules were meant to be broken," Jackal stated defiantly.

Regal froze as his conversation about Keir's first meeting with Viraine came back to him. The angel had been concerned about Viraine's accusation that Jackal and Gloria were guilty of breaking the Heavenly Laws. Regal was certain that they were both noble enough to follow their own rules. Had he been wrong to put such faith in them?

Jackal looked over at Regal and pointed at the ground beside him. "Come here, now."

"Regal, don't go if you are having doubts," Sauda warned, glancing over her shoulder back at him. "Do what's right for you."

"He doesn't have a choice in the matter," Jackal said angrily. "He is my son, and he is returning home."

Does he really want me back? After all of this? Regal thought dizzily as sirens began to wail above them. The sudden break-in had notified the guards within Purgatory. Soon they would be coming to fight off the intruder, unaware that the trespasser was Jackal himself.

"Regal, are you certain you want to go back?"

"Of course he wants to go back. He isn't a traitor, unlike you."

"Quiet! I can't think!" Regal shouted, covering his ears with his hands.

The sirens turned off, and the murmur of voices outside the room was the only thing they could hear. Regal knew that there wasn't much time to make a decision at all. *What the hell am I going to do?*

The golden door opened. Jackal, Sauda, and Regal turned to face it. Regal was expecting an army of Purgatory soldiers to flood in, but instead, a single woman walked inside before closing the door behind her. Beside him, Sauda dropped to her knee and bowed to the woman who entered.

The newcomer was of average height, extremely curvy and heavy set. She had dark skin and deep brown eyes. Her frizzy black hair was styled into an afro with lilies woven within. It looked like a dark halo crowning her head. Her frilled tank top, jeans, and heels were pure white, contrasting against her flawless skin. She wore golden jewelry that glistened in the light of the room. She walked across the room, her heels clicking against the granite floor.

"If you'll excuse us," she said simply to Sauda with a smile. Although her voice was soft, it rang with authority and power.

The Archangel of Patience nodded and sheathed her weapons. She glanced toward Jackal as she stood up, her eyes narrowing as if she expected him to drag her back to Hell. Her eyes then locked on Regal's. He was begging her silently to stay—she was the only one who could relate to him. She frowned sadly and broke contact, then left through the golden door to leave the three of them alone.

The woman smiled and locked her eyes on Jackal. Her eyes seemed warm and welcoming, but they were filled with spite. Regal noticed that Jackal shared the same expression.

"Let's all have a seat, shall we?" she said as she gestured to the table. A third chair appeared. "Regal, you can sit here."

Regal felt compelled to listen to her and sat down in the new chair. Jackal took his place, sitting down in the seat in front of Hell's door. The woman sat down across from him, her chair in front of Heaven's door.

"Now, I think it's time we tell Regal about his heritage. Don't you think?"

"Whatever you think is best, Gloria," Jackal growled lowly.

Regal felt his stomach drop and his heart immediately began to pound. Sitting in a small room with the two strongest beings in the universe was the last place he wanted to be.

The trio sat quietly for a moment, glancing between one another as time slowly passed by. Jackal and Gloria were staring at each other coldly, rivalry and animosity flashing in their eyes. Regal could tell they were having a silent conversation with the way their facial features would twitch slightly as if they were in a heated argument. It was eerie knowing that they were talking about him and he couldn't hear them.

Gloria let Sauda become an archangel... Jackal let Sauda ascend... did Jackal fight to keep Sauda? Gloria banished Gabriel's wife... and stepson? Would Jackal ever banish me? Why is Gloria insistent on discussing my heritage? Is this about my destiny? Regal's thoughts were swimming, and he was beginning to sweat due to how anxious he felt. He didn't like being so close to Gloria, and his father didn't give him much comfort, either. His stomach was twisted in knots and his mouth was dry as his brain tried to make sense of everything that had happened. He groaned and rested his head in his hands.

"Someone has to talk," Regal said once the tension became too much. The silence was weighing hard on him and all he wanted were answers; but speaking up, out of turn, was not a smart move. The two monarchs quickly looked at him, causing him to slink in his seat anxiously. Jackal looked about ready to rip his throat out, while Gloria just seemed extremely annoyed.

However, She sighed and shook Her head. "He's right, you know. It's not like he can throw in his two cents. I'm sure you haven't told him a thing about his legacy or his destiny."

"He doesn't have to know," Jackal argued harshly. "He's a demon and that's it."

"Life is far more complicated than that," Gloria mused. She looked over at Regal and smiled. "How much as your father told you about your birth?"

Regal glanced over at Jackal for a moment, catching the menacing glare that was given. Although Jackal wasn't speaking to him telepathically, Regal could tell that his father didn't want him to answer; but Gloria's expecting stare made him speak up out of fear.

"I know that I'm the third of his children... and that I am the only one with naturally-born wings," Regal said timidly. He could hear Jackal growling, but Gloria merely reached over and smacked the back of Jackal's hand to hush him.

"Good, that's a place to start." Gloria leaned back and looked over at Jackal. "Did your father tell you about natural demonic anatomy?"

"No, I didn't tell him. There was no reason to, Gloria," Jackal interjected. "He's a demon at heart, and that's all that matters."

"And what about all the other stuff? You honestly don't expect him to believe forever that demons are granted feathered wings at birth," Gloria said firmly. "Surely he must have noticed that the other incubi don't share his gift."

"He's special that way, because that is how I wanted him to be," the ruler of Hell argued.

Gloria scoffed, crossing Her arms over Her chest as She glared harshly at Jackal. "You mean that's because of how you *changed* him to be."

"He was born for only one reason, and that reason is to be my heir. That is his destiny, and I will not let you take you from me."

"Like how you took him away from Gabriel?"

"Slow down!" Regal shouted, overwhelmed by the amount of information being thrown at him. He buried his head in his hands and ran his fingers through his hair roughly as he tried to process everything. "Please... stop arguing and tell me what you're talking about."

Gloria looked back over at Jackal and quirked her brow slightly, leaning back in her seat. "Ball is in your court, Jackal."

Jackal looked over at Regal guiltily, a saddened expression on his features. The ruler of Hell seemed to deflate, his shoulders sagging as anger was replaced with concern and fear—something Regal rarely saw from his father.

"Regal... I haven't been completely honest with you."

"Apparently."

"I just couldn't bear to tell you. I only want what's best for you. You're my son, and although I don't show it well, I do love you," Jackal explained painfully.

"You or Erebos?" Regal snapped. Jackal looked visibly hurt at the accusation. "If you care for me and want the best for me, tell me the truth."

Jackal sighed and looked over at Gloria for a moment, nodding solemnly as She watched with soft eyes.

"All right..." Jackal replied, his voice hollow. "I'll tell you."

CHAPTER *Thirty-Three*

ORMALLY, DEMONS DON'T have feathered wings," Jackal began, lacing his fingers in front of him. "I'm the only demon with that privilege because Gloria made sure I inherited Satan's wings when Erebos' soul merged with him. You, too, have the gift of naturally feathered wings, but, you didn't inherit that from me..." Jackal paused and looked over at Gloria.

"You were born as an angel, Regal," Gloria cut in. "You were originally an Angel of Patience destined to become one of the strongest Guardian Angels in history. You had the power and potential to protect dozens, if not hundreds, of people at a time rather than being tied down to one human soul. You were merely a baby, hardly old enough to crawl..." Her voice was filled with the sorrow of a mother who lost her child. Her expression then switched to resentment as She glared at Jackal. "But Jackal had sensed that power within you and decided to bend the Laws of the Ethereal Kingdoms to steal you and convert you to a demon."

Jackal cringed. "I had to strip away all of your virtues and feed you sins. By the time Gloria noticed you were gone..."

"You were already being bred as an incubus, and I could not save you." Gloria frowned. "Unlike Jackal, I have standards and I will play by the rules."

"Rules?" Regal asked numbly.

"We are not supposed to take denizens away from each other, but I saw so much potential in you," Jackal explained. "So I stole you and raised you to be an incubus. Over time, you proved yourself to be a powerful demon, and I knew that my decision to make you my son and the Prince of Lust was the right choice."

"I was just a pawn in your game?" Regal asked, hating how his voice sounded broken.

"You were, but now you have another chance to choose your fate, instead of having someone else decide for you," Gloria added softly. "You can go back to your true home, to Keir, to your father."

"Gabriel..." Regal slumped in his seat, taking a deep breath as he stared at the bowl of fruit on the table. He felt like he had been kicked in the stomach with Keir's halo for a second time. *I'm Gabriel's son?* He turned the thought over and over in his mind, barely able to believe it. Yet something inside of him knew it was true.

"Regal," Jackal started, looking over to his son.

"Is that even my name?" Regal asked sharply as he cut off Jackal. He looked over, his eyes burning with anger.

The ruler of Hell looked taken aback at the comment. "Of course that's your name."

"Just making sure; after all, I've been lied to my entire life. Who knows what else isn't true," Regal snapped, his voice growing more venomous.

"I was only trying to do what was best for you."

"Best for me?" Regal asked as he stood up and slammed his hands on the table. "You kidnapped me and molded me to what you wanted me to be. You destroyed lives because you wanted me as a pawn in your sick game!"

Gloria stood up, walking over to rest a hand on Regal's shoulder. "I know that this is hard to soak in..."

"And you," Regal barked, turning to back away from Gloria's touch. "If I was so important why didn't you try your hardest to take me back?"

Gloria's brow furrowed slightly. "Of course I tried to get you back, but the laws that Jackal and I follow made it impossible

329

for me to take you back by force. Once an angel is converted, he cannot be forced to change again unless it's through free will, and even then there is a limit on the number of times an ethereal being can convert. I didn't know how to get you back until Keir told me he loved you, and that he would do whatever it took to save you and bring you to Heaven."

"Is that why you let him come after me?" Regal asked.

Gloria paused for a long moment. "I wouldn't necessarily say that..."

"That is the reason. You don't actually approve of demons and angels being anything but enemies. You only wanted your pawn back! I bet Gabriel doesn't even know I'm his son!"

"No, that's not it at all," Gloria said quickly. "I wanted you back because I love you."

Jackal stood up from his seat. "And I love him as well."

"Hard to believe," Regal growled bitterly.

Jackal looked over at Regal with a sad expression darkening his eyes. "It's true that I initially fought to keep you because I saw the potential in you. But over time I grew to love you. Not Erebos. Me." Jackal moved closer to his son, but Regal stepped back and kept his distance from both of the lords. Jackal frowned as his shoulders sank. "You're my son, Regal. Regardless of what you were before," he said softly, trying to coax Regal to come back to him.

However, Regal was not falling for any more tricks. "What made me your son?" Regal asked bleakly, his eyes narrowing as they welled up with tears of frustration.

"When you took your first steps," Jackal murmured. "When you learned to fly, when you first called me "dad," when you won your first fight with a lesser demon."

Regal bit his lip, trying hard to fight back the urge to fight, scream, cry, and wake up from this nightmare.

"Please forgive me, Regal. Please come back home," Jackal pleaded as he moved closer, trying to close the gap. Gloria moved as well, not wanting Jackal to get too close.

"Regal, the sooner you relax, the more sense this will make. It'll be easier to decide your fate once you calm down," Gloria said soothingly, hoping that the child could regain composure.

Regal took a deep breath and let it out slowly. Being weak wouldn't do him any good. He had to be brave and take it like an adult. He stood up straighter, staring at Jackal and Gloria fearlessly. The ruler of Heaven was right; everything was clearer when he was calm.

He understood now that his entire life was built upon that moment when Jackal took him. If he had never been stolen, he would have ended up an apprentice to an archangel. He never would have grown to be thick-skinned and cunning. He would have never learned how to defend himself from other demons through brute force. He never would have met Keir—and even if he had, he never would have learned to love him in the way that he did over the last month.

Despite knowing the reasons behind Gloria and Jackal's actions, he was furious at both of them. But, Keir had taught him how to forgive and move on. He was tired of running. He had run from Keir for a year, and from his inevitable ascension. If this decision was Regal's destiny, he wasn't going to flee any more. This was his ultimate test, and he was determined to pass with flying colors as the species he was meant to be his entire life.

He glanced over at the doors to his left and his right; one leading to Hell—the place he had once called home, and the other leading to Heaven—his true birthplace. This was where he would make his choice free of chains and restrictions. His fate was in his own hands for the first time in millennia.

"I will not listen to either of you," he murmured quietly, his voice failing to live up to his expectations to sounding brave. "Both of you are trying to influence me to join you, and I am tired of being tugged on like a children's toy." His voice began to grow stronger as he felt bolder and more confident. Assurance and pride welled up within him, giving him the courage to stand up to the two strongest beings in existence. "Both of you are children."

He looked over at Jackal for a moment, reading his expression as nervous and frightened. After all, he could be losing his son in just a few moments. However, he couldn't give into his father. He couldn't let his emotions take control.

"The love you claim to have for me is violent and ruthless. Instead of showering me with affection, you whipped me until I feared your wrath and sought your approval. You abandoned me when I needed you most," he said as he stared at Jackal.

His gaze then shifted toward Gloria soon after, causing her to raise a brow. "And the love you claim to have only shows when it benefits you. Where were you when Keir was dying from Viraine's attacks? Where was your love for him? You're no better than Jackal."

Regal flared his wings, the feathers a strange shimmering gray of neutrality before he decided his fate. "I will no longer be a pawn or an item to either of you. I am going to be what I was destined to be all along, in the place that is my true home."

With a deep breath to calm his nerves, he turned sharply and threw open the door behind him, stepping inside before Jackal or Gloria could try to influence him anymore. The door slammed shut behind him as he was forced through the portal. With a rush he was swept downward, blinded by the stark darkness. Almost as quickly as the darkness came, bright light blinded him for the rest of his descent.

He hit the ground hard. Groaning, he rubbed his head and rolled into his back. His wings ached from being tugged in the vortex and his eyes were struggling to adjust to the new lighting. He looked up, squinting as the sun shone brightly in his eyes. He could feel the grass underneath him and the wind tugging at his hair. He smiled.

He was free.

The halls outside of the infirmary were usually quiet, but today Keir could hear a commotion. The mixed voices of anxious chatter and the shadows of angels and saints passing the stain glass doors made him nervous. Why was everybody suddenly so worked up? Was the news about him and Regal spreading through the kingdom? Did Regal ascend?

He sat up, ignoring the aching pain he felt in his body. Even after two days of rest, his wounds weren't completely healed, but he wouldn't let that stop him from figuring out why everyone was distressed. Keir used his wings to help lift him, and for the first time he saw his wings in the reflection of the main doors. They were a perfect white once again. The saints did a great job of healing him back to full health.

Are Regal's white now, too?

The doors opened and Gabriel stepped inside. For a moment, the gossip that was spreading through the kingdom grew louder, and Keir could almost pick out different words: mission, ascension, infirmary. Gabriel closed the doors behind him, muffling the voices before walking over to Keir.

"What's going on?" Keir asked.

Gabriel grabbed a pillow and propped it behind Keir's back before sitting down on the edge of the bed next to Keir's. "Your mission to find Regal is no longer a secret. Once word spread that you were no longer missing and that there was a demon who was going through the process of ascension, angels put the pieces together."

"Do they know why I was searching for him?"

"No. They think you were sent on a mission from Michaelangelo to test your skills, even though you're too young to be doing missions that dangerous. He'll take most of the blame for your actions."

Keir looked out the window and sighed. At least no one knew the truth. If they did, they would treat him like a traitor... a monster. He shuddered. They wouldn't be wrong.

"Let Michaelangelo know that I'm very grateful to him."

"I will," Gabriel promised. "Regal's ascension is also finished."

"What was his decision?" Keir asked, his voice sounding hopeful. Although he knew Regal felt more like himself as a demon, part of him hoped that Regal had chosen to join the hierarchy of angels. Then they could be together, and the other angels would see Keir as a savior or hero... but would they ever accept Regal as one of their own, especially when he is one of Jackal's direct kin?

"Well..." Gabriel started, rubbing the back of his neck. "He didn't choose."

"What?"

"He took the door to Earth."

"Why would he do that?" Keir asked. It didn't make any sense. Why wouldn't Regal choose Hell when he had the chance?

"We're not sure." Gabriel began to check Keir's bandages. "Your wounds are healing quickly, and your stitches will be removed in a few days."

"That's great news," Keir said halfheartedly. He couldn't bring himself to feel happy knowing that Regal had chosen to give up being a demon. *What happened to make him change his mind about going home?*

"I have better news," Gabriel added. "Gloria feels that you've been through a lot more than She had anticipated when you decided to run away. Angels of your rank don't normally have to live amongst demons, fight off their influences, and battle against a pack of them." Gabriel continued. "It's impressive."

Keir blushed. Gabriel didn't know that he didn't actually run away, that he and Gloria had made an agreement to allow him to track Regal. Still, he felt guilty and embarrassed for his actions. However, he also wasn't used to hearing so much praise, and he felt that he did show Gloria and the other archangels that he was capable of handling demons.

"Which is why," Gabriel continued, "Michaelangelo and Gloria have decided to appoint you as Michelangelo's deputy."

Keir blinked in astonishment, his jaw dropping. "Really?" he asked in shock. He was being appointed as deputy? They were the angels directly under archangels on the scale of power. If something were to happen to the head archangel, the deputies were expected to take command and continue their duties. Michaelangelo was the last archangel who had yet to choose a predecessor. Keir wasn't entirely sure he was the right angel to choose.

"I... I really don't know what to say."

"A thank you is enough," Gabriel said with a smile, although his tone was a bit stern. "Have a little bit of pride; it's not always that bad. Many dream of having this rank and never achieve it. Your strength, experience, and devotion to the virtue of kindness allowed you to be the perfect candidate."

"Oh... thank you! It's an honor!" Keir exclaimed. He beamed up at Gabriel, wishing he felt well enough to reach out and hug him. He was going to be deputy, and the youngest angel to ever be appointed in that position! He would work hard to prove that he was the right angel for the job.

"Oh, and you'll need this." Gabriel pulled out a small pendant from his pocket.

"My shield," Keir said as he took it from Gabriel and attached it to his necklace.

"We retrieved it when we went back to clean up the mess at the hotel." Gabriel stared blankly at Keir, his teal eyes unfocused, before he looked back at Keir's bandages. By the way his mouth pursed, Keir could tell he was deep in thought.

"What is it?"

"Well... I shouldn't be telling you this," Gabriel said quietly. "But you deserve to know. Regal is missing."

"Missing? How?"

"We're not sure. Gloria thinks She knows why She can't see him. She's sending me on a mission to find him and bring him back to Heaven for judgment."

Unease washed over Keir. "Why does he need to be judged? He made his choice."

Gabriel paused for a moment, clearing his throat. "Due to the fact he didn't choose Heaven or Hell, he is technically neither an angel nor demon. Now that he is a half-breed, we fear he may align himself with Chaos, and he is considered a threat until we find him and prove otherwise."

I can't let that happen, Keir thought immediately. It was obvious that Regal didn't want to be aligned with the Ethereal Kingdoms if he chose to go back to Earth. Something had happened to make him change his mind. "I want to help you."

"We can't allow that."

"Why not?" Keir asked angrily. "You just told me that I've got special experience with demons. I've tracked him down for the last year. I've been bonded to him! He's my..." He paused. What was Regal to him? Boyfriend? Lover? Soulmate? He couldn't find a term that defined their odd relationship.

"Your relationship with him makes you a threat, as well."

Then why was I appointed to deputy? Keir thought bitterly. He forced the thought out of his head before Gabriel could pick up on his suspicion.

"I've been in your position," Gabriel said sadly, his stern exterior softening. "Many times. My son disappeared days after he was born. I chose to bury myself in my work to cope with the pain instead of working through it with my wife. She couldn't handle it alone and cheated on me with a mythos on Earth. I couldn't save her from succumbing to Chaos. I felt that it was all my fault..." The archangel sighed, haunted by the choices he had been forced to make. "Many things that we don't expect happen, and we have to make difficult decisions. I know it doesn't make sense right now, but trust Her judgment. She is doing what is best."

"I understand," Keir replied. *I just don't agree with it.*

Gabriel walked over to the window and drew open the curtains, allowing the breeze to come in. "It's a beautiful day. Everything is back in order. Soon you'll be able to begin your training and become an official deputy."

"I can't wait..." His reply was hollow. He was excited to start training, but his heart still burned with loneliness.

"Good to hear. Rest well, and I'll see you later." The archangel smiled warmly at Keir before leaving the room.

Keir sighed and laid back in his bed, staring out the window to his left. The last year had been a rollercoaster: hunting and marking Regal, living and travelling with him, the fights and the conversations, the heartbreak and the immeasurable joy... Keir wouldn't trade it for anything.

He certainly wasn't going to give it all up now.

The angel would train to be a deputy. He would redeem himself and make Gloria proud. Most importantly, he would find Regal and protect him.

Even if it sent him straight to Chaos.

ACKNOWLEDGMENTS

Back in 2012, I decided to participate in Camp NaNoWriMo: a virtual "summer camp" for writers that challenged them to write a novel over the course of a month. It wasn't my first time trying to write a book. Believe me, I crashed and burned at my first few attempts. However, this time I was *serious*. More importantly, I was prepared: I wrote up an outline of where I thought my story was going to go, stuck to my word count goals, and didn't give up when I was hit with writer's block.

After a month of writing daily, I had reached my goal of 50,000 words, but the novel was only half way done. So, I spent another month writing, and after another 45,000 words the first draft of *The Art of Falling* was complete. Then for the next five years, I spent every waking moment re-reading, editing, and re-writing until I felt it was ready to be on the bookshelf.

Throughout it all, I couldn't have done it without the help and support of several important people, and I wanted to take the time to thank each individually:

Gwen Gades, for deciding to take on this book (and consequently, the dozens of other books in this series that I will write.) Your faith in my work has been a blessing, and I am so thankful to have found a publisher that really puts the story first. I know that I made the right choice going forward with Dragon Moon Press.

Sandra Nguyen, for working with me each step of the way when doing the final edits for the novel. Without your keen eye, quite a few simple typos and errors would have slipped through the cracks!

Adrienne Frances, for being one of my first editors and a great friend. I'm very lucky that we happened to be in the same creative courses at Oakland University. Your input as a fellow author, both in and out of the classroom, has made a huge impact on my writing.

Sharon Cicilian, Annie Gilson, and Dawn Newton, for being some of the best instructors I had during my college career. Not only have I become a better writer after taking your classes, but I have also learned how to be a better editor. You all taught me how to grow a thick skin, and prepared me to throw myself into the publishing world. For that, I am humbled.

Eddie Bunch, for putting up with my constant brainstorming. I'm very lucky to have a best friend and fiancé who is willing to bounce ideas, as well as read and edit my work. Many of the "Ah-ha" moments I had while writing were from you poking holes into my plots and forcing me to think deeper. Not only that, but when I felt like I wasn't good enough, you were there to dig me out of my own insecure hole.

Mom and Dad, for always supporting me with my creative endeavors, and for giving me advice and criticism along the way. Though I probably don't say it enough, thank you and I love you. I hope I can make you proud.

Kaylen and Tryst, for being there from the very beginning. If it weren't for you two, I wouldn't have gotten into the world of roleplaying and writing. Many of my characters would have not been born. We always said that one day our stories would be made into books and movies. I think our pre-teen selves would be excited to see how far we've come.

Finally, thank *you*. The fact that you are holding a copy of this book means the world to me. Your support will help me achieve my dreams of being a published author. I honestly can't do it without you.

Now you'll have to excuse me. I've got a sequel to work on.

Dani Cojo

ABOUT *the Author*

Dani Cojo is an aspiring author with an expansive library of novels that have yet to be written. An avid reader herself, she hopes that her stories will give book-lovers the escape that they crave, and book-loathers the exciting and unyielding desire to read a book from start to finish in one sitting.

A proud Oakland University alumna, Dani spends most of her free time writing, or playing Dungeons and Dragons with her fiancé and their friends. She currently lives at home with her parents and two cats in Macomb County, Michigan.

Follow Dani on her website: Danicojo.com

Made in the USA
Las Vegas, NV
02 February 2022

42852019R00204